Diamond Sky

Annie Seaton

Porter Sisters 3

Porter Sisters series
1. *Kakadu Sunset*
2. *Daintree*
3. *Diamond Sky*
4. *Hidden Valley*
5. *Larapinta*
6. *Kakadu Dawn*

This is a work of fiction. Characters, institutions and organisations mentioned in this novel are either the product of the author's imagination or, if real, used fictitiously without any intent to describe actual conduct.

Aboriginal and Torres Strait Islander people should be aware that this book may contain images or names of people now deceased.

ISBN 9798418667052

Annie Seaton lives near the beach on the mid-north coast of New South Wales. Her career and studies have spanned the education sector for most of her working life, including completing a Masters Degree in Education and working as an academic research librarian, a high-school principal and a university tutor until she took early retirement and fulfilled a lifelong dream of a full-time writing career. In 2014 Annie was voted Author of the Year and in 2015 was voted Best Established Author in the AusRomToday.com Readers' Choice Awards. In 2016, *Kakadu Sunset* was shortlisted by the judges of the Romance Writers' Association of Australia for the Ruby, in the long book category.

In 2018 *Whitsunday Dawn* finalled in the ARRA Awards and was voted Book of the Year in the AUSROM Readers' Choice awards.

Each winter, Annie and her husband leave the beach to roam the remote areas of Australia for story ideas and research. She is passionate about preserving the beauty of the Australian landscape, and respecting the traditional ownership of the land. For those readers who cannot experience this journey personally, Annie seeks to portray the natural beauty of the Australian environment—its spiritual locations, stunning landscapes and unique wildlife.

The Kimberley of Western Australia – the setting for *Diamond Sky* – is one of the world's last wilderness frontiers. The beehive domes of the Bungle Bungle Range are a relatively recent discovery; the Purnululu National Park was established in 1987. The stunning landscape is protected as a natural heritage region but is still threatened by human activity.

Readers can contact Annie through her website, annieseaton.net, or find her on Facebook, Twitter and Instagram.

Also by Annie Seaton

Standalone Books

Whitsunday Dawn
Undara
Osprey Reef
East of Alice
Porter Sisters Series
Kakadu Sunset
Daintree
Diamond Sky
Hidden Valley
Larapinta
Kakadu Dawn

Others
Four Seasons Short and Sweet
Deadly Secrets
Adventures in Time
Silver Valley Witch
The Emerald Necklace
An Aussie Christmas Duo
Pentecost Island Series
Pippa
Eliza
Nell
Tamsin
Evie
Cherry
Odessa
Sienna
Tess
Isla
Richards Brothers Series
The Trouble with Paradise
Marry in Haste
Outback Sunrise

The House on the Hill series
Beach House
Beach Music
Beach Walk
Beach Dreams
Sunshine Coast Series
Waiting for Ana
The Trouble with Jack
Healing His Heart
Second Chance Bay Series
Her Outback Playboy
Her Outback Protector
Her Outback Haven
Her Outback Paradise
The McDougalls of Second Chance Bay

Love Across Time Series
Come Back to Me
Follow Me
Finding Home
The Threads that Bind
Love Across Time 1-4 Boxed Set
Bindarra Creek
Worth the Wait
Full Circle
Secrets of River Cottage
Bindarra Creek Duo
A Place to Belong

The Augathella Girls Series
Outback Roads
Outback Sky
Outback Escape
Outback Wind
Outback Dawn
Outback Moonlight
Outback Dust
Outback Hope

An Augathella Surprise
An Augathella Baby
An Augathella Spring

5

As always to Ian, my ever-patient and loving husband.
You are always there for me

We steered this morning through a splendid country, rocky and undulating, which for twelve miles maintained the same character . . . the creeks we crossed were perfectly dry. To the Northward, several small ranges appeared in the distance.

Kimberley explorer, Alexander Forrest, in his Journal of Expedition from Degrey River to Port Darwin.
Perth, 1880.

Chapter 1
Matsu Diamond Mine – East Kimberley, Western Australia

Apart from soft music from the radio in the kitchen as the staff prepped for the day, the only sound interrupting Drusilla Porter's solitary breakfast was the occasional clang of a mop in a bucket as the cleaner washed the hall leading to the mess room.

'All by yourself, Dru?

Dru jumped as the chair beside her slid across the floor with a high-pitched squeak. As she looked up she bit back the groan that rose to her lips. 'Hi Jennifer.' Dru reached back and rubbed her neck to ease the tight muscles. After she finished her coffee and checked her emails, she planned on heading to her room to crash for a long sleep. Talking to Jennifer—an administrative assistant in the security section—was the last thing she felt like doing.

After a twelve-hour night shift out in the heat on the perimeter of the diamond mine, the cool and the solitude of the staff mess had eased her inner tension but her muscles were still taut. She had come straight to the mess after she'd signed off, hoping to avoid the rush of the night workers from the processing and crushing plants after the changeover of shift and get back to her room more quickly. The day shift staff had already been through for their breakfast.

Like the rest of the mine, the staff mess was run like clockwork, although the work boots of fifty day staff had already wreaked havoc on the shiny floor tiles. A fine layer of East Kimberley red dust covered most things at the mine, both inside and out.

'Early breakfast for you, Jennifer?' Dru gestured to the empty chair across from her; one thing their mother had instilled in her three daughters was good manners. Tiredness tugged at her muscles and she yawned, but ten minutes chatting was a small concession to make;

maintaining a pleasant relationship with a nosy staff member didn't take much. She knew Jennifer would keep the conversation—and the site gossip—going while Dru drank her coffee and listened. The occasional nod and sympathetic murmur would keep the young woman happy and then Dru could make her excuses and get away.

'I'm on early start today. Night shift for you, was it?' Jennifer's smile was sympathetic as she took in Dru's face. She'd had a quick splash in the washroom outside the mess but hadn't worried about the streaks of red dust where she'd wiped away the perspiration through the night. A long hot shower would clean that up when she got back to her room.

Dru nodded and sipped the steaming hot coffee as she looked over Jennifer's shoulder through the huge glass window to the low foothills of the Matsu Range. Even though it was only seven-thirty, the blue shimmering heat haze formed a distinct line at the base of the range. Scrubby trees and hundreds of termite mounds, small and large, dotted the flat plain that stretched between the mine and the hills. Nothing moved in the morning air; the nocturnal creatures had retreated for the day, and the kangaroos were hidden away, lying in the meagre patches of shade provided by the occasional boab tree. Here and there, patches of yellow grass soothed the eye as they broke the monotony of the red dust.

'How come you're not flying out today? Everyone's headed to the airport. Bus just left.'

Dru turned her attention back to Jennifer as the young woman pierced her egg and the bright yellow yolk ran over the plate.

'Oh, gross. I'll be so glad to get out of this place and back to civilisation.' Jennifer turned her lips down in a pout.

This time Dru's murmur was noncommittal. Jennifer always found something to criticise; the food here at the Matsu Mine was excellent. Dru had her pegged as a short stay staff member. It took a certain personality to make it on the fly-in fly-out jobs, so despite the rugged and isolated location, management made sure that workers had the best of everything. The perks and the excellent salary ensured that staff turnover was lower than other mining companies.

Although the salary was nowhere near what she'd been earning in Dubai. A cold shiver ran down Dru's back as she thought of her previous workplace. Pushing the feeling away, she smoothed back the loose strands of hair and picked up her spoon, using it to gesture to her bowl of muesli. 'Muesli's good if the eggs don't suit.'

'Not for me. Chook food, my dear old grandpa used to call it.' Jennifer stirred the runny egg with the tines of her fork and looked at Dru. 'So you didn't say why you're not on the morning flight out.'

'I've got an extra seven days on this work block.'

Dru gave up on any chance of a peaceful breakfast as Jennifer settled in for a chat.

'Me too. I only said yes because I'm going to Bali with my boyfriend for my next two weeks off. Apparently there's a new work safety guy who needs to learn the system, and the overtime I get will pay for our flights.' She let out an exaggerated sigh. 'Always, work, work and more work here.'

'Yep.' Dru uttered the monosyllable and tried to look interested.

Jennifer went on. 'I don't know how long I'll last here. I might go back to Perth soon. There's plenty of work there. You've been here a while now, haven't you? How long do you think you'll stay? Rooms in the dongas are tiny, aren't they?' She fired off a volley of questions and Dru concentrated on slowly chewing her breakfast, and flashed her co-worker an apologetic smile. It wasn't too difficult to talk to Jennifer but Dru knew she'd seize upon any information that could be embellished and passed on. Life was pretty tame on site most of the time, and the gossip machine loved to run with stories.

'Never mind. I think we started the same month. About nine months ago.'

Dru nodded as Jennifer drew breath and waited for the next barrage of questions to avoid.

'It's so crazy that I have to fly to Perth and then go north again. I did think about getting to Darwin but it's too hard.'

'North?' Dru frowned. She'd lost the thread of the conversation. 'To get to Bali.'

'Oh, of course.' Dru gave another sympathetic nod. 'Yes, it's a long drive.'

Jennifer put her knife and fork down and stared at Dru. 'What about you? Where do you go for your time off?'

'Just home.' Dru's phone pinged with an incoming message and she glanced down at it. 'Excuse me for a second.' She picked the phone up from the table and glanced at the screen.

Probably Emma or Ellie trying to do the family thing and set up one of their lovey-dovey family chats. God, she hated it, but no matter how much distance she tried to keep, her sisters insisted on keeping her in the family fold.

Sweet. It was Megan, not her sisters. But Dru's relief was short-lived when she scanned the text.

You have to come to our wedding. NO EXCUSES. Read this and think about it. SERIOUSLY. PLEEEEAASE. xxxxxxxx.

The rest of the message filled the screen. She turned the screen off and put her phone back on the table; she'd save it for when she was back in her room.

'So where's home for you?' Jennifer persisted as Dru picked up her coffee mug.

'Darwin.'

'Darwin? So that's why you don't ever get the Virgin flight back to Perth. I wondered why I hadn't ever seen you on the plane.' There was a brief pause in Jennifer's inquisitive chatter as she screwed her face up in a frown. 'So how do you get to Darwin?'

'I drive to Kununurra and fly from there.'

'Wow, you're brave.' Admiration filled the young woman's expression. 'You drive out over that?' She gestured to the wide expanse of desert that surrounded the mine. Red dust, scrubby trees and heat haze as far as you could see in every direction.

Dru nodded and put her spoon down, forced a false yawn and covered her mouth with one hand. But she wasn't quick enough, and

Jennifer moved closer and lowered her voice. There was nobody else in the room with them apart from the kitchen hand singing along with the radio.

Here we go. She wasn't going to get away without the latest gossip. Dru resisted rolling her eyes.

'Did you hear? There's another two new staff coming in on the flight today as well as the new work safety guy.' Jennifer looked around before she spoke. 'Big changes are about to happen here.'

Dru raised her eyebrows. 'Like what?'

'Big changes.' Jennifer sat back and folded her arms. 'Apparently they're talking about drilling a second underground mine.'

Dru sat up straight and stared at Jennifer who was now smiling, obviously pleased that she had her attention. As much as she hated gossip, she *was* interested in the mine and its future. *Her future.*

The open pit mine had closed down three years ago and the diamonds were now extracted by underground mining. Dru was working on the rehabilitation of the land to the south of the open pit. This job had been tailor-made for her and it ticked all of her boxes.

After two years living and working in Dubai, the isolated outback of Western Australia's East Kimberley was heaven.

And it was a place to hide out for a while until she felt safe again.

'Another underground mine. That's good news.' This time the interest in her voice was genuine. Her main worry had been that the mine would wind up before she was ready to move on. But how much factual information Jennifer was privy to was a matter for debate. Nothing had been mentioned at the staff engineers' weekly meeting last week, so any changes that were in the wind were either confidential—or purely gossip.

'Apparently the block cave thingy has been so good, another one is in the wind. I was doing some data entry the other day and I overheard the boss talking about it in his office.' Jennifer was whispering, although there was no one else in the room. 'So don't tell anyone, it's all hush hush.'

A block cave *thingy,* for God's sake. This time Dru couldn't help her eye roll. 'I won't say anything but if that's true, it could mean a lot to our jobs here.'

'How come?' Jennifer stared at her.

'Block caving is the underground version of open pit mining. Undermining an ore body, allowing it to progressively collapse under its own weight.' Dru nodded slowly. 'I was reading an article about that just the other day. The new technology means we can do real-time monitoring of sensors in the block cave. It really would make a second mine feasible.'

Jennifer's eyes widened. 'Wow, how *do you* know all about that?'

'I'm an engineer.' Dru tempered her short response with a laugh.

'An engineer? I thought you just looked after the gardens and stuff.'

'No, I'm an environmental engineer.'

'What's that?' Jennifer screwed up her nose and frowned.

'Rehabilitation. I look after the mine site. In a nutshell I make sure that everything we do will eventually be put back the way it was before we mined.'

'And you had to go to uni to do that?' Jennifer's voice was loud, and the kitchen hand looked up with a grin. 'It must be deadly boring. Is that all you do out there?'

'I also liaise with the local indigenous groups to make sure the mining doesn't impact on their culture.'

Jennifer's eyes were wide. 'Out there? What culture? None of them even live near here.' Once again a dismissive hand waved at the arid landscape.

Dru suppressed her irritation. 'It is traditionally owned land and there *are* settlements close by. Some of our indigenous workers live out there and drive in each day—or night— for their shifts.'

A few days ago she had received a personal call from John Robinson, the CEO of the mine, asking her about the mood at the weekly meetings she held with the local Aboriginal community. She'd been surprised at the time, but maybe it was because of a proposed expansion. The mood at the meetings hadn't been good and she'd passed that onto John. But a new underground mine would make a lot of the permanent staff happy. She focused her attention back to Jennifer.

'And the cultural stuff is really interesting too. One of the cultural things impacts on this site very much.'

'Oh?' There wasn't a lot of interest in Jennifer's tone as she wiped the egg from her plate with a crust of toast.

'Did you know we're not allowed to take diamonds from within a two-metre circumference of the boab trees on site, even with the mining lease?'

'No. Why not?'

'The tree is important to the Aborigines of this region. They call it *larrkardiy, and they believe i*t has a strong spiritual presence.'

'God, you do know a lot, don't you? And here I was wondering why you gardened on the night shift. You can't see much out there at night!'

'You can, you know. I was lying on the dirt watching termite mounds last night,' she said drily. 'Even though it was stinking hot, it was quite beautiful out there in the moonlight.'

'Even hot out there at night?'

'It averages thirty-eight to forty-two in the day at this time of the year. If you leave a metal tool in the sun for more than a minute or so, it gets burning hot.' Dru held her right hand up to show Jennifer the blister that was healing on her palm. 'That's why we work mainly night shift through the spring and summer.'

Jennifer pulled a face. 'I forget when I'm in this air con all the time how hot it gets in the desert. I don't know how you do it. It's such an ugly mess out there. How can the land possibly be put back the way it was? It's been dug up for years.'

Dru forgot how tired she was as she gave Jennifer a potted version of her role on site. Her team's brief was the restitution of both flora and fauna and landscape features that preserved the value of the site for the Aboriginal community. Dru loved her job at the mine. Rebuilding an ecosystem that blended with the undisturbed landscape was challenging, and immersing herself in her work had helped put the fiasco in Dubai behind her. Even sitting watching termite mounds in the middle of the night was preferable to being back there.

And a hell of a lot safer.

'I heard something about you finding a big diamond off the ground your first week here.' The young woman narrowed her eyes as she interrupted. 'Or was that just goss?'

'No, it really happened. Rocky Cardella was showing me the boundary line of the mine and I spotted a big one on the ground lying near a boab tree. It was a pretty exciting start to my job.' Dru smiled as Jennifer's expression filled with interest. 'Rocky took it into the plant.'

'That's way cool. Rocky's an Aboriginal, isn't he?' Jennifer asked curiously. 'Is that why he was allowed to pick it up?'

'Yes, that's right.' Dru pushed her chair back. 'It wasn't a fine quality gem . . . the clarity and colour were lacking. It was just a cognac but you're right, it was pretty cool. Anyway, time I got some sleep.' Dru forced a smile to her face as she stood, and then looked down at Jennifer. 'Enjoy your trip to Bali. See you around.'

She could talk environmental rehabilitation for as long as Jennifer could gossip, but if the glazed look in the young woman's eyes was anything to go by, she'd been more interested in diamonds than the description of restoring the land. Besides, this morning's text message from Megan about the wedding was forefront in her mind, and her stomach was churning.

She stepped outside of the air-conditioned staff mess and paused on the verandah that looked over the pool. Her gaze settled on the mountains in the distance and she drew a deep breath.

Each time she drove from Kununurra towards the mine after her rostered two weeks off, she always arrived with the same feeling: safe and secure away from the frantic pace of civilisation. Not that you could call Darwin frantic after Dubai, but it was still full of wide, open spaces and even in her luxury apartment on the harbour she felt exposed. But once she entered the vast red bowl of the Kimberley and drew closer to the huge open-cut mine halfway between Lake Argyle and the beehive monoliths of Purnululu National Park—known for a long time as the Bungle Bungles—the sensation that she had cut ties with the rest of the world filled her with a satisfying sense of being invisible and untouchable.

Even though the arid wind from the mountains rendered the site a dust bowl in the dry season, and the dumping of the torrential rain turned it into a hot humid pool in the wet, Dru had appreciated every minute of her nine months at the mine. Her small staff apartment was one in a long row of dongas on the side of the hill above the mess building. It was tiny but she still preferred being here than in her three bedroom, two bathroom apartment overlooking the beach and recreation lagoon at Wharf One on Darwin Harbour. The dongas at Matsu were small box-like rooms with a king-single bed, a desk and a small en-suite bathroom for each. A coffee table and a television were the closest things to luxury items.

Dru had spent the past months out on the mine site or in her room and if she felt like conversation—which was rare—she'd wander down the hill to the staff mess. With two weeks onsite and then two weeks in Darwin, the time had passed quickly. Last time she'd spoken to her sisters, Ellie had made some smart remark about her being antisocial and Dru had shrugged it off. So what if she preferred her own company? So what if she didn't particularly like spending time with her family? That was her choice and that's the way it was.

To her mother's incessant hints that there was plenty of work for a environmental engineer in Queensland mines closer to the family—not that there was much left of that after Dad died and the sisters had scattered to the winds—she would always reply that the excitement of working in a diamond mine was unbeatable. Maybe she was a loner, but Dru was much happier away from Ellie's intense looks and Emma's need to control everyone; family wasn't necessary to her. She was an adult and forging her own independent life. She was in control now.

And here at the mine she was *safe*.

The roar of a jet engine filled her ears as the daily plane appeared over the open cut mine to the south. It was later than she'd thought. Dru headed for the seclusion of her room.

Chapter 2

September
Head Office, Matsu Diamonds – Perth, Western Australia

'We're prepared to pay double your going rate if you –'

'Before we discuss my rates, I need you to tell me more about the actual theft please, John.' Connor Kirk kept his voice polite. 'I know the documents you had couriered to me in Indonesia were just an overview of the case. I understand you didn't send them electronically because of the confidential nature of the investigation, but now I'd like to hear the actual details. I need you to take me through what happened step by step and explain how you discovered there had been a theft at the mine itself.'

John Robinson, CEO of Matsu Diamonds, steepled his fingers in front of him. 'Okay . . . but before we get to the details, *if* you accept the contract, just let me –' He paused as the door opened and his assistant entered with a tray set with two fine china cups and saucers, a coffeepot and some sandwiches. When they were alone again, he continued. 'Just let me say at the outset that I'm very pleased that you . . . that your firm is considering taking on this investigation for us, and very pleased that you would be the man on the ground, so to speak. You have an excellent reputation, Connor.'

Connor nodded and leaned back; he was the best in his field, but he didn't need to be flattered. If he decided to take this case on—it was very different to his recent experiences—it wouldn't be because of the opinion of the CEO or the company. He did things his own way and he didn't want his perceptions to be influenced by anything other than fact. However he forced a smile to his face as Robinson continued.

'Your company—and you in particular—have a stellar reputation for your results and your discretion. We want you to take on the investigation for us. No matter what it costs.' John leaned forward and looked at him intently.

Connor stared back at him without commenting. Robinson didn't know—and he didn't need to know—that Connor *was* the company. In the field he worked alone and that was the way it would stay.

'I'm aware that this sort of investigation is different to the cases you usually take on, but we want the best.'

'So ... John, a diamond theft?' Connor bit down on his impatience and turned the conversation to the case in hand. He directed the CEO back to the actual theft. Robinson was right, a diamond theft in Australia was very different to his usual type of job, but maybe it was time to ease back. Lately he'd been pushing the boundaries with risk taking in Indonesia and he was tired. One wrong decision over there could be deadly. This job would be a nice change from risking his life busting drug rings in South-East Asia.

Robinson continued. 'So far we've kept our investigations very quiet at this end. We don't want the thief or thieves tipped off. It has to be an inside job of course.' John reached for a folder from the desk in front of him and handed it to Connor. 'There are three staff who are of particular interest, the –'

Connor put the folder down without opening it. 'Before we talk suspects, tell me more about the theft.'

John stopped talking and stared past Connor to the glass window that overlooked the Perth CBD. Connor had glanced briefly at the magnificent vista of blue sky and the river running along the expressway earlier. The outlook was good, but in his opinion too distracting for an office view.

'I want to know exactly how you found out that the diamonds had bypassed your security. And where they ended up.'

John shook his head. 'I'm sorry. I'm still having trouble getting my head around it. The discovery was a shock. The mine has state of the art monitoring equipment in place; it cost us millions to install. Comprehensive searches at the point where the diamonds leave the recovery room, a body scanner at the exit gate, and X-raying of luggage before they fly out, a bulletproof vehicle that takes the bags of rough diamonds to the flight each day, cameras all over the site and a twenty-four-hour security shift.'

'Certainly sounds tight.' Connor sat still; John hadn't answered his question. 'So when were you first made aware that there had been a theft? Tell me exactly what happened please.'

John nodded and reached for the coffee pot. Connor waited patiently as he filled both cups, adding two sugar cubes to his own and stirring it slowly. The clinking of the teaspoon against the fine china tinkled softly in the quiet room.

'Last month, the personal assistant of an international businessman turned up at an exclusive jeweller's in Antwerp with six of our violet diamonds and an order for a necklace.'

Connor frowned. 'There was nothing about that in the file you gave me.'

'I was holding that information back until I met with you personally.' John stared at him over his glasses before he lifted another folder from his desk and passed it over. 'The contents of this file are very sensitive and highly confidential. Please don't share it with any of your colleagues.'

'I won't.' Connor nodded and glanced down at the file in his hand. 'So tell me. What's so unusual about a customer bringing some diamonds to be set in a necklace?'

'Nothing normally, except that every Matsu diamond is laser etched with a unique identifier before being released to market. Fortunately, Hughie Van Hoebeek, the jeweller, has a very close relationship with our company. As soon as he realised that these six diamonds hadn't been laser etched when they were cut, he contacted us. When we went through our database, we had no records of those particular diamonds ever being on site. Of even more concern, this man's personal assistant brought with him a pair of earrings that he wanted the necklace matched to. Again our diamonds, and again no etching.'

'So where does the businessman come from? Is he Australian?'

'No, he's lived around the world but he's currently based in Dubai, in the United Arab Emirates. That's where he was born and where most of his companies are registered.

'Where are the diamonds now?'

'Still in Antwerp. Hughie Van Hoebeek has secured them all. The theft has been reported to the World Diamond Council and Interpol have been notified.' John put his cup down and his frown deepened. 'So you can see why we need professional investigative help here. We can't afford to have our security breached. There are potentially billions of dollars worth of diamonds to be compromised here. The stolen diamonds are some of our biggest—Hughie has sent photos as well as weights. The value of each individual stone would be at least one million dollars.'

Connor let out a low whistle.

Steely determination glinted in John's eyes. 'No one has been interviewed on site because we don't want whoever is responsible to know that we're aware of the thefts. I want you to take this on, but very discretely.'

Connor's interest was fully engaged now. One million dollars for a single diamond was a lot of money. 'As I said before, this is very different to my usual brief. You'll need to give me a lot more background information.'

'Most of it is in the files here.' John gestured to the folders on the desk. 'But I'll be available twenty-four seven to answer any questions you may have.'

'Okay. First up, tell me how the diamonds can be unequivocally identified as being from Matsu.'

'Do you know anything about diamonds, Connor?'

'Not really. Our usual line of work is industrial espionage.' Not exactly truthful but that was the public face of his company.

John picked up his cup and sipped his coffee. He put it carefully in the saucer and placed his hands in front of him on the desk. 'The Matsu diamond pipe is a diamondiferous olivine lamproite diatreme with an age of about 1178 million years. Coloured diamonds, such as the Matsu violets, have what is known as a defect centre, where one or more of the carbon atoms in the diamond lattice may be missing, or may have been replaced with a different element. The crystalline structure is unique to our diamonds.'

'Okay. Now put that in layman's terms for me.' Connor sat back and folded his arms, trying to get his head around the scientific stuff.

'There are only three other places in the world where pink diamonds are found, but violet diamonds are unique to us. That's what makes them so valuable. Matsu violets can be priced anywhere from three hundred thousand dollars up to over two million dollars per carat.' John pursed his lips before continuing. 'This is obviously an inside job. There is no way that anyone can get onsite at Matsu unless they are staff. And as I said, security at the mine is state of the art. We've put a lot of money into securing the site.'

But obviously not enough, thought Connor. There was always the human element. Where there was money to be made, there was human greed and anything could be bypassed if the right palms were greased. He'd lost count of the number of times he'd seen that in the last ten years.

'To help you understand the certainty that these are our diamonds—apart from the colour of course—I'll show you what they look like.' John picked up a pencil and began to sketch. 'It's the crystalline structure that makes them easily identifiable as being from our mine. While some coloured diamonds get their colour through the addition of a chemical impurity, this is not the case for our violets. Violet diamonds get their colour from a distortion in the crystal lattice structure of the stone.' The pencil flew over the paper and an intricate shape appeared. John held it up and pointed to the centre of the lattice shape. 'This distortion in the crystal structure leads to internal graining in the stone. It is believed to occur after the diamond has begun to grow rather than at the point of formation. But it's still all hypothetical and we're still putting a lot of money into research.' He put the paper down and stared at Connor. 'But we *can* identify the source of these diamonds unequivocally. They are from Matsu. There is absolutely no doubt that some diamonds are bypassing our process.'

'Is it possible that a visitor might have found the diamonds? You do have daily tours of the plant in the dry season.' Connor had read up on the mine; the historical, the economic and the tourist perspectives. 'Outsiders are frequently on site.'

'Tourists can be discounted. When you're there, you'll see the security in place. And anyway, the tours go nowhere near the recovery area.' John shook his head, but Connor thought he was being naive if he thought any security system was perfect.

'So talk me through the process from the beginning.'

'The diamonds are normally mined here –' John gestured to several large photographs of a tiered open cut mine along the wall beside the desk '– and then processed onsite and shipped out to our cutting facility in Perth. That's where they are laser etched for further identification.'

'What's laser etching?'

'Laser inscriptions are grading report numbers, inscribed on the girdle of the diamond. A very precise laser beam transforms the micro thin layer of diamond from its transparent form to a form that is visible under magnification.'

'So not easily seen?'

'No. Not visible to the naked eye. Usually ten to twenty times magnification required before you can see them. The diamonds in Antwerp had been cut and not etched, so did not go through any of our usual processes.'

Connor nodded. 'So what you're saying is that the diamonds were mined on site, but removed by someone before being recorded or going through the usual etching process.'

'That's correct. And cut elsewhere.'

A dozen possibilities flashed through Connor's mind, but he pushed them aside.

Facts first. He turned his full attention to John as the man outlined the internal investigation that had been undertaken so far.

'As I said before, this whole issue has been kept very quiet. The last thing we want to do is tip off whoever is taking the diamonds from the recovery area.'

Connor nodded. 'That goes without saying.'

'There is another possibility. Very unlikely but probably needs mentioning.' John's voice was low and Connor leaned in closer.

'While we previously retrieved the gems from the open cut mine, and we now mine underground, the weathering and erosion of the pipe still releases diamonds.'

'How do you mean releases them?'

'They're washed down the creeks that drain from the pipe, and this means that diamonds can simply lay on the ground until someone stumbles across one.'

'What? You mean just lying there ready to be picked up? So if someone picked one up on site, they could just pocket it and walk out?' Connor shook his head. Security be damned.

'Yes, hypothetically, they can be picked up from the ground.' John raised his hand and held his fingers flat, staring at them as though he was holding a diamond on the flat of his palm. 'But the chances of doing that six times? Not likely at all. Even if that had happened, the X-ray, body scanning, and search processes should have prevented them being taken offsite. That's where our problem is. It should be impossible to get them offsite.'

'Well it's obviously not impossible. It seems there is a way to get them out. Is there a way to leave the mine site without going through security?'

'Highly unlikely. The terrain is almost impassable south, east and west. When you see the terrain, you will understand why we've discounted any connection there.'

Connor held up the folder. 'I assume it's outlined in here?'

'That's correct.' John stared at him and the worry lines etched into his forehead eased a little. 'You also need to know there are some cultural issues concerning the tailings dam at the moment. There's some strong talk of the traditional owners wanting the site back, and although that's unlikely to be related to the theft, you do need to be aware of it.'

'Would that create difficulties for the mine?'

'Too bloody right it would. But that's another issue we can discuss later. I'm going up to Matsu in a couple of weeks for a meeting with the local Aboriginal community. When you have a look at the files, there's a mention of one of our indigenous staff in the list of suspects but I don't believe he should have been included. If you take the job on, we'll talk more about the staff who've been flagged.'

'Okay.'

'The head of our security operation there is Don Finlayson. He's the best in the business. If you take us on, he has suggested a way for you to go in undercover.'

'Can he be trusted?'

'Of course. I'd trust Don with my life. He's been a close, personal friend for many years. He's the godfather to our eldest son. He was the one who suggested your firm to me; he's as perturbed by what's happened as the rest of us.'

Perturbed? An interesting way to put it. When there were billions of dollars at stake and you were responsible for the security system that had been breached, you'd be more than bloody *perturbed*. Connor filed that information away to look at later. Everyone was a suspect for him, no matter whose godfather they were.

John pulled a handkerchief from the pocket of his trousers and mopped his brow. 'There's been a spate of workplace accidents over the past weeks and that's why your presence onsite won't raise any eyebrows. Don will set up a position for you, a workplace safety role. That way you can be all over the site without raising suspicions. Your brief will be to get in there and find out how the security is being breached. The initial contract is for three months. So what do you say?'

John's profile was in shadow as the late morning sun streamed through the window, but Connor saw the tension leave his shoulders as he stood and reached over to shake the CEO's hand.

'When do you want me to start?'

Chapter 3

At around lunchtime that day, Connor straightened in his narrow seat as the Virgin Airlines charter plane banked to the left on the approach to Matsu Diamond Mine. The plane was full of workers flying in for their two-week roster of twelve-hour shifts. He had requested a seat by himself and had watched with interest as the staff greeted each other when they'd boarded the plane, before settling down in their seats with headphones to keep themselves occupied for the three-hour flight.

Being an observer was an integral part of his job. His hippie mother had always attributed his acuity and keen perception as being handed down in some sort of mystical way. She'd called it the sixth sense. But what he'd known and done naturally since he was a child had been defined for him by his studies of psychology. Connor preferred to put it down to simple intelligence and using his senses to form a coherent response to another human being by observing their actions and body language. No hocus pocus about it; it was logical and scientific. The biggest mistake he'd ever made had been following instinct. He shook his head and forced that time from his mind. That was in the past and he'd moved on.

Connor looked down at the landscape below. A couple of narrow creeks in the far distance glinted silver in the sun as the plane began its descent.

He thought back to that initial discussion with John Robinson. Once he'd agreed to take on the job, it had only taken days for the contract to be drawn up and a hefty deposit for his fee was paid into his account. The balance at the end of the investigation would set him up for a couple of years. It was time to take a break; Connor was well aware he was on the road to burnout if he kept up the pace he'd set for the past few years.

But worse than that he was losing his edge. The last couple of busts in Thailand had been more dangerous than usual and he'd taken too many risks. Chasing down a diamond thief would be a walk in the park compared to the past few cases in South-East Asia.

He'd met with the CEO again, and Don Finlayson had flown down to Perth to outline the undercover role he had set up for Connor.

Their internal investigation had identified three suspects. John had outlined the three staff who had been flagged as persons of particular interest.

'It's a starting point,' John had said before he'd turned to Don. 'I'll hand over to you, Don.'

Connor prepared to take notes as Don clicked on his iPad.

'First up, there's Liam Carruthers, one of the truck drivers.' Don Finlayson had a strong Scottish accent. 'He's been flashing around photos of a couple of properties he's bought on the Gold Coast recently. And during most of his rostered breaks he travels overseas. In the past four months, he's met his partner in –' Don referred to his notes on the iPad in front of him on the table '– Paris, Las Vegas, Singapore and Hong Kong.'

Connor lifted his head. 'No other source of income identified?'

'That's over to you. Just the bragging about the money and showing photos of the casinos he visits,' Don said. 'He's definitely being bankrolled by somebody. We pay well at the mine, but not well enough for the lifestyle he's recently taken up.'

'I'll check him out thoroughly.'

'Second on the list –' Don glanced back down at his iPad '– Rocky Cardella. He's a long-term indigenous employee who works across a few different sections in –'

'Why have you flagged him?' John Robinson had mentioned Cardella at their initial meeting, but Connor recalled that he had dismissed him. Connor didn't want to know the work details, only the reasons he had been flagged initially, but Don continued in the same slow, deep voice.

'He's been with us since the early days. The very beginning, in fact. Cardella was actually working with the geologists who discovered the first diamonds on the site back in the late seventies. He's the longest serving employee onsite and he knows the place like the back of his hand. Because of cultural considerations he has a little bit more freedom in how he comes and goes off site.' Don sat up straighter and rested his elbows on the table. 'He might know a way off site without going through security, but we haven't picked anything up on the security cameras. And we've been watching him closely since the diamonds surfaced. There are some other issues there, but I won't go through them now. You'll find them in his file.'

'What do you mean by "cultural considerations"?'

Don went to answer, but John interrupted him. 'Rocky is a member of the indigenous board—the traditional owners that we liaise with. Don's added him to the list because of his freedom to come and go. He belongs to the *Gija* and *Miriuwung* people and he was a primary influence in the drawing up of the Matsu Participation Agreement. I told you about the issues that are being raised up there at the moment and I suspect he is behind them. I don't know what his motivation is. Could be genuine. Could be a cover for something else. I've argued with Don on this because I don't agree with his inclusion as a suspect, but I realise I can't be swayed by my gut feeling.'

Connor nodded. Suspicions and gut feelings weren't good enough on their own. 'Worth looking at if he can leave without going through security.'

'I doubt very much if he is involved. Working at the mine for so long, he has a balanced view and he was invaluable when we were negotiating the new agreement with the traditional owners. But yes, I know I have to keep an open mind.'

Don and John had exchanged a significant glance when they'd moved on to the next flagged staff member.

'The most likely suspect in both our minds is someone who came from Dubai just over nine months ago—Dru Porter.'

Connor's interest quickened and he nodded. 'Dubai? What's his position here?'

'It's a she. Dru is short for some long female name.' John picked up another file from his desk and flicked over a page. 'Drusilla Porter. She's an engineer and she was working on the *Ain Dubai*—you know that Ferris wheel project in Dubai? There was very little information about why she left the company and she was quite adamant at her initial interview that her connection to Dubai remained confidential.'

'There's a big difference between working in Dubai and here. I imagine the salary and the perks in Dubai would be much better.' Connor nodded thoughtfully. He'd make his own decisions, but John was right to flag this Porter woman.

'She halved her salary to come here.'

'That's noteworthy,' Connor said.

'There's not a lot of information in her file, but she was employed in an environmental capacity in Dubai, same as here. This is only her second job. She's a fairly recent graduate and we don't know much about her.' John handed over to Don.

'On site, she's efficient, does her job well, and keeps very much to herself.' Don glanced down at his iPad. 'She did express an interest in being a part of the cultural committee and as part of her role she consults with the traditional owners regularly to ensure that the rehabilitation is culturally appropriate.' He lifted his gaze to meet Connor's eyes. 'What may be of interest to you is the only person she seems to have struck up a friendship with is Rocky Cardella.'

Connor nodded and drew a connecting line between the two names.

Don glanced at John as he spoke. 'There's one more thing you need to be aware of.'

'Yes?' Connor said.

'Over the past six months, we've had problems with the security cameras onsite. Persistent choppiness of the feed, and intermittent freezing of the video. We've had the technicians up from Perth a number of times, but the problem always reappears a few weeks later.'

'Are the cameras hard-wired or wireless?' Connor asked.

'Wireless,' Don replied.

'Okay, I'll have a look at that too.'

'The dates and times of the interference episodes are in one of the reports in your file.' John added. 'It may be significant, or it may not. That's your brief.'

Connor sat back and folded his arms. 'Okay, so just to summarise where you're up to . . . only the three persons of interest? What other evidence do you have?'

'That's the problem. We have nothing more. Nothing apart from supposition and tenuous links and coincidences. Rocky and Dru are the only ones who may ever have opportunity.' John shook his head and then stared at Connor. 'I want you to get the evidence so we can put a stop to this as quickly as possible. As well as the cultural issues, there are other problems affecting our share price at the moment. If news gets out that there has been such a significant theft, our stocks will plummet, and that could impact on the approval for the second underground mine. Do whatever it takes . . . and do it fast.'

Don stood and shook his hand. 'You need to know I'm taking some personal leave for a month. While I'm off, Adam Hennessey, my second-in-charge is running the security section, but John and I have both agreed that he doesn't need to know about the thefts, or your undercover role.'

'The less who know the better,' John added.

Connor had left the meeting deep in thought. He had lot of information to sift through, as well as reading up on what his undercover role as the workplace health and safety officer would entail. Being a compliance officer on a working mine site was a far cry from the old occupational health and safety committee he'd been on ten years ago in the Federal Police.

Now he looked around the plane but didn't recognise any of the faces. John had provided photos of Carruthers, Cardella and Porter. Three very different people in a large staff. If those leads turned out to be dead ends, it might prove to be a longer and more difficult job than the CEO hoped for. The camera issue was one that he would prioritise.

The landing gear of the plane lowered with a whir and a thud; Connor's eyes widened as he took in Matsu Diamond Mine below. Much bigger than he'd anticipated; it looked like a small town from the air. Dozens of buildings dotted the large site and a network of roads surrounded the mine on three sides. Several car parks surrounded the various buildings and three bulk storage tanks. On the western edge was a large hill that brought to mind the pyramids of Egypt. The plane completed a circle over the site in preparation for landing. On the second pass over Connor realised it was the regular terraces of an open cut mine that gave the hill the look of a pyramid.

The wheels hit the tarmac and the thrust reverse engaged with a roar. A fence covered in purple bougainvillea flashed past as the plane slowed to a taxi and turned towards the terminal.

Chapter 4

Dru rolled over and opened her eyes with a start, feeling like she'd barely slept. After reading Megan's third long message in as many hours, her daytime sleep had been fitful and filled with crazy dreams. She'd been dreaming about rocks crashing into a huge digger with three buckets but the constant banging in her dream was someone pounding on her door.

'Seven o'clock start and bring your dough with you, love.' Rocky's dry laugh reached her as his footsteps passed by her window. 'Gonna wop your butt tonight, lady.'

She turned and buried her face in the pillow with a groan. Her eyes were gritty and her throat was dry. Opening one eye, she lifted her head and squinted at the clock.

A quick swim in the pool and she'd still have time to shower and grab an early dinner before she met the guys. A bit of fun would take her mind off the problem that Megan's request had presented. The last thing she wanted to do was go back to Dubai; she wasn't prepared to take the risk.

Please, Dru. I'll just die if you won't be my bridesmaid.

A reluctant smile had tugged at her lips as she'd read Megan's message. Even though she was a drama queen, Megan had been a great friend to Dru for the two years she'd spent in Dubai. Sam, her fiancé, had been one of Dru's colleagues on the *Ain Dubai* project and she'd met Megan the first week she'd arrived in the city. But although they had developed a close friendship, she had only ever told Megan a little of what had happened; she wasn't sure that anyone would even believe her. Dru had been mortified that she had let things get to the stage they did. Zayed had been so jealous of her friendship with Sam and Megan, and he had even threatened Sam's job once things began to get nasty.

The thought of seeing Zayed terrified her. She closed her eyes again and pulled the shutter down on those thoughts as her heart skittered up a few beats and the familiar clamminess prickled at her neck. She rolled over and lifted the loose hair from her collar as she picked up the phone and read Megan's most recent entreaty for the third time:

Dru darling, we'll look out for you. Promise, promise, promise. We won't leave your side. Oh, please, please, please, Dru. I've found you the most gorgeous cerulean blue pants suit. It will go so well with your blonde hair and your fair skin. I know you won't wear a dress and heels . . . although I don't know why. You are way too self-conscious about your height.

Don't say no straight away, think about it. PLEEEASE xxx

Email me and tell me when you are off shift and I'll call. Please be a sweetheart . . . it would mean the world to me. You've got two weeks to let me know. How generous am I? Love Megs xxx.

Megan was burying her head in the sand if she thought there'd be no risk if Dru went back to Dubai; but it was a problem Dru would sort out later. Right now, she had a poker game to go to. If there was one thing guaranteed to take her mind off her constant worrying it was a poker game with the guys. Rolling over, she climbed out of bed, grabbed her swimmers and slipped them on before knotting a sarong over the top and tucking her braid into a baseball cap.

When she reached the pool, Dru was pleased to see she was the only one taking a late swim. The final shards of sunlight were playing on the desert; the scrubby savannah grasslands picked up the yellow hues from the setting sun and the occasional splash of red flowers of the sticky kurrajong trees glowed brightly against the spinifex grass at the base of the Matsu hills. The Kimberley desert was the opposite of the manmade artificiality of Dubai; she knew where she preferred to be.

The warm air caressed her skin as she slipped the sarong off and placed it on one of the chairs with her baseball cap. As she kicked her thongs off and crossed to the diving blocks, the sun set in a golden flash and the sky faded. The evening star appeared as a pinprick in the indigo sky. Blue, golden and white; she'd been fascinated with the stars growing up. She and her sisters had often lain on their backs in the backyard of the family farm in the Territory watching for shooting stars, ignoring Mum's dire warnings about snakes.

Mosquitoes were the only bites they'd suffered back in those wonderful childhood days. Dru closed her mind and refused to let the memories drift in.

Stepping up onto the diving block, she stood with her toes over the edge of the pool, tucked her chin down and stretched her arms over her head. She rocked gently, anticipating the moment when the cool water would slide over her heated skin before pushing her feet from the diving block and gliding almost soundlessly into the cool water. She broke the surface and took a deep breath before setting off on the first of the twenty laps she had time for before the card game.

***

On arrival at Matsu, Connor met with the site manager and filled in the appropriate paperwork before being shown to Adam Hennessey's office for a security induction. Hennessey was out on the mine site and his administration assistant, Jennifer, settled him at a small desk beneath the window with three large folders.

'Adam's been trying to get rid of this induction role; especially with Don on leave, he spends most of his time out on the site. You can't go out there until you've read them all and signed off,' she said with a smile. 'But I guess that's second nature to you, being a safety officer.'

Connor smiled back. 'I probably wrote the templates they're based on.' Might as well immerse himself in the role from the start.

'Well, I won't say anything about them being boring then.' The young woman flicked him an appreciative glance before leaving Connor to read. 'Happy reading. I've put some biscuits out for you and there's a coffee machine over in the kitchen up the hall.'

He nodded and settled in to read through the documents. *Yep, boring as batshit, but essential on a worksite.*

After reading the security induction in depth, Connor fired up his laptop and made notes on possible security weak points. There were a couple of extra places where the security could be breached additional to those Don and John had identified.

By five o'clock he had an excellent understanding of the processes at the mine. The compliance documents for each department had given him a clear overview of how the site worked. He still had to get his head around the jargon so it sounded as though he knew what he was supposedly checking up on as he roamed around the site. But over the past three weeks, Connor had read up on the safety officer role so he was confident he could carry it off without alerting anyone to the fact that he was in there in an undercover capacity.

Half an hour later the door opened and Jennifer leaned around holding a set of keys.

'Almost done?'

'Yes, all read and signed.'

He walked across and handed the signed documents over to her as she stepped into the room.

'Thanks. Adam asked me to convey his apologies. They're having trouble with one of the cameras at the fuel depot where the tourist buses refuel and he's not going to be back anytime soon.' She held the keys out to him. 'He asked me to give you these and directions to the village. He's set you up with an office along the corridor here and he'll show you tomorrow. Meanwhile there's a ute for your use. The number is on the key. It's in the car park outside this building. And you're in Apartment 16.' She grinned at him. 'Lucky you. Right near the pool.'

'Apartment with a water view?' Connor closed his laptop and took the keys with a smile.

'Yeah, in your dreams. More like a box overlooking a puddle. Anyway, welcome to Matsu.' Jennifer smoothed her hands down her work trousers and shot him a shy smile. 'If you're ever at a loose end and want a coffee, give me a call. I live down in the staff village too.'

'Thanks. I'll keep that in mind.'

'Oh, I almost forgot.' She turned as she reached the door. 'Adam said to walk down to the staff mess after you get settled in your accommodation and he'll meet you for dinner. He always sits at the table beside the coffee machine. After six he said.'

It only took a few minutes for Connor to find the ute matching the key number, throw in his duffel bag and briefcase and head back along the road towards the airport. The turn-off to the staff village was halfway along to the left. He crested a small hill and parked the ute next to another twenty or so identical vehicles.

The prefabricated buildings were situated in six rows from the top of the hill down to a large grassy area that surrounded a small swimming pool and tennis court. In an-L shape at the end of the pool, a building with a flat roof butted onto the pool enclosure. Connor assumed it was the staff mess. Collecting his bag, he followed the signs until he reached the end of the second row from the bottom. Apartments ten to twenty were in that row. Five minutes later, he'd stowed his bag and checked out the single bedroom, tiny bathroom and double sofa and coffee table that made up the accommodation. On a small table beside the sofa was the electric kettle and two cups with some packets of coffee, sugar and three tea bags, and small containers of long-life milk. He shrugged. It didn't matter; he'd be spending all of his time out on the site.

The walls of the donga pressed in on him—the room *was* too small to be called an apartment—so he pushed open the door and stood on the tiny covered landing at the top of the three steps. The night was quiet, with only the muted roar of machinery coming from the west where the mine was situated about three kilometres away. A movement below caught his eye and he watched as a tall woman strode to the edge of the pool and stood on the diving block. Slim and lithe, she barely made a splash as she broke the water. He watched her swim a few laps before he closed the door and headed down towards the building at the bottom of the hill. When he reached the mess, he turned as he heard the occasional splash from the pool. The lone swimmer was still there, turning gracefully as she reached the end and flipped over to commence her next lap.

Once you were off shift, he guessed there wouldn't be a lot to fill your time at Matsu mine. He'd go stir crazy if he had to work in a place like this all the time. He shrugged again and turned towards the building behind him.

Hennessey was waiting for him where Jennifer told Connor he would find him. He stood and held out his hand.

'Connor. I'm Adam Hennessey. Welcome to Matsu. Sorry I wasn't around to meet you before.'

Connor shook his hand; Hennessey had a firm group and held his eye steadily. He sat back down and picked up the large mug on the table as Connor pulled out a chair. 'I'm just having a coffee and then we'll eat. No after work beer here, unfortunately,' he said.

'Goes with the territory,' Connor said as he pulled out a chair. 'No coffee for me. I'll grab a juice in a while.'

Hennessey grimaced and held his mug up. 'It's about the only thing keeping me going at the moment. 'We've been busy here over the past month. Bloody breakdowns across the site almost every day. Luckily I only have to worry about the security equipment. The mechanical engineers have had to address so many breakdowns, they've flown in another couple of engineers from Perth.' He drained his coffee and put the mug on the table. 'Things usually run like clockwork here.'

Connor's nod was noncommittal. They chatted for a while and Connor listened as Adam dominated the conversation. Happily, he was a talker and it seemed he liked to talk about himself. Within minutes, Connor had heard about his wife and three children back in Brisbane, where he'd worked before and how happy he'd been to pick up the job here at Matsu.

'How long have you worked here?'

This is my third year in the job,' Adam said. 'I usually love every minute of it, but the past couple of months have been particularly busy and I've put in longer hours than I like to.'

The door opened with a soft slide and a buzz ran through Connor when a tall blonde woman walked into the dining room.

Dru Porter. He recognised her immediately from the staff photo on the file John Robinson had given him. And he now realised, she was the woman he'd seen dive into the pool. He stared at her for a moment and turned at Adam's chuckle. He was looking at Connor with a smile on his face.

'Good looker,' Connor commented with a grin. He inclined his head over towards the counter where she stood reading the board. Dru Porter had to be over six feet tall. Her long blonde hair was damp and hung to her waist, brushing the top of her knee-length khaki cargo pants. Her calves were toned and when she lifted her arm to point to the board, the muscles flexed in the top of her arm.

A strong, fit and—he thought reluctantly—very attractive woman.

'Don't waste your time.' Hennessey stared across the room with him.

'Oh?' His comment surprised Connor. For a moment, the jovial demeanour had slipped and there had been a slight tinge of hostility in Hennessey's tone.

'She's not into men. Some of the staff say she thinks she's too good for the rest of us. A few of the blokes have tried their luck but she always lives up to her nickname.' He shook his head. 'Or so the site gossip goes. Not that I know personally.' Hennessey lifted his left hand and his gold wedding band flashed. 'Like I said, I've got the noose around my neck.' This time he laughed. 'But I wouldn't have it any other way.'

Connor nodded and looked away from Dru. 'What's the nickname?'

'The ice queen.'

Connor turned back to the counter as Hennessey's phone buzzed on the table.

He watched Dru Porter chat to the kitchen hand while Adam took the call. Moments later he hung up.

'Damn, we've had a video freeze up in the processing plant. A quick feed and it's back to work for me.'

'Jennifer said you had a problem with a camera earlier today?' Connor probed. 'What's the problem?'

'Mate, if I knew the answer to that I wouldn't be working the long hours I have been. Cheap Chinese shit. You'd think a company making mega dollars could spend some of it on decent gear, wouldn't you?'

'You would.' He nodded and tried to sound sympathetic. 'And boy, that could impact on my job too. If there's second rate equipment on site.'

Adam looked at him curiously. 'With all the recent breakdowns I guess that's why we're having a safety audit.'

'Yep, safety. That's my brief,' Connor replied.

Chapter 5

Having showered after her swim, Dru stood at the blackboard in the staff mess hall reading the pearls of wisdom that someone had put up above the day's menu.

'Every now and then, go away have a little relaxation, for when you come back to work, your judgement will be surer. Go some distance away and then the work appears smaller . . .'

'Soup or pasta bake, love?' Jeff, the chef, held the ladle over the hot food in the bain-marie.

'Leonardo da Vinci?' She pointed to the loopy chalk writing on the board.

'Huh?' He screwed his face up before he glanced up at the board and read the credit beneath the quote. 'Oh, apparently it is. That's one of Julie's quotes. She was raving on before about restoring harmony or some such thing when she wrote it up this morning.'

'Good advice for a two-week on, two-week off workforce though. Serve the others while I decide.'

Dru looked at the hot food laid out in front of her. It smelled appetising but her stomach was still roiling with worry. Should she listen to Megan and go back to Dubai on her two-week break next month? How could Megan and Sam possibly stay by her side the whole time? It was their wedding, for goodness' sake. Maybe she could fly in one day, and fly out the next? Megan was a good friend, but to do a twenty-eight-hour return trip like that in a couple of days was stretching it. Jeff interrupted her thoughts.

'What'll it be?'

She slid her tray along towards the refrigerated area at the end of the counter. 'Got any salad left?'

Jeff pulled open one of the fridge doors that ran the length of the stainless-steel bench. 'You'll need more than salad in your stomach if you're joining up with that lot over there tonight.' He nodded towards the small group of men sitting at the table in the far corner of the large eating area. 'Can't tempt you with the pasta bake?'

'No thanks . . . and why more than salad?'

'Poker night, isn't it?' He winked as he handed over the salad. 'To soak up the alcohol.'

Dru shot him a puzzled smile. 'Alcohol-free worksite, Jeff. Salad will be plenty to go with my coffee.'

'Sure it will, love.' He winked again as he turned back to the kitchen. 'I'll give you a yell if I see the new bloke heading across to you.'

'New bloke?'

'The work safety guy. That's him over behind the coffee station with Adam. Not a good first impression if he springs you drinking. Not to mention the cigar fumes if those blokes light up. I've already spoken to that bloody Rocky. They'll be escorted off site before you can snap your fingers.'

Dru threw a quick glance across the room. During her site induction, Adam Hennessey had tried his best to entice her to join the social activities down at the mess. There was always something being organised—'Corporate Wellness' was the catch cry. In the time she'd been at Matsu, organised activities had ranged from walking and jogging groups, a baseball team and a touch football team. For the more sedentary workers, there was yoga, darts and pool competitions and cooking classes.

In nine months, the only team she'd joined was Rocky's poker game and that wasn't one of the formally organised activities. She preferred to work out alone, and her daily swim kept her fit, as did the kilometres she walked around the site each shift.

Dru placed her bowl of salad on the tray, then added a bread roll and crossed to the coffee machine. She'd be no good in tonight's game without a good kick of caffeine. Jeff was wrong about the alcohol; the poker games might sometimes be loud and raucous but they weren't fuelled by alcohol. A group of hard-working men—and one woman—

letting off some steam didn't need alcohol to relax them. Besides, getting caught with alcohol on the mine site—whether it was in the working areas or in the staff mess, or even in the privacy of the staff accommodation—meant instant dismissal.

Hitting a double shot of espresso to fill her cup, Dru took a sip and waited for the buzz to flood her system.

'Hey Dru!' Adam called across to her from the table closest to the coffee machine.

A ripple of unease ran through her when she turned. The new guy was staring at her intently. She straightened her shoulders and stared back as his eyes held her gaze without wavering. The guy's expression was hard to read and she lifted her chin as her own eyes travelled slowly over him—more for her own confidence than any interest.

What was it with these guys who had to prove themselves? Another one who objected to a woman in what many men considered should be an all-male worksite. In the couple of years since she'd graduated, Dru had come across sexism in the workplace on more occasions than she could count, although Matsu was nothing like what she'd experienced in Dubai.

She was not going to be the first to look away. His mid-brown hair was sun-tipped and neatly cut, and the short back and sides framed an angular, chiselled face. The short-sleeved collared shirt and navy tie stood out like a sore thumb in the mess where the workers usually wore hi-vis tinged with a layer of red dust. As she continued to stare, his lips lifted in an appreciative smile but it didn't reach his eyes. It wasn't helping her equilibrium one little bit that his eyes reminded her of Zayed's. A different colour but the same intensity, the same look that said 'I know what you are thinking.'

How dare he? Well, by the look on her face, he'd know that she was thinking he was crossing the line with his stare and his smart-arse smile. She stood there until it became too uncomfortable to take it any longer. Her heart was pounding and her temper fired. How could she let one simple look get her into this state?

Finally she was the first to look away. Gripping her tray tightly, she took the few steps to the table and ignored the rude newcomer. 'Hello, Adam.'

'I thought you were off to Darwin. Wasn't your two-week roster up today?' Adam's grin was welcoming. He was a stocky man with fair-skinned ruddy cheeks, and even though he always had a friendly greeting for her, she'd tried not to get involved in conversations. 'I thought I'd missed you.'

'I'm staying on.' Dru balanced the tray as she stood there avoiding looking at the new guy. 'We've got some new procedures coming online this week and I wanted to be here to supervise.

'No wonder I can't keep up with who's around. Rosters are non-existent here.' Adam stood and shook his head, his grin getting wider. 'Anyway, I wanted to ask a favour.' He reached over and took the tray. 'Here, let me take this for you. You're heading across to the poker game, I guess?' He gestured with his head across the room.

'Yes, I am. Thank you.' Dru frowned when he turned back to the table.

'Sorry mate, how rude of me. You don't know Dru yet, do you?' Adam looked from one to the other. 'Of course, you don't! You only arrived today and you've been locked up doing your induction.' Adam balanced the tray on one hand as he turned back to her. 'Dru Porter, meet Connor Kirk.'

Dru nodded silently as he pushed his chair back and stood.

'Hello, Dru. Pleased to meet you.'

'And you. Welcome to Matsu.' She turned back to Adam. 'Why did you want to see me? Is there a problem with my section?' There'd been a few meetings recently. 'Another meeting I need to know about?'

'No, nothing like that. All good.' He grinned at her and his eyes crinkled. 'I have a personal favour to ask.'

'Personal?' Dru wondered what he could mean.

Adam followed her as she headed to the table where the poker boys were waiting for her. She glanced back. Connor had sat down and was looking at his phone. Since Dubai her comfort zone meeting new people had hit rock bottom and he'd made her feel very uncomfortable.

'What I wanted to ask you—' Adam's phone beeped and he put the tray down on the table and turned away. 'Excuse me.'

Dru waited while he took the call.

'I'm on my way.' Adam disconnected and shoved the phone into his shirt pocket. 'Sorry, Dru. I have to run. Good to know you're around for the rest of the week. I'll catch you later.'

'Okay. I'm leaving next Friday.'

'I'll call by and see you before then.' Adam nodded at the others. 'Enjoy your game. Playing for cattle stations again?' His laugh boomed around the room and Dru was aware of the new guy's interest as he watched them.

'Yep, high stakes game tonight.' Rocky Cardella waved the cards in his hand as he grinned. 'Don't think coffee's going to give the queen the edge tonight, Adam.' Rocky nudged the guy sitting on his left as Adam hurried away. 'Thinks she's the queen of the card table, doesn't she, mate.'

Dru pulled out a chair. 'Hey, guys. Good to see you all too.' She sat down and reached for her coffee as she looked around at the motley crew. Rocky's dark curly hair was sticking out in tufts as always, and his T-shirt was stained where he'd spilled something down the front. A pile of gambling chips lay in the centre of the table. Gary was tapping his fingers on the table as he waited for the game to begin. Dave and Liam were both glued to their phones but there was no sign of Paul, the most serious member of the group who made sure no one cheated.

'And yep, I'll keep my crown, until—what was it you yelled through my door before, Rocky? That's right, I'll be keeping it until someone wops my butt.' She forced herself to smile as she lifted her damp hair from her neck, letting the cool air circulate on her overheated skin. Normally she braided her waist-length hair because it was so hot in the desert heat but she'd washed it in the shower after her swim and was letting it dry. She'd plait it later, before her shift tonight. Reaching into her pocket for her lucky shade, she pulled it on over her loose hair, more at ease now that she was with people she knew. Her heart rate had settled down and she took a deep breath.

Dad had taught her to play poker and she had taken his lucky shade and put it in with her school things when the house had been packed up soon after he'd died. Dad had spent a lot of time with Dru and her sisters when they'd been growing up on the farm. He'd taught them to drive an old bush bomb in the flat paddocks by the river in their early teens, and he'd taught them all to drive the tractor. Ellie had been his apprentice farmer, Emma had loved being in the kitchen with Mum, and Dru had been his card-playing mate at night.

Dru's poker nights with Dad had been hers alone. Lifting her cup, she closed her eyes and let the precious memories steal over her as she sipped the steaming coffee.

'Finished your maths homework, love?' Same question every night, and she'd nod and pick up the cards and head for their card table outside. Nights like that Dru had felt special, even though they all knew Ellie was Dad's favourite. Funny, she could still picture Emma sitting in the swing chair reading, but Ellie didn't figure much in her memories. Maybe because they'd had such a difficult relationship since Dad had died.

Dad had been the master of the poker face and he'd taught her well out on the enclosed verandah where they'd played cards most nights. In the wet season, the rain had drummed on the tin roof and made it a cosy place to spend time with Dad.

'The luck of the draw isn't important.' She could still hear his deep voice over the plopping of the mango chutney on the stove as Mum stirred the huge, stained pot. The volume of the television in the small lounge room was turned up loud so Mum could hear the ABC news over the heavy rain pounding on the roof.

'The second most important thing that will let you take control of a game is your face. Don't move a muscle. Don't give one flicker of an eyelid.'

Dru had jutted her chin out and matched his bland gaze. Her face would be set in a stiff mask, her eyes wide and her mouth straight. They'd sit like that until the first one cracked with a tilt of lips, and the other would collapse into fits of laughter.

'Gotcha!' Dru had learned her poker face quickly and Dad was usually the first to give in.

'Okay, chicken, you've got the face right. Now you have to master the most important thing.'

Dru had stared at him as the gentle warmth of his voice washed over her. They were what she focused on; his poker face and his deep voice kept her rational when the bad memories tried to push in.

'You have to control your emotions. And that's the trick. We're not wired to deal with probability and randomness, so you have to control your emotional reaction. Don't follow your gut. You must make the correct logical play every hand, no matter what you've been dealt, and that is one of the hardest things to do in poker.'

Logic. That was what had led her into an engineering career. If only Dad had been around to see her graduate. He would have been so proud. And he would have told her to wake up to herself, get over this stupid fear. She could just hear him now. 'Control your emotion. You can do it in a poker game, now apply that to your life.'

Well, not only had she learned to control her emotions, Dru had managed to bury them so deeply since Dubai that she didn't feel much at all these days.

All she had to do now was learn to stop worrying about things that were out of her control.

'Up for a big one, Dru?'

She jumped as Rocky's gravelly voice interrupted her memories and she opened her eyes and put her cup down.

'Nah, I'm on shift at eleven. What about you lot?'

Rocky's grin stretched his facial muscles in a wide arc. 'We're all on day shift. So we can go all night if we want.'

'That's if you have any money left after I've taken it all from you.' She turned to him with a cheeky smile and Rocky shoved the stub of a cut cigar towards her. 'Light that up for me while I cut the cards, will ya, love.'

'Jesus, Rocky. If you want to smoke, you know you have to go outside.'

'Let's take the game outside, then.' Rocky pushed his chair back and stood up and Dru shook her head.

'Don't be silly. It's still stinking hot out there and the mozzies would carry us away.

'Ah.' He flicked her a sidelong glance. 'But there's a few other fumes to cover up.'

'Fumes?' Dru looked across as Liam and Dave surreptitiously lifted a pair of hip flasks from beneath the table. She frowned as she shook her head. 'Look guys, I don't want to be a killjoy, but you know what happens if you get caught, don't you?'

'Worth the risk.' Dave looked around before he took a swig from the small flask and shoved it back in his pocket. 'And we've got a full twelve hours before we go underground. A couple of early drinks won't hurt.'

Dru rolled her eyes and then sat back and listened as the guys joked with each other. It was the first time she'd seen the guys drinking and it didn't sit comfortably with her.

'Where's Paul?' It would be a loud—and long—night if Paul wasn't there to keep the guys in order. She began to wish she'd turned down the offer of tonight but she had a reputation to uphold.

'He's gone to the bog.' Rocky sat back down and held his hand out to Gary for the cards and then tapped his fingers restlessly. 'And he wants to get a move on. I ain't waitin' all night.'

The sliding doors opened at the entrance and Dru looked over, but it wasn't Paul. More workers from the day shift walked in, all showered and dressed in shorts and T-shirts—men and women. They'd finished work for the day, hair damp, and no sign of red dust as they headed over to the buffet for the night meal. The noise in the room increased as a few other groups settled into card games.

Someone turned the television on over in the corner and Sky News blared across the room.

As well as the new guy that had been with Adam, there were other new faces in the mess. The staff at the mine was large and itinerant, but Dru wasn't interested in knowing who worked where. Working in an environment where the staff came and went suited her just fine. Casual relationships and a game of cards now and then kept her at the distance she wanted. No one up close and personal wanting to know her business, and no one knowing that her brash exterior was a mask for the uncertainty that dogged her most of the time. Her work was her life and that's all she needed. She had her small crew and didn't interact with the other sections, spending most of her days out at the southern end of the tailings dam.

As they waited for Paul to come back, Dru stared out into the deepening dusk over the Matsu Range, thinking of the message waiting on her phone. Megan had been a great friend to her, and when things had gone to shit in Dubai, she and Sam had helped her. If it hadn't been for their quick thinking, she could have ended up getting caught in a more difficult situation than they knew.

Rocky's curse interrupted her brooding and Dru looked over at him. The room had filled but there was still one empty seat at their table.

'Jesus, where is he?' Rocky put his beefy hands on the table and pushed himself up. 'I'm not waiting anymore. I'm gonna go see where that bastard's got to.'

'Wait up.' Dave lifted his head from his phone. 'I just got a text from him. He's gone back to his room. Doesn't want to play tonight. He's got the runs.'

'Ah, fuckin' oath. We're not playing with five.' Rocky scowled as he slumped down into his chair. Dru was used to his quirky ways; she'd learned to read his face and could easily guess what his hand was by the scowl or the sneaky look that crept across his face if he had a good hand of cards.

'Suits me. I'll go and get some more sleep before I start my shift.' Dru went to stand but Rocky put his hand on her chair.

'Nah, we're here now. I'll ask one of the boys over there. ' Rocky pushed his chair back while Dave and Liam argued.

'Three hundred mate.' Liam dug into his pocket and pulled his wallet out. Dru had noticed before that the truck driver always liked to flash his cash around.

'No way.' Dave shook his head. 'You might be able to afford to lose that sort of money but my missus'd skin me alive if I did.'

Liam would bet on anything. He apparently had more money than brains; one night she'd seen him betting on flies crawling along the window sill. She tilted her face to the cool of the air conditioning pumping through the vents and looked out the window at the desert. now shrouded in darkness. Focusing on the view brought her to the now and she pushed away thinking about the decision she had to make.

'Hey guys, I found us another victim.' Rocky laughed. 'Ah, sorry, Connor, I meant to say player. Guys, this is Connor Kirk. He's happy to stand in for Paulie.'

Great. Just bloody great.

Dru forced herself to look up as Rocky gestured to the chair opposite her. The light was behind Connor's head and his dark eyes were shadowed but the silhouette of his frame showed off his height and broad square shoulders. She hadn't noticed how tall he was before; she'd been too busy trying to evade that piercing stare. Mum, and Ellie and Emma were tiny, but Dru had thrown back to Dad's side of the family. She towered over most guys she met but Connor was so tall she had to tilt her head back to make eye contact with him. Her antennae went back to high alert; he exuded the same air of authority and cockiness that she'd seen so many times in her engineering career, and they always turned out to be dickheads.

Adam was standing beside him. 'Connor, good to meet up with you. Enjoy the game. Meet me in the security building tomorrow at eight and I'll show you around.'

'Pull up a pew, mate,' Rocky said. 'Time to get this show on the road.'

Connor nodded and as he sat in the chair across from her, Dru caught his eye. A slow lazy smile quirked his full lips and he raised one eyebrow as he leaned tanned forearms on the table.

'The token female?' His voice was slow and deep with an undercurrent of something unspoken beneath his words.

Yep, a dickhead.

Before she could come back with a smart reply, Rocky butted in. 'Don't be too hasty. Dru here is the queen of the poker table.'

He held out his hand and nodded. 'Hi, Dru. Good to meet you . . . again.'

It would have been rude to ignore him. She half-rose and shook his hand briefly, then held his gaze as she slowly wiped her hand on the side of her jeans.

'Dave and Liam are over there, and that's Gary on your right.' Rocky, social as ever, made the introductions all round. Connor shook hands and then settled into his chair. As Dru watched, he took off his tie and shoved it in his pocket, then undid the top couple of buttons of his shirt. Dru looked away and folded her arms, waiting for Rocky to go through his usual card shuffling ritual.

He shuffled and counted and muttered and Dru looked up to find Connor watching her again.

Bloody hell, she was so over this guy of the intense stares. Talk about obvious.

'Are you right there?' she said jutting her chin out.

'I am. Why do you ask?' His voice was deep and he kept his eyes on her. She could swear his chin lifted a bit too. Belligerent as well as being a smart-arse.

She folded her arms and leaned back in the chair before she answered him.

'No reason.' She kept her voice light.

'I'm pleased,' he said.

Great, just the way she wanted to spend the night. Two guys with alcohol hidden in their flasks, a pissing contest and way too much testosterone. And a new guy who obviously had something to prove. The only fun tonight would be wiping that knowing smirk off his face, although if truth be known she'd have been way happier back in her donga watching a movie.

Liam's chuckle covered the sharp click as Rocky split the cards on the table.

'So what section of the plant are you working, mate?' Liam asked.

'All of it. I'm doing a workplace safety and compliance audit.'

Dave and Liam spluttered and looked at each other as Rocky dealt the first hand.

Dru picked up her cards. It was going to be a long night, but it would be far worse for the guys sitting at the table with the workplace safety officer and their hip flasks burning a hole in their pockets. She couldn't help the grin that crossed her face when she caught Rocky's eye.

Chapter 6

'Right are we ready? Finally?' Rocky's husky voice ground out.

The first couple of hands were slow and Dru let her usual focus slide. Connor had got under her skin, and Megan's message was still at the forefront of her thoughts. She stared at her diminished pile of chips; it was time to get her act together and start concentrating on the game. She sat up straight and watched Rocky lick his lips as he checked his cards. He pulled them close to his chest, then looked up and caught her eye.

Too late, Rocky. The lip licking was a dead giveaway; he had a good hand this time.

Dru glanced down at her cards and her gaze roamed over the others, except for Connor. Liam was peering at his cards impassively. Dave, who didn't bluff and as a result never won, was tapping his leg, a sure-fire signal that he had something worthwhile. But he surprised her when he put his cards down and said, 'I'm out.'

God, she was really off her game tonight.

Dru looked down at the cards on the table before she finally forced herself to look at Connor. She'd processed what was there; it was highly unlikely that anyone was holding a better hand than she was. Keeping her face blank, she waited until the final card was turned. The back of her neck prickled and she looked over to Connor. His eyes were alight with a smile.

Stuff you, Mr Smart-arse.

She sat up straighter and raised the bet to twenty dollars. Rocky grunted in disgust, then put his cards down. Liam and Gary sat quietly until Connor spoke.

'Fifty dollars.' His voice was clear and smug.

Dru knew he was bluffing. Putting on the big man act.

'I'll see you.' She moved the same number of chips to the middle. An unpleasant shiver ran down her as Connor held her gaze.

It was as though he was toying with her, like a cat torments its prey before pouncing. His expression reminded her of Zayed's, and that unnerved her even more. She held back the need to swallow to ease her dry throat, and sat perfectly still, refusing to be intimidated.

Liam and Gary spoke together. 'I'm out.'

Dru fanned her cards on the table and smiled as she displayed a full house. As she scooped the chips over, she bit back a satisfied smile as Rocky crowed proudly.

'Told ya, matey. Our Dru's the queen of the table.

***

After Dru won the hand, Connor relaxed and looked at the group sitting around the table. He knew better than to put anything down to luck *or* coincidence. It was a large staff and to find Dru Porter, Rocky Cardella and Liam Carruthers all in the one place on his first day on the job was more than coincidence. It appeared that the three staff flagged by John Robinson were all known to each other. On a site this size, that had to be more than coincidence.

It was a shame Hennessey had been called away. Connor had missed the end of the conversation about the favour between them when Adam had carried Dru's tray across the room for her. But he'd be following that up.

Being asked to join the poker game had been an unexpected bonus; he was already getting a fair idea of personalities from watching the play and he'd make the most of this opportunity to see what made them tick away from the worksite. He could smell the grog on Carruthers' breath, but he wasn't going to mention that. Keep them onside; he had a lot more to look for than an illicit swig here and there. Not his problem, but it did say a lot about the workings of the site. If security was lax in one area, the problem was sure to be widespread.

It was a matter of finding the weak points—he'd identified a few of them from the paperwork alone—and then identifying who had created them, and was using them to get the diamonds off site. It might be one person, but logic told him there had to be more working together.

Illicit alcohol aside, and Hennessey's comment about cheap equipment, the visible security on the site was equal to the best he'd seen. On the way over to the staff dongas, he'd noticed the cameras on every building and every road intersection. He'd asked Hennessey about the cameras in the brief talk he'd given him about safety when he'd first joined him at the table. Apparently, they were monitored twenty-four seven from the large windowless security building and at the Matsu head office in Perth. Those cameras could prove problematic as he moved around the site when he didn't want to be observed. But Don Finlayson could probably sort that if it became necessary.

Liam dealt the second hand. Connor sat back and watched Dru as she picked the cards up and stared at them without a change of expression. A frown had wrinkled her brow since he had first looked at her.

'Sour' was the word that came to mind. The one time she'd grinned her face had come alight but it hadn't lasted long.

He looked down at her hands holding the cards. Square cut fingernails and no rings on her fingers. No wedding ring or jewellery of any sort; not even her ears were pierced. Despite the frown and her pursed lips, she was still a beautiful woman. Her face was strong; fair skin, lightly freckled, with high cheekbones and lush full lips. In contrast to her almost white-blonde hair, her lashes and brows were dark. Her eyes were a pale blue; almost an ice-blue that matched the look that she'd shot him when he'd deliberately dropped the sexist comment.

When Cardella challenged her in the next hand, Connor could have sworn he saw her lips tilt slightly. Maybe not, blink and you'd miss it.

'Well?' Her voice was husky and throaty and it held a hint of mirth for the first time.

'Raise you,' Cardella replied with a chuckle.

'Nup. It's all yours.' She fanned her losing cards on the table and a huge grin crossed Rocky's face.

'Looks like I've got a chance tonight, sweetheart.' He rubbed his hands together gleefully as Gary dealt the next hand. 'Mugs away.'

'Don't get too fucking cocky, Rocky-boy.' She flicked Connor a glance as she swore. Not as cool as he'd first thought; the look was a dead giveaway. She was putting on an act for him.

The tension built with each hand and despite Connor's intention of staying detached, a measure of distaste settled in his gut as Dru's language matched that of the men. The way she held herself and the way she interacted with them projected an extremely confident woman, a woman who was very comfortable in a man's world.

Hard as nails. From this first impression, he reckoned Dru would be capable of anything. She oozed confidence. Maybe she was someone who would have the guts to steal diamonds and smuggle them out of the mine. He was aware that she was watching him from beneath lowered lids as he threw his cards on the table. She won the next hand.

'Jesus, Dru, anyone would think you were playing for a fucking cattle station.' She grinned at the whine in Rocky's voice.

'Maybe we will be one day, Rocky-boy. Maybe we will.' Her laugh was husky like her voice.

Connor's attention wandered as he thought about her choice of career and work location. There was a big difference between working in an international city like Dubai, and here in the isolated wilds of the East Kimberley. And John had said she'd taken a fifty percent drop in salary to come here. He'd be looking closely at Dru's records and references. *Was* she here for the takings? Salary and more?

'So, are you still in?' Her voice broke into his thoughts. He looked up and she lifted her chin and stared him down. He pushed back his irritation, forcing a smile. She rubbed him the wrong way but he wasn't going to give her the satisfaction of a reaction. Before he could find out if she was involved, he would have to win her trust, and getting her offside on his first night at the mine was not the way to go about it. He sensed he'd already upset her with his scrutiny and he hoped she'd take it as purely male interest.

'Sure am.' He glanced down at his cards, lifted his chin and held her gaze. 'I'll raise you.'

From that point, the poker game became a battle between the two of them. Connor ignored her cursing as the tension grew but he figured she was probably doing it to distract him from his game. He stayed calm and cool. When she reached for the cigar that Rocky offered, she let her gaze swivel around to his and raised her eyebrows.

'I thought there was a no smoking rule in here,' he said sardonically.

'But I'm not smoking,' came the quick reply. 'Just holding a lucky cigar.'

But not so lucky for Ms Dru Porter tonight.

Connor had played cards with the best, and he knew he was the master of the poker face. He gathered his winnings a few hours later, as Cardella and Dru walked across the room, deep in conversation. A brief nod was all he'd got from her in the way of goodnight, but the three men had been gleeful that someone had brought the queen of the poker game down.

'Consider yourself the newest member of the Matsu Mine poker club. Paulie can piss off.' Liam punched him on the top of his arm.

As he pushed his chair in, Dru looked back and held his gaze.

Chapter 7

Even though it was much later than she'd planned to get back to her room, Dru wanted to call Megan and tell her she'd let her know as soon as she made her mind up. Mobile phone service in the isolated Matsu Ranges was excellent even though they were over two hundred kilometres from the nearest town—one of the perks of being a mining centre. She glanced at the time; there was about half an hour before her shift started and all she had to do was slip on her hi-vis vest over her jeans and long-sleeved work shirt, braid her hair and pull on her socks and steel-capped boots.

She dialled Megan's number and closed her eyes as she waited for her friend to pick up. It would be early evening in Dubai, and Megan and Sam would be getting ready to go out for pre-dinner drinks as they did every night after work. Dru had been uncomfortable in that world from the outset. Living the high life in a luxury block with the other expat professionals had never sat comfortably with her. It was a long way from the mango farm in the Northern Territory where she'd grown up.

Working in Dubai had been surreal, almost like living in a bubble. But it had been a false picture; the city of perfection, blemish-free, with its massive shopping malls, indoor ski slopes and the constant round of socialising had made it easy to overlook a lot of things.

Dru shook her head and ignored the strange feeling in her fingers. Despite the cool air pumping from the air conditioning, sweat still trickled down her neck as the call went to voicemail. It was going to be hot out in the desert tonight.

'Hey, Megsy, it's me. I'm off to work now. I'll talk to you over the weekend.' A sense of relief flooded through her; she could put off her decision about going to the wedding for a while longer.

After braiding her hair, Dru sat on the step and pulled on her work boots, and then let out a groan of frustration as she looked over at the car park. Liam's ute was behind hers and he had parked her in. She knew it was his because the M decal on the back of the tailgate had come off. Liam thought it was hilarious that his ute read ATSU. Liam and Paul had been fooling around during one poker game making silly phrases from the acronym. In hindsight, they'd probably been drinking that night too. They'd almost fallen off their chairs as they'd giggled like a couple of teenage girls.

'This mine is an "absolute total screw up",' Liam had said.

'Nah.' Paul had barely been able to get the words out between howls of laughter. 'We work in "a total shit unit".'

'I can do better than that,' Liam had snorted. 'Forget the diamonds. We're "all towing shit uphill", mate.'

Later the same night Paul had had a go at her about having her personal car taking up a car space in the car park. Tempers always frayed towards the end of the two-week roster.

Dru glanced down at her watch. There was still time to catch one of the staff buses that ran over to the mine site each shift. She slipped off her room key and buttoned it into her top pocket before throwing her car keys back inside and closing the door quietly behind her. The last thing you wanted when you were lying on the hard ground of the desert was to roll over on a bunch of keys. She'd had those bruises before.

She couldn't help the grin at that thought. Mr Workplace Safety probably had a rule about keys in your pocket. Robin had said there was to be a blitz on work safety over the next month, and he looked like just the type who would enjoy enforcing every regulation. A looker, but obviously a total jerk.

And he'd beaten her at poker too. Although her mind hadn't been on the game tonight, he'd still been good. His face and body language had been totally unreadable, but despite that she got the feeling he'd judged her and she'd been found wanting. And she'd played up to it with the language and the cigar. At least it had taken her thoughts away from Dubai for a while.

The walk to the bus stop would normally clear her head and get her focused on the night's work. But tonight, no matter how much she tried, that sardonic grin stayed with her. When she'd pushed her chair back and stood beside the table after the game, he'd risen automatically and fleeting surprise had run through her.

He had manners.

The bus was almost full when it stopped at the street at the end of her unit block and she stepped up and nodded to the driver before settling into the last vacant seat behind him. She pulled her ear buds from her shirt pocket and slipped them in, leaning back on the headrest for the short trip to the processing plant where she would sign on for her shift.

She managed to avoid any long conversations as she signed on, grabbed the keys to one of the plant utes and walked across to the car park. A few minutes later Dru was alone in the clear and silent night.

The moon was rising over the Matsu Range to the east as she parked the vehicle at the top of the last hill, and she caught her breath as the fat yellow orb cleared the top of the low mountain. Creamy moonlight spilled over the expanse of desert below her and peace stole through her as she stepped from the vehicle. The silence was so complete she could hear the soft night wind puffing across the desert and the occasional rustle of the leaves as it picked up the heat from the ground. She stood still, letting her gaze wander over the flat earth that surrounded the tailings dam to the southwest. The slight wind had kicked up a few waves and the water shimmered silver as the moonlight bounced off it. Tonight, she planned on systematically working through the termite mounds in a grid from the edge of the road to the dam to see if they had been repopulated since the mining activity had ceased in this section of the mine two years ago. As it was the switchover day, she'd rostered herself on alone, but that suited her well tonight.

Dru turned back to the ute, the stony ground crunching beneath her feet as she walked to the flat tray at the back and opened the tool box. Retrieving a small shovel, she lined up half a dozen empty glass vials for the soil samples in a small wooden carry box. As she walked down the hill and paced out the hundred metres to the first mound, she focused on the haphazard line of dark structures between her and the dam. Twenty-six mounds to sample should just about take the whole shift.

Just as she reached the waist-height mound, a shower of small rocks skittered down the hill behind her and she turned. Holding the wooden handle, she scanned the brightly lit terrain for the animal that had disturbed the silence, ready to record the sighting in her log.

This job was great; it was so different to working in the huge team she'd been with on Bluewater Island. There was a big difference between restoring an ancient desert landscape and working on a reclaimed island in a huge, overdeveloped, bustling and wealthy modern city. In Dubai, the ever-present noise of construction machinery on the island had necessitated the wearing of earmuffs. Here in the desert, it was quiet and peaceful, and working alone in the moonlight was soothing. She had plenty to do each shift, there was no time to dwell on the past and that suited her just fine.

Dru looked around again but there was nothing moving. She was careful out here, day and night, knowing how termite mounds could also be home to snakes and goannas as the mounds were often the only reliable ecosystem present in this arid desert. She put down the shovel and reached into the deep pocket of her work trousers and pulled on a pair of thick work gloves. No point getting bitten, and if that workplace safety guy wanted to check on her, she'd be kitted out as per the safety regulations.

Lifting the shovel, she turned back to the termite mound and gasped as a dark figure loomed in front of her.

***

Even though it provided for every need a worker could possibly have, the mini-city of Matsu was still a sterile artificial environment. Connor was glad to head out of the air-conditioned mess once the card game had finished. It had been most informative observing the staff he was interested in, but he'd found it hard to be sociable. It was the first time he'd found himself in a social situation in many months.

This job was going to be very different from chasing the drug runners he'd exposed over the past few years. He still wasn't exactly sure why he'd taken this case on. Maybe he was finally letting go of the past and his crusade to make up for what had happened. Maybe he was tired and just needed a break from the constant danger.

He had lots to think over after seeing the three suspects, and he'd already planned his internet search strategy to drill into their pasts—and their current activities. If people realised how transparent their lives were these days they'd give up their phones and never log on to a computer. Or maybe that was just his jaded viewpoint; it seemed to be that most people took pride in sharing the minutiae of their boring daily lives on social media.

Through a couple of hackers he knew from his time in the Australian Federal Police, he had access to more databases than the normal Google search would retrieve. Maybe not ethical—or legal— but he didn't care. Connor's belief in ethical and legal practices had gone to shit a few years back—along with his career—and whatever it took now to get a job done, he'd do it. Deeper access to banking data was beyond him, but his former colleague Greg didn't mind doing him a favour every so often, and he'd called with his list of requests for each name before he'd come on site.

One of the things Connor was keen to do was to follow up Dru's travel arrangements. As the conversations had washed around him during the game, he had gleaned little nuggets of interest.

'Good drive in last trip, Dru?' Carruthers had asked halfway through the game as Connor had dealt the cards. 'I'm going out that way tomorrow.'

'Yeah. The creeks are still dry, so it's easy getting across.'

'Yeah, me mate's working over at Smokey Creek and he said the roads were much better now. You should be able to get out through the wet this year. I hear they've built up a few of those low bridges over the winter.'

Dru had caught Connor's glance and made a noncommittal noise in response to Carruthers' comments. She'd looked back down at the cards in her hand.

Robinson had mentioned that Cardella drove on and off the site—apparently his home settlement was only a few kilometres away. Connor had assumed that Dru came in by air from Perth with the rest of the fly-in, fly-out workforce.

Make no assumptions; first rule of the game. His interest in her was stacking up but he wouldn't jump to any conclusions based on personality. No matter what his gut reaction had been.

After Dru had left, Cardella had returned to the mess, where Connor had stayed back after the game on the pretext of making another coffee. It was an opportunity to talk to the other guys. The look on their faces was priceless when they realised he was going to hang around, but there was no sign of the hip flasks he'd seen earlier when he'd left the table briefly to grab a Coke from the fridge.

'Great job tonight,' Liam said.

Connor raised his eyebrows. 'How's that.'

'Taking on the ice queen.' Liam's voice was harder than it had been when Dru was at the table. 'The bitch needed taking down a peg or two.'

Before Connor could comment, Rocky stepped over and grabbed Liam's shirt. 'Watch your mouth, boy.'

Liam shrugged him off with a jerk of his shoulder and stuck his face up against Rocky's. 'What? You getting a bit are you, old man?'

Connor grabbed Carruthers' shoulder and pulled him back. 'Settle down.'

Carruthers glared at Connor with a dark look on his face. 'Well, she did need taking down. Cocky, sullen bitch. Aw, fuck this. I'm going to bed.'

Now Connor walked slowly back to his own apartment deep in thought.

Interesting. Carruthers had a temper and Cardella had come straight in to defend Dru. There was a relationship of sorts there; he'd noticed that they were very comfortable with each other during the game. More so than he would expect work colleagues to be.

After throwing his keys and wallet onto the table near the door, Connor walked into the tiny bathroom and filled his hands with cold water. He sluiced his face and hair.

Christ it's hot in these tin boxes.

He changed into dark pants and T-shirt before picking up his keys and heading out to the car park at the end of the row of dongas.

He'd accessed the rosters online and knew that Dru was working over near the tailings dam this shift. He drove out of the staff car park and along the road to the eastern side of the mine with his headlights on low beam, passing a couple of other vehicles and two trucks as he headed past the processing plant. He had an explanation ready if anyone pulled him up tonight, along with the security tag that Hennessey had left for him with Jennifer. In his 'safety' role, Connor had free access to the whole plant with the exception of the diamond recovery room.

It was the first time he'd driven further than the administration and security buildings and Connor let out a low whistle as the scale of the mine became apparent. It had looked big from the air, but on the ground it was much larger than he'd realised. He passed a small power station, and a fuel depot with three large fuel tanks. The size of the site would make checking for any holes in security difficult.

He followed the road until he reached a Y intersection and slowed the car. The sealed road appeared to wind around the fence on the southern perimeter of the site and a wide gravel road to the right led up a steep hill. A huge dump truck was parked at the top. Connor turned the ute to the right and the engine revved as he accelerated up the hill. There was one vehicle parked beneath a security light over on the eastern edge of the cliff. He slowed the car to a crawl and killed the lights, then turned behind the truck and parked his ute on the other side away from the lit area. He climbed out of the car and checked that his vehicle was hidden from the road. The truck was huge, with six massive tyres. Each one had to be at least twice his height.

Satisfied that he was well hidden, he reached into the car for his night binoculars and small torch. He put the torch in his pocket; there was enough moonlight to see where he was going. Hopefully his dark clothes would hide him from any curious eyes.

Despite being after midnight it was still bloody hot outside and there was an eerie light bathing the desert landscape. The muted roar from the processing plant a few hundred meters away reminded him of a science fiction movie setting.

He stared down to the base of the hill. He could see Dru moving around, her bright vest glowing in the moonlight. He shook his head; she was alone. That was a red flag. It wasn't safe for anyone—male or female—to be working on their own in the desert at night. In his role as safety officer, it would be within his brief for him to bring that up. She did the rosters—he'd already looked at that—but he'd assumed she'd have at least one offsider out here with her at night.

Maybe she worked alone because it gave her the opportunity to look for rogue diamonds? Stupid . . . or very clever. It was the closest point to the tailings dam where John Robinson had told him it was possible for diamonds to wash down from the open pit. Hard to believe a multimillion-dollar facility was built to mine the gems and you could wander around and be lucky enough to pick one up off the ground.

But not six.

A large sign to his right along the top of the northern face of the cliff flashed in the light of the rising moon and Connor walked over to the fence. As he read the notice, he realised this was the tourist lookout over the open cut pit. Below and above him, the bright moonlight highlighted the edges of the horizontal tiers that had been cut into the face of the mountain. According to the sign, the pit was over two kilometres long and a kilometre wide, and covered over three hundred hectares. As his eyes became more accustomed to the darkness, he leaned over and looked down the terraces below him. The pit stretched along the edge of the mountain into dark shadows. From his memory of the map, the tailings dam was down the other slope at the southern end of this hill. He shook his head slowly. Securing this site would be a nightmare.

Over the hum of the processing plant up the hill, the engine of another vehicle revved at the bottom of the road. Connor stepped back into the shadow of the truck and lifted the night binoculars to his eyes. So far there'd been no sign of anyone else, and he'd assumed that one of the utes parked over by the fence had been driven up there by Dru. The bright lights of the vehicle lit up the truck and he pressed himself against the tyre and they flicked past him as the ute parked at the top of the road.

He stayed still and held his breath as he waited for the car door to open. Finally the door closed quietly and footsteps crunched on the gravel, heading away from him.

He stepped around the front of the truck, taking care to tread lightly and not make any noise. There was no one in sight. Connor crept forward, keeping along the northern side of the hill along the fence line until he reached the southern escarpment.

Rocky Cardella was making his way quickly down the hill just to his left. He shouldn't be out here, Connor thought; Cardella was definitely not rostered on this shift.

Carruthers and Cardella were on the eight o'clock start in the morning, and he'd assumed they'd gone back to their rooms after the game. This top level of security that Robinson had assured him was in place at Matsu seemed to be full of holes wherever he looked.

As he kept the man in his line of sight, there was a sudden loud, long drawn out metallic screech from the processing plant behind them and then silence. Connor sat still and watched. The moonlight was getting brighter as the moon rose and it was easy to see Cardella picking his way between the scrub and the mounds at the base of the hill. As Connor observed his progress there was a movement about fifty metres ahead. Dru Porter was bent over in front of a high mound and her back was facing Cardella.

She turned around just before he reached her, and snatches of conversation drifted up the hill to Connor. Her voice sounded agitated and for a moment Connor considered following him down, but thought better of it.

No rush. Slow and steady.

'You . . . What . . . shouldn't be here . . .?'

For a moment before a cloud obscured the moon and the light dimmed Connor could read her agitation from her gestures. She had dropped whatever it was she'd been carrying and her hands were on her hips as she towered over the shorter man.

She moved her hands to her chest, and stepped closer to Cardella. Connor sat down at the top of the hill, waiting to see what would happen.

Chapter 8

'Sorry, love. Didn't mean to give you a fright.'

'I thought you were on day shift. You scared me, creeping around like that.' Dru narrowed her eyes and stared at Rocky with her hands on her hips. 'And you've been drinking too! I can smell it. Do you want to lose your bloody job?'

'May not be any jobs here soon.' He tapped the side of his nose and Dru frowned.

'What do you mean?'

'End of the mining boom, maybe.' He shrugged casually.

She lifted her head and turned towards the processing building. 'Did you hear that screech? The conveyors have stopped running.'

The only sound was the eerie whistle of the wind; the constant hum that ran from the processing plant twenty-four hours a day had ceased. Clouds scudded across the sky as the wind picked up and a whirlwind of gritty dust filled the air around them.

'Must have been a breakdown.' Rocky folded his arms and his teeth flashed in the dim light as Dru coughed.

She covered her mouth with her hand to block the swirling dust. 'That's unusual. I wonder what happened.' Unease snaked through her chest and the familiar fear that was always close to the surface began to flicker through her veins. She shook her hands in front of her and took a deep breath. It had been a peculiar day and it didn't seem as though she was going to have the peaceful nightshift she'd anticipated. 'It's never quiet like that. First time it's shut down since I've been at the mine.'

Rocky shrugged again as he moved past her. 'I dunno. Really. Anyway, nothing we can do about it. Have you noticed there's been a lot going wrong on this place lately? Breakdowns, tools getting pinched, workers getting hurt, and a lot of the new staff aren't staying as long. Strange times.' But despite his words, he didn't seem unduly concerned. 'Rumour is the mine will be closed down within a couple of years.'

Dru chose not to pass on Jennifer's gossip about the new drilling tunnel she'd heard was being proposed. She would be interested to hear if that gossip had reached the local Aboriginal community, but she'd wait for the meeting at Wipporing later in the week to suss that out. 'I hadn't noticed anything different. I did hear that one of the night foremen in the processing plant suffered a hand injury a couple of days ago.' Dru stared at him. 'What else has happened?'

'One of the truck drivers broke his leg this morning. Pretty nasty break. Didn't you hear the chopper come in?'

'No, must have been when I was asleep. Maybe that's why that new guy's here. To investigate the accidents,' she said thoughtfully.

'Could be. The medico has been busy here all right. Anyway, I'm off. Places to go, people to visit, I'll see ya later.' Rocky lifted a hand and turned away.

'What places? Where are you going now?' Dru brushed the dust from her face with the back of her gloved hand as her breathing settled to a normal rate.

'Got some business down near the dam.'

'Rocky, what the hell are you up to? You know you're not supposed to be out on site if you're not working.'

'On site?' His voice was sharp. 'Nothing you need to worry about, love. I'm just making sure that things are as they should be. I've got a meeting over by the dam in a while. And as well as being "the site" it's my place. My land.'

'A meeting! At this time of night? Who with?' Dru screwed her nose up as she stared at him. 'What the hell is going on?'

'Nothing you need worry about. Some of my people have come down to see me, and because I'm working in the daytime, we're going to have a meeting over the other side of the dam tonight.' He grinned and his teeth flashed in his dark face. 'It's nice what you've done over there, with the trees and the grass. They'll be pleased to see it. And I do know you understand. I see how you care for our land. We're just making sure things are put back the way they should be.'

'What do you mean?'

'Just what I said. Things haven't been done right by us here, and we're making sure that the traditional owners of the land get what they are entitled to.'

'Meaning?'

'My people have had our power taken away by the legal talk and the big money. Along with the loss of access to our land we've lost our spiritual connection to our country.' He lifted his hand and pointed and Dru tracked the direction of his raised hand, but she couldn't see anyone.

'What are you pointing at?'

'Some of the women from my clan are already over there.'

'Are they allowed here?' Her voice was soft. 'It's Matsu land.'

'It won't be if we get our way. The flat on the other side of the dam is a sacred women's site so they have the freedom to come and go.'

Dru shook her head. 'No, it's not. I've met with your people and I've seen the site maps. There's no mention of sacred sites anywhere near the mine.'

'That's exactly what I mean by making sure things are set right.' His voice was full of determination. 'We have some serious business to talk about, and you'll hear about it soon enough. So you go on counting termite mounds and we'll get on with the important stuff. See ya later, love.'

Dru narrowed her eyes as Rocky strode towards the dam. As far as she could see there was no one else over there to meet with him as he claimed. There was nothing out there apart from the new trees that they'd planted last month. Beyond that was a vast expanse of desert to the horizon.

In the nine months she'd been at the mine, Rocky had looked out for her. It was not what you could call a friendship but they'd definitely established a mutual respect. Dru had always felt comfortable with him, probably because he reminded her of Bill Jarragah, Dad's workman back on the farm when she'd been growing up in the Territory.

Now she bit her lip as curiosity tugged at her. Surely if it was a sacred women's site, she'd know about it—and Rocky wouldn't be allowed there. He was definitely up to something.

For a fleeting moment she was tempted to follow him, but she shrugged and picked up her shovel.

***

Watching Dru make her way from termite mound to termite mound was mind-numbingly boring. There'd been no sign of Rocky Cardella after he'd disappeared into the hills on the other side of the tailings dam and Connor decided he was wasting time that could be spent better elsewhere. He gave up shortly after 3.00 am. He was hot, tired, and sick of sitting on the side of a hill peering through his binoculars.

As he drove back to the staff village, the loud noise from the processing plant could be heard through the closed windows of the ute. Whatever the problem was, it had been fixed. He looked up as he drove past; the conveyor belt was in action.

Connor unlocked the door of his donga and put his binoculars and keys on the table. He made a coffee and pulled out his laptop, bypassed the Wi Fi provided to mine staff, and logged on with his secure dongle through his company. There was an email from Greg.

More useful stuff here. Call me.

Connor grunted. The smiley face at the end of the message didn't temper his frustration one bit. If there was information, he wanted it now, but he'd have to be patient. He trusted Greg and if he wanted him to call there would be a reason. Since they'd left the force and Connor had started his business, Greg had been more than happy to use his skills to retrieve a variety of information for him. They always used email or phone to communicate, and occasionally postal mail for the more sensitive items.

A quick check of the rest of his email provided nothing of interest so he turned to the printed staff files that John Robinson had provided. Dru's file only had a few pages; those of the male staff were far bulkier as they had been employed by the mine for a longer period of time. He put them aside and focused on hers, ignoring the certainty that was building. He was sure she was involved but he had no evidence yet apart from the Dubai connection. It could be purely circumstantial but there was a tingling at the back of his neck that told him to keep digging.

Motivation. Opportunity. Proof. He needed to establish all three, and in that order.

Motivation—the diamonds and the wealth that came with their sale to the right person.

Opportunity—he had a bit more work to do there but he already had identified some gaps in the security.

In the investigations Connor had been involved in since he'd left the Federal Police, money had almost always been the prime motivator, with the exception of one white-collar crime in Sydney that had been motivated by revenge after a marriage breakdown.

It was usually the simplest mistake that set him on the path to finding who he was after and that's what he was hoping for here. From experience he knew that extreme confidence—like Dru had displayed—and the almost delusional belief in one's ability to escape detection were characteristic of the criminal mind. Connor was proud of his work and he knew he'd made a difference to the quantities of drugs coming into the country from South-East Asia over the past few years. This investigation should be easier than that work; all he had to do here was work systematically through the evidence until he found the flaw in the security of the mine.

Proof—That was going to be the hard part, unless he caught someone with the diamonds in their hand. But that was unlikely. A crime of this magnitude wouldn't be an opportune, spur of the moment incident. Hopefully Greg had found something for him in his computer search.

Connor clicked the mouse and scrolled to the next screen, his frustration building. The lack of information on Dru was fanning the flames of his suspicion, and he had to make a conscious effort to pull his thoughts back into a logical order.

He could trace her digital footprint right up until she left university and moved to Dubai, and he only knew about that position from the files that John Robinson had given him. There was no record of her in any of the public databases and no connection with Dubai at all. He pulled up the social pages of some Arabian newspapers and magazines and ran a search on her name, but there was nothing documented.

Her university records were accessible—to him anyway. He accessed the server at James Cook University with a string of MS DOS commands Greg had taught him when they'd worked together in the Force. Pulling up past student records from the archived files, he raised his eyebrows as he scanned through her results over the four years she attended. A high distinction average had guaranteed her the pick of the engineering jobs at the end of that year.

He pulled up the server of her last employer, but didn't log in once he managed to reach the company's log in screen. The *Ain Dubai* was a top-secret project; state of the art engineering, and he didn't want his illegal access to be traced as he was sure it would be. He'd have to use other means to find out why she left. He jotted down a note on the pad on the desk to call the company. Surprisingly the direct approach often revealed more information than he'd expected.

Resorting to a basic Google search, Connor retrieved a few newspaper articles that were over five years old. He read the screen, nodding slowly. Dru had been involved in a few sports clubs around Townsville. A series of photographs from her university days showed her hanging from cliffs, jumping from planes and scuba diving. No matter what she was doing, she looked serious and intense. That's what he'd noticed about her tonight. She rarely smiled.

A few later photographs were of her abseiling, and the most recent one was of her receiving an award for completing her tenth sky dive with a North Queensland company.

And then it came to a dead end. Absolutely nothing. No hits in the search engines that were more recent than her university days. He'd have to get Greg to look even deeper than her financial records. When he could get hold of him.

He pulled up Facebook but the three Dru Porters who were listed bore no resemblance to her. He picked up her staff file again and looked for her full name.

Drusilla Maree Porter. He typed it in and searched again.

Bloody hell. *Nothing.*

Connor leaned forwards as Dru Porter, Engineer, came up on LinkedIn and a spurt of excitement fired briefly but it was another dead end. There were no details apart from her name and qualifications, but they were useless. He already had those from the university search and the Matsu file.

Connor clicked his tongue in frustration; he was going in circles. He leaned back in the chair and took a deep breath, cleared his mind, and then let his thoughts come back randomly.

How were the diamonds being taken off site?

The likely scenario was that they were taken from the recovery room before they were registered in the Matsu computer system. But if that was the case there had to be involvement by one or more of the security staff.

Finlayson? Hennessey? Or someone else who had access to that part of the site and could tamper with the cameras? Or was there someone out on the plant pulling the rough diamonds from the conveyor belt?

He'd read up on the process; his next step was to go to the plant under the guise of checking their compliance with the policies and watch the process in action. What security was in place there, he wondered. According to the documents, there were more cameras in the recovery area than anywhere else on the site. All employees and visitors to recovery had to undergo a random search every time they left the building to ensure no diamonds were being smuggled out, but what did *random* mean? How could that guarantee security?

It had to be an inside job.

With all of the cameras around the site, it would be near impossible to just pick up a diamond at any point in the process.

Were any of those other staff members highlighted by Robinson likely to be able to do that?

Adam Hennessey could be a possibility, but there was no evidence of his involvement; he'd been upfront about the camera problem. He'd been at the mine for a few years and until now there'd been no problems. But Connor wasn't going to discount him.

Don Finlayson had carte blanche access to the whole system too. Was it significant that he had chosen to take leave at precisely the time when there was such a security issue at stake?

Connor yawned and reached for his coffee cup, and grimaced as the cold strong liquid hit his tongue. He glanced at the time on the bottom of the screen. It was 5.00 am. No wonder he was making no headway.

As he prepared to shut down the laptop, the Arabian newspaper he'd searched earlier filled his screen. Reaching for the file that Robinson had given him, he flicked through the pages until he came to the information provided by the Belgian jeweller. How the diamonds were being removed from the mine was a problem he could explore later. He'd try working backwards for a while.

They had been presented to the jeweller in Antwerp by the personal assistant of a businessman . . . he turned the pages slowly, searching for the name that he had been given in Perth.

Zayed Al Tayer.

Connor turned back to his laptop and initiated another Google search. He let out a low whistle as he read the public information that filled the screen. Bingo! One of Al Tayer's companies held the contract for the entertainment precinct on Bluewater Island where the *Ain Dubai* was located.

The *Ain Dubai*. Dru had worked there before she came to Matsu. He flicked from screen to screen and read Al Tayer's background until a series of images filled the final screen.

Zayed Al Tayer was a lot younger than Connor had expected from the background biographical information. A tall dark man in a Western dress, he looked more like an Englishman than an Arab. He'd been educated in Dubai and then continued his studies in the United Kingdom where he graduated from Sandhurst and later studied economics at Cambridge University.

'Fucking hell.' Connor widened his eyes as he stared at the screen.

The caption read: 'Zayed Al Tayer at the opening of the new aquarium at Atlantis, the Palm.'

A photograph of a social occasion in Dubai showed a group of people in evening dress surrounding the tall man. Beside him was an equally tall young woman in a close-fitting midnight blue dress, with her blonde hair pinned artfully to the top of her head. She towered over the rest of the women in the group as she smiled at the camera. Connor clicked on the top right of the browser and zoomed in. Al Tayer's hand was just visible above the woman's hip as he held her close to him, but it would not have been obvious to the casual observer.

Well, well, well. Nerve endings fired all over Connor's body.

Drusilla Porter and Zayed Al Tayer were known to each other.

Just how well, he was about to find out.

Chapter 9

In the days that followed it seemed like wherever Dru turned, someone was in her face and wanting something from her. All she wanted to do was graph the termite mounds. She'd changed to day shift and it seemed her mornings and nights had been filled with phone calls and meetings.

Nothing out of the usual had been discussed when she'd driven off site to attend the weekly aboriginal meeting at Wipporing. So much for Rocky's assertions about changes in the wind. The meeting was just a laid-back chat over the usual cup of tea. Sometimes she wondered if it was necessary to attend, but it was part of her duty statement.

While she'd been off site and her phone out of range, Mum and Ellie had both left messages about setting up a 'family chat'. And Emma had called this morning as Dru was about to leave for work, demanding to know where she had been for the last three weeks because Mum was worrying about not hearing from her.

The fingers of anxiety that were always inside Dru tightened their relentless grip as she pressed her phone against her ear. 'Hello, I have a job, remember . . . and I've been on nights a lot. You know, work at night, sleep in the day,' she said to Emma. Even though she was ready for work and had half an hour to spare, her words were clipped. 'I'm about to leave to catch the bus now.'

'Okay, no need to be snarky. I know all about shift work. But look, just give Mum a quick call and let her know you're okay. Please.' Emma's voice was calm and measured and the usual spike of guilt tangled with Dru's anxiety.

'All right.'

'She worries about you.'

'There's no need for anyone to worry. I'm a big girl now.'

'You know that, and I know that, but you'll always be Mum's baby. She'd been so well lately, I don't want her to worry about anything.'

'*Okay*. I'll call tonight.' Dru clenched her jaw and attempted to inject some interest into her voice. 'So how's things with you?'

'Busy. Like you. Jeremy's been away up at the Cape for a week, and the clinic's been hectic.' Dru couldn't help smiling as Emma's laugh tinkled down the phone line. The knot in her chest loosened a bit. They'd got on well when they shared an apartment in Townsville when they were both at uni. 'Sorry, I have to go. George is coming across the river. And Dru?'

'Yes?'

'Love ya.'

'Yeah. Whatever. I'll ring later.'

Tears pricked Dru's eyes as Emma hung up. Discomfort—or guilt—settled in her chest; any talk of love made her uncomfortable. If Mum and Emma and Ellie knew what had happened last year, they'd worry about her even more. Mum would have another nervous breakdown, and Dru didn't want that on her conscience. She could handle it herself. So maybe she was the bitch of the family. That's just the way it was.

The past few years had been so lonely until she met Megan in Dubai, and she'd been the first person that Dru had let breach her defences since Dad. Okay, so lonely was not good, but it was safe and she should have stayed there; accepting Meg's overtures of friendship had been a huge mistake. At uni, the tag 'ice queen' had suited Dru fine. She'd focused on her studies and even though she'd joined what everyone called the high-risk clubs—abseiling, rock climbing, sky diving, rodeo riding—she'd mostly kept her distance from her fellow adventurers. She knew that she'd earned the same nickname here at Matsu. She smiled grimly. At lease she was consistent.

If no one got close, she couldn't lose them.

So yeah, Meg had been a mistake. It had opened a door to her emotions, and look where that had ended up. For a few months Dru had let go of the bone-chilling emptiness that she carried within and her heart had unfurled like a flower in the desert heat. Not only friendship with Meg but a whole new world had opened up when she met Zayed at a function for new staff not long after she'd started her contract.

It had been more than a physical attraction that had led to her downfall, and it wasn't love but trust that had been a huge part of it. Dru had been trying to make sense of where Zayed had figured in her life when her whole world had come crashing down around her.

She should have kept doing what she'd always done and used her loneliness and emptiness as a shield. She should have stuck with her usual reticence—ice queen, bitchiness, whatever—call it what you like.

It was *safe*.

If she'd done that she wouldn't be hiding in another desert thousands of kilometres away.

Don't think about it.

'Dru? You home?' Dru put her hand to her chest as she jumped up. Someone was knocking at the door. She'd been miles away.

'Who is it?' Damn, she hated this jumpiness. It was time to pull up her big girl panties and get over it.

'It's Adam.'

She crossed the room and opened the door. Adam Hennessey was waiting on the path at the bottom of the two steps.

'Hi, Dru. I hope you don't mind me catching you so early. I checked your roster and saw you were on day shift.' He smiled and looked up at the clear sky. 'Gonna be a hot one today. The heat's coming quickly this wet season.'

'Looks like it.'

'I wanted to run that favour by you I mentioned the other night. I've been working around the clock and haven't had a chance to catch up with you.'

'What sort of favour?'

'I know you drive to Kununurra to catch the plane to Darwin. Are you heading back there later this week?'

'Yes,' she said slowly. Last thing she wanted was to give someone a lift and have to make conversation for two hours. She thought quickly, searching for an excuse.

'Do you have much time in Kununurra before your flight?'

'Yeah, I'll be there overnight Friday. My flight goes out at noon on Saturday.'

'I was wondering if you'd have time to do some shopping for me. I'm stuck on site for an extra week.' Adam reached into his pocket and pulled out his wallet. 'Look, it's my wife's birthday in a couple of weeks and all she's been talking about is this amazing stuff they sell at the diamond gallery in Kununurra. She even wanted me to take her there for a holiday.'

'Jewellery?' Dru stared at the handful of fifty-dollar notes that Adam held out to her.

'No, it's this exclusive face cream. Four hundred friggin' bucks. She read about it in the Qantas magazine last time we flew to Bali, and she'd been on about it ever since. I'm sure it's an advertising scam but I know she really wants it. It's supposed to be a paste made out of diamonds that is a skin rejuvenator.'

Dru couldn't hold back the laugh that bubbled up in her chest. 'Diamond face cream? Four hundred dollars. Are you serious?'

'Yup, and only available at Pentecost River Fine Diamonds in Kununurra. I can get it online but Cathy would see the online banking record. I want it to be a surprise.' He held out the notes. 'I have no other reason to go to Kununurra. Do you mind picking up a jar for me?'

'Yeah, I can do that. But I won't be back here for two weeks.'

'That's okay. Her birthday isn't for a few weeks. I really appreciate it, Dru. She's a pretty special person.' His voice softened and he held her gaze steadily. 'Gets a bit hard for the wife and family with me living up here. And now I won't be home before her birthday, it's the least I can do.'

'I can imagine. Of course I'll get it. I'll have plenty of time. There's not that much to do in Kununurra.' As Dru took the notes and looked down at the wad of cash in her hand, the door to the next apartment opened and Connor stepped out and locked the door behind him. She hadn't realised he was next door to her. That donga had been empty for a couple of months and she hadn't heard anyone moving about in there.

'Morning.' He nodded at them both before he headed across the narrow road to the small staff car park.

'Morning.' Dru shot Connor a tight smile and waited till he was out of earshot before she turned back to Adam. 'Want it gift-wrapped?'

This time the grin was sheepish. 'Yes please.'

'Four hundred dollars!' She shook her head. 'It must be good stuff. Maybe I'll have to try it.'

'I'll let you know if it works. Thanks, Dru, I really appreciate it.'

Dru went back inside and put the money into the side of the bag she was taking home with her.

She shook her head again as she pulled on her work boots and headed for the staff bus.

Bloody hell, she thought. Not even Meg would spend four hundred dollars on a jar of face cream.

By the time the bus reached the small building where the rehabilitation team was based, Dru was focused on the day's tasks ahead. They'd made a lot of progress on the area between the processing plant and the tailings dam, and she wanted to draw up a schedule of work for the upcoming shifts while she was off. The focus for the coming dry season was to prepare the terraces where the open cut mining had destroyed the habitats and creeks. The last meeting with the Participation Committee had resulted in an agreement to re-establish vegetation on the bottom terraces to stabilise the sub strata and minimise future erosion. There was an expert on local flora flying in from Darwin to look at the site this week.

She looked across past the temporary staff shed that had been set up when they started work in this area. The team was already halfway down the hill working in the heat.

Rocky was sitting in the small kitchenette when she pushed open the door.

'Morning, boss.' He raised his coffee cup in greeting. 'Kettle's hot.'

Dru looked across to the small meeting room adjacent to the kitchen. 'The crew's out early today.' A lot of the labourers were indigenous and drove in from Wipporing where Rocky lived.

'Yeah, they've been out there for a while.' Rocky watched as she put a tea bag in the cup that had BOSS written on it. 'They're all ready for the change of shift this afternoon.'

'And you're not?'

'Nuh, I'm going to hang around for a few more days. I want to see that plant bloke as much as you do. See if he's the expert he's supposed to be.' Rocky's grin was wide.

'First time you've been interested in plants that I can recall.' Dru raised her eyebrows as she opened the fridge and grimaced. 'No milk?'

'Nup. Have to have it black.' He stared at her over the rim of his cup. 'Are we having a meeting today?'

'Yes, that's why I was hoping I'd catch everyone. Never mind. At morning tea break will do.' She pulled up a chair and grinned at him. 'So how come you're really hanging around?'

'Family's gone away to Wyndham fishing, and there's a few things I want to do over at the dam.'

Dru blew on the steaming liquid and waited for it to cool. 'What things?' She hadn't mentioned her plans to work on the terraces to any of the staff yet.

'Don't worry. Nothing to do with the mine or your work. It's on the land on the other side of the boundary. 'There's a few stands of vegetation over there that are seeding, and I'm going to collect the seeds.'

'What? You're collecting seeds?' Dru took a gulp of her coffee and cursed as it burnt her mouth. 'Shit, that's hot.'

'Yeah, what's wrong with that?' His lips were set in a thin line as he stared back at her. 'Just because you're the engineer with all the fancy university bits of paper, don't think I don't know what's going on here. I've been here since day one of this place and I'm going to see that the right thing is done.'

'I'm sorry.' Dru put her hand up. 'I didn't mean anything like that. It's just that I've never seen you out doing that sort of stuff.'

'I'm one of the traditional owners of this land and I've got more interest in getting it back the way it was than any of these experts that come in their fancy suits.' His voice was proud as he sat up straight in the chair. 'Bloody condescending bastards. They think they make it right. Throwing money at us and sending our kids down to the university, to learn about soil and all that shit. And the weekly *mantha?* What a joke.'

'*Mantha*? I'm sorry, I don't know what that is.' Dru kept her voice soft. She'd never seen Rocky fired up like this before. Something had obviously happened to upset him.

He stared at her and his dark eyes were coal black. 'That meeting you go to. The smoking ceremony when the mine staff "interacts" with my people every week.'

'Oh, I didn't know what it was called.' Dru put her hand on his arm. 'I've never seen you like this before. Every time we talk about what the mine is doing in the partnership deal, you've agreed. The pastoral lease that's on trust and all the restoration work that we're doing, you've always seemed happy with it. How did your meeting go the other night?

'Yeah, it was fine.'

'What's upset you so much today, Rocky?'

'Not what, who. Creeping Jesus, that's who.' He jutted his chin out and waved towards the door as a vehicle pulled up outside. His laugh was bitter. 'Speak of the devil and he turns up.'

Chapter 10

The hostile atmosphere surrounded Connor as he pushed open the door and stepped into the small building.

'Morning.' He nodded at Rocky and then turned to Dru. 'Morning, again. I wanted to see you at the plant before you came down here but I got caught up.'

'Sticking your bloody nose in there, too,' the older man muttered as he stood and pushed past them. Rocky Cardella was a different man away from a poker game.

Over the past three days, Connor had created a smokescreen by sitting through several meetings with other sections as they'd gone over the safety polices of the mine. He didn't know how anyone did this sort of thing for a job. If he had a dollar for every time he'd said 'safety policies and procedures are only effective if you make sure they are properly implemented and enforced', he could probably retire. One good thing was that everyone seemed to accept he knew what he was talking about. All the department heads were eager to show off their compliance procedures. He didn't mention the number of times he had seen them breached as he visited various sections of the plant. What the policies said and what the practices were appeared to be very different.

There had been a spate of silly accidents over the past few weeks, but most department heads were still falling over themselves to convince him that the policies were in place. No one had been seriously hurt, but there had been an inordinate number of breakdowns and lost time.

But Dru was in his sights today.

'What's wrong with him?' Connor injected a light tone into his voice as the aboriginal man slammed the screen door behind him.

Connor had put a lot of thought into how he was going to deal with Dru without arousing her suspicions. Until he had proof that she was involved he was going to play it very cool. The first thing was to try and establish some sort of working relationship. And try to be amicable. It was normally hard for him to be sociable and friendly but he knew he had to do it. His usual cynicism about relationships and friendships had to be put on hold.

He waited for her to answer.

Her eyes were ice-blue, and this morning her long hair was braided and pinned to the back of her head beneath a baseball cap. She was a far cry from the elegant woman in the stiletto heels and slinky dress in the photographs he'd found on Friday night. After Connor had come across the first photograph, he'd searched other online magazines and hit the jackpot.

Time Out Dubai had provided a wealth of information and several more photographs of Drusilla Porter with Al Tayer. She'd never been named in any of them, which was why the Google search hadn't pulled her up. Once he'd stumbled on the first photo, he'd done an image search on Al Tayer. He'd found photographs of Al Tayer in meetings in Dubai, and in two of them Dru had been sitting at the same long table. Made him wonder what a newly appointed environmental engineer would be doing in high-level meetings about an entertainment precinct.

Dru's husky voice brought him back to the woman standing in front of him.

'Nothing. He's just being Rocky. He's a moody bastard. Don't take it personally.' Her words seem to serve as a warning for her own attitude. 'So what can I do for you, Mr Kirk?'

'Connor, please.' He gestured to the kitchen. 'Mind if I grab a coffee?'

'Sure. Help yourself.' She sat back and waited as he flicked the kettle on and searched for a cup on the shelf above the small sink. 'There's no milk.'

He could feel her eyes on him as he waited for the water to boil, but when he turned around and carried the steaming drink across to the table, she was flicking through a bound document on the desk.

'It's all here ready for you.' She pushed the booklet across the table, and her eyes challenged him.

It would take balls to steal millions of dollars worth of diamonds, and she sure had them. When he reached for the file, she sat back and crossed her arms, her voice clipped and her expression closed. 'It's all there. I'll leave you to read it while I get out to the team. We've got work to do.'

Connor held up his hand. 'That's why I was trying to catch you before. I want you to take some time to go through the procedures with me.'

'It's all in there.' Her voice was disinterested but Connor raised his eyebrows as he noticed her hands. They were clenched together and her knuckles were white.

'*We* need to go through it.' He shook his head slowly; he was going to enjoy this. 'Together.'

'All right. But let's make it quick. I have *work* to do.'

'I'm sure you do. But so do I.' Connor lifted his cup and paused as he sipped at the coffee. 'Bloody hell, that is hot.' He crossed to the small sink and topped the coffee up with cold water from the tap. She could wait.

Connor turned and leaned against the sink. Dru was really bringing out the worst in him; he would have to be careful that her antipathy towards him didn't make him overreact and taint his judgement.

'My brief here has a focus on compliance, quality assurance and implementing change and improvement processes.' Connor bit back a grin as he continued with the spiel he had memorised. After the first five minutes, her eyes had begun to glaze over.

Finally he pulled out a chair and sat across from her with a smile. 'So you understand how all this impacts on your role as chief engineer of the rehabilitation team?'

'I do.' She had relaxed into her chair and he sensed a softening of her attitude.

'Look, I know this can be boring, but it's all about preventing accidents, fatalities, injuries and occupational disease.'

'And improving profit.' The cynicism in her voice sent a ripple of surprise through Connor.

'Of course.' He nodded. 'That's what business is about. We'd be naive if we thought anything else.'

'Look, Mr Ki – *Connor*.' This time her voice was strong. 'I love my job and I take pride in doing it properly, and seeing that my team does too. I'm happy to answer your questions and tick the boxes, but I want to do it quickly. Okay? I've got a lot of work to get through out there today before it gets too hot.'

'So as far as you are aware, you follow the mandatory safety procedures that the company has set?'

'I do. We all do here.'

He picked up the manual and flicked through to the relevant section. He'd prepared well for this meeting because he wanted to catch her unaware. 'Section three paragraph two: "At all times when working in the field an employee will have a work buddy within sight."'

'And your point is?' Back to the icy glare.

'The other night when you were on shift after the card game, who was rostered on with you?'

'I'm the team leader.'

'So, *you* are above the policies? I don't think so, Dru.'

'Of course I'm not. Wait a minute. How do you know I was out there by myself?'

'I saw you. You were alone. Apart from the few minutes that Rocky was with you.'

'Creeping Jesus,' she muttered.

'I beg your pardon?'

This time she stood and he had to look up at her as she towered over him. 'Is part of your brief to spy on the staff while they are trying to do their job?'

'My brief is to ensure that all staff are complying with safety policies, and it appears to me that your section pays lip service to them.' He dropped the folder on the table with a thud. 'Easy to write it down and tick the boxes. A whole different matter when the boss doesn't follow it. A couple of you seem to be taking your responsibilities very lightly. Do you think you are above them?'

'No. I don't.'

'What if you'd had an accident out there? What if you'd fallen? Been bitten by a snake?'

He stood and she was eye to eye with him. 'Look, Dru, this isn't a pissing contest to see who's the strongest. It's about safety. It's about your people not wandering over the site however they please.'

'I'll see to it.' Her voice was as hard as her eyes and that did piss him off. Connor hadn't been going to come in for the kill but he had exposed her soft underbelly and it was time to strike. Dru had presented him with an opportunity to rattle her and he took a gamble.

'I have a question for you. Is that the reason you lost your job in Dubai? Non-compliance with company policy?'

Despite her fair complexion, her face paled even more as she took in her breath in a quick gasp. The freckles on her aquiline nose stood out and her mouth stayed open as she stumbled back to the chair and dropped into it. Something akin to sympathy ran through him as she stared up at him, her breath coming quickly. Her hands were still clenched together and for a moment he was sure that it was fear that crossed her face.

Fear that she was going to be found out?

Her eyes closed and he could see her throat working.

Connor moved across to the sink and filled a glass with water.

'Thank you.' Her voice shook and her expression was still one of distress as she took the glass from him. 'How do you know I worked in Dubai?'

He waved a dismissive hand. 'Someone mentioned it the other night. I can't remember who it was exactly.'

Even after she had drained the glass empty her breath came in deep gulps.

'Are you all right?' Fake concern edged his words as he watched her reaction. Not what he had expected at all. Had she twigged that he was onto her? Or was she just a bloody good actress? Putting this on him to gain his sympathy?

'I will ask you one more time.' Her cheeks had two spots of colour high on her cheeks and this time her voice was composed. 'How did you know I worked in Dubai?'

'I can't remember.'

'You're lying,' she whispered as she put the glass back onto the table so hard Connor was surprised it didn't crack. 'It is none of your business. It's nobody's business.'

Connor was left alone as she strode to the door and pulled it shut behind her.

Chapter 11

'Everything looks good, Jim.' Connor nodded at the supervisor of the processing plant as they stepped out of the sorting room the next day. 'And ah ... your area has been accident free for a twelve-month period, and the documents are all in order. Signage is good, and I can't see a problem with anything here this afternoon.'

'Thanks, I'm proud of the tight ship we run here. We had a breakdown the other night, but it was mechanical. Nothing to do with the safety procedures,' Jim said. 'An absolute pain in this part of the plant because of the security.'

'How's that?' Connor looked at him curiously as they walked past the processing plant. It had been stinking hot in there. The sides of the plant were open to allow the noise and the dust to escape, but even so, the temperature must have already been in the mid-forties. It had been a relief to step into the air-conditioned sorting room.

'The paperwork takes me hours. Who was on shift when it broke; who dismantled the equipment; where it's going; if it's coming back; who took it out; who drove the truck. Bloody ridiculous.'

Connor filed that statement away.

Jim turned to him. 'Now before we go, we both have to go through the search regime down in the search room.'

'You too?'

'Yep. Everyone.'

Connor let surprise cross his face. He'd set up this safety check of this part of the plant specifically so he could go through the sorting room and come out through the search room. After examining every process on site, he'd come to the conclusion that this was the weakest link in the security.

Jim stepped back to let Connor exit the building ahead of him. 'You probably noticed there is only one entry and exit. Anyone who comes into the building goes through a search regime at the end of shift or whenever they leave the building for any reason. Even the CEO gets searched when he comes to visit.'

Two men were waiting outside a corrugated iron building in front of the exit. It looked more like a barn than a search facility. Jim nodded to them. 'Sorry guys, do you mind if we jump the queue?'

'No problem, boss.'

'You can go first, Connor. I know you've got a meeting to get to after this.'

The door creaked as Connor stepped into the search waiting room. Jim waited outside chatting to the workmen.

A tall man in an orange hi-vis vest greeted him. 'G'day mate, I'm Peter Allendale.'

Connor shook the hand that was extended to him. 'Connor Kirk, Safety Officer.'

'You've just been through the highest risk building on site, where we recover all the diamonds. This is the search waiting room where all the workers gather at the end of shift. First off we'll check your boots to make sure you haven't inadvertently picked up any diamonds in the soles.'

Connor lifted each foot in turn, while the other man checked his boots.

'All good. Now we go into the search room.' Peter pointed to a door in the middle of the back wall.

They stepped into a small anteroom and Peter nodded to a man sitting beside an X-ray machine on a small, wheeled trolley. 'That's Steve.'

The only other furniture in the small room was a desk that held three metal boxes and one chair. A poster-sized photo of the Matsu mine hung in the centre of the wall beside a clock. Connor nodded at Steve and got a brief nod in return. Peter locked the door and Connor raised his eyebrows in surprise.

'Policy, mate.' Sometimes we do a strip search, so the rule is lock the door so no one can walk in accidentally. We always have a witness to every search,' Peter explained. 'Steve will sign off to say that I have done the search, and he'll also sign that the X-ray is clear if we need to X-ray anything.'

Connor's mind began to tick over with possibilities. His instincts were screaming that this was the most likely scenario for bypassing the system. And ironically it was where the security was ostensibly the highest. What if there was collusion between the men that were supervising this search regime? He'd ask John about the process of selecting the men who worked here.

He paid close attention as Peter reached over to the desk and handed him a small plastic cylinder with a handle on the top. 'What we have here is a shaker. Grab the handle. Give it a good shake and turn it upside down over the desk.'

Connor took it and gave it a shake. A yellow ball bounced out of the shaker onto the desk and Peter scooped it up.

'Yellow, Steve.'

The witness guy made a note on a card.

Peter turned to Connor with a grin. 'You're in luck. Yellow means lowest level search, a partial removal. All you have to do is take off your shoes and socks and I'll give you a pat down.'

'Not what I expected.' Connor nodded at the shaker.

'It's a random way of checking. Blue ball means shirt off search. Green is a strip down to your undies.'

'I guess I'm in luck then,' Connor said. 'Although it seems like a bit of an archaic system.'

Peter shook his head. 'The shaker is sealed. The result is totally random. It can't be tampered with or predicted. And we're being recorded.' He nodded at the cameras in each corner.

Connor nodded but remained unconvinced.

'Okay, shoes and socks off. Shake your socks; make sure there's nothing in them.' Connor rested his hand on the desk and obliged.

'Okay, all good. I've checked the soles of your boots again. Boots are clear.' He nodded to Steve who made another note on the card.

'Now turn your pockets out, and then I'll do a pat down search.'

Connor put the keys to the work ute and his iPhone on the desk, along with his handkerchief and a packet of gum.

Peter picked up the gum and ran his fingers over the flat wrapped strips. 'Still sealed.' He nodded as he commented to Steve.

'Now put your arms out, and I'll run around your collar, across the back of your shoulders, down your back to make sure there's no belt or anything strapped around your torso.'

Connor obliged as he was patted down. When Peter finished, he turned around to face him and Connor looked at him curiously. 'Can I ask you a couple of questions?'

'Sure can.' Peter smiled at him. 'We heard that there was a compliance check across the whole site. Too many accidents lately. His grin widened. 'I guess we're a part of it too but there's not much chance of accidents in here.'

'Unless you fall over taking your boots off,' Steve said.

Connor laughed. 'Don't worry, Jim's already passed over the workplace safety policies for the search regime process.'

'Great.' Peter nodded.

'So from a safety point of view, when do you use that?' He gestured to the X-ray machine.

'If anyone has a packet of loose tobacco or a tube of cream or the like that's impossible to search, they get put through the machine. If your gum had been opened, we probably would have run that through too. Any diamonds will fluoresce under the X-ray.'

'Have you ever picked anyone up in here with a diamond on them?' Connor waited as Steve handed the card over for Peter to sign.

'Never.'

'So no X-raying of workers themselves?'

Peter shook his head. 'No, under health regulations we can't do that.'

'What do you do about someone who leaves the building a few times a day?'

'Doesn't matter if it's once or ten times. We go through this search regime with everyone leaving the building, every time they leave.' He handed the card to Connor for his signature. 'Sign the search report here and then you can put your shoes and socks back on.'

'Thanks.' Connor signed the card and then bent over and quickly pulled on his socks and shoes.

'Any more questions?' Peter filed the card in a small metal box on the desk.

'Just one. Do you ever do a body cavity search?

Peter laughed. 'With the gloves and the works? No mate, not on your Nellie. If it got to that stage of suspicion, the police would be called and a medical officer would do that part of the investigation.' He pointed at the door marked exit. 'You're right to go. Good to meet you, Connor. Might see you over in the mess later.'

Connor walked out slowly. He was going straight back to his room to log his thoughts. That had been a worthwhile exercise.

Chapter 12

After Connor had left the office earlier that week—when she finally convinced him she wasn't going to pass out like a weakling—Dru had managed to catch up with the team. They'd worked hard all week, the guy from Darwin had great ideas, and even Rocky had approved of his amendments to the re-vegetation plan. Now the schedule for the next two weeks was prepared and the three landscapers had a plan to follow until she came back on site after her two-week break.

If she came back after her break.

Dru had barely slept since Connor had asked her about Dubai. Her stomach had been churning, and her hands wouldn't stop trembling. She'd been clumsy and slow out on the site, and that had pissed her off even more. She'd called Mum like she'd promised Emma, and had pretended to be fine, but the whole time her thoughts had been on Connor.

How the hell did he know she had worked in Dubai, and what did it have to do with a safety officer? What did he mean by how she'd lost her job there? No one at the mine knew where she had come from before this, and no one apart from Zayed and his personal assistant knew why she had left Dubai so suddenly. Well, Meg knew a little, and Sam knew a bit less, but they wouldn't have told anyone.

Dru hugged her privacy to her like a protective cloak. All she had shared with the other staff was that she lived in Darwin, and some of her rehab team knew she'd done her degree at James Cook University. Not even Rocky knew about her time in Dubai.

The only Matsu staff who knew her background—and a sort of reason why she left Dubai—were the HR people in Perth who had interviewed her. All she had told them was that Dubai had not been what she expected. Whether they had believed her or not was irrelevant; her immediate supervisor had given her a glowing reference when she'd left—of course she hadn't asked Zayed for one—and she'd nailed the interview. She had explained to the Matsu Human Resources officer that she would prefer that her previous employment be confidential due to the confidentiality agreement she'd signed when she had joined the *Ain Dubai* project. There was to be no link from Dubai to Matsu. As far as she was concerned, that time of her life was gone and she'd attempted to wipe it from her mind. What she buried deep, she couldn't talk about in error. In hindsight, she realised she had been naive. Human resource records these days would be electronically stored on a staff database. Anyone with the right clearance could access them.

She had become too complacent. Someone had accessed her information. And that person had shared it with Connor.

On Friday afternoon Dru stood at the window of the staff building and pressed her forehead against the hot glass. What did it have to do with Connor? There'd been no safety breaches or accidents in her section since the day she commenced work at Matsu. Over the months, her time at the mine had fallen into a pattern. A pattern that soothed her and kept her calm and she didn't want anyone threatening that.

Day shift, sleep at night.

Night shift, sleep by day.

Pretend to be sociable when she had to. Converse with her team. Play cards once a week. Try to keep the fear locked away. That was the hardest part.

Now her past had followed her. No matter how much he had insisted someone had told him, Connor was not speaking the truth. He must have accessed her staff records, but why would a safety and compliance officer need to do that?

For one irrational moment, Dru wondered if Zayed had sent him, but she gave a hollow laugh. That wasn't his style at all. He wouldn't send someone in under the guise of a compliance officer. If Zayed knew she was working at Matsu, and if he still wanted her, he could have sent one of his henchmen in to deal with her. Or to take her back to Dubai. That was the greatest fear that hung over her, day and night. And that was why Dru had kept her mouth shut and continued to do so.

Zayed's beautiful dark eyes had burned into hers that last day. 'This is my choice and it is the best thing for you,' he'd said. 'You'll love life here with me.'

How had she ever found him attractive? She'd fallen for his charm like the naive woman she was, and stayed for two years until the emotional manipulation had her trapped in a cycle.

No more. She would trust no one.

Goosebumps rose on her arms and she blocked Zayed's face from her thoughts. Despite the forty-degree heat, by the time she had clocked off and driven back to the apartment to get changed and collect her bag, Dru was still shivering. All she wanted to do was get away. Put distance between her and the events of the week while she thought about what she should do. As much as the mine was her safety net, and kept her cocooned her from the outside world, when she drove out through the security gate near the airstrip today it would be a relief.

The fear had lodged in her chest like a rock. Her eyes flicked from left to right as she drove down the hill from the staff village towards the airport. Despite the bright sunshine and the waves of heat shimmering off the tarmac as she drew closer to the exit and the freedom of the desert, she imagined shadowy figures wherever she looked. Maybe she needed to talk to someone professional about this fear that dogged her.

When she'd told Megan about Dad being murdered, it was as though a light bulb had switched on.

'Oh, sweetie, no wonder you're so uptight. How many people go through that sort of emotional trauma, and especially when you were still a kid? You poor thing.'

Maybe it was time to dig a bit deeper and face her fears. Ellie and Emma had got on with their lives, so why couldn't she? Even Mum appeared to have got herself sorted when she'd spent that time with her in Port Douglas after she'd come back from Dubai.

'Afternoon. Pull over please.' The security guard—a new staff member that Dru hadn't seen before—waved her off the road and stood beside the car.

Dru drummed her fingers on the steering wheel. All she wanted was to hit the highway and get out in the open spaces.

She forced a smile at the guard as she got out of the car. Three mine utes and a small delivery van were lined up in front of her on the approach to the building at the exit gate.

'Is that all you've got?' He looked at her bag on the back seat.

She nodded.

'Can you grab it out and pop the boot please?' Dru frowned when he pointed into the office behind the gate.

'New procedures. Updated X-ray machine in the terminal to replace the old one we had here at the gate. Just take your bag inside, thanks. Have you been offsite in the last week?'

Dru shook her head.

'There's a new body scanning process too,' he explained. 'Don't worry. We're not allowed to X-ray staff. The scanner is the same that you go through at any airport.'

Five minutes later, after her bag had been X-rayed in the terminal and she'd been through the new body scanner, Dru turned onto the unsealed road that would take her west to the Great Northern Highway, where she would then turn north and head to Kununurra almost two hundred kilometres away. A cloud of red dust hung in the air along the road in front where the delivery van had turned ahead of her. She slowed down until the dust settled. The other utes had turned south at the gate along the road to Wipporing from where the indigenous workers did their daily commute.

As she drove, Dru's nerves settled and she turned the CD player on, attempting to soothe her mood with some mellow classical music. Her thoughts were jumbled and she forced herself to look at the problem logically.

Connor—or Creeping Jesus as Rocky had christened him—didn't have anything to do with Zayed. He was just a collar and tie man who took his job seriously.

Creeping Jesus. She bit back a smile. Maybe she'd lived under a rock for a while, but she'd not heard the expression before and when she was out on site she'd asked Rocky what he'd meant.

He'd stared at her for a moment, still in his bad mood. 'Someone who puts on a big act to impress the bosses. They creep around watching what you do, and they're dying for a chance to stab you in the back. Don't be surprised if a heap of us get fired after his visit. It's happened here before and you mark my words, that bloke's been put in here to clean the staff out. Safety, be buggered. He's up to no good.'

He put his hand up to his wrinkled face and squinted. 'Bet you didn't know he was watching you with night binoculars when you were out at the termite mounds the other night. I saw him on my way back in. He watched you for hours.'

Dru reached up and wiped her face with the back of her hand and grimaced when it came away streaked with red dust. 'I did actually.'

'No shit? How did you find that out?'

'He told me. I got hauled over the coals for being out there by myself.' She grinned ruefully. 'And he was right. I wouldn't have let another crew member do it. But you know what? He was more interested in what *you* were doing out there over at the tailings dam.'

Rocky had spluttered and walked away kicking the rocks in disgust. 'Told you, he's up to no good. I've worked here for bloody thirty years, so he can bugger off back to wherever he came from. If I want to work by myself, I don't care if it's bloody dawn or midnight, I will. No slimy bugger's going to tell me I can't.'

Dru reached over and turned the air conditioning up. Even though the sun was low in the sky, the heat of the desert was still warming the interior of the car to an unbearable level. Ahead the sky glowed red as a pall of smoke hung low from a fire at the Smokey Creek Station, the only outpost of civilisation between the mine and the Great Northern Highway. Twenty more kilometres and she'd be off the dirt and sharing the main road with the never-ending stream of grey nomads on their way north from Purnululu National Park.

At one point earlier that afternoon, she'd broken into a cold sweat and her thoughts had got the better of her. What if Zayed had tracked her down and someone was waiting for her in Darwin at her apartment? If anything happened to her she wouldn't be missed until she failed to report back to the mine in two weeks' time. Sure, Mum would be worried when she couldn't get in touch with her, but her family was used to it. As she let her imagination run wild, the familiar anxiety lodged in her throat. Maybe she needed to put something in place? Tell Meg she'd text her every couple of days and if she didn't hear from her there was something wrong. If she said that to Emma, her overprotective sister would insist she move to Queensland. She'd not mentioned a word to Emma, Ellie or her mum about why she'd left Dubai, even though she'd spent a couple of weeks at Port Douglas before coming to Matsu. Jeremy and Emma had just got back together and had been the focus of everyone's attention, and Dru was happy about that. She'd never been one for talking about herself so Mum readily accepted that she simply hadn't liked living in the Emirates.

She clamped her fingers on the steering wheel and she shook her head, angry at the direction of her thoughts.

God, I need this break.

An hour and a half later, she turned into the small bustling township at Kununurra. With wariness still clutching at her, she bypassed her usual motel—no point being predictable—and headed for a caravan park at the edge of the small lake on the southern side of the Victoria Highway.

What would she find in her apartment in Darwin? Could Zayed have found her? If Connor knew where she'd come from, maybe it was just as easy for Zayed to find where she'd gone? The things he had said to her that last afternoon still made her tremble. If it hadn't been for Megan and Sam getting her on the late Qantas flight, she'd probably still be there in Dubai. With Zayed's money and connections, anything was possible.

Another piece for his collection of beautiful things.

She needed help. She needed to talk this out with a professional. Megan was right. It was the way they'd lost Dad that still put bogeymen in every part of her life. God, for years she'd almost jumped at her own shadow.

'Just the one night? I've got one cabin left but it's one of the dearer ones down by the lake with a view of the water. Is that okay?' The receptionist smiled as she waited for Dru to answer. She'd just caught the office before it closed up for the evening.

'That's fine. She quickly filled out the paperwork and took the key that the young girl handed over.

'Have a good evening. There's a pizza night on over by the pool tonight. It's already started but it'll go for another hour or so.

'Thanks.'

Dru parked outside the cabin and grabbed her bag from the car. As she stood on the steps of the compact one-bedroom cabin she drew in a deep breath and looked over the lake. Above the water, the setting sun had painted the sky a palette of soft gold and misty blue, the low line of dark trees on the other side of the lake creating a perfectly symmetrical reflection that provided a border between the silver water and the sky. Small birds with long beaks were dipping in and out of the water on her side of the lake and a family of ducks glided past silently. Soft laughter reached her from the lawn as the grey nomads' happy hour got under way. Serenity trickled in slowly and she took a deep breath. Rational thought overcame her worry and for the first time since Connor had asked her about Dubai, the pressure on her chest lessened.

Her fears were irrational. How could she possibly take a leap of imagination and link a safety officer at the mine with Zayed in Dubai? Connor had thrown her with his question. There would be a simple explanation for how he knew she'd worked in the Emirates. He'd probably sussed out all the staff leaders before he started his job, but she still wasn't happy about anyone having access to her information.

But why did he mention Dubai specifically? Was he just trying to get a rise out of her? Thoughts went round and round her head as she stood beneath the shower trying to scrub away the sweat and the red dirt. She washed her hair, wrapped the second towel around her head and pulled a cool halter-necked dress from her bag. Pizza by the pool would be easier than driving into a grocery store in the small township. She'd noticed the restaurant at the edge of the garden; it would do her good to blend in with the crowd and relax for a change. Her flight didn't leave till one pm tomorrow and that would give her plenty of time to sleep in and pick up the gift for Adam's wife before she headed for the airport to catch the commuter plane to Darwin.

Dru squeezed the excess water from her hair and brushed the knots out. Water from her damp hair trickled down her bare back as she slipped on a pair of sandals. She stepped out onto the verandah and took a deep breath, the evening air heavy with the smell of fresh mown grass. Not a particle of red dust to be seen here apart from the fine covering that had stayed on her car. No point getting it washed; it would go into the car park at the airport at Kununurra for the two weeks she was in Darwin, and then she had to traverse that road again on the way back to Matsu.

Locking the glass sliding door of the cabin, Dru put the key into her money purse and walked down the steps. A small village of swags and tents dotted the lawn at the edge of the water and she glanced curiously at the cars parked at the end of the row. There were a couple of Matsu utes parked beneath the trees, the company logo recognisable in the fading light. She shrugged; it was a big staff and maybe some of them came up here for a break instead of flying west.

Bamboo torches flared into soft flickering flames defining the path from the cabin to the outdoor eating area by the pool. Country and western music with twanging guitar riffs and mellow voices filled the air. Purple insect zappers crackled at each end of the long bar as the night insects launched themselves at the light. The pool glistened in the soft light as the last swimmers climbed out and the buzz of conversation was loud over the music.

She slipped onto a stool at the end of the bar closest to the door; God help her, before Dubai she had never even thought of escape routes. Now she was filled with disgust at her own weakness.

'What can I get you, love?' Interest flickered in the eyes of the barman as he waited for her order, but she looked down at the wooden counter top. It had been polished to a high gleam and she ran her fingers over the smooth timber.

'White wine, please. With a glass of ice on the side.'

He nodded as he pulled a glass from the fridge and filled it with ice.

'Are you eating here tonight? Good seafood pizza on. Fresh prawns just down from Wyndham.'

'Sounds good.' She looked up and let herself smile.

Lighten up, Dru.

'Go and find yourself a table. We're busy tonight but there's a couple of places left over by the pool. I'll bring your drink over. You'll have to share a table. Just ask, we're all friendly here.'

Dru looked at the ground as she made her way to the pool. She was well used to the attention she got; not many women were over six foot tall. Once upon a time she'd stood straight and enjoyed the looks, but now she'd give anything to be pint-sized and able to blend into a crowd.

Maybe in her time off, she'd go and see someone in Darwin. Maybe it was time she admitted her weakness and stopped putting on this brash exterior.

'Two seats here. Are you by yourself?' A middle-aged woman with a tanned face and a chin-length bob of blonde hair patted the empty chair at the end of the table where two couples were seated.

'Thank you, and yes I am.' She pulled out the plastic chair. 'I'd be happy to join you.' Her voice was hesitant. 'If you're sure?'

'Don't be shy. Rob and June are at the end here, and I'm Chrissie and this is my husband, Pete. We're all on the road together.'

'Nice to meet you. I'm Dru.'

She sat and smiled at the barman as he followed her and put her drink on the table. He pulled out an order pad and looked around but his gaze settled on Dru.

'So folks, pizza all round? How about I just bring enough for the whole table?'

Chrissie looked over at Dru and put her head to the side. 'You happy with that, Dru? You're not quite a grey nomie, but it's what we do. You're more than welcome to join us.'

'What some of us do,' her husband interrupted. 'Don't forget the others cooking in their vans.'

Chrissie waved her hand dismissively. 'You meet all kinds on the road, but we know how to have fun.'

'They're the ones who'll have a longer trip than us because they don't eat out every night.' He nudged his wife affectionately.

Dru smiled as the happy banter and teasing washed around her. It was comfortable . . . and safe. Normal.

A family with three young children were at the table beside them and Dru watched as the youngest clambered up onto her father's lap. A shaft of nostalgia pierced her chest as she remembered the few family holidays they'd had when her life had been normal.

'Stop brooding' Meg's voice interrupted her thoughts and for a moment it was as though she was here next to her. She looked away from the family and focused on the conversation at the table.

'So Dru, do you have an RV, or are you a backpacker?'

She frowned. 'An RV? Oh, I know. You mean like a Winnebago? One of those easy ones that you don't have to tow?'

Pete laughed over at Rob. 'That's right. We've got an RV but this bugger here has an almost thirty-foot long van.'

Rob smiled at her. 'He's exaggerating as usual. It's a twenty-footer.'

Dru laughed along with them. Sweet relaxation flowed through her and she leaned back in the chair. 'I have to confess. I'm not camping, I'm in a cabin. I'm just here for the night before I fly to Darwin tomorrow.'

'So we were all wrong. As soon as you appeared at the bar, we had you pegged as an RV driver. We're a pretty boring lot. We're all experts at labelling people as we travel around. Keeps us entertained.'

'Sounds lovely and uncomplicated to me.' Dru's hair was almost dry now and she reached into her pocket for a band and pulled it into a ponytail. Her hands were steady and her heart was beating a steady and slow comfortable beat.

She smiled again as Pete, who appeared to be the wag of the group, described some of the characters they had come across on the road.

'Disco Dan was at Litchfield over near Katherine. He didn't ever come out of his van and he played Abba songs at full volume until midnight every day.' Pete's voice was full of mirth.

'And then Wally the Wanker was parked behind the four of us in Darwin.'

Chrissie wagged her finger at her husband. 'Don't be rude, Pete. Dru doesn't need to know all about that.'

'Well, he was. He was a know-it-all, and besides that, he wore all those gold chains and all he wanted to do was tell us about his real estate all over the country. Not a real bloke in my books.'

'Your intolerances are peeking out again, darling.'

'Didn't believe a word he said. Anyone with that sort of dough wouldn't be staying in a caravan park. All he wanted to do was tell us about his trips to Bali and the stuff he imported for the stores he reckoned he had.'

'I bet I know what he was really importing.' Rob grinned. 'Lots of call for that funny weed in Darwin.'

This time it was June who chastised her husband. 'Look you pair, it's all right for you to joke around when it's just us –'

Dru picked up her drink and rubbed her thumb up and down the wet surface of the glass. There was a strange buzzing in her ears, and

June's voice faded into the general noise of the outdoor area. She closed her eyes as the back of her neck prickled.

'Dru?'

She startled as the deep voice came from behind her. Icy fingers clutched at her heart as she turned and looked up into the serious face of Connor Kirk.

Chapter 13

Lakeland Village Caravan Park – Kununurra, Western Australia

Connor stood at the bar and scanned the crowd. Dru was sitting at a table on the far side of the manicured lawn with a small group. She was wearing a brightly patterned dress tied around her neck, and her damp hair hung low on her bare back. He worked his way past the crowded tables in the bistro and walked along the path that led to the pool. As he drew closer to her table, her laugh reached him and he paused for a moment. She was a damn attractive woman.

Connor forced himself to chill, quickly arranged his lips into a grin and kept his voice warm and friendly as he approached the table. 'Dru!'

She turned to him with wide eyes.

'What a coincidence,' he said. 'I thought you flew out to Perth this afternoon?'

All week he'd been thinking about Dru's reaction to the question he'd asked her about Dubai. Was it fear? Or guilt? He'd rung the company since, but gleaned little information apart from the fact that she'd worked there at some point in time, and no, sir, unfortunately we cannot share any further information without legal reasons.

He knew that he'd rattled her, and now that several days had passed, he regretted mentioning it. He'd given too much away. But the damn woman pushed his bloody buttons. She had an answer for everything and he'd wanted to see her reaction. And he'd sure got one. She'd almost dropped her glass when he'd spoken and her cheeks flushed a rosy pink.

He nodded to the others at the table. 'Hi everyone, I'm Connor Kirk. I work with Dru down at Matsu.'

The older man at the end of the table pointed to the empty chair. 'Take a seat. The more the merrier.' He introduced the others sitting at the table as Dru sat straight, her face devoid of expression. Connor pulled out the chair and sat down before she could voice the objection that he knew was on her lips.

Despite what he'd said, he'd known that she hadn't been on the flight out to Perth. Not only had he pulled up her flight booking from Kununurra to Darwin, he'd slipped a GPS tracking device beneath the bumper on her car before she'd left the mine site, just to make sure she did come this way. Dru's flight was at one pm. Luckily for him, a earlier flight ran at eleven am on Saturdays to cater for the tourists heading to Darwin for the weekend. – it would have been a bit hard to stay out of Dru's sight on an eleven-seat plane. He'd follow her from the airport and see who she met up with, plus he'd got her Darwin address from the staff database. She was in his sights for the next two weeks

He'd had no luck in his investigation of the other staff that John Robinson had flagged. He'd started deep internet searches on them but not yet unearthed anything suspicious.

There was no other reason to suspect Liam Carruthers apart from the money he'd been bragging about. As a truck driver he had no access to any of the places on site where the diamonds were held. Nothing yet on Rocky Cardella either, but he was still a person of high interest.

He'd added two more names himself—Adam Hennessey and Don Finlayson, but to date he'd not looked deeply into either of them. Hennessey had been more than co-operative showing him through the security section, and his safety manuals and procedures were the best on site, but there was something not right about him. He had more digging for Greg to do into both Hennessey's and Finlayson's backgrounds before he cleared them.

At the moment Connor's money was on Porter, with maybe Cardella as an accomplice. Although nothing had come up in the X-ray scan as she'd left the site, he intended keeping a very close eye on Dru.

Don't trust anyone. Don't take anything at face value. If he'd learned that earlier in his career, he'd probably still be in the Federal Police force.

'Connor.' She nodded briefly and half-turned away from him.

'So you work down at the mine, Dru.' The older man shot Connor a curious look.

'We thought you were on holidays,' Chrissie chimed in. 'Just goes to show you never get it right, Pete.' The other woman laughed and Dru joined in.

'We took a flight down to the diamond mine last week. It's a very interesting place,' Rob said.

Dru nodded and the couples looked at her expectantly. Connor sat back and folded his arms. Social chitchat always made him uncomfortable. He preferred his own company to spending time with casual acquaintances—people he'd never met before and would probably never encounter again. If he was honest, he preferred his own company full stop. The only time he'd lived with a woman and been a part of her social world had been difficult. In that way, it had been a relief when he'd walked out.

'Yes, it is. There's a couple of planes come in every day with tours.' Dru appeared to have regained her composure and the flush had faded from her cheeks. Her voice was soft though, and Connor had to lean forward to hear her response over the buzz of conversation in the bistro.

'What do you do there?'

'I'm an engineer. In charge of site restoration.' Her voice grew in confidence.

June nodded and smiled. 'I really enjoyed the tour but I felt guilty the whole time. As though I was being watched. The security there is amazing.' Her eyes were wide. 'The tour guide told us what not to do. You're not allowed to pick up anything off the ground, or take photos of the security cameras. I was barely game to get off the bus.' June giggled.

'But you enjoyed your time in the diamond shop, didn't you, darling.' Rob's smile was gleeful.

June leaned over and nudged her husband. 'I did.' She looked across at the other couple. 'Tell Dru and Connor what my lovely husband bought for me, guys.'

Chrissie laughed and shook her head. 'He's such a generous guy, is our Rob. He bought us all an ice cream!'

The happy banter continued between the two couples, and it ensued that Pete had been in a similar occupation before he'd retired. 'But a zinc mine is nowhere near as exotic as diamonds, is it Pete?' Chrissie chipped in.

'My work is really not that different to any other site restoration project,' Dru said. 'Out in the heat of the desert, and a lot of the work can be boring.'

'Where else have you worked?'

Dru lifted her gaze and looked at Connor. He could have sworn her chin tipped up a little as she stared at him. 'I was overseas for a couple of years before I came here.'

'Nothing like seeing the world when you're young. Then you can see Australia when you're our age.'

Pete was greeted by a chorus of protests. 'Our age!'

The conversation turned to travel as a waitress brought two large pizzas to the table.

While the others shared out the pieces, Dru turned to Connor, and her whispered words were terse. 'What are you doing here?'

He frowned and pretended not to know what she meant. He gestured to his plate. 'I'm having dinner. Are you?'

Dru reached for a slice of pizza. 'You know very well what I mean. Why are you following me?' Her whisper was harsh but her voice cracked a little as she spoke.

Guilty conscience kicking in? he wondered.

He raised his hands in front of him and played dumb. 'Whoa, right there. Why on earth would I be following you? I thought you were on the flight out to Perth, remember?' He shrugged. 'I was as surprised to see you as you seemed to be to see me. I don't recall seeing a car in front of me as I negotiated that bastard of a dirt road. Maybe you were invisible?'

Her expression was closed and her lips set tightly together. He jutted his chin out to match her tilted chin and they were silent as the battle of wills played out.

Finally, she lowered her eyes to her hands. They were clenched in her lap, and she was squeezing them so hard her knuckles were white from lack of circulation. She was hiding something; he had no doubt of that, but an unfamiliar surge of sympathy appeared from somewhere within him. The two men were still immersed in conversation, but the women sent a couple of curious glances their way.

'Sorry, that was a bit rude.' He shrugged and spread his hands in an attempt to allay her suspicion. 'Look. I'm on a short break too. I thought I'd have a look at the Kimberley while I'm here at the mine. So I drove to Kununurra. Found the best caravan park, and here I am. Simple as that.' The lie came easily.

'Where are you staying?' Her voice was still low. She reached for the pizza and nibbled around the edges as he watched.

'I told you. Here in this park'

'I got the last cabin.' Her gaze challenged him.

'I'm on a grass site down by the lake. Camping. In my swag.' Dru didn't need to know that he'd tried to get a cabin and when there was nothing available apart from an unpowered site he'd gone into town and bought a swag at the camping store. He was well used to roughing it in Indonesia.

'Oh.' She put the pizza back on her plate and fluttered her fingers against the patterned fabric on her thigh. The brashness he'd observed in her previously had disappeared completely. The woman sitting in this casual outdoor area was very different to the hard, confident card player the night he'd met her. Softer, more feminine. And putting on a vulnerable act with the big eyes and the soft voice.

Maybe she was trying to use her feminine wiles to distract him. But there was Buckley's chance of that happening. Fluttering eyes, sexy looks and poses, and tears; over the years he'd learned every trick that a woman could use to get her own way.

Maybe it was because Dru was out of the work clothes he was used to, but there was an aura of something lingering around her tonight.

Sadness? Uncertainty? Vulnerability? Even fear.

As he fought to kill the sympathy and recover the steely determination that drove him, she stood and placed her hands on the table.

'Well, it was lovely to meet you all. Enjoy the rest of your trip. I'll pay my share of the meal on the way out.'

'No, our shout,' Rob said.

'Thank you.' She nodded to the two couples before turning to him. 'You too, Connor. Watch out for the midges down near the water. They'll eat you alive in a swag.'

She sounded as though she hoped they would.

***

Dru's heart was thudding and her fingers tingling as she hurried back to the cabin. Until Connor had turned up, she'd managed to relax a little bit and had even been beginning to enjoy herself. She should have known better than to let her guard down.

Was it merely a coincidence that Connor was here? True, he'd been nowhere near her on the road and she'd told no one where she was staying so she had to accept it was just that.

A bloody coincidence. Of course it would be her blasted luck that something else happened to shake her just when she had started to calm down.

After she'd changed into her PJs, Dru turned the light off and stood by the window. Lights flickered from a couple of the tents and the soft strumming of a guitar came from the area where three Wicked campervans were parked in a small circle. A bit like a wagon train. She smiled despite the regret that pinged through her; how nice would that be? To be comfortable with friends like that and enjoy being on the road. Good company, safe and secure; confident in your own world.

It was time to do something about this fear that was always waiting to consume her. She couldn't spend the rest of her life living like this.

Dru was about to go to bed when she caught a movement in her peripheral vision. Connor was sauntering casually down the road, and as she watched he turned right at the end of the road onto the grassy verge by the lake where she'd seen the Matsu ute earlier. LJ 203; she memorised the large yellow letters on the side. She still didn't trust him.

As he reached a light at the end of the road down to the lake, he stopped and turned around and stared directly at her cabin. Dru stepped back behind the curtain. Her blood turned to ice and she swallowed as her stomach churned.

He knew which cabin she was in.

Chapter 14

Connor slept lightly that night; his acute hearing was attuned to the sound of a car leaving from the direction of Dru's cabin. What he hadn't counted on was the mass exodus of RVs, campervans and caravans from sunrise on. He grabbed his towel and strolled up to the amenities block. Dru's blue car was still in the carport next to her cabin, and the curtains remained firmly closed.

An hour later, they were still closed and there was no sign of life as he packed up the swag and placed it in the back of the work ute he had borrowed. John Robinson had cleared him to use any of the mine facilities, although the security guard at the gate had raised an eyebrow when Connor had signed the vehicle out.

'You're lucky. Unusual for a newbie to get a work ute to take off site on their break.'

'Good to hear.' Connor had stared the man down until he looked away. 'I'm pleased that policies are being followed.' Let him think what he liked, Connor reported to no one apart from the CEO. But he knew it would cause talk, so he tempered his words with a casual comment and a wide smile. 'And yeah, it makes my life easier. Had to get to Darwin for some personal business and the boss agreed as a one off.'

He waited in the ute until he saw the curtains open in Dru's cabin. He knew that he had made her uncomfortable and he wanted to allay any suspicions she might have. Last thing he wanted was to have her watching *him*. He kicked himself; for the first time in a long time he'd let a suspect get under his skin. Despite her size and confident bearing, Dru's strength was overlaid by an air of vulnerability. A sadness that seemed to be a part of who she was.

For God's sake. He was letting his emotions be affected. It was threatening his judgement.

Connor started the car and cruised slowly past her cabin towards the gate. He wasn't going to give her any more reason to be wary of him. He'd seen her flight booking and he'd booked a seat on the plane that left an hour earlier; there was an extra flight on Saturday mornings to cater for demand. Once they got to Darwin, he'd make sure that she didn't see him at all. His surveillance would be much more discreet.

He knew her address; but he was going to hire a car and follow her from the airport and track her movements. For all he knew she could meet someone there before she went to her apartment, though he hoped that wouldn't happen. Once she parked her car at the airport at Kununurra, he had no way of tracking her. He'd have to wait at Darwin airport and follow her when she disembarked. He'd just have enough time to collect the car before her flight landed.

Outside the caravan park he turned left and drove into town, parking the car in a car park in the middle of the shopping precinct. Being a Saturday morning, there were markets in the town park and he soon lost himself in the crowd. At the edge of the park, a coffee stall was set up and there were a few vacant plastic chairs beneath the huge trees. He ordered a coffee and positioned himself in a chair up against one of the wide tree trunks. Pulling out his smartphone, he logged in and opened the tracking software. Dru's car hadn't moved. She was still at the caravan park.

Shit. What if someone was meeting her there? He had left too much to chance here.

Keeping half an eye on the screen, he sipped his coffee and took in his surroundings. It appeared that many of the people who'd left the park early were here at the Kununurra markets. A long convoy of caravans and RVs filled the side of the road from the edge of the park out to the highway.

He expelled a relived breath as the blue circle on his screen finally began to move. She probably wouldn't go straight to the airport; there was plenty of time before she needed to check in and the airport was only a couple of kilometres west of town. He concentrated on the screen as the software tracked her route. She was heading towards town. If she ran into him, so be it, but he would try to stay out of her sight. He could only claim so many meetings as coincidences.

The blue dot stopped a couple of streets away from where he was sitting in the park. Connor switched his screen to street view and let his breath out in a low whistle.

A coincidence?

Dru had parked in the car park outside Pentecost River Fine Diamonds. Pushing his chair back, he threw the coffee cup into a nearby bin and took off for the store at a brisk walk. Maybe that was the connection. He was certain she had no diamonds with her this trip—she'd cleared the X-ray point—but there could be a link. Maybe that was where she usually dropped them off?

By the time he reached the front of the shopping mall across from the diamond outlet, there was no sign of Dru, but her vehicle was in one of the parking spaces out the front. Connor stood outside a real estate agency focusing his interest on the window, keeping the reflection of the store in his sight. As he watched, the light caught the sliding doors as they opened and Dru walked out with a short man. Connor stepped back to the side of the building and stood in the shadows observing the interaction.

She held up a small bag and put her other hand on the guy's arm. An animated conversation ensued until with a final wave, Dru crossed the road and headed in the direction of the markets, the bag clutched firmly in her hand.

Connor waited until she turned the corner and was out of sight, and then crossed the road to the store. He slipped his phone into his shirt pocket and walked through the automatic sliding doors. They closed noiselessly behind him. The air pumping from the air conditioner was cold and the room was bathed in bright light. Two L-shaped showcases were at the back of the store and tall glass cabinets lined each side wall. Four three-tiered free-standing display units were placed symmetrically in the open space in the centre of the store.

Crossing to the first cabinet on the side wall, let his eyes move from the top of the case to the bottom. The shelves glistened with a variety of jewellery and he held back a whistle of surprise. The pink diamond necklace draped over a stand on the top shelf held a discrete price tag of over three hundred thousand dollars. Not what he expected in a small town at the edge of the Kimberley. He glanced up, not surprised to see three cameras placed at regular intervals along the top of each wall. Turning slowly, he looked up. Four more cameras were positioned above the door, and he was sure there would be smaller cameras hidden throughout the store if that necklace was an indication of the value of the jewellery in here.

'Can I help you, sir?' A woman in a black skirt and pale pink shirt had appeared by his side. The other women behind the counter wore the same uniform. Elegant and understated. There was no sign of the man that Dru had been speaking to outside.

'Yes, I'm looking for a present for my mother.'

Her perfectly plucked eyebrows rose as she nodded, and he was enveloped by a cloud of nauseatingly strong perfume.

'Jewellery?'

He followed the direction of her arm as she gestured to the showcases in the middle of the room.

'We also sell diamond-based cosmetics, as well as an array of accessories such as business card holders and clutch bags with pink diamond chips set into the edge.'

'No, definitely a piece of jewellery.'

'Certainly. Our diamonds are all local pink and violet diamonds, with some cheaper cognacs in the counter display. Do you have any particular piece in mind?'

'Perhaps some earrings?' Connor smothered a grin. His mother would have laughed at the idea of him spending money on 'baubles' as she'd called them. Never leaving her alternate lifestyle behind as most of her friends had done when it was no longer trendy to be a hippie, she'd be happier with a necklace made with string and a couple of beads.

'Depending on what you need, we have readymade sets in this cabinet –' she gestured to the cabinet to his left '– or if you prefer you can choose your own Matsu diamond and the jeweller can set it for you.'

'You have a jeweller on site?'

'Three.' Her voice was very cultured and Connor wondered idly if she was a local. She was more suited to Toorak than a small town in the East Kimberley. 'We have a twenty-four-hour turnaround on anything you may order. If necessary, the jeweller will work all night to finish a piece for a specific order.' The woman took a step back as the door opened and more potential customers walked in. 'I'll leave you to browse, shall I? Often a piece will speak to you as soon as you see it.' Her voice became more posh as she spoke.

Connor had noticed her check out his leather shoes and Rolex watch. Obviously a good saleswoman who assessed the customer and then moved in for the sale. 'Thank you. If something speaks to me I will be sure to call you over personally.' Again, he bit back a smile. Bloody hell, if only the diamonds at Matsu could speak to him, he'd solve this case and be out of here on the first plane. He glanced down at his watch; it was past time to check in for his flight.

It only took a couple of minutes to drive to the airport at Kununurra. Connor parked the Matsu ute at the back of the car park and crossed the hot bitumen. Even though it was just before ten o'clock, the heat was rising from the ground in waves. He put his finger in his collar and loosened it, keeping an eye on the road. He didn't think Dru would be here yet; her plane was scheduled two hours after his. He sat in the airport lounge and kept his smartphone in his hand. He logged into the tracking program but her car was still stationary in town.

When his flight was called he stood and lifted his bag, and the small blue circle began to move on the screen. She was on the road to the airport. He switched his phone to flight mode and slipped it into his pocket, wondering how Dru usually travelled from Darwin airport to her apartment. He knew little about her personal life; maybe she had a partner who would pick her up. Maybe she'd get a cab.

As the small plane took off, about ten minutes behind its scheduled departure, Connor leaned across and looked down. Below him on the edge of the small township, the mango and sandalwood plantations on the fertile plains of the Ord River formed a wide green fringe at the edge of the red desert. The silver ribbon of the fast-flowing river snaked across to the manmade Lake Argyle to the east, and the diversion dam to the west of town.

He turned away from the shimmering view to concentrate on the job at hand. He needed to figure out was what she was doing in the diamond store at Kununurra and why the jeweller had followed her outside.

****

The deep vibration of a plane taking off filled the air as Dru turned onto the airport road. Her eyes were gritty and her limbs leaden. She'd tossed and turned all night, worrying about the coincidence of Connor being in the same small town.

What did they call it? She'd looked it up once, not long after she'd got back from Dubai. A persecution complex? The delusion that someone was out to harm her. Well, someone was, she knew that, unless her memory was embellishing what had really happened.

When she thought about Dubai, it always triggered her recurring nightmare about Dad.

As Dru had lain there drifting on the edge of sleep, old memories pushed into her thoughts and she broke into a sweat. Her legs stiffened and she clenched her fist against her mouth as that picture rewound. The same picture, the same people, the same outcome.

She'd tried to move the packing crates, but Mum had pulled her away.

'Peter, Peter.' Her mother's sobs had been guttural.

Eyes bulging, red spots in Dad's cheeks. His tongue protruding from his open mouth, as though he was trying to talk to them.

Help me. Dru had imagined the words coming from his mouth.

'Dad,' she had screamed. But they could do nothing to save him. It was too late.

She'd dragged her mum to the house and made her sit in the lounge. In the end Dru had to climb into Mum's lap and sit on her to stop her going back out there to that fucking shed while they waited for the police and the ambulance to arrive. The call to her sisters had been one of the hardest things—no, it had been the hardest thing— she'd ever done in her life.

She could still remember every second as though it was yesterday.

Ellie and Emma had grieved too, but they had never understood the depth of pain that Dru carried inside and how it impacted on her every day.

Her relationships, her trust, her damn wellbeing. Her whole fucking life. There was no way she was going to call it mental health— even to herself. She had found Dad, and Mum had come to the shed just behind her.

Dru hadn't been able to save him. Her wonderful, loving father. She knew she couldn't have saved him, but that didn't stop her from blaming herself. It was easier to stay away from her family and keep her grief buried deep along with every other feeling that wanted to surface. She could forget most of the time. But sweet Jesus, would that picture of her dead father ever leave her?

Hot tears had spilled from her eyes and she let them fall onto the pillowcase.

Finally, she slept deeply for an hour before dawn until the sound of departing caravans woke her.

The humidity was building and she sat in the car for a long moment, enjoying the cool air pumping from the dashboard vents. She closed her eyes and took a deep breath. Shopping at the diamond store for the gift for Adam Hennessey's wife and then wandering around the Saturday markets had eased her tension for a short time, but now her fingers began to tingle and her heart beat heavily. Taking another deep breath, she switched the ignition off and opened her door. She slipped the package into the side pocket of her soft bag, and put it onto the ground as she leaned across to get her backpack from the front passenger seat of the car. The jeweller had come outside at the same time she had, and he'd been interested to see that she'd bought a jar of the face cream. 'As you can guess, we don't sell much of it,' he'd said.

'It's for a friend,' she'd replied.

As she looked across the airport car park, Dru spotted the white Hilux ute parked in the very back row. Picking up both of her bags, she walked to the end of the row and stood looking at the number plate.

LJ 203. Connor's ute.

Anger filled her and she strode into the terminal. Suspicion solidified in her stomach. He *was* following her; of that she was now certain. A couple of businessmen in suits sat in the departure area, their phones to their ears. Three couples, Indian and Japanese waited by the counter but there was no sign of *him*. Connor Kirk.

She waited in the line, her heart now beating a staccato rhythm in her chest. When the flight service officer was free, Dru stepped forward and took her e-ticket from her backpack. With a smile, she inclined her head to the car park.

'I thought I was on the same flight as my . . . er . . . friend, but he doesn't seem to be here? Connor Kirk?'

The girl smiled back at her and glanced down at her computer. 'I'm sorry. I can't give out passenger information but there was another flight to Darwin earlier. We run two flights on Saturday mornings and they're both always full.'

A spike of uncertainty ran through Dru's chest and settled in her stomach. Her thoughts ran in circles for a few seconds and she clung to her e-ticket as the girl held her hand out for it.

She swallowed and injected a brightness she was far from feeling into her voice. 'In that case, there's no point me getting there after him.' She knew she was babbling and her words made no sense. 'Different meeting times.' Her words ran on top of each other. 'We must have gotten confused. Look I'll catch him later. Please cancel my ticket. No point me leaving now.'

'Are you sure?'

'Yes.' Dru's nod was jerky. She knew her eyes would be red-rimmed and the usual purple shadows would be there. 'I'll catch him later. Just cancel my booking. Don't worry about the refund. It's fine. I'm not worried. I have to go. I'll see you next time. Thank you.'

She was aware of the girl's curious gaze staying on her as she picked up her bags and turned to the door. Let her think it was a lover's tiff. Or—closer to the truth—that Dru was a nutcase.

She took slow and steady steps and it felt as though she was moving through quicksand. Her sweating hands slipped on the straps of the bag and she had to grasp them tightly. Okay, maybe she was being totally irrational and hysterical, but better to be safe than sorry.

Darwin was an international airport and it wouldn't be hard to get her onto a flight to Dubai. If Zayed had employed Connor to take her back, he would have passports and whatever was needed to get her there.

Okay. Maybe she was totally crazy, but she was not going to go home to her apartment. It was time to disappear for a while. She just had to figure out where to hide for two weeks.

Maybe longer.

'They need one more to join the tour or they're going to cancel.' The English accent was strong.

Dru slowed as she passed the tourism office on her way out of the airport. Two young women were standing in front of the counter looking at each other.

'Oh no. Really? We wanted to see the Bungle Bungles and we're flying back to England next week.' The taller one's voice was laced with disappointment.

Dru put her bag down and approached the counter. She'd been thinking about going back to the mine; at least she knew she was safe there. But she wasn't rostered on for two weeks, and what if Connor came back there looking for her? She needed another option.

'Excuse me. What's the tour?'

The tour operator looked down at the computer screen. 'A safari camp in the Bungle Bungles. It's supposed to head out this afternoon, but it's about to be cancelled.' She shrugged and gave an apologetic smile. 'I'm sorry, but we need a minimum of fifteen to run it. It's one of the last tours of the season. It's a bad time of the year with the wet coming on. We have trouble filling some of the tours and it's disappointing when it doesn't go ahead at the last minute. The Kimberley is usually a one-off visit for most tourists, especially the backpackers.'

'That's us.' The red-haired girl shook her head. 'It was going to be our last tour before we headed home.'

'Maybe I can help.' Dru glanced at the two young backpackers with a smile before turning back to the guide. 'Tell me more about it.'

'Six days down in the Bungle Bungles. A lot of hiking with an indigenous tour guide and everything is supplied. Safari tents and all meals. Five star "glamping". All you need is some energy and the desire to have a good time.'

Dru smiled; the woman was a good salesperson.

'Okay, sounds good to me. Sign me up.' Dru even surprised herself with her quick decision. She reached into her bag and pulled out her wallet. 'I needed something to fill in this week. What do I need to bring along?'

'Just a few changes of clothes and your toiletries. A towel, a pair of swimmers and a pair of sturdy boots. Everything else is provided.'

Dru handed her credit card over.

'Oh, and a wide-brimmed hat and sunscreen too.'

After the payment was processed, the tour operator handed Dru her card. 'Be back here by quarter to one. It's a four-hour drive and you'll get there just in time to set up camp tonight. Park your car over in the long-term park. No charge for tour members.'

The two young girls grinned at her. 'That's way cool. Thanks so much.'

After heading into town to pick up what she didn't already have in her bag, Dru was back at the airport with time to spare. Knowing that Connor had left on the flight to Darwin eased her tension and she'd stopped looking for shadows that didn't exist. She put her new Akubra on her head, locked her bigger bag in the boot and picked up her backpack before heading for the small tour bus parked on the other side of the car park.

As they sailed past the turn-off to the mine a couple of hours later, Dru settled into her seat with a smile. A week where nobody knew where she was; a week where she would be one hundred percent safe.

Chapter 15

Darwin, Northern Territory

A string of curses left Connor's lips as he stood at the side of the arrivals lounge at Darwin airport and watched the passengers disembark. He waited until the flight crew left the plane and then realised that Dru had somehow duped him. Or maybe she'd never had any intention of getting the flight to Darwin. Maybe she was one step ahead of him and a lot cleverer than he had given her credit for. It was a multimillion-dollar heist that he was investigating, and he'd been acting like an amateur and had underestimated her. Her looks and her confidence had thrown him that first night, and then the vulnerable act that she'd put on last night had got to his emotions and sucked him right in.

He pulled out his phone and switched it on, and quickly scrolled to the tracking app. The blue circle indicating the co-ordinates of her car was stationary in the car park at Kununurra airport.

So maybe she'd missed the flight just in and was catching a later one. He looked up at the flight board listing the arrivals. There was one more regional flight due in from Kununurra mid-afternoon. He'd sit and wait. There was nothing else to do.

Damn, damn, damn.

While Connor waited for the next flight to arrive from Kununurra, he opened his bag and pulled out his laptop. At least he could spend the time productively.

The faulty cameras were part of the theft; he was certain of that, but who was interfering with them was still an unknown. He emailed Greg and asked him to run a couple more background checks—on Don Finlayson and Adam Hennessey.

A new list appeared on the screen as he put his thoughts down. He typed D. Porter at the top and tapped his finger on his lips as he added to the list.

Opportunity. That needed a bit more work. Like the other suspects, as far as he could see she had no access to the processing plant or the recovery room.

Secrecy about her background. That was a big red flag.

And the Dubai connection. A photograph taken with the guy who'd bought the diamonds. That alone was enough to have her interviewed by the police. But had he bought them? There was no evidence of a purchase; only the word of his PA to the jeweller in Antwerp.

Connor had almost completed his preliminary investigations at the mine, so it was time to take the investigation a bit wider. A trip to Dubai and Antwerp to interview the key players was his next step. Zayed Al Tayer, his personal assistant, and Hughie Van Hoebeek, the Antwerp jeweller.

When the final flight arrived from Kununurra and Dru wasn't on it, he stood and pushed his laptop back into his bag, frustration blurring his thoughts for a few seconds. He forced himself to calm; he'd had plenty of harder cases than this over the past few years.

Dru wouldn't come to the party; so he'd go and check out her apartment. He plugged Dru's Darwin address into his phone and pulled out the key to his hire car.

He had no trouble getting into her place. As soon as one of the tenants had buzzed him into the foyer—all he had to do was say he was a deliveryman—he was inside her apartment within minutes. The location had made breaking in even easier. It was on the top floor overlooking the harbour and her entry door was hidden from view.

He knocked on the door for safety's sake—as far as he knew she lived alone—and then used his tools to pick the lock. As he turned the knob, he waited for a security alarm but all was silent. He stepped into the foyer, slipped his shoes off and let out a whistle. A huge glass window overlooked the sapphire blue water of the harbour. A low white leather sofa fronted a huge television screen recessed into a small alcove at one end of the room. At the other end was a kitchen with glossy black countertops.

Careful not to touch anything, Connor stepped into the first bedroom. As he looked around at the luxurious apartment, he realised what was missing. The apartment could have been a holiday let. There were no personal items on display; no knick knacks, no photographs, no books.

Nothing.

Connor stepped into the en-suite bathroom and opened the cabinet.

Empty.

A cold feeling settled in his gut. Christ, what if he'd broken into the wrong apartment?

Walking slowly toward the front door, he glanced at the last door at the end of the wide hallway. He turned and stepped down the hallway, the white tiles cold beneath his bare feet. Opening the door, he found a room filled with cardboard boxes. A hairbrush sat on the low cupboard beneath the window. He picked it up. A couple of stray long, blonde hairs were caught between the fibres.

He was in the right apartment.

Most of the boxes were sealed with packing tape and although he was tempted to open them, he didn't want her to know that he had been in the apartment. He lifted the lid of a couple that were already open but they only held an assortment of books and clothes.

Frustration gnawed at him again. She'd led him on a merry chase and it was a bloody waste of time looking here. He wasn't going to find anything. Biting back his temper, he went back to the entry and slipped his shoes on.

It was time to go deeper, and to visit the place where he knew there was information waiting for him. He'd take the first flight back to Kununurra in the morning.

The drive to Wyndham the following afternoon took just over an hour. The road from Kununurra was sealed the whole way and

Connor was surprised by the lack of traffic. He ignored the temptation to turn onto the famous Gibb River Road and head down to El Questro and Zebedee Springs. Apparently, he and his mother had spent some time along the Gibb River Road when he was a child but he had no memory of it.

What he could see so far appealed to him—wide open spaces, little traffic and no habitation. He shook his head as he slowed the vehicle to avoid a large bird pecking at a carcass in the middle of the road. He'd spent the first five years of his life in a kombi van moving from place to place wherever his mother's mood took them. Maybe that explained why he found it hard to settle on one place now. Maybe he'd take some time off after this job was done; hopefully things would go his way and it wouldn't be long.

Despite being tired—and if he was honest, a bit jaded—Connor knew he was on the right track. He'd set himself a punishing pace over the past ten years but he'd had a business to build up—not to mention demons to keep at bay.

He could pinpoint the date and time that this bloody restlessness had begun to consume him. The seventeenth of April, 2005—his twenty-eighth birthday.

Up until then, he'd been content with the three-bedroom house in the suburbs of Canberra while he built up his career in the Australian Federal Police. Until a betrayal of mammoth proportions had taken his job, his fiancée and everything Connor had believed he wanted. He'd left it all behind without a backward glance, and tried to put it behind him.

For a while he thought he had, but since the two Australians had been executed on Bang Kwang last year the nightmares had returned.

Truth, integrity, justice. There was no such thing. But in his immaturity and naivety, he'd believed they existed.

A road sign informed him that Wyndham was ten kilometres ahead. He glanced in the rear-vision mirror; there was no traffic following so he slowed the car, keeping a look out for a turn-off to the right. Five minutes later, he reached the five kilometre sign and realised he'd missed the turn he was looking for. He checked for traffic before pulling onto the middle of the road in a U-turn, and headed back the way he'd come. This time he kept his eyes on the scrub at the edge of the road.

To the west, flat saltpans glinted in the late afternoon sun, stretching as far as he could see, broken only by occasional clumps of mangroves. The salt flats were dry white cracked mud, so vast it created a mirage. The Cockburn Ranges bordered them to the south, incredibly tall, brilliant orange sandstone rising to over six hundred metres. The occasional derelict and abandoned boat lay in the mangroves and the only things moving were plovers scurrying across the tidal flats in search of food. A fragment of memory tugged at him; how did he know they were called plovers?

He turned back to the eastern side of the road and lifted his foot from the brake, but slammed it down hard as a large vehicle and caravan appeared in his side mirror right up behind his back bumper bar. It whizzed past with a toot of the horn, and as he indicated to go back onto the bitumen, the sun flashed on something a short way into the scrub just ahead. This time he pulled further off the road and nosed the ute into a low stand of trees. A slow smile lifted his lips. From his new vantage point, he could see a thick chain linked to a small steel post on each side of a narrow sandy track. Opening the door, he climbed out and picked up his Akubra hat, shoved it on his head and then reached across to the back seat for the brown paper bag containing the two bottles he'd purchased in Kununurra.

On the top of one of the posts ahead was a hand painted sign. Daubed in white and red paint on an old piece of corrugated iron, rusty and jagged at the edges, was a warning.

'Enter at your own peril. Bugger off. Or go out in a box.'

He'd arrived.

Locking the car, Connor climbed over the chain and headed up the sandy path that led to his destination. Putting his hand up, he tilted the brim of his hat down and shaded his eyes. He peered ahead but there was no sign of any habitation between the road and the next low hill.

Striding out, he kept his eyes on the track as it climbed to the top of the hill. He gave a short grunt of satisfaction when he spotted faint tyre marks in the mound of sand that the wind had blown to the side of the track. The distant sound of dogs barking broke the silence and he squinted into the bright sun. Ahead and about two hundred metres to the left, a bright flash split the afternoon sky. Connor slowed his pace and kept the direction of the flash in his sight as he stepped off the track and headed that way. He'd approach the dwelling from the bush; it was safer that way. Knowing the temperament of the man who lived there, and how rarely Connor—or anyone—visited, he'd probably have the dogs set on him before he got anywhere near.

Or worse. Connor came to a dead stop and raised his hands as the cold nudge of metal pressed through his shirt into his left kidney.

'Don't take one more fucking step.'

The gravelly voice brought a smile to Connor's lips. He'd know that voice anywhere.

'Can't fucking read, hey bud?' The rifle pushed harder into his back.

The smell of unwashed man wafted across to him on the slight breeze and he slowly turned around. 'Better than you ever could, Gregory,' Connor retorted. 'I thought you might like some company. Especially with the house-warming gift I brought you.'

Connor stepped back as Gregory Francis opened his arms wide. 'I said to call me. I didn't expect you to pay a personal visit.'

'Wasn't hard, Greg. I could smell you from the road.' He held out the bottle of Glen Livet. 'Now are you going to invite me in? Or set the bloody dogs on me? You said you had something for me so I came to get it. I don't have an address at the moment. Not one for sensitive stuff anyway.'

Greg took the bottle from him. His hands were filthy and the rank odour got stronger as he stepped closer. He wore a tracksuit with a hooded top, even though it had to be over thirty-five degrees out here in the afternoon sun. His hair was matted and greasy and his beard, long and tangled. A shaft of anger sliced through Connor's chest and he closed his eyes.

Fucking Nina Smythe. She could take full responsibility for the wasted human being who stood in front of him. Not only had Greg walked away from his career that day; he'd dropped right out of society. Connor had walked too, on his career, on his workmates and on his conniving deceitful fiancée who had shafted them both.

Never trust a woman.

He should have listened to Greg's mantra before it was too late. Connor had started up his business and become a loner, only being able to persuade Greg to work with him from this hideout over the years.

But I could have ended up like this, he thought. And the thing that frightened him most was that he still could.

***

An hour later they were sitting on the verandah of the old hut on the side of the hill. It was a small dwelling with an outside concrete tub that doubled as a bathroom. A composting toilet was situated about fifty metres into the scrub at the back of the hut. A couple of chooks clucked around and a mangy ginger cat stretched itself along Greg's lap. Connor leaned back in the creaky rocking chair and looked out over the view. The road was hidden by the tree-covered hill between the house and the coast. The sun sat low in the sky and the salt plans glistened with a ferocity that hurt his eyes.

'It's a peaceful spot here,' he commented. The dogs had stopped barking once they'd come through the gate and were settled beneath the tree beside the house lazily snapping at flies.

'Yeah, and no bugger bothers me. Usually.'

Greg had washed and changed after Connor had refused to drink with him until he cleaned himself up. He lifted his glass and looked at Connor over the rim. 'You're looking a bit stressed, Kirkie. You still working yourself into an early grave?'

'Still working. Don't know about the grave.'

'Still doing your bit to make amends though?' Greg's voice was quiet but it held a hard edge.

Connor stared past him but didn't take in the view. He didn't answer for a few minutes. 'Yeah, but I'm not sure it's about making amends anymore.'

'So what's with the company ute out there?'

'Undercover job.'

Greg nodded and then picked up the whisky bottle, holding it up to the light. Fragments of light splintered and danced across the old weathered beams holding up the tin roof. 'You up for a big night? I've got a cold carton in the fridge out the back.'

'Why not? Might help me sleep.' Connor's voice was bitter.

Greg slammed his glass onto the table beside his chair. 'Did you see what that bitch said the day after they were executed?'

'Yep.'

'"The organisation cannot predict where an investigation might lead as no two scenarios are the same."' Greg put on a high-pitched voice with a plum accent. 'Or some bullshit along those lines. She swore it didn't start with a tip-off.'

Connor leaned back on the chair and it gave a gruesome creak. 'We have to let it go, Greg. We did our bit. We got shafted but life goes on.'

'Fucking hell. I was the one who got the tip-off and set up the travel alerts for when they hit customs.' Greg's eyes were wide. He picked up his glass and swallowed another hefty slug.

They sat in silence for a while before Greg spoke again. 'I guess it was doubly hard for you. You were sleeping with the bitch.'

Connor gestured inside the house with a nod, ignoring Greg's comment about Nina. 'You got a spare bed in there?'

'How long for?'

'Couple of days, maybe. As long as it takes you to chase up some more information I need.'

'Couple of days? Where's your faith in me, mate?' Greg blew out a plume of smoke.

'Tell me what you've got already.'

'Chasing up some drug baron? That Liam Carruthers bloke you got me to delve into works at a diamond mine.'

'That's where I'm based undercover.'

'A change for you, mate. Carruthers recently inherited a shitload of money. I'll show you later. And by the way I've had a look at that Finlayson and Hennessey already.'

'Why did you want me to call you?'

'Technology problems. Fixed now. Anyway, Hennessey's pretty ordinary too, nothing jumped out of the box there, but I probably wouldn't have emailed the stuff I found out about Finlayson so it's just as well you turned up here.'

Connor sat up straight. 'What did you find out about him?'

'I got into his private email.'

'And?'

'He's got a big secret. And like we both know, anyone with a big secret is open to blackmail.'

'Spill.' Connor finished his drink and put his glass down.

'Your man is married. Couple of kids. Nice house in Perth.' Greg reached for the Scotch and held it up but Connor shook his head.

'Not yet, I want to keep my head clear until we do a bit more work. Keep talking.'

'Your choice. So back to your man. By all accounts, he's a fine upstanding bloke.'

'But? His finances came up dodgy?' Connor was hoping.

'No, not at all. Thing is, he's got another house, one I wonder if his wife knows about. Leads a bit of a double life, does your Don Finlayson.'

Connor sat up straight and wrinkled his brow. 'Like what?'

'He's gay. And he's got a partner that no one seems to know about.'

'Damn.' Connor stared at Greg.

'Damn what?'

'That's nothing like I was expecting.'

'Remember, Kirkie. When there's some deceit, there's sure to be more. And he's open to being blackmailed with that sort of secret. Is this another drug investigation?'

'No. I've taken on something a bit different. A diamond theft. Having a bit of a holiday up here in the Kimberley.' Connor ran his hands though his hair. 'Shit. Maybe that takes one of the suspects off the hook a bit. But I'll still get you to look into his finances later. I've got a few more jobs for you. Up to it?

'Pleasure.' Greg smiled and stood with the Scotch bottle tucked beneath his arm. 'Long as you keep the whisky flowing, I'll do whatever you ask.'

Connor shook his head as he stood and pushed the flimsy plastic chair back. 'I need to track someone's bank account over a couple of years. And maybe tap into a company database in Dubai. A bit more than I can handle.'

'Piece of piss, mate.' Greg flashed him a grin and for a fleeting moment, it was like looking back to the carefree face of his partner in the Australian Federal Police ten years ago. 'Now tell me what else you want and we'll go and have a look.'

Walking through the crooked doorway of the old hut was a bit like stepping into Doctor Who's TARDIS. The dwelling was composed of a single room with a double bed in one corner and a low bench running along the back wall. Three computer screens blinked as Connor stood in the room. He shook his head as Greg ambled across to the large leather desk chair in front of the middle screen.

'Pull up a pew, mate. You'll have to bring in one of the chairs from outside.'

Connor stepped back onto the verandah and looked around. There was another old plastic chair in the corner and he picked that up and carried it inside. He shook his head. 'I can't believe you've been here five years.'

Greg leaned back in his chair with a grin and put his hands over his hefty paunch. 'What? You don't like my choice of abode? The payout I got from the force paid off the missus and left me enough to buy my computers.'

Connor didn't comment on the reference to Greg's wife. He knew it had almost broken him when she'd walked out with the kids after the incident that precipitated their resignations.

Greg rolled his chair closer to the desk. 'All the creature comforts covered. Bed, food and beer. Not a lot of spare cash around this month though. I did my dough at the salt flat races a couple of weeks back. So now what else can I do for you?'

Connor checked underneath the chair for spiders before he sat down gingerly. The flimsy plastic legs moved and he redistributed his weight to the back of the chair.

'I need to find some bank accounts. Australian and maybe foreign. Some maybe Dubai based.'

'What name?' Already his fingers were flying over the keyboard and the middle screen changed to an MS-DOS command prompt. He moved to the screen on the left and brought up Google.

'Drusilla Porter.' Connor watched as Greg started a Google search. 'There's not a lot there on her. Just some uni stuff.'

'Clever woman. If she's savvy enough not to have a digital footprint we might start at the uni. Which university and how long since she was there?'

'James Cook and I'd say about three years.'

Greg moved back to the centre screen and typed a string of commands. Connor wasn't surprised when a student database filled the screen.

'Campus?'

'Townsville.'

The clicking of the keyboard filled the room and the screen burst into colour. A photo of a young Dru Porter appeared in the centre. Her ice-blue eyes stared at the camera but her mouth was tilted in a smile. She looked happier than the times he'd spoken to her.

'Hmm. What's she into? Something to do with the diamond theft?'

Connor gave a short laugh. 'A suspect high on the list. But my money is on her. As sweet as she looks there, she's as hard as nails.'

'Mate, after what we saw I'd believe anything.' Greg grunted and his fingers flew over the keyboard. 'Her uni fees were paid through a local building society account back then. Most people keep their early accounts.'

Connor watched as the screen filled with rolling text.

'Yep. She's still with them. There's the account number.' Greg lifted his hands and rubbed them together. 'Now for the fun part; finding her password. Grab us a coffee, Kirkie. We might be here for a while.'

Connor raised his eyebrows. 'No more Glen Livet?'

The response was a wave of an arm. 'Time for that later. You have me intrigued here. Need a clear head to get into the international stuff. Once I get her personal details from the building society, we can go searching deeper. Kettle's out the back on the fridge. Go down to the creek to get the water. I found a dead possum in the tank yesterday so the water in there is a bit dodgy.'

Connor stepped out onto the verandah. Since they had gone inside the sun had dropped below the horizon and the evening sky was shot with streaks of purple and vivid orange. He took a deep breath and watched as the vapour trail of a jet heading north dispersed in the high winds. It turned into a golden line on the purple velvet backdrop of the brilliant sky. Where was it going? It would do him good to board a plane and head off somewhere new for a while.

After this job is over.

Connor let the peace and quiet of his surroundings seep into his soul. Greg had the right idea. Find somewhere to live where no one bothered you, and where you had no stress to tug at you constantly. Nothing to achieve and nothing to prove.

He walked around to the back of the building and found the kettle plugged into a double power point above the old rusty fridge. Two towers of tinned food balanced precariously next to the kettle and he lifted it down carefully after he'd unplugged it. He opened the fridge and frowned. Nothing but a carton of milk and a dozen cans of beer. If he was going to stay here a couple of days, he should have brought some supplies with him.

By the time Connor had found the creek and filled the kettle, then returned and made the coffee it was pitch dark. Night came quickly in the tropics, as did the mosquitoes that buzzed around his head as he came back into the light.

He put the coffee down on the desk beside Greg and walked back over to close the door to keep the insects out.

'Bring the bottle in too.' Greg gestured towards the door with his head.

'How's it going?'

'I'm almost done here. Put a slug of whisky in my coffee.' The laugh was pure evil and Connor couldn't help but smile. He'd enjoyed working with Greg in Canberra; they'd had some great times together and they'd been good mates.

'You'll need it to kill the taste of that instant coffee. Black and Gold? Where did your gourmet tastes go?'

'Same place my income went. Speaking of which, you might like to take a look at this.' His voice was serious. 'A very organised lady, this Drusilla Porter.'

Connor pulled the plastic chair closer to the screen. Greg had a spreadsheet open.

'Four accounts.' Greg highlighted part of the document and made the font larger so it was easier to see. 'The original one that she appears to pay her bills from. And an investment account with the same building society.'

'Fifteen thousand dollars balance. Not a huge investment.' Disappointment laced Connor's voice as he read off the figures.

'There's more.' The screen scrolled down. 'An account in Dubai with forty thousand *dirham* in it.

'Now you're getting somewhere.'

'No, that's only about fifteen thousand Aussie dollars too. But look here.'

Greg scrolled to the final page. 'I've downloaded the transactions for this account. It's an account with another bank. Two transactions about eight months ago. A deposit of nine hundred thousand dollars. It sat there for three days and then was withdrawn and went to a solicitor's trust account.'

'Holy shit.' Connor leaned forward as his adrenaline spiked. He was right, Dru was the one. Forget the gut feeling that she was involved; here was the proof. 'Where did the deposit come from?'

Greg's teeth glinted in the light from the screen as he smiled. 'Dubai.'

Chapter 16

Kununurra

Six days hiking in the Purnululu National Park with fourteen carefree backpackers helped Dru relax more by the day. She wore herself out physically, slept like a baby and regained her equilibrium. It truly was 'glamping'; she'd smiled when she'd seen the double bed and solar shower and toilet in her tent.

The enormity of the beehive domes, and the giant scale of the rock formations helped put her problems into perspective, as did the nights spent at the bush camp. Sitting around the campfire, sharing stories, and laughing at what some of the group had experienced in the outback was cathartic.

On the last night of the tour, Dru walked out beneath the stars along the Cathedral Gorge Trail lost in her thoughts. She had always recognised that her father's murder ten years ago was at the root of her insecurities. Back then, she'd refused to see a counsellor and had buried her grief in wild and risky behaviour during her final weeks at high school in Jabiru. Non-stop partying, underage drinking and unprotected sex; it was a wonder she'd passed her Certificate of Education. It was a miracle that she hadn't fallen pregnant or caught something, but thankfully she'd avoided causing her mother any more grief.

Not that Mum would have known about it anyway, dosed up on anti-depressants and hiding away in the house most of the time. Emma had done her best to guide Dru into safe behaviour, but she had been wasting her time. By the time Dru left school a few weeks after Dad's funeral, they'd moved from the farm into Jabiru, and that had made it even easier to get to the parties. But after a few scary experiences Dru had even frightened herself with the risk taking and finally she had given herself a stern talking to when she headed off to uni.

A new Dru, a new reputation in a fresh environment. The only risk taking there was in her choice of sports. She pushed herself, needing the buzz that the danger gave her. While ever she was doing that the dreams and the bad feelings left her alone. She joined the abseiling and sky diving clubs. The rush she got from standing at the top of the mountain and jumping from a plane had filled the emptiness that constantly dogged her.

By the time she'd graduated and got the dream job in Dubai, Dru's restlessness had mostly settled. Her friendship with Megan had been the next step in confronting her fears. In Dubai she had finally opened up to Megan; the first person who had ever got her talking about herself—and her past—and in a way Meg's pseudo-psychoanalysis had been cathartic.

'You know it's because you lost your Dad when you were young, don't you?' Megan had put her hands on the table and stared at Dru as they sat in one of the bars at Atlantis, the Palm, looking out over the azure waters of the Persian Gulf. Dru had been more interested in the logistics of building the huge man-made island that the hotel was situated on, but Megan wouldn't give up. 'You're scared of losing someone else. That's why you shut down so quickly. The cold response is a barrier.'

'Cold?' Dru had almost spat the cocktail—her second—over the huge circular table in the Ossiano bar. She quickly regained her composure and looked away from the view, past the huge column towards the other side of the room. 'That aquarium is amazing, isn't it?'

A huge spotted stingray glided through the myriad of brightly-coloured fish, closely followed by a shark. Dru pretended to be interested in their progress through the water.

'Don't change the subject.' Megan sat back, put the cocktail glass on the table and folded her arms. 'You put up this big ice queen front, but you don't know how challenging that is to some men.'

Dru pursed her lips and turned back to face Megan. 'You're talking rubbish.'

'Don't look at me like that. I know the real you and I know you care about people, no matter what you hide behind. Plus being stunning looking just adds to the challenge.'

Dru almost spat her drink again at that comment. 'Yeah sure. Okay, so what do I hide behind, Ms Psychoanalyst?' A slow simmer of anger had begun to burn in her throat and she took another slug of her mango cocktail.

'Good, get cranky. It'll do you good to talk about it.' Meg reached out and put a perfectly manicured hand on Dru's wrist.

Dru bit her lip as she stared down at the red, tapered nails. In contrast, her own nails were trimmed and unpainted. Practical.

'You work your butt off to be the best at what you do. You're trying to prove something.'

'Being good at my job is important to me.' Dru couldn't believe that tears were pricking at the back of her eyes.

'But why is it so important to you? Have you ever wondered?'
Trust Meg to cut to the heart of it.

'I don't have to wonder. I know why.' Dru pulled her hand away from Megan's touch and shook her fingers in front of her chest. 'My job is all I've got. No one can take it off me if I do it well.'

Meg lifted her hand and grabbed at one of Dru's hands. Dru was still opening and closing her fingers slowly.

'Why do you do that shaking stuff with your fingers? I've noticed you do it a lot.'

Dru stared down at her hand that was now firmly clasped in one of Megan's.

'It's a nervous thing.' She kept her voice low, ashamed to admit to any weakness. 'When I get stressed, I get this feeling in my hands.' All of a sudden, her vision blurred. 'Like butterflies in my fingers. Crazy, aren't I?'

'It's okay. No need to be stressed here. I'm here for you, hon. And I will be whenever you need me. Just talk when you want to, okay?'

Dru nodded. It had been a long time since she'd talked to anyone about how she felt.

Meg gestured around the luxurious bar. 'Gawd, look at this place. Opulence unlimited.'

Dru took a deep breath and reached for her drink again, hoping that Megan had changed the subject, but she hadn't finished.

'You know what causes your stress? You've got family issues. You should hear yourself. You talk about your sisters as though you don't care but then you refer to them all the time. Emma did this and Ellie's a helicopter pilot. Yada, yada, yada. You might be fooling yourself, but you haven't fooled me.'

Megan's lecture had made Dru take more notice of her family for a while. When she fled Dubai, it made it easier to go home to Mum's place in Port Douglas.

The mournful call of a night bird in the gorge brought her back to her present. She stopped on the trail and stared down the rock walls below her. These incredible sandstone formations were thought to have been forged over 350 million years ago from the sediment of an old riverbed. The unique orange, grey and black stripes were lit by the faint light of the new moon in a clear sky. She lifted her head and looked up at the stars. The velvet black sky out here in the desert was not tainted by light pollution. Thousands upon thousands of pinpricks of light were visible to the naked eye. What had Dad used to call it?

A diamond sky.

'When you feel as though your problems are overwhelming, go outside and look up at the night sky. It puts them all in perspective. Each of us is just one little spot on one planet orbiting around just one of how many million stars that are out there.' Dru could almost hear Dad's voice as he'd lain on the grass beside her looking at the night sky. Remembering his words she looked up at the sky again; the awesome grandeur and the complex magnitude of the solar system reinforced how minuscule her problems were. The tranquillity of the night sky and the serenity of the rocky landscape held her motionless;

Dru let her thoughts return to another desert ten thousand kilometres away.

Since she'd left there her fears had come back tenfold. But it was all in her head; none of it was real. She turned and walked slowly back to the camp. Surely her recent fears were unfounded and Connor had just been an unknowing target of her paranoia. Megan was right; she had overreacted in Dubai and thrown a good job away. There was little chance—even if he knew where she was—that Zayed would even be interested in getting her back there. He would have moved on by now. It was time for a fresh start and to get over this stupid fear that dogged her everywhere she went. Life would be unbearable if she didn't get over it.

And she *would*. Today was a new start.

Tomorrow she'd head back to Kununurra with the group. She'd collect her car and head back to the mine a couple of days early. She was good at her job, and she enjoyed it. The money might be less than Dubai but it was still a generous salary for a recent graduate. And now she had the apartment in Darwin, she could start saving again.

From now on she'd apply the same analytical skills that she applied to her work to her emotional turmoil. Her first task would be to ring Megan and accept the offer of being bridesmaid, and tell her she'd be there. Then she'd get her flight to Dubai sorted. Dru pushed away the tiny niggle of nerves that fluttered in her fingers and clenched her fists. No more finger shaking. No more stress. She looked up at the sky.

Serenity and tranquillity. That would be her new mantra.

With a happy grin she walked back into the camp and headed for her tent.

Chapter 17

Matsu Diamond Mine

'So?' Meg's hopeful voice brought a smile to Dru's face. Since she'd left the National Park and returned to Matsu a couple of days before, she'd been feeling upbeat and managed to keep her nerves at bay.

'Yes, I'll be there. But just for three days.' The new Dru was still wary.

'Oh my God,' Meg's voice was so loud Dru pulled the phone away from her ear. 'Really? You'll really be my bridesmaid?'

'I will. But the deal is I don't wear a dress or heels.' Dru's voice was dry.

'You got it, babe. I told you I have a killer pants suit picked out for you already. Oh, Dru, I am so happy. You've made my day.'

'That's good. I'll book my flights but I want Sam to pick me up at the airport and take me straight to your place. Okay? Nowhere else. Your place, the wedding and then the airport. I might be being silly but I'll feel more comfortable if we do it that way.' Even though Dru had come to terms with her irrational fear, she still wasn't going to hang around Dubai. She'd see Meg and Sam, do the bridesmaid bit and come back to Darwin for a while. Heck, maybe it was even time to go and visit Mum. Perhaps she could fly back via Cairns International Airport.

'Got you loud and clear and not a problem, we'd already thought of that and done better. We've booked a few rooms at the Atlantis and we'll look after you. We'll both be there for a couple of days before the wedding. All the family are flying in and we don't have enough room at the apartment.' Megan squealed. 'Oh. I am so happy you said yes!'

'So what are we going to do about this "killer pant suit". Remember I'm not an off-the-rack size.

A quick discussion about measurements and dressmakers satisfied Dru that Megan had the outfit well under control She agreed reluctantly that Dru could pick her own shoes.

'A little heel maybe?' Meg cajoled. 'Just a teensy one?'

'Don't push your luck, sweets.' Dru laughed. 'I'll see you in a couple of weeks.'

***

There had been no sign of Connor in the staff mess or around the site since she'd come back, and Dru wondered if his work at Matsu had finished already. She shrugged as she headed out to the ute. She was keen to head out to the rehabilitation site and see what had happened while she was off. Before she could do that, there was a meeting with the traditional owners to attend in the administration block. She'd been surprised to see the extraordinary meeting notice in her email when she came back.

Dru parked in the front car park and made her way to the building. Outside the main door a couple of unfamiliar men in suits were deep in conversation with Rocky. Unusually for him, his trousers were pressed and he was wearing a collared shirt. His hair was slicked back with oil and he was clean-shaven. As she pushed open the door and entered the foyer, John Robinson, the CEO of the company nodded at her. She'd only met him briefly once before and didn't know him well enough to start up a conversation, so she walked to the water cooler under the pretext of getting a glass of water. The door opened again as more committee members arrived. Finally Rocky came inside with the two men and John ushered everyone into the meeting room.

The chairman called the meeting to order as soon as everyone was seated around the U-shaped table. The secretary from the main office was sitting on John Robinson's right, taking minutes on a small laptop.

'I'd like to welcome you to this extraordinary meeting. The traditional owners have requested this meeting in relation to the proposed expansion of the mine. The legality of the current Participation Agreement has been called into question, and we are taking this opportunity to listen to the concerns raised in a letter to the committee –' the chairman glanced down '– dated the first of November.'

He read from the letter in his hand. 'The *Gija* and *Miriuwung* People are the traditional owners of their ancestral lands in the Eastern Kimberley, and the Matsu Diamond Mine has been in operation on their land for the past ten years. We hereby register our objection to the proposal for a second underground shaft. This further incursion on our traditional land will continue the destruction of our ancestral homeland, irreversibly devastate our cultural heritage, and offer little in return for such a massive loss.'

He put the letter down and opened the meeting for comments.

Rocky raised his hand. 'I want you all to know about our main concerns. This meeting has been called by the *traditional* owners of this land.' Dru jumped when he slammed his fist on the table. 'Not the imposters who signed this agreement ten years ago.'

The chairman looked over his glasses at Rocky. 'Would you please clarify what you are trying to convey, Mr Cardella.'

'What I –' he glanced at the two men sitting on each side of him. 'What *we* are *conveying–*' his voice dripped with sarcasm '– is that the original agreement is not legal. It was a set-up.' Rocky reached up and ran his finger around the collar of his shirt. 'Some of the original signatories were not members of our people and our two legal representatives here today can prove that was the case. We have proof that the agreement was signed without the agreement of the genuine and true owners of our land, and further we have proof that some signatories received payment for signing the agreement.'

Dru examined the faces of the men sitting alongside the chairman. A few frowns could be seen, but John Robinson's face was the one that caught her attention. His eyes were as cold as flint and his mouth was set in a straight line.

The man on Rocky's left cleared his throat and raised his hand. 'My name is Tom Wari, and I represent my people. We are prepared to be reasonable with the negotiations to address this matter—and please rest assured that there *is* an issue. We are not saying that Matsu Diamonds was behind this; we are looking into the situation from our side. However, no matter how the signing off was done, our major concern is that a sacred site on the southern side of the mine has been compromised.'

Dru sat up straight. That's where she'd been working recently. And it was where Rocky had been spending a lot of his time wandering around. She paid close attention to the ensuing discussion.

Tom continued to speak with passion. 'Land is fundamental to the wellbeing of our people. It's not just soil or rocks or the mineral wealth in the ground. The land sustains our people, and in return our people and culture sustain that land. Our country, and our sacred sites, are at the core of our relationship with our land.'

John Robinson's voice was cold. 'May I ask why it has taken ten years for this issue to be raised?' His tone implied disbelief. 'Our agreement was the result of a structured –'

'That's all good, mate. And too bloody right the structure was there.' Rocky interrupted. 'But what we're saying is that some of the signatories were not the traditional owners. It was dodgy.'

Robinson ignored him. 'As I was saying, our agreement resulted from a structured negotiation process.' He picked up the water glass in front of him and drank. 'There were ethnographic and genealogical studies of the area, heritage protection agreements, the execution of a land use agreement, and we examined the traditional culture –'

Rocky's voice drowned him out. 'You can go on all you bloody like. Sitting down there in your office in Perth or wherever, the agreement is still illegal.'

'There was no mention of any sacred sites within the defined boundaries.' Robinson's voice was dismissive and Dru watched with interest as Rocky stiffened in his chair. 'So what do you want, Mr Cardella?'

'We are going to lodge a dispute with the National Native Title Tribunal.'

The room was silent.

Tom Wari leaned over and whispered in Rocky's ear. Dru looked from him to John Robinson; whichever way this issue went it might not have a good outcome. For the expansion of the underground mining—or for anyone's job here at the mine.

'Before the dispute is lodged and goes to arbitration, we, the traditional owners, are prepared to come to a compromise agreement. As a traditional owner representing my people, I have been given authority to raise it here today.'

'A true traditional owner,' Rocky muttered but loud enough for everyone to hear. Tom Wari put his hand on Rocky's arm.

'Go ahead,' Robinson nodded to Tom to continue.

'We will not object to the new drilling on one condition. We know the importance of the mine for the economic development of our state, and we appreciate the employment and the educational support that our people have received over the past ten years. We also appreciate the effort that has gone into the rehabilitation of the site.' He looked at Dru and nodded slightly.

Rocky butted in. 'At the time of signing there was pressure to accept because they'd seen what happened in other places. People were afraid that if we took too long to agree, the land could simply have been taken without our agreement.'

Tom took over. 'And at the time of the signing of the original agreement, there was an attitude of getting some of the "whitefella money". You have to understand that even in recent years, many of our people were still paid in food and clothes. The prospect of getting paid for the land led to the making of some unwise decisions. We are not opposed to either the mining of diamonds on this site or further development. What we are opposed to is the continued destruction of our heritage, our sacred sites, and our culture in an atmosphere of bullying that seems to go hand in hand with mineral exploration and mining.'

John Robinson looked down and fiddled with the papers on the table in front of him.

Tom's voice hardened. 'We will remain immovable on any negotiations that attempt to ignore our single condition.'

'And the condition is?' John Robinson's lips were set in a straight line and perspiration dotted his brow.

'The sacred site on the southern boundary will be compromised no longer and the south-eastern corner of the mine, where the site is located, must be returned immediately to the traditional owners.'

Much discussion ensued after Tom dropped the bombshell ultimatum, and Dru was surprised that John Robinson was prepared to listen. 'Of course, it will have to go to much wider consultation and negotiation, but I am willing to initiate discussion.'

Rocky had a wide grin on his face by the time the meeting drew to a close and Dru made her way outside. It was what he had been telling her that night at the termite mounds. She'd doubted him at the time, but he had trusted her enough to tell her the truth.

As she crossed the foyer, surprise brought her to a stop.

Connor was standing by the water cooler where she'd waited before the meeting.

Okay, no time like the present. She drew a deep breath and straightened her shoulders, ignoring the nervous churning in her stomach.

'Hello, Connor.' She injected as much brightness into her voice as she could. Reaching out, she touched his arm lightly.

He turned and regarded her silently. She moved her hand back, dismay flooding through her. His face was closed but his eyes were intense. After a moment, his lips tilted in a brief smile of acknowledgement but if she'd blinked she would have missed it.

'Dru.' He nodded curtly. 'What can I do for you?'

Embarrassment played havoc with her resolve but she swallowed. 'Oh, I just thought I'd say hello. I haven't seen you around since I came back from my rostered time off. I thought you must have finished here on site.'

'No,' he drawled. 'I'm here for as long as it takes.' He reached for a plastic cup and filled it. He stepped back and drank the water before crushing the empty cup and dropping it into the bin.

'So how's the safety audit going?' Dru was determined to make conversation.

'Good.' One word and he stood there, his arms folded across his chest.

This time she'd wait him out until he engaged in a conversation. If that didn't work she'd done her best. He looked across the room as a couple of men came out of the meeting room. She stood beside him quietly. She swallowed and ignored the shaky feeling in her hands as her discomfort grew. This long drawn-out silence was embarrassing. Dru was about to speak when he broke it.

'So, did you have a good break?' he said finally.

'Oh yes. I went on a tour to the Bungle Bungles.' Dru's confidence grew and relief flooded through her. 'It was the most amazing experience.'

'Sounds relaxing.'

'Have you ever been there?'

Again, his gaze was intense and the penny finally dropped for Dru. It was nothing to do with her; he was as uncomfortable as she was making social chit chat. And she could sympathise with that. How stupid had she been, seeing Connor as a threat? She must have been in a state to link him with Zayed.

'No.' His gaze narrowed. 'Or maybe I have. When I was a small child.'

Dru smiled widely although it was getting hard to keep up this one-sided conversation going. 'Are you around tonight?'

'I am.'

'Come down to the mess. I'll get a card game going and tell you all about my trip.'

His expression was closed but he agreed. 'I'd be interested to hear all about it.'

'Great.' Dru put her hands together and nodded. 'Seven o'clock in the mess. It's a place you must visit. Gorgeous scenery. Good for the soul.'

And God help her, she winked at him.

She was conscious of his gaze on her back as she headed to the door. When she reached it, she couldn't help looking back but he was deep in conversation with John Robinson.

Chapter 18

'Come to my office. It's too public out here.'

Connor followed John Robinson across the foyer to the stairs leading to the top floor of the administration building. John nodded to his secretary as he opened the door to the office. 'No interruptions, please.'

'Yes, sir.' She put her head back down to her computer.

Robinson sat behind the desk and gestured to the other chair. 'Thanks for coming to see me, Connor.'

Connor sat and nodded. 'Thank you for coming on site. I was going to fly down to Perth to meet with you.'

John pulled out a handkerchief and mopped at his brow. 'Sounds like you have some information for me. After the past couple of weeks here, I'd appreciate some positive news.'

Connor waited until he had John's full attention. 'I've had a look at your three suspects and while there is no evidence that we can use at this stage, I think you were spot on with your suspicions of Dru Porter.'

'Excellent. Time to call the police yet?'

'No, not yet.' Connor put his hand up. 'As I said, I have no evidence that could be used in a court of law, but all of the indicators are pointing to Porter as the guilty party.'

'Okay, tell me what you have.'

'A direct connection to Zayed Al Tayer, and a substantial deposit into her bank account a few weeks before you said the diamonds surfaced in Antwerp.'

'That's surely enough.' John's voice was brisk.

'Give me a couple more weeks. I want to find out how she's getting the diamonds out. With any luck, we'll catch her red handed.'

'Okay.' John nodded. 'I want to ensure that it can't ever happen again. Our security obviously has a weak spot and we need to seal it.'

'Trust me. I'll have it for you. She's booked a flight to Dubai for her next break.'

'Jesus.' John slammed his hands on top the desk. 'You think she's taken more?'

'Either she has got them already or she's about to. Don't worry, I'm watching her closely and I'm hoping I'll get the evidence for you soon. If not, I'll follow her to Dubai. I intended going there to interview Al Tayer and then to Antwerp to meet the jeweller.'

'Do whatever it takes. Charge the flights to the mine.'

'Will do. I've put myself onto the same flight as a precaution just in case I do have to follow her.' Connor pulled out his phone and scrolled though his notes. 'While you're here, I have a couple of questions I noted down to ask you.'

'Go ahead.'

'I'm sure she's not working alone here. Despite the weak points I've identified, the security is too good for that.'

John nodded slowly as he listened. 'That's one positive, I suppose.'

'I've identified two suspects who may be helping her, and I want your thoughts on both of them.' Connor looked up from his phone. 'Some of the information I have retrieved is quite . . . ah . . . sensitive.'

'Yes?'

'First off, she has a relationship—a friendship—with Rocky Cardella, and they seem to spend a bit of off work time together. I had no luck whatsoever tracking down his finances, so I have nothing there but the fact that they spend time together.'

John rubbed his hand over his forehead. 'Cardella *is* causing some problems for us at the moment. Rabbiting on about sacred sites and handing part of the mine back to the traditional owners.'

'Do you think it might be connected to the thefts?' Connor said. 'Something else to take the focus off the investigation? I want to raise something else with you. The sudden increase in accidents and breakdowns. It's too much of a coincidence in the time frame we're looking at.'

John shook his head and his smile held no mirth. 'You think it's to take attention away from the diamonds getting off site? I suspected that the recent workplace incidents are more than that. It's a ploy to discredit the company. The share price has dropped a bit and we're—confidentially—looking at expansion with a second mine. We can't afford any setbacks at the moment. Accidents or thefts.'

'And the land issue?' Connor asked.

'It all came together for me in that meeting. They want the tailings dam back because they think it's full of diamonds.'

'Is it possible that he got the diamonds there and gave them to Dru to take off site? I have seen him wandering around down there.'

'It's quite possible. The processing equipment we use at Matsu was originally designed only to recover diamonds down to about one millimetre in size. Any diamonds smaller than this have ended up in the tailings dam. No process is perfect and in the early days when the ore grade was higher some larger diamonds probably did get through our filters. But six in such a short time frame? I doubt it.'

Connor made a note to research more about the tailings process as John continued.

'Anyway, whatever they expect they've got no chance of changing the original agreement. We'll dredge the dam to get the residue out as part of the finalisation process a few years down the track.' John leaned back in his chair and frowned. 'So the other person you want to ask me about? Is it Carruthers?'

Connor shook his head. 'No, we've checked him out and he came by his money honestly. An inheritance. We've discounted him as a suspect.' As well as having an honest source of his money, being a truck driver Liam Carruthers had no opportunity; he worked well away from the processing plant and the recovery room.

Greg had let out a low whistle when they'd gone through his bank statements together. There was more there than he'd first noticed. 'How come the bastard still works?' he'd said.

'A million's not a lot these days, Greg. And at the rate he's going through it, he'll need a job sooner than later.'

Connor leaned back in his chair. 'Tell me what you know about Don Finlayson.'

'Know?' John's tone was wary.

'I've come across some information that may put him in a position to be blackmailed. As head of security, he could possibly turn a blind eye to the comings and goings of anyone who needed to get off site if they were privy to this information.' The only thing that Connor hadn't established was a connection between Dru and Finlayson, and that bothered him.

John pushed his chair back and walked across to the window. He stared outside for a few moments before turning back towards the desk.

'You're good. There's no doubt about that. I knew it when we approached you. ' He dropped back into his chair. 'I presume you're talking about Don's sexuality.'

Connor was surprised. He stared across the desk at the CEO.

'I can guarantee that Don is not open to blackmail. It may not be known publicly, but his wife and family know, as do his closest friends. Myself included.' He let out a long sigh. 'Don's partner is a high school principal and until he retires, he prefers to keep his private life just that. Private.' He held Connor's eyes with his. 'I told you before that I would trust him with my life, and I do. He still lives with Gloria, but they have an arrangement. It may be unusual but unless you've found direct evidence of his involvement with the theft, you can discount Don from anything to do with it. He's not travelling very well at the moment and that's why he's taken leave despite the investigation. I fully expect him to retire.'

'Very well.' Connor was surprised, but he was prepared to accept what John said.

'I'm pleased with what you've told me today, and you've raised some issues that I need to look at more closely. I think you are on track with Dru Porter. Not so much with Cardella. I think he's got another agenda. Is there anything further that I can offer to help you wrap this up?'

'The only way I can see the diamonds being moved off site is by someone who has direct access to the recovery room. If someone on the security staff is letting them out.' Connor gave a dry laugh. 'From what you've said, it doesn't sound like someone is just fishing them out of the tailings dam.'

'It has been known to happen at other mines, Connor. But six is beyond the realms of possibility—and that doesn't take into account the earlier diamonds either. By their size, they all have to be coming from the processing plant.'

'Well, that leaves me with Dru Porter then. I'll check out the Dubai and Antwerp connections and see where they lead.' Connor stood to leave. 'I hope to have this wrapped up for you in a couple of weeks.'

Chapter 19

Dru lay on her back with her feet up on the sofa, her phone pressed to her ear as she chatted to Megan that evening; the floor tiles were cool against her skin. The air conditioner hadn't been on for long since she'd come back from her day shift and the heat that had been trapped in the donga during the day hadn't dispersed.

The temperature had peaked at forty-two degrees this afternoon; summer was coming quickly. They were rushing to finish the southern corner around the tailings dam before the wet arrived. Although if things went the way that Rocky and his people wanted, maybe they wouldn't finish up down there at all.

She glanced up at the clock and was surprised to see she'd been talking to Meg for almost half an hour. 'I'll have to go soon. I've got a poker game tonight.'

Meg's laugh trilled down the phone and Dru smiled. She'd been feeling so much better over the past few days.

'I swear you're just one of the boys at that mine of yours,' Megan said.

'It's a good place to work. I'll call you one more time before I fly out next week. I'm driving to Darwin when I finish my shift.'

'Email me your flight details. And don't worry; we'll have a welcoming party for you at the airport. Oh, that reminds me. I wanted your opinion on a couple more things for the wedding.'

'Fire away.' Dru pushed the button on the air conditioning remote with her free hand and ramped up the fan speed a couple of settings. It was getting even hotter as the last rays of the setting sun hit the wall through the high western facing windows.

'The table centrepieces. I can either have glass bowls with sand and shells, and make it a beachy theme or just –'

'Whoa, girlfriend. It's your wedding, you have whatever you want.'

'You really think so?'

'Of course. You're the bride. You get to pick what *you* want.'

Megan's laugh tinkled down the line. 'Really?'

'Why do I get the feeling this is leading to something?' Dru dropped her feet from the sofa and sat up. She only had a few minutes to get down to the mess before the poker game.

'Well . . . they just have a tiny, teensy heel, but they are perfect for your outfit, and seeing as I'm the bride . . . '

Dru put on a dramatic sigh. 'So you get to pick everything, including the bridesmaid's shoes? You are one master manipulator, Megan Smith, but I fell for it, didn't I?' She pushed herself to her feet and threw the air conditioner remote onto the coffee table. 'I guess it saves me going shopping for shoes. Over to you, size ten.'

'I know. I've already bought them. They're gorgeous.'

'I'll take your word for it. As long as they don't make me ridiculously tall. Or I should say, ridiculously taller.' Dru walked across to the door and slipped her sandals on. Her *flat* sandals. 'Have to go, Meg. I'm running late.'

'I can't wait to see you. Twelve more days.'

'Not long now. Say hello to Sam for me.' Dru opened the door and put her hand to her eyes as a blast of hot wind swirled up the road.

'Love ya, babe. It's so good to hear you sounding so upbeat.'

'Bye.' As Dru turned to shut the door, she looked up at the air conditioner. The light had gone out on the unit and the fan had stopped whirring. For a minute she thought the power had gone out but she flicked the light switch and the light came on. Must be something wrong with the unit. She pushed the door open wide. It would be too hot to sleep tonight if she left the place closed up while they were playing cards. With a bit of luck, the movement of the air would cool it down a fraction.

She grabbed her laptop and locked it in her car. It was the only thing of any value in her room. Shoving her phone in her pocket, she ran lightly down the steps and down the hill to the staff building. She was late. The outside door was closed and Dru pushed it open and hurried into the cooler air, barrelling straight into the man standing just inside.

She grabbed for the handle as she overbalanced but a strong arm went around her waist as his mobile phone clattered to the floor.

'You *are* eager to play poker.' Connor's deep voice was full of humour for a change and Dru stepped away from his supporting arm. Heat rushed through her as she untangled herself.

Connor leaned down and picked up his phone. He put it to his ear. 'You still there? Sorry about that. I'll call you later.' He hung up and slipped it into his shirt pocket.

'I'm sorry. I was running late.' Dru fanned her face with her hand. 'And you know what Rocky's like if you're late for a game.' She shook her head. 'No, of course you don't. Anyway, it's unacceptable to be late for a Matsu poker game. Rocky's rules.'

'I saw what happened last time I played.' His gaze was intense on her. 'You get discarded and replaced.'

When they reached the mess, Paul and Dave were sitting at the usual table and they both greeted her with a wide grin.

'Hey, guys.' She crossed to the fridge and pulled out a bottle of water.

'Hey, Dru. Good to see you back. Have a relaxing break?' Paul leaned back in his chair.

'Really great, thanks.' Dru sat down and looked around. Connor had taken the seat opposite her. 'No Rocky or Liam yet?'

'Liam's working but Rocky said he'd be here in a few minutes. He left his bag out on the site and had to go back up the hill.' He shot a sly glance at Connor. 'Told us we had to be on our best behaviour because you were playing tonight, Connor.'

Dru was surprised when Connor laughed. 'No need to do that. I'm off duty for twelve hours.'

'You've sure had your work cut out for you lately.'

Dru watched as Connor replied with a grin. 'How's that?'

Maybe it was just women he had trouble relating to. She'd done her best and tried to be friendly, so he could take it or leave it. She stared past him out the window. Darkness was falling quickly and the lights of the buildings up the hill lit up the night sky.

'All the breakdowns in the past week,' Dave said.

Dru lifted and rolled the cold-water bottle over her forehead. Now that she'd got used to the cooler temperature in here, she was feeling hot again. 'What's happened?'

'You name it; it's probably broken down this week.' Paul pointed in the direction of the plant. 'The processing plant was out for twelve hours one day while you were rostered off. They had to get the data restored from the backup in Perth before it could run again.'

Dave joined in. 'There was a batch of bad fuel at the depot and two of the dump trucks broke down too. Luckily it was the same day the processing plant was out.'

'Do they know what's happening?' she asked. 'Or is just coincidental?'

Connor turned to face her. 'Could be to do with the electricity supply to the site. Most things here are computer driven, so once the computers get spiked, there's a problem.'

'Might explain why my air con's carked it,' Dru said with a grin. 'Although that's pretty small in the scheme of –'

Her words were cut off by the scream of a siren from outside.

'Bloody hell,' Paul exclaimed. 'That's the mine rescue siren.'

They jumped to their feet as one and the outside door slid open. A man Dru didn't recognise ran in.

'We need some manpower up at the top of the hill, guys. One of the utes has gone over the pit and there's someone trapped in it.'

A cold feeling lodged in Dru's stomach. As they reached the door, she put her hand on Paul's shoulder. 'Didn't you say that's where Rocky was going?'

Chapter 20

Connor's ute was parked outside the staff mess. 'Do you want to come with me?'

Dave and Paul opened the back doors and jumped in. Dru ran around to the passenger side.

'Can you please stop halfway up the hill at the dongas?' she asked as Connor slammed the ute into gear. 'I need my boots.' He roared up the hill and swung past the dongas before coming to a sudden stop.

She jumped out and he waited, tapping his fingers on the steering wheel. She came out carrying her boots and a pair of work pants. She jumped back in and threw them on the floor as they sped across the plant toward the pit. He wondered what the hell had happened. As soon as he'd heard that Cardella had gone back out in the mine site—which was against policy—his suspicions had been aroused. And Dru's sudden attitude change had his bullshit meter swinging high. That night at the caravan park she could barely tolerate his presence, but now she was trying to engage him in conversation every time he turned around. He looked across at her, wondering if somehow, she had twigged that he was onto her. Her forehead was creased in a frown and she was staring intently ahead through the windscreen. A convoy of vehicles was making its way up the hill.

He parked the ute next to one of the big trucks. Paul and Dave were out before he'd even killed the engine. Dru jumped out and reached in for the pair of work pants she'd thrown onto the floor with her boots. Her cheeks were flushed and her hair had come loose from her braid.

She caught him looking at her but she looked away and laced her boots up. 'God, I hope he's all right.' Her voice was low and intense.

'It mightn't be him.'

'How the hell could a ute go over the edge of the pit?'

Connor shook his head. 'It's got me beaten how a lot of things happen on this site.'

'What do you mean?' She jogged along beside him to join the group of workers in hi-vis vests who were lined up at the edge of the hill.

'Too many accidents.'

At the top of the hill there was a jagged break in the wire fence. He pointed down the slope. Three spotlights were shining on one of the terraces about fifty metres below them where one of the Matsu utes was on its roof.

'It's Rocky's ute, I'm sure.' Dru's voice shook.

Dave ran back over from the covered area where the tourist information was. 'The mine rescue guys are already down there with him. They don't need us.'

Dru's voice shook as she clutched his arm. 'Any word on how he is?'

'I don't know anything else, love. That's all I heard.'

'Oh God. What if he's –'

Sympathy flooded through Connor. It was an unfamiliar emotion. He took her arm before he could change his mind; her distress was growing the closer they walked to the edge. 'This way, Dru. We can wait at the top of the hill. They'll bring him up that way.'

He was surprised when she let him lead her over to the shelter. He tried to distract her by pointing to the signs with the information about the mine for the tourists. 'I didn't know any of this was up here.'

She lifted her head and the sheen of tears glinted in the moonlight. 'A lot of the cultural stuff there is Rocky's work. He's proud of his association with the mine. And he's proud of his heritage.' She let out a short laugh but there was no mirth in it. 'No matter what a rude old bugger he can be sometimes.'

'He's a good man.' Connor kept his voice calm. He still held Dru's arm lightly, even though she'd stopped shaking. 'He thinks very highly of you. I heard him defend you in the staff mess one night.'

'That'd be Rocky. He reminds me of an old friend who worked on our farm when I was growing up.' Her voice hitched. 'I feel comfortable with him.'

'Where did you grow up?' Connor hadn't delved into her past before her university days.

'In the Territory. On the edge of Kakadu.' Her voice was soft as she stared at the lights flashing around them. The lights of the mine ambulance lit the signs in regular flashes of red and blue. The onsite medico climbed out of the passenger side and walked around to the back of the vehicle and opened up the doors.

Just then there was a cheer from the edge of the hill. 'The stretcher's on the way up.'

Dru grabbed at Connor's arm with her free hand. 'Oh, please, let him be okay.'

'If they're bringing him up rather than sending the paramedics down the hill that's a good sign.'

'It is, isn't it?' She pulled away from him and folded her arms tightly across her chest. 'I'll be sure to give him a serve when they get him up here.' Her voice hitched again and once more something akin to sympathy ran through Connor. He tried to tell himself that this woman was his chief suspect and that the injured man was quite likely to be her accomplice, but he was having difficulty focusing on that. All he could see was Dru's pale face and her lips trembling as she stared up at him, her eyes shadowed as the flashing lights moved away.

He put his hand out and then pulled it back before he could touch her. The smell of her perfume lingered on his fingers from where he'd held her a moment ago.

The radio inside the ambulance crackled into life and they both turned to listen. 'Patient is in a stable condition. Conscious and lucid.

He's insisting he wants to speak to Dru Porter. Can someone get her up here?'

Dru's eyes widened and Connor followed her as she stepped toward the paramedic. 'I'm here.'

The radio crackled again. 'We can't do a proper examination because he's clutching a bag to his chest and hanging onto it for dear life. Won't let go. Says it's for Dru Porter and no one else.'

Connor stood stock still. Maybe this was the evidence he'd been waiting for. He turned to Dru and kept his voice neutral, hiding the excitement that had fired in him.

'What's in the bag?'

She shrugged but her voice was hesitant. 'I have no idea.'

They waited a few more moments and another cheer came from the group by the fence, louder this time.

'Easy does it.' Two of the mine rescue team appeared over the lip of the drop and pulled themselves up and over. 'One more level and we'll have him out.'

Connor put his hand on Dru's shoulder as they waited; he was not going to let her take a step away from him. For a brief moment guilt ran through him when she turned with a grateful smile.

'Thank you. I'm sorry I got so upset before. I . . . I . . . it made me think of something that always upsets me. I don't handle medical stuff very well.'

'Happy to help.'

She held his gaze for a moment and when she reached up and squeezed his hand, it was all Connor could do not to express his disgust with a smart retort. She was a consummate actress. All she was worried about was losing her offsider. He recalled the pictures he'd seen of Dru in Dubai with her fancy Arab boyfriend. This woman in work clothes with dust smeared on her face was a long way removed from the elegant creature in those photographs with almost a million dollars in her bank account.

Yes, she was good. Bloody good. Equal to the best he'd seen.

Remember that, Connor. Don't get sucked in. A pretty face led to your downfall last time.

***

Dru held her breath as the two men reached down and took the end of the stretcher as it was lifted over the edge of the drop. Slowly they pulled it up from the man out of sight on the level below. The indentations in the pit were each only two metres high, and Rocky was only a small man so the weight of the stretcher would be manageable. The spotlights were angled around and she dropped her head as the brilliant white lights were directed onto the stretcher.

'Jeez, turn those bloody lights down. You tryin' to blind a bloke?'

Dru sagged with relief and stepped away from Connor's protective grip as Rocky's voice reached her. The two men on the top level slid the stretcher over the last few metres.

'Bring the ambulance closer,' someone called out.

Dru hung back, reluctant to get in the way of the medical staff, but also torn, wanting to see for herself that Rocky was all right.

'Give me the bag, mate. I need to open your shirt.'

'Get your hands off me and leave my shirt alone.' Rocky's voice was loud. 'I only bumped me head. The rest of me is fine.'

'Just let me hold it for a minute? Please?' The paramedic had stepped forward. 'We want to check out your heart.'

'I'll give it to Dru. Go and get her and then you can do whatever you want.'

'I'm over here, Rocky.' Dru stepped forward and felt Connor follow right behind her. 'What on earth have you done? How the heck did you end up down there?' Her voice shook again as she thought of how bad it could have been. She looked down at the stretcher as the paramedic leaned over Rocky. Blood had trickled from a cut on his temple and she drew a quick breath. Maybe he had a head injury. She let her gaze travel down from his face and saw that he was gripping a small hessian pack to his chest.

'Come on over here. I'm sorry I missed our poker game, but I had to get my bag.' Rocky's voice was getting fainter and alarm ignited in Dru's chest.

'What bag, Rocky?'

'This one.' As she leaned over him he held it up and put it in her hand but didn't let go. 'It's really important, Dru, I know you'll look after it for me, if anything happens. You'll know where they have to go.'

Dru sensed movement in front of her and looked up as Connor walked around to the other side of the stretcher. He looked at her, his face unreadable.

'Promise me you'll look after them. You know who to give them to, don't you?'

Dru had no idea what Rocky was talking about but she nodded to soothe his agitation. 'Of course, I will. And as soon as you let these guys get you down to the clinic and look after you, the quicker you'll get better and you can have them back.'

Whatever 'them' was, she wondered.

'Good girl,' he muttered and his voice was slurring. 'Knew I could trust you. But no other bugger around here.' Finally, he relinquished his hold on the bag and Dru held it close.

'Don't trust anyone,' Rocky said. 'You know who to give them to.'

Chapter 21

Dru walked back to Connor's ute after they'd loaded Rocky into the mine ambulance. The medical officer had assured her that as far as he could tell, Rocky's injuries weren't serious and the slurring was most probably from shock. He'd hit his head on the side of the ute cabin as it had rolled but the cut wasn't deep. They were more worried about concussion than anything else.

Connor's was one of the last vehicles to go down the hill back to the staff village. He had waited silently beside her while they'd examined Rocky and got ready to take him to the clinic.

'Come on, I'll drive you back down.' His voice was quiet.

She took a deep breath as she climbed into the passenger seat. Paul and Dave had already walked back down the hill.

As they drove past the administration building, the ambulance pulled into the bay near the medical clinic. Dru let out a sigh and slumped down in the seat. 'I could have done without that tonight.'

'Shout you a cup of coffee back at the mess?' Connor asked with a quick glance across at her. She looked back; his face was shadowed and although his tone was friendly, as far as she could see his expression was set in its usual stern lines.

For a moment, Dru was tempted. Connor had been friendly tonight and she was grateful for the sympathy he'd shown her. When the flashing lights had lit up the night earlier, all she'd been able to think of was the ambulance that had taken Dad away from them. It had taken all of her self-control to stop a full-blown panic attack coming on. Connor's quiet words and sympathy had kept it at bay.

'Thanks. But I'm tired. I think I'll go straight to bed. I want to get up early and go down to the clinic and check on Rocky before I start my shift.'

'Make sure you look after that bag of his, won't you.' Connor's voice was friendly but she sensed the undercurrent of curiosity. Hell, she was intrigued too but Rocky's words about not trusting anyone stayed with her. She probably should have agreed to have a coffee and look in the bag down in the mess with Connor, but something held her back.

'I will,' she said lightly.

He pulled up outside her donga and gestured to the front. 'Your door's open.'

Dru was surprised by his tone.

'Yes. I left it open. My air con's broken, remember? There'll be fresh air in there at least.'

'Not very safe.'

'It's safe here. Besides there's nothing worth stealing in my donga.'

'Pleased to hear that,' he said. 'Make sure you look for any critters that might have come in.'

'I will.' Dru shivered as she climbed out of the ute. 'And Connor, thanks again. I appreciated your support tonight.'

He nodded. She stood and watched as he drove down towards the staff car par before she turned and went inside. She put the bag on the table and looked around as Connor had suggested, relieved to find no wildlife taking refuge in her donga. She picked up the bottle and took a swig of the water she'd left on the bench and pulled a face. It was lukewarm too.

Too bloody hot for everything, she thought, pushing her loose hair back as she mopped the perspiration from her brow. Dru took another drink of lukewarm water before she went back into the small living area and sat on the now not-so-cool tiles.

She pulled the bag over to her, wondering what on earth Rocky had been up to, and what was so important. For a fleeting moment she worried that he'd been picking up rogue diamonds from the ground, but she quickly discounted that. If that was the case he wouldn't have been so insistent about giving them to her in front of so many onlookers. Dru lifted the bag; her arm lowered as the weight of the contents pulled her hand down. She put it on her lap and slipped open the two metal clasps, pulling the straps through before she looked inside. There was a single piece of paper and a bundle of cloth in the bottom of the bag, along with a few handfuls of loose dirt. She pulled out the paper and looked at it curiously. Latitude and longitude co-ordinates were written in heavy lead pencil and there were grubby fingerprints over the edges of the paper. A grid of twelve squares had been drawn in the centre of the paper, and five of them had been shaded in. The square at the top left had a big circle around it and there were two small drawings in the margin.

She turned the paper upside down. Rocky—if it was his work—had drawn some sort of implement. Staring intently, she turned the paper around to the other side. It was a sketch of an axe head.

She carefully reached in, pulled out the cloth bundle and unwrapped it. Inside there were three other pieces of cloth. Two were light with barely any weight to them. The third was large and heavy and she unwrapped that first. It contained a lump of basalt and on it there was a chalk mark.

E4.

Dru picked up the map and looked closer. In the bottom of each square there was a key and the square E4 was the one that was circled. Glancing at the co-ordinates, she crossed to her desk and pulled up a map of the mine site. The square that Rocky had marked sat in the middle of the rocky area beside the tailings dam. The same place he had been wandering around and supposedly meeting tribal members. The same place that the traditional people had requested be returned to them because it was a sacred site.

Her excitement grew as she reached for the two smaller cloth bundles. Picking up the first one, she held it gently in one hand. Carefully folding the cloth back, she stared down at the piece of stone nestled on the soft cloth. She lifted it between her index finger and her thumb and turned it over. It was a small piece of basalt, and the top edge was smooth and glossy. It looked like an axe head. The shape of this fragment and the way it was highly polished on one side showed it had been worked into that shape. It was not a natural feature of the stone.

Bloody hell, Rocky. What have you found?

Dru put the sharp piece of carved stone back into the cloth and turned to the other one, taking care to be as gentle as she could. Unrolling it, she placed the cloth on the coffee table and looked at the artefacts in front of her. Six shell beads between five and ten millimetres long nestled together on the fabric. They had been made from the front end of the shell and three had a circle of natural grooves around the spheres that were a deep ochre colour. Residue of some sort? The largest bead still held a fragment of fibre. Dru picked it up and held it up to the light. Had it come from the string that originally held the beads together?

Whatever Rocky had found was of great significance and he'd obviously known that. No wonder he wanted to make sure the bag was safe. He'd said she would know what to do with it.

Dru thought over the options. Hand the bag over or keep it for now? She decided to keep it with her until the next weekly meeting with the Aboriginal community in Wipporing; it all depended on Rocky's recovery. If he was recovered by then, she would give it back to him. If not, she'd seek out Tom Wari's details and get it to him as soon as she could. In the meantime, she would hang onto it. The bag could stay in the donga when she was here, and when she was at work, she'd lock it in the glove box of the ute.

So Rocky had been telling the truth all along. There was a sacred site of great significance next to the tailings dam. His find was going to have huge ramifications for the mine. She wasn't sure what yet, but she wouldn't let him down.

Dru locked the door and headed for the bathroom. She stood beneath a cool shower for five minutes. Lifting her face to the water, she let the tension seep from her shoulders. It had been a strange day but she felt she had made some progress with Connor. Switching the taps off, she gave a dry laugh. He'd almost been friendly to her. As she stepped from the shower, the cloying heat of the donga surrounded her once again. She pulled on a pair of boxer shorts, but threw her T-shirt back onto the chair before she lay on top of the bed. Exhausted from the heat and the events of the night, Dru fell asleep quickly.

Strange dreams peppered her sleep; she was in the desert in Dubai. Rocky was following her and picking up diamonds from the sand dunes and wrapping them in Christmas paper. The paper crackled as he folded it over the huge purple diamonds.

Dru woke suddenly and turned over onto her back. Her heart was pounding, and she caught her breath as the crackling noise from her dream continued. Something was in the room with her. She lay perfectly still and opened her eyes slowly. She held her breath as a large shadow crossed the wall on the other side of the room.

No, it wasn't an animal. Damn it, there was *someone* in her room. Her throat dried and she froze, conscious of her bare breasts exposed as she lay on her back. The sheet was draped over her legs and her arms were rigid at her side. The only light spilling into the room came through the door that was now open wide; she'd double-checked it was locked before she turned the light out. Her thoughts raced furiously; there was nothing close by that she could grab to defend herself.

The shadowy figure headed for the door and Dru let out a shuddering breath as it disappeared through the gap. As she watched the door was pulled shut and closed quietly.

Her pulse was racing as she swung her legs over the side of the bed and grabbed the T-shirt that she'd left on the chair. She pulled it on and tiptoed silently across to the door. Taking a deep breath, she put a shaking hand to the knob, trying to work up the courage to open the door. She turned the knob slowly so that it didn't make a noise.

There was no movement in her immediate line of sight, so she took another shuddering breath and put her head out a fraction. The road was deserted; no lights were on anywhere and there was no sign of life from any of the other dongas. As she waited, she heard a door click shut but it was too far away to tell which building it had come from.

Whoever had been in there had to be in one of the dongas in this row. How the hell had they got into her room? She spun around and crossed to the table where she'd left Rocky's bag. Letting her breath out in a whoosh, she relaxed. It was as she had left it; nothing had been touched. With a frown, she looked around the darkness of the room. There was nothing else of any value in here apart from her phone, and that was still on the table where she'd left it. Dru crossed to the door, and checked the lock again. This time she wedged a chair beneath the doorknob.

It took her a long time to get back to sleep. All she could think of was Connor's curiosity about what had been in Rocky's bag, and that he was in the donga next to hers. Did he have access to the master keys as part of his role?

Chapter 22

Dru's eyes were gritty from lack of sleep when she started her ute the next morning. In the early hours she'd finally convinced herself that she'd had another nightmare; the worry of Rocky's accident had wound her up. No one had come into her room. A night terror; that's all it had been. She'd suffered from similar nightmares for weeks when she'd first left Dubai. But from now on, no matter how hot it was, she wouldn't be leaving the door open.

Rocky was sitting in the foyer of the medical building when she called in on the way to work.

'Hey, there,' Dru said with a smile. 'You're looking much better this morning.' The only sign of an injury was a piece of sticking plaster on the side of his forehead.

'Thanking my lucky stars, I am. If I can get a lift back home, I can get out of here right now.'

'I'll take you. I'm due for a visit out to Wipporing.' Dru lowered her voice. 'And you need to tell me all about that bag you handed over on Monday night.'

Rocky looked at her, his one good eye wide open. 'Where did you put it?'

'Don't worry; the bag's locked in the glove box of my ute.' Dru smiled as the paramedic came back over. 'I looked inside. It's a pretty impressive find.'

'It is, and thanks for keeping it safe. When I get home, I'll give Tom a call. He's got the right contacts.'

'Now any dizzy spells or headaches, you get yourself straight to a doctor.' The paramedic helped Rocky out to Dru's ute and settled him into the passenger seat. 'You were a lucky bugger. If you'd gone any further down the levels –'

'Wasn't my time. I've got a few good poker games left in me yet, hey Dru?'

'You sure have.' She waved to the paramedic who waited till they drove away. 'I was just wondering. Does anyone else know what you had in that bag?'

'Nope. Only you. Why?'

'Just curious.' She slowed the ute down as they approached the fuel depot. 'I just have to top up the diesel.' Before she got out of the car she asked him casually, 'Do you think there'll be a problem taking those artefacts offsite?'

'There'd better not be. They belong to my people. They're not diamonds so anyone who tries to stop me can go take a flying leap.'

'Okay,' Dru said slowly. 'I hope there's no problem.'

After fuelling up, she took the turn to the left past the staff village and headed for the main gate. 'So what happened, Rocky? How the hell did you end up over the bank? It frightened the life out of me when we heard the rescue siren and someone said it was you in the ute.'

He looked sideways at her. 'I was so bloody excited about finding them, I couldn't believe that I left them on the table up there.'

'Why were you up there in the first place?'

The sheepish look stayed on his face. 'Promise you won't laugh?

'Promise.' Dru glanced across at him.

'I found them just before sunset yesterday. There's a small cave at the edge of the sacred site, and I dunno, I just got this feeling I needed to go inside.' He turned his head and looked at her. 'I know you get me, Dru. You've told me all the stories about growing up with my people up your way in Kakadu. I just sort of had to go in.'

'And what happened?' Dru changed back a gear as they approached the main gate.

'It was like someone had just laid them out for me. Sitting on a bit of ground on the other side of a rock at the back of the cave.' He rubbed his eyes with the back of his knuckle. His voice was thick. 'When I drove back up the hill, I stopped at the top there. You know? That place I showed you when you started work here.'

Dru cast her mind back to her first day out on the mine site. After her induction, Adam Hennessey had called Rocky to the main office to take Dru across to the rehabilitation site.

'Rocky here knows this place like the back of his hand.' Adam had smiled. 'He's the head of your crew over on the rehabilitation site works.'

Dru had shaken Rocky's hand and followed him to a Matsu work ute. On the way to the rehabilitation site, he'd asked about her background but all she'd told him was about growing up at Kakadu and how much she'd loved it.

'I bin there when I was a young fella,' Rocky had said. 'Like in Kakadu, we have a strong spiritual attachment to our land.'

Dru had nodded. 'We had an aboriginal worker on our mango farm. Bill taught my sisters and me so much about the land.' As they drove past the open pit, Dru had pointed to the mountains in the distance. 'Even though it's a desert landscape, it's still beautiful.

Rocky had nodded. 'You in a hurry?'

Dru shook her head. 'I've got all day to look around and see the site.'

'Good.' Rocky had turned off the road after they passed the open pit. 'I'll show you just how special this place is.'

He'd driven her up the hill where the dump trucks were parked next to the tourist area overlooking the open cut pit. Dru had wandered over to the signs near the covered shelter.

'That's our Dreamtime story of where the diamonds come from.' Rocky pointed to the painting that depicted the story along the edges of the sign. 'Barramundi Gap is one of the resting places of the female Barramundi Dreaming being.'

Dru stood quietly for a few moments and read the story on the large sign. 'What a beautiful way of describing it.' When she reached the end, she turned to Rocky. 'So according to tradition, when the Barramundi escaped from the wall of rolled spinifex pushed through the water by the Dreamtime women to entrap her, she lost some of her scales?'

Rocky had taken his hat off and wiped his brow. 'Yes, when the geologists discovered the diamonds they thought they were the first to know about them. But through the Dreaming we have always known that the diamonds have been there. The success of the mine is due to the power of the Dreaming.'

'Tell me more about the story. I'm sure that's just a part of it.' Dru had loved hearing Bill's Dreamtime stories about Kakadu.

Rocky smiled. 'The Barramundi's escape is evidenced by the gap in the range where the mine is located. And also the colours of the diamonds proves her escape. The diamonds are said to be her internal organs, transformed. The pink diamonds are her body fat, and the cognacs and champagne-coloured ones are from her lungs and liver, and the grey and green are from her guts.'

'It makes you wonder why we have to take them from the earth, doesn't it?' Dru said thoughtfully. 'And it has such cultural significance to your people, it's essential we restore the landscape.' She shrugged. 'Even though the diamonds are no longer there.'

'Come over here with me and look at this. I want you to know this land, and to remember what I am saying as you lead the rehabilitation project.' He turned his back to the pit and walked across to the other side of the flat area at the top of the hill. It was early autumn and the sky was hazy with smoke. In the distance the Matsu Ranges broke the flat landscape.

'Over there is the range where diamond exploration first started. Some of us were invited to join the venture as we knew our land so well. We followed Smokey Creek from the foot of the range for twenty miles until we reached this point. Would you believe we were picking up diamonds from the top of termite mounds, and when we sieved gravel from parts of the creek, we'd get up to thirty-five stones in our trays?'

Dru had stared out over the landscape. It was almost ethereal in its beauty. The blue shimmering haze hovered over the desert and the red mountains edged it in the far distance. Nothing moved; there was no sign of any wildlife nor was there any indication of human habitation.

'It's very beautiful.'

Rocky had put his hand on her arm. 'Now turn around. I want you to remember what you just looked at.'

She turned slowly and looked to the north. Tier after tier of slashed red earth met her gaze as the open pit mine filled her line of sight in each direction. Dust hung in the air as the dump trucks collected the olivine lamproite ore which they trucked to the processing plant for crushing and separation.

'I see what you are trying to say. There's no need for words.

Now they'd reached the main gate, Dru brought her thoughts back to the present.

Rocky looked ahead at the buildings that dotted the landscape as Dru pulled up at the security checkpoint.

'When I found the artefacts yesterday, I wanted to go back and remind myself of how it was before,' he said.

'And?' She put the car into neutral and let the engine idle.

'I went up there and looked at the landscape and then I stupidly left the bag up there on the ground. By the time I remembered it, I'd had a drink or two and I put my foot on the bloody accelerator instead of the brake after I went back up there to get the bag.'

'You were very lucky.' Dru shook her head as she waited for the boom gate to go up. 'You've got to stop drinking on site. You'll lose your job.'

'You know, Dru. I don't know if I want it any more. It breaks my heart to see this landscape devastated. Our land. Once we get that site returned to us—and I have no doubt that we will—I'll work on that land.' His sheepish grin took on a sly tinge. 'And it won't hurt us to have the tailings dam handed over sooner than later.'

Dru raised her eyebrows as his grin got wider. 'Why's that?'

'It's full of bloody diamonds. Why else do you think John Robinson wants to "negotiate" and "consult" and bloody procrastinate. It belongs to my people.'

Before she could respond to Rocky's bombshell, Dru's attention was pulled away as the security guard waved them over.

'Morning. Sorry, we'll be a bit slower getting you through today. Another breakdown so we've got a manual check inside.'

'What the bloody hell's a manual check?' Rocky scowled and pointed to his head. 'I'm crook, mate.'

'Sorry. Just a shoe check and turn out your pockets. Thank God there's no plane going out today.'

Luckily there were only a couple of others in front of them. It didn't take too long, despite Rocky whinging about being injured.

'I'll just take a look in the back of the ute. No bags?' the guard asked.

'No, I'm heading to a meeting at Wipporing, and then I'm coming straight back.' Neither she nor Rocky told him about the artefacts locked in the glove box.

The guard walked around the ute and then waved them through. 'You're good to go.'

As she put the ute into gear, ready to drive off, Adam came out of the building and waved her to stop.

'Dru!' He hurried across the road to the car.

She turned the motor off, opened the door and stepped out to wait for him. His face was shiny with perspiration and his fair skin was flushed.

'Hi Adam, what's up?'

'I just wanted to catch you before you left. I've been so bloody busy with these camera breakdowns I haven't had a chance to come and see you.' He wiped his face with the back of his hand. 'Are you heading to Kununurra today?'

'No, Rocky and I are off to Wipporing for the meeting with the elders.'

'Oh, that's a relief.' He smiled. 'I haven't got any cash on me.'

Dru frowned. 'What's the problem?'

'I posted that face cream stuff to Cathy. She loved it and she wants me to send over another jar for her sister.' He screwed his nose up and shook his head. 'Honestly, she doesn't understand the distances over here. She just thinks I can pop across to the shop and do her Christmas shopping for her.' Despite his expression, his words were light and he chuckled. 'I've been flat out here and can't spare half a day to drive out. I was going to ask you to pick up another jar next time you go to Kununurra, if it isn't too much trouble?'

'No, that's fine. Happy to help. I'm going out in a few days. Do you want me to post it for you?'

'No, I won't impose on you. ' He waved his hand. 'I'm just grateful you'll collect it for me. I can post it from here.'

'Consider it done.' Dru smiled. 'Are you okay, Adam? You look frazzled.'

'Busy days. But no more than most of us here, hey?' As Adam turned away, he grinned. 'As soon as Don's back from his leave I'm taking a month off. I'm spending all of January at the beach with Cathy and the kids.'

'Sounds like you need it.'

'Make sure you catch me before you head out and I'll give you the cash.'

'Will do.' Dru got back into the ute and fastened her seat belt.

'What'd he want?' Rocky turned to watch as Adam went back into the security booth.

Dru started the car. 'Just some shopping.'

'Poor bugger looks frazzled,' Rocky said. 'Haven't seen him at the mess or at a card game for a while.'

'Apparently there have been more camera problems.'

Rocky grinned. 'I guess the artefacts aren't going to be an issue then.'

'Just as well we don't have diamonds,' she replied. 'The whole site seems to be going to the dogs.'

Dru frowned as she turned towards the main road.

Breakdowns and injuries.

Maybe Connor better hurry up and get on with his safety audit.

***

Connor had spent the night in his room intent on finding the link he was overlooking. He'd emailed Greg and set him another series of tasks, particularly trawling though any financial records they could find for Rocky Cardella.

If it was Dru and Cardella, there had to be a third person working with them. But if Cardella was involved, why would he hand a bag of diamonds over so publicly to an accomplice? After much thought, he concluded that whatever was in that bag must be unrelated.

Connor shook his head. He knew from past experience that it was rare that an illegal conspiracy involved more than two people on a site. The probability of being caught increased with each person involved. He sat back and closed his eyes. If there was a third person involved, it would have to be either someone in the security area, or in the diamond recovery room.

Don Finlayson? John Robinson was adamant that it wasn't him.

Adam Hennessey? He had overheard Hennessey asking Dru for a favour, but apart from that he'd never seen them together since that first night in the staff mess.

Or was there another person in security who was still unknown to him?

He snatched a couple of hours sleep and then headed for the staff mess. The room was full of workers heading off to day shift, but there was no one of interest there; he'd been hoping to come across Dru but there was no sign of her. Restless, he went back to the donga and gathered up some safety manuals.

The medical clinic also was unattended and Dru's ute was gone from the car park. Perhaps she had gone out to the site early before the heat became unbearable. A niggle of something worried at him. If the medical clinic was closed, that might mean they had taken Rocky off to hospital somewhere. Dru had been in a state last night and Connor hoped she was okay this morning.

Christ. What was with this unwanted concern for Dru? He pulled open the door of the ute with more than the necessary force and threw the documents across to the passenger seat.

What the hell is wrong with me? Connor climbed in and started the engine, but before putting the vehicle in gear he put his head back and closed his eyes. For the first time in many months, he summoned up Nina Smythe's face.

She had similar coloured hair to Dru, and a long nose but Nina was olive skinned where Dru was fair. Their voices were similar, both with a husky undertone. He had to remember and keep drilling into his mind, they were both women.

And not to be trusted.

There was no room for feelings of sympathy. He was here to do a job; to find the diamond thief or thieves, and resist this bloody attraction that threatened to deter him from his path. Hell, he should have learned that lesson well enough before.

Connor opened his eyes and wrenched the steering wheel to the right, pointing the vehicle out of his parking spot and up the hill to the security block.

Women are not to be trusted.

He would keep that at the forefront of his mind until he'd delivered those responsible to John Robinson and was out of here.

***

'I can't afford to lose my job. I've got a mortgage mate. The wife is already unhappy. Please just let it go.'

Adam Hennessey's office door was wide open and Connor glanced inside before he tapped on the open door. The guy from the X-ray machine in the search room—Connor couldn't remember his name—was sitting beside Hennessey's desk.

'Last chance, Steve. Just remember what I said.'

Adam screwed up his face in a grimace when he saw Connor about to knock. He turned to the guy. 'So you've got all that? Loud and clear?' He moved around the desk and stood over the guy.

'Yes, Adam. Appreciate it.' He bolted out of the chair and scurried out the door with a brief nod in Connor's direction.

'Come in, Connor.' Adam stood and removed the hip flask that was sitting square in the middle of his desk before he gestured to the chair that Steve had vacated.

'Problems?'

'Jeez, tell me about it.' Adam sat back in the chair and pointed to the silver flask that he'd put on the small sink in the corner of his office. 'I'm tempted to get one of them myself. Seems every other bugger on site has one.'

'And you're telling that to the safety officer?' Connor raised his eyebrows. 'I saw a couple around myself in the staff mess my first night on site.'

'I know it's tough. The guys here work hard and to be here in this unrelenting heat for fourteen days straight makes it very tempting to sneak a drink. An alcohol-free worksite is almost impossible to police.' Adam shook his head and then ran his hand though his short, sandy hair. 'Honestly mate, the last few weeks have been hell here. How do you tell a guy that his job is gone if he breaks one more rule? The bugger's got a huge mortgage and three kids in fancy private schools. Sole income—although a bloody good one—and his wife has expensive tastes.'

'Do you think he'll heed your warning?'

Adam looked up and stared him square in the eye. 'I have no doubt of that at all. If I had chosen to come down on him, Steve Jarvis would've been heading for the gate now. But don't worry, I'll be keeping a close eye on him.'

Connor nodded as he filed the guy's full name into his memory. He held out the booklet he'd brought with him. 'Have you got time to go over a couple of safety issues with me?'

'Why are you so interested in safety in the security department?' Adam's gaze was quizzical and Connor huffed a sigh. *Track covering time.*

'I know, mate. It gets a bit tedious. It's a full site safety audit. Bit like Steve there, if I don't do a proper audit my job's on the line too.' He shrugged. 'Besides, what I overheard flagged an immediate safety issue.'

'Look, if he'd been on duty, it would have been an instant dismissal. I saw him with it in his ute last night. I asked him to bring me the flask and I gave him a dressing down.'

'Anyone else you know of? Drinking on site? Or not "every bugger on site", like you said.'

Adam shook his head. 'Not recently. I was exaggerating. I'm bloody tired. I've been extra busy with Don on leave.'

'Okay. Look I won't bother you with any more questions. I can find what I need to know for my report out of your documents.' Connor held up the file he'd brought in with him. 'Take it easy, mate.'

'Thanks.' Adam was already staring at his computer screen as Connor let himself out of the office.

His mind was ticking over. Walking in on that conversation had been most opportune. Steve Jarvis had looked as guilty as hell, and Connor recalled that the afternoon that he had been through the security check in the recovery room, he hadn't seemed particularly interested in what he was doing. A weak link in the recovery area that his instincts kept telling him was the place he should be looking.

He pulled himself up. Forget the instinct. Go with the facts.

He pulled out his phone and messaged Greg:

Steven Jarvis. Security worker at mine. Finance check please.

That was the logical path of investigation to follow and as he let himself out of the security building and glanced at the cameras mounted on the outside of the building, he knew he had identified another one. He would contact John Robinson and find out how he could get hold of the footage of each camera before it went out.

Chapter 23

Connor flew to Perth on Wednesday morning and spent the rest of the week reviewing the security footage at head office. While he was there he discovered an interesting correlation. He met with John Robinson before he flew back to Darwin, ready to head to Dubai and Antwerp.

'I've had a breakthrough, John. Still no specific evidence but I'm sure I know how they're getting them out of the recovery room. Also, what I've found is sure to be of interest to you with the plant breakdowns.'

'What's that?' John followed the direction of Connor's finger as he pointed to the graph on a whiteboard above the desk.

'Look at the dates and then look at the colour coding below them. A red square means a plant breakdown and loss of production. The yellow means camera interference. I've written the plant location below each incident. There's a definite correlation between the interference and the location of the equipment breakdowns.' Connor pointed to the dates.

John scanned the month of dates that were written in a vertical column. 'I see what you mean. But why? What's your take on it?' He moved forward to take a closer look.

'My take?' Connor stepped away from the whiteboard. 'First up someone has a device to deliberately interfere with the cameras. There are many things that can interfere with a wireless signal but your wireless cameras are engineered to switch channels to find a clear one in the event of interference. But if there is another wireless device in the close vicinity, one designed to switch a signal, this will result in persistent choppiness or intermittent freezing in your video feed.'

'You think it's deliberate? It couldn't just be someone with a phone or some other sort of communication device in their pocket?' John stared at the whiteboard.

'My theory?' Connor had put a lot of thought into this before he raised it with John. 'It's a decoy tactic. The malfunctioning of the cameras is a small issue when you look at the impact of some of the breakdowns. I'm even wondering whether your thief is even aware that he is interfering with the cameras as he moves around the site. The equipment breakdowns are only in two buildings, so we can look closely at the staff who work those buildings. Somewhere hidden in all that data will be the times where there was interference in the recovery room and your thief has picked up the diamonds.'

'But we've got the random search procedures.'

'The yellow, blue and green system?' Connor shook his head. 'Only as good as the staff working it.'

'So, you're saying the thief has an accomplice in the recovery room security.'

'I'd put money on it. Ten different staff in there and I'm looking closely at each of them.

'It's more than a coincidence, isn't it?' John Robinson looked weary and frustration laced his voice. 'You really think there's a connection to the missing diamonds?'

Connor's voice was firm. 'I'm sure there is. Everyone is concerned about the breakdowns too. The site managers have been in my ear about safety.'

A rueful smile crossed John's face. 'Seems like we picked the wrong cover for you.'

Connor waved his hand dismissively. 'The right one I'd say. All this focus on the breakdowns has meant I can look more closely into the areas I think the diamonds are being picked up.' He injected confidence into his voice to reassure the CEO. 'Anyway, I'm off to Dubai and Antwerp in a few days, and I'm hoping to wrap this investigation up for you quickly. My colleague is looking closely at the names I've given him.'

John expelled a long breath. 'That would be good. And then I can focus on the breakdowns onsite. Our share price has been a bit volatile in the last two weeks and that's one thing we don't need.'

As the two men shook hands, Connor looked at John Robinson's weary face. He wouldn't want a job like that, no matter what it paid.

On Friday morning Connor called Greg as he waited for the flight to Darwin to pick up his international connection. 'I've just had a call from Al Tayer's personal assistant. He's agreed to meet me.'

'Did you tell him what you wanted to talk to him about?'

'Of course not. I'm a businessman looking for an opportunity. Technically correct. I just didn't elaborate.'

'That's great. I hope it's worthwhile. It's a long bloody way.'

'So you've got all the details for me?'

'Yes, mate. I'll message them to you now.'

Greg had retrieved Dru's flight details but it had taken him a bit more digging to find out which hotel she was staying at in Dubai. Greg had reserved a room for him on the floor above Dru's at Atlantis, the Palm, on Jumeirah Island, and booked him in business class on the same flight.

'She's right at the back of economy so if you board late and get off first, you can stay out of her sight.'

Connor kept an eye on the departures board as he spoke. 'I'll have to time it carefully. Last thing I want is to have my name called over the airport system and warn her.'

'I'm sure you'll handle it.' Greg's voice was cheery. 'Two nights in a luxury hotel in Dubai. I hope Matsu have given you a good expense account.'

'Don't worry,' Connor said drily. 'I'll claim it on my tax.

Chapter 24

Dubai, United Arab Emirates
Dru picked up the face cream for Adam at Pentecost River Fine Diamonds in Kununurra before she flew to Darwin. She stayed the night in her apartment and put a note on the fridge to remind her to take the cream back to the mine when she returned to work.

By the time she'd packed her small Longchamps carry-on bag and called a taxi to take her to the airport, butterflies were jumping around in her stomach. She pushed away her nervousness about going back to Dubai. The wedding would be fun, it would be great to catch up with Megan and Sam and she'd be back home in Darwin in just a few days. As she stood at the Emirates check-in counter, she was tempted to ask if there was space in first class. She hated long haul flights and the exit row seats in economy with extra leg room had already been taken. She bit back the temptation. It was a waste of money; she'd grin and bear it.

The plane was full and the flight to Dubai was uneventful. Between movies, Dru managed to catch up on some sleep. She was squeezed into the middle seat on the window row so by the time they landed in Dubai fourteen hours later, her legs were aching from the cramped space. But that at least took her mind off the butterflies in her stomach. After the plane taxied into the terminal, she stood in the aisle with her carry-on luggage over her shoulder, waiting for first and business class to disembark. Finally, the queue moved and the heat slammed into her as she stepped onto the bridge leading into the arrival's hall.

'Dru!' Megan's squeal reached her across the huge tiled expanse and Dru immediately forgot about her sore legs. Any remnants of trepidation fled as she held out her arms to Megan.

'You really came!' Megan hugged her back.

'Of course, I did. I promised, didn't I?'

'I had my doubts.' Megan's smile was wide. 'We're taking you straight to the hotel. You've got time for a shower and to get changed before the rehearsal lunch.'

'Look at you, Megs. Gorgeous dress and beautifully made up.' Dru looked down at her own rumpled cargo pants. 'A shower will be great.'

Sam pecked her on the cheek and held out his hand to take her carry-on bag. 'Which luggage carousel?' he asked.

'That's it. I'm only staying three days, and you've got my wedding clothes—and shoes,' she darted a laughing glance at Megan, 'so I didn't need to bring much more.'

'Two days?' Sam looked at her curiously. 'Barely worth coming.'

'Oh yes it is.' He kept looking at her and finally he shook his head. Nerves fluttered in Dru's stomach. 'What? What's wrong?'

'I can't believe you came here for two days and what? One night? You'll spend as much time in the air as you will here.'

'Couldn't miss the wedding, Sam.'

***

Connor figured it was safe to leave the airport without following Dru to the hotel. He'd disembarked with business class and then watched from the level overlooking the arrivals lounge as she was greeted by a young couple. He knew where she was heading and where the wedding was being held. Meanwhile he was looking forward to the interview with Zayed Al Tayer.

On the flight he'd tried to prepare the questions he would ask, but deleted more than he kept. Working in an area where his knowledge was limited was making it more difficult. Connor wasn't satisfied with any of the answers he was coming up with.

After an hour in a taxi he was ushered into a large office on the twenty-fifth floor of a modern building in the financial district of Dubai. As he waited, he crossed to the window and watched the busy river traffic on the wide waterway known as Dubai Creek. The heat from the desert shimmered in the air and it was difficult to see more than a few hundred metres away. He turned as the door opened and two men walked in.

A tall man impeccably dressed in conservative grey suit, Al Tayer, crossed the room and held his hand out. Connor examined him as he returned the firm handshake. Zayed Al Tayer would have fitted into a boardroom anywhere in the world. He oozed self-confidence yet beneath the sophisticated veneer, Connor sensed arrogance.

'Connor Kirk? Pleased to meet you. I'm Zayed Al Tayer. Welcome to Dubai.' His accent was British and his expression was inscrutable. He directed Connor to one of the comfortable sofas near the window.

'Thank you.'

The other man stood quietly in the background until Connor and Al Tayer had sat in opposite chairs.

'Thank you, Najeeb. You may sit.' Al Tayer's voice was deep. He glanced down at his diamond-encrusted watch. 'So, Mr Kirk. You have fifteen minutes. Normally I wouldn't meet with anyone without more background information, but as you are from Australia—from the mining industry, I believe—your request intrigued me. I am also curious as to why you requested the presence of Najeeb at our meeting.'

'You are interested in Australia?' Connor asked.

Al Tayer waved an elegant dismissive hand. 'I employ many Australians in my businesses and I admire them for their work ethic and their honesty.'

'That's a good thing to hear about my fellow countrymen.'

'And women,' Al Tayer added. His expression closed even further as he waited for Connor to speak.

'I work in the mining industry,' Connor said. 'I believe you have recently purchased some Matsu violet diamonds to complete a matching set.

'That is correct.' Al Tayer nodded to his personal assistant. 'Najeeb purchased the diamonds on my behalf. And yes, it is to complete a beautiful set for my wife. We are about to celebrate our tenth wedding anniversary and it is my way of showing her my love and appreciation for being a wonderful wife and mother.' He looked at Connor with a challenging glint in his eye. 'But I do not understand why a *miner* –' his tone was disparaging '– from Australia would be interested in my jewellery. Unless you wanted to purchase it perhaps?'

'Perhaps,' Connor replied, his voice steady. 'Is the set for sale?'

'No. When the jeweller completes this necklace, it will be a part of my collection. And there it will stay.'

'So you have not seen it yet?'

'It is on the way back to me.'

Connor hid a smile; Zayed was either lying or he didn't know the diamonds were now in a bank vault in Antwerp. According to John Robinson, Al Tayer had simply been told that there was a delay in the making of the necklace. The resolution of the diamonds' ownership would probably play out in a lengthy court case once the theft was resolved.

Al Tayer sat straight and his voice hardened. 'Now Mr Kirk, I'd like to know why you are really here. You don't look like a miner, but I very much doubt you are a diamond trader.' This time his face wore an open sneer as he regarded Connor from top to toe.

It appeared that his creased denim jeans and black T-shirt did not meet Al Tayer's dress code.

'I am here to discuss the Matsu diamonds with you on behalf of my employer,' he reiterated. 'We believe the diamonds may have been stolen.'

'Ah, so you are an investigator. Najeeb could not, find any mention of you as the businessman you claim to be. What do you want from me? I know nothing about any stolen diamonds.'

He held Al Tayer's gaze, sensing that he was getting under his skin. 'My employer would like some information. Who did you purchase the violet diamonds from?'

Al Tayer waved his hand again. 'I do not know. Najeeb purchased them on my behalf. I am too busy to worry about trivial details such as that.'

Connor deliberately widened his eyes. 'Come now, Mr Al Tayer. A six-million-dollar purchase is surely not a trivial detail.'

Al Tayer's face was smug. 'It may not be to someone such as you, but I can assure you, in my world, that is trivial.'

Connor's gut clenched as he was filled with disgust. He could not imagine Dru with this guy, but he'd seen the photographs. There was a lot of game playing going on and he decided to up the ante. 'Perhaps Najeeb can tell me?'

'Certainly. I have nothing to hide. Najeeb . . .' Al Tayer nodded to his personal assistant.

Najeeb's accent was strong and Connor had to concentrate on his words. 'The Australian trader I bought the small diamonds from, she contacted me again and told me she had more beautiful diamonds.'

'She?' Connor interrupted. 'Do you have a name?'

'Her name is Cat, and the name of the company is GCH,' was the quiet reply.

'And the company is a registered diamond trader?'

Najeeb nodded but his eyes skittered to the left. 'I believe so.'

Connor let that pass. 'You said she contacted you *again*? What did you mean by that?'

'Mr Al Tayer entrusts me with the task of finding gems for unique pieces of jewellery to celebrate special occasions. His collection is very well known in the diamond world.'

'I see,' Connor said, aware of Al Tayer's narrow-eyed gaze.

'I was contacted by this trader after Ayisha's birth earlier this year. She knew of the collection and she said she had some beautiful violet diamonds.'

'This Australian woman, Cat. Do you have a last name for her?' Connor probed.

'I am sorry I do not recall it.'

Connor didn't take his eyes from Al Tayer as he spoke. 'Perhaps the name Drusilla Porter would jog your memory?'

The look on the man's face was one of instant fury. His eyes narrowed to slits and his cheeks reddened. He turned to Najeeb and spoke to him quietly in Arabic. Najeeb stood and left the room, closing the door quietly behind him.

Al Tayer turned back to Connor. 'Unfortunately, my personal assistant has another pressing engagement and cannot answer any more of your questions.'

He stared at Connor for a full minute before he continued. 'Are you insinuating that there is an issue with my ownership of these diamonds? Because if you are, and if you—or your *employer*—have shared that information anywhere else, I will ensure you do not work again and I will cripple the company.' His voice was cold and his stare was deadly. 'Believe me, Mr Kirk. I am a man of my word.' This time his voice rose and his expression was challenging.

Arrogant bastard. So he was going to take on Matsu Mine, was he? Connor clenched his fists beside his thighs, resisting the temptation to wipe the smirk off Al Tayer's face.

'I will not have my reputation tarnished. I will say this once. No matter what you may think, I paid for those diamonds, and I paid very well. If there is any issue with their provenance, that is nothing to do with me. Do you understand?' Suddenly his voice reached screaming pitch and the posh accent disappeared.

'It appears that I was incorrect.' Connor stood to leave. He turned for the door, but then paused. 'I have one more question for you, Al Tayer. Why did Dru Porter leave your company?'

This time, Al Tayer's smile was feral. His lip rose in a sneer and his eyes were cold. 'Unfortunately she left of her own accord before I could reward her for her excellent work.'

'Perhaps you can reward her yourself,' Connor said. 'She was on the same flight as me this morning.'

***

Soon Sam had loaded Dru's bag into the SUV and they were heading along the motorway. As they drove towards the hotel on the manmade island, Dru looked around with trepidation at the vibrant city. It was a clear day and the smog was less than usual. The beautiful buildings of Dubai filled the skyline and she leaned back into the seat and tried to relax. But all the old fears rose and threatened her composure as they passed familiar places; the restaurants, bars and the huge hotel on the beach—one of Zayed's favourite places—where he'd paraded her around like a trophy.

'Many from work coming to the wedding?' she asked Sam casually.

'A couple of the engineers from my department,' he said.

Megan twisted around in her seat and caught Dru's eyes. 'Don't worry, hon. We haven't told anyone you're coming. Not even our families. They'll be happy to meet you. They've heard so much about you.'

Dru rolled her eyes as embarrassment took over. 'I can imagine.'

'Only good stuff.'

'What's the big deal about keeping your visit a secret?' Sam glanced over to her. 'Megs swore me to secrecy. That is, when she finally told me you were coming.'

Dru didn't answer for a while. 'Long story, Sam. I'll tell you all about it when you come over and visit me.

'I'll hold you to that,' he said.

'But you know what? I'm pleased I came.' Dru reached forward and squeezed Meg's hand.

'We are too. Wait till you see your shoes!' Meg laughed as she turned back around to the front and Dru chuckled.

The wedding celebrations had already begun and as soon as she'd checked into her room and freshened up, Sam and Megan headed to the private bar for the rehearsal lunch and pre-wedding family drinks. Dru's stomach was still fluttering and full of butterflies.

'Mum, Dad, this is Dru.'

Dru nodded and smiled as she was introduced to Megan's parents and then her sisters, the other two bridesmaids, and then to Sam's parents. Despite the happy atmosphere and the small group, she felt distracted and couldn't help keeping an eye on the door that led out to the hotel.

Dru was not one for sentimental gushing, but the next afternoon her eyes pricked with happy tears as Megan stepped out of the dressing room in the huge suite at the luxury hotel on Jumeirah Island. The high-necked lace wedding dress was accentuated by the fancy upsweep that the hairdresser had completed a few minutes before.

'Ha! Caught you crying, Dru Porter.' Megan grinned as she crossed the room to where Dru was standing.

'I'll admit it.' Dru dabbed at a tear. 'You look gorgeous, Meg. Sam is one lucky guy.'

'I am so happy you came over. I really, truly appreciate it you know.' Megan opened her arms. 'And thank you for wearing the shoes. They look great!

'We made a deal, remember. You come and visit me in the Kimberley as soon as Sam gets some time off.' Dru hugged Megan back.

'Promise. As soon as we can.'

Dru watched as Megan's mother fiddled with the bridal veil. 'Come on, darling. Your father's waiting outside.'

Dru picked up the bridal bouquet and handed it to Megan. 'Come on, Megs. It's now or never.'

The wedding was a short civil ceremony held in one of the private function rooms at the luxury hotel. No expense had been spared; the flower arrangements in the room outnumbered the guests. The official part only went for fifteen minutes before the bridal party moved onto the terrace for photographs. Once that ordeal was over—Dru hated everyone watching as the official photographs were taken—they joined the guests in the restaurant next to the huge indoor aquarium for the wedding breakfast.

Nerves skittered in her stomach as the patrons in the public section of the restaurant watched the wedding party walk across to the private dining room. The choice of the reception venue was unfortunate; Dru had never told Megan that this restaurant was where Zayed had brought her for dinner the night he had locked her in his Mercedes.

It all seemed like a horrid nightmare now. He'd sworn it was an accident and she'd accepted his explanation at the time, and for a while after that his behaviour had been charming again.

Tendrils of panic tried to wind their way around her as she passed their usual table but she swallowed and took a deep breath. As she lowered her head, a man passed by her; for a moment she'd thought it was Najeeb, Zayed's assistant. She drew another shuddering breath, kept her head down and continued walking. Before she entered the private dining room she turned around and looked back, but there was no sign of him.

Taking the chair at the end of the family table, Dru slid down as far as she could, her hands still shaking from the fright she'd had. She felt so exposed, sitting up at the front of the room next to the bridal table, although she was thankful she hadn't been expected to sit with Sam and Megan in full view of everyone. Megan's parents and sisters joined her at her table, and chatted to her as the first course was served. But the unsettled feeling lodged in her stomach like a stone and she barely picked at the beautiful meal in front of her. Fighting to keep calm, she focused on her breathing and reminded herself that this panic was all in her head.

As Sam had said, a couple of the engineers from the *Ain* were present, and they'd greeted her casually as she'd passed their table. Seeing old workmates had added to the unsettled feeling. Even though Megan had said Zayed wouldn't be there, Dru kept looking around the room, half expecting him to burst in. They'd attended many functions at the Palm, and it would be just like him to big-note himself and drop into the wedding uninvited.

She sat back and closed her eyes, willing herself to relax as the table was cleared.

Deep breaths.

Her hands were tingling so she clutched them tightly in her lap. The conversations washed around her as she thought back to the day her world had changed.

Chapter 25

Two years earlier

Megan had taken Dru shopping at the Dubai Mall to buy a new dress for a company dinner. In her first few months in Dubai, her life had been exciting. The job—and her responsibilities as a new graduate—had exceeded her expectations. Zayed, the owner of the company took a keen interest in the staff and he was often on site. He'd spent hours in her new office explaining the history of the *Ain* from the concept up and telling her how proud he was of the initiative. She had fallen for the charm and the flattery and when he'd asked her to help him out, she'd believed everything he'd said.

'And maybe some fancy lingerie?' Megan had nudged her and smiled as they'd looked through the clothes in the Victoria's Secret store.

Dru smiled back. 'Don't be silly. There's no need for that. He's married, remember. He just needs a partner for the social functions he attends. A man of his standing needs someone to accompany him. He told me his wife is very shy, and she is busy with the children. And she's expecting again. I was flattered when he asked me.'

The look Meg directed her way had been hard to read. 'So what's the function tonight?'

'Oh, it's only us tonight. He wants to talk to me about my dress for the ball coming up next month.'

Despite what she'd told Megan, Zayed had wanted more than just a partner for social occasions. But although he had charmed her, Dru had so far resisted his attempts to get her to spend the night with him. Of course, she'd been flattered that a man with his wealth, charm and looks was attracted to her. He'd been amused at her prudence—as he called it—and Dru sensed that her reluctance to fall into bed with him had made her all the more attractive to him. Every time they went out he bought her a gift of some sort.

One day he sent flowers to her office and then he'd arrived at her desk just before five. 'I was passing and I thought you might like a ride home.'

'I have my car here,' Dru said.

'No matter.' He'd dismissed her comment with a wave of his elegant hand. 'I need you to help me with some shopping. Rihanna has asked me to buy her some Venetian glass—did I tell you we spent our honeymoon in Venice?'

'That would have been very romantic.'

'It was. Drusilla?' His eyes held hers intently. 'I love my wife very much and she appreciates you helping me at all of these social events.'

'It's a pleasure,' Dru replied. And it had been for a while. When Zayed was warm and being a perfect gentleman, he was fun to be with. 'So where are we shopping?'

'Thank you, dear one. I told Rihanna you would help. I'll send a car to get you to work tomorrow. Leave your car here.'

They were driving along Al Mussallah road towards the Dubai Mall when Zayed glanced over at her. 'Where's the watch I gave you?'

'Oh, it's too fancy to wear to work.'

'Make sure you wear it from now on please, Dru.'

Dru was quiet as Zayed turned the Mercedes into the Dubai Mall. The car park was busy and she looked at the brightly coloured billboards advertising the stores as the car climbed from floor to floor. Finally on the seventh floor after passing many vacant car spaces, Zayed parked the car at the end of a row. He climbed out and then looked back. 'I'll go and get the parking ticket. Wait for me at the elevator.' He pushed his door shut.

Dru reached down for her purse—she was not going to let Zayed pay for anything today—and as she did the remote locks of the car clicked into place. She tried to open her door but it was locked. She shook her head; sometimes Zayed's protectiveness was too much. Picking up her phone, she checked for messages as she waited for him to return.

After five minutes, she put her phone away and turned around to look through the back window. There was no sign of him or anyone else in the car park. The windows were closed and it was getting hot in the car. She began to perspire and regretted that she hadn't brought her large handbag where she always carried a bottle of water. She opened the refrigerated console between the two front seats but it was empty. She climbed across to the driver's side hoping he might have left the keys on the ignition, but they were not there.

Half an hour later panic had set in. Zayed hadn't returned and her head was aching. Her mouth was dry and when she turned her head to the side, dizziness took over. She yawned and swallowed, trying to get some moisture into her body.

By the time the door locks clicked open, Dru was disoriented and on the verge of tears. She had been locked in the car for forty-five minutes. She opened the door and stumbled out into Zayed's arms.

'Where did you get to, Drusilla? I told you where to meet me.' His voice was full of concern.

'What? No you didn't.' Her voice was thick. 'You locked the car door. I couldn't get out. I need a drink.'

'Oh, I am so sorry, my dear. It was not intentional. When you weren't at the elevator I took it to the top floor. I couldn't see you. I've been looking in all of your favourite shops.'

As Zayed led her to a coffee shop on the top floor of the mall, Dru felt silly. She sat quietly as he ordered their coffee.

'When we finish our drinks we'll go and get the glass and then I'll buy you a dress for the ball. I want you to be the best dressed woman there.'

Dru put down the empty glass; she'd drunk almost the whole carafe of water that the waitress had put on the table. She was sleepy and feeling too ill to argue.

'And then we can go to the Palm for dinner.'

***

A few nights later they had dinner on Bluewater Island where the *Ain* was being built, to have one final look at the ballroom set-up. If there was one thing Zayed insisted upon, it was perfection in everything he was involved in.

She had met him in the hotel earlier in the evening and he was particularly attentive. He looked at her warmly as they left the function room; he was satisfied with the preparations for the ball. Dru was feeling relaxed and had convinced herself that his locking her in the car had been unintentional.

No one would do that on purpose.

A strong wind was blowing off the Gulf as they stepped onto the open balcony that led to the bar, and he placed his hand on her waist to support her. When they entered the restaurant, he kept his hand there.

'On Sunday I have a special treat for you.'

'That sounds interesting.' She tipped her head to the side and looked at him. He really was a fine-looking man. His smile was wide and Dru tried to ignore the warm feeling that suffused her.

'Rihanna and I are taking the children to the aquarium at the Palm Hotel and we would like you to join us. Rihanna wants to thank you for everything you are doing while she is unable to join me at these social events,' he said.

Dru nodded and accepted, although one disloyal thought crossed her mind fleetingly. If Rihanna was able to travel so far from their home, and go out to a restaurant for lunch with Zayed and four young children, why wasn't she able to accompany him to the occasional social event in the evenings? From what Zayed had said of his home life, there were nannies and housekeepers employed to look after every detail of their life.

The trip to the aquarium had been a very pleasant afternoon; Rihanna was delightful. Warm and friendly and interested in Dru's background and most impressed that she was an engineer. Her black *abaya* was elegantly embroidered with gold thread and her beautifully made-up eyes twinkled in a smile as Dru answered her many questions. Their two small daughters were dressed in identical party frocks. Soft pink knee-length dresses fell in a swirl of frills past their knees, and they each wore a headband in a matching colour. The two little boys were also well behaved and after the meal, they became more used to Dru. She held the two little girls' hands as they watched the fish.

Zayed was a perfect father and husband. His warmth and sense of humour had come to the fore, and they'd spent the afternoon laughing as he teased the children.

The only niggle was that Rihanna didn't mention Dru accompanying Zayed; but Dru convinced herself that she had forgotten.

The car incident had been the first time she had wondered about Zayed. But after the Sunday lunch, his behaviour became more controlling each time they went out. To her embarrassment, one night he presented her with an expensive diamond bracelet. His reaction to her refusal to accept it led to a tense evening and she saw an aggressive, insistent side to his personality that at first made her slightly uncomfortable, and soon began to frighten her.

'But why not, Drusilla?' he'd said. 'I can afford to give you a hundred like this.' His lips had set in a truculent line.

She tried to explain her reluctance, but he insisted. 'I love beautiful things, and you, my dear, are exquisite.'

He put the bracelet down and picked up her hand, and turned it over in his palm before kissing the inside of her wrist.

'It's not the cost—although that is a part of it. It's just not right for you to be giving me gifts. You have a wife and family and I'm simply helping you out.'

'We do things differently here. I want you to take it.' He held her gaze with his as he picked up the bracelet and placed it on her wrist. Despite the smile on his lips, his eyes were dark and he held her wrist so tightly that Dru was unable to remove her hand. When she removed the bracelet later that evening, her skin was bruised from the punishing grip.

The next month had been a nightmare for Dru, but she hadn't shared any of what was happening with Megan until she knew her position at the *Ain Dubai* had finished.

She began to decline Zayed's invitations and tried to ignore the ever-increasing number of texts that arrived on her phone. Then he turned up unannounced at her apartment, but she refused to buzz him up. He phoned her incessantly, and worst of all, he would come into her office at work and act as though nothing was wrong. He wanted her in his life whatever it took, and the more she resisted him, the more he persisted.

Finally, she accepted a dinner invitation. She hoped that face-to-face she could talk to him and extricate herself from this situation. She couldn't have been more wrong.

'I don't like the colour of your dress. Don't wear it again.'

'There won't be an "again".'

Zayed waved a waiter over and ordered a bottle of expensive champagne. When the man retreated, he turned back to her. 'You are being very silly, Drusilla.' His voice was gentle but insistent.

'No,' she said firmly. 'I am not being silly. I'm here to work, not to get involved with a married man.'

His laugh was light. 'Involved? All I am asking is that you come with me to some functions. You are overreacting, my darling.'

When the waiter had poured their drinks, he raised his glass. 'To you, Dru.' He took a long sip, then put the glass down. She hadn't touched hers. 'I do not like it when you disobey me.'

Dru stared at him as his dark eyes gleamed. 'Disobey you?' she said slowly.

'If it happens again, you will find that your visa to work in the Emirates is withdrawn.'

'Are you threatening me?'

He ignored her and took another sip of champagne. 'Let's order. I think we will both have Wagyu beef tonight. I must visit Australia again soon. With you, of course.'

'No, that won't be happening.'

'I think you had better give that some more thought, my dear. Your friends wouldn't want to lose their visas, would they?'

Dru was quiet—and compliant—as he ordered their meals. What else could she have done? He owned the company she worked for.

By the time she finally broke and told Megan how he was harassing her, Dru was in a near constant state of heightened anxiety.

The final straw had come one morning in her office. She was immersed in the project plan for the next stage of work when her office door had closed quietly. She'd been leaving it open deliberately over the past weeks. Zayed had called in every day since he had threatened her visa.

Her mouth dried and her pulse accelerated when he crossed to her desk and placed a large bouquet of flowers in front of her. Hanging from the tag was a circular key ring that looked as though it was encrusted with small diamonds. Dru swallowed. Knowing his style, they wouldn't be fake. Zayed walked to the window without speaking and stared out over the blue water of the Gulf. The blue-black sheen of his dark hair glistened in the morning sun. Dru dug her nails into her palms as she sat behind her desk.

'Is there something *work-related* we need to discuss, Zayed?' She kept her voice neutral as she pushed the chair away from her desk and stood. 'I have a meeting upstairs shortly.' She looked at her watch pointedly.

He turned slowly and his eyes travelled slowly from the top of her head and down her body. His expression was set, his mouth fixed in a straight line. 'There *is* something we need to discuss.'

Dru held herself straight and met his intense gaze. His brown eyes softened as his mouth lifted in a smile. 'I have overcome our problem.'

'Which problem is that?' Dru looked over at the whiteboard on the wall of her office where the month's goals were written up.

'It's rather a shame because you are one of the best in your field. You do have a good career ahead of you. Maybe we can find you another position here. In a few years.'

His smile widened and Dru tensed as she waited to hear the solution to whatever problem he was talking about.

'I am terminating your employment on the *Ain Dubai* project as of this morning.'

Dru grabbed for her desk as the room suddenly tilted. She closed her eyes and waited for the dizziness to pass before she asked slowly, 'What did you say?'

Her breath caught as Zayed took her hand firmly and smoothed her skin with his thumb. He leaned in closer and his breath brushed her cheek. 'I did hope you would be here to see this project finished. It will be amazing. An expanse of the Gulf transformed into an island with high class dining and entertainment and the beautiful *Ain Dubai* at its centre. But be assured you can still share it with me. We can celebrate its conclusion together. And in the meantime, you will not have to go to work each day. You will be available when I need you.'

'I don't understand.'

'You are no longer employed by *my* company.'

'You can't do that.' Dru stood straight and for one satisfying moment she looked down at him. It was one of the rare occasions that she took pleasure in her height.

'I can do whatever I want, Drusilla.' For a moment, his smile was cold. 'I own the company. *I* say who is employed. And *I* don't want you on the *Ain* project any longer. Your friends can stay for the time being.'

'What the hell are you talking about?' Dru stood stock still as shock coursed through her. 'Terminating my employment? You can't. I'm on a contract.'

His voice was calm and smooth. 'If you're not working here, you won't have to worry about our relationship any longer.' Still holding her hand in a tight grip, Zayed reached across the desk and pulled the key ring from the stem of the flowers. He dangled it in front of her face with a smile.

'This is the key to your—to *our*—new apartment.' She tried to resist but he dragged her across to the window and pointed to the north. 'It's on the northern tip of Bluewater Island and you will be able to see our work from our penthouse once the *Ain* is completed.' His face was set and although he smiled, aggressive determination emanated from him. Fear flooded through Dru but she found the courage to argue as adrenaline coursed through her.

'No. I want to stay here. In my job. I . . . I . . . haven't agreed to this.' Wariness made her choose her words carefully. 'I don't have to agree to it.'

'You don't have to agree.' Zayed shook his head and pressed the key into her hand so hard it hurt. 'It is all arranged. I have filled the apartment with beautiful things from my collection. You will be the crowning piece.'

His grip tightened and Dru looked down as blood seeped from her palm where the cold metal had cut her skin. In that moment, she knew he was crazy.

He was hurting her, but she refused to show it. She thought desperately for a way to convince him. 'Zayed, I'm extremely flattered by your words.' Dru swallowed and fought to keep her voice steady. 'It's nothing to do with us working together. In my culture, it is inconceivable to share a man.' She kept her voice calm and quiet and looked at him from beneath lowered lids. 'You already have a wife . . . and children.'

'I know I am already married, and I appreciate that you may have a problem with that. But it will be good. In my culture taking another wife is accepted. As long as a man can prove he is able to support two families.' Zayed shook his head. 'But we are getting ahead of ourselves. I am inviting you to be my partner only—perhaps we will marry eventually.'

Horror gripped Dru in its relentless hold. This was surreal; she was in her office, the place she had worked in as an engineer for two years. Through the frosted glass beside the door, she could make out the figures of the other engineers as they went about their work. Where the hell had this crazy scenario come from? What was she going to do? What should she say? How should she react? Fear crawled up her spine; she had witnessed Zayed's ruthlessness firsthand in meetings and she had no doubt he meant what he said.

He glanced at his watch. 'I have a meeting until late this afternoon. Finish up what you are doing, and pack up your desk. I'll pick you up at five and we'll move your things over to the penthouse tonight. This is my choice and it is the best thing for you.' Zayed leaned over and brushed his lips across her mouth. 'For us.'

'Zayed.' Dru forced herself not to tense. 'I want to keep working on the project. I love my job.'

'No. You no longer have a contract.' He reached for Dru and pulled her close. His fingers were hard and cruel on her shoulders, and his cologne surrounded her. 'I'll pick you up at five. After we move you in, we'll go out for dinner. You can choose the restaurant. *Tayeb*?'

'Okay,' Dru said.

'I will have to teach you some Arabic,' he said as he turned away. '*Tayeb* means okay. So what do you say, Dru?'

'*Tayeb.*' Her throat closed as she nodded mutely, not strong enough to disagree with him. Her mind was whirling and she was finding it difficult not to be sick. She gripped the key in her hand to ground herself as the door closed behind him.

Chapter 26

Atlantis, The Palm – Dubai (present day)

Thinking about that last day in her office had brought the crushing fear back to Dru. By the time Zayed would have arrived at the office to collect her, she had been in an A380 on the tarmac of Dubai International Airport waiting to take off. As soon as she was sure Zayed had left the building, she went straight to Sam's office, numb and shaking. She had told Sam that she had an emergency at home and had to leave that day. Megan had met them at the airport and Dru had taken her aside as Sam carried her bags in from the car.

'Don't tell anyone that you and Sam helped me. Lie, do whatever it takes, but tell Sam to say he had to go home early today because he was sick or you were, or something.' Dru wrapped her long cardigan around her. She couldn't stop shaking. 'Don't mention me at all. Promise me that!'

Luckily, Sam had found her a seat on the next flight out and Dru had flown to Brisbane and then up to Cairns. She'd called Megan from her mother's house and been relieved to hear that there had been no consequences for Sam—yet.

The two weeks she'd spent with Mum at Port Douglas before she'd applied for the job at Matsu had been a blur. Emma had come down to visit with Jeremy, and Dru had sat back quietly and let them be the focus of attention. She had instructed her solicitor to submit her formal acceptance of the termination of her employment on the *Ain* and had been amazed when the company had paid her out immediately, under the terms of the early termination of her contract.

Dru was pulled back to the present as the MC tapped on the microphone and the formal part of the evening commenced. She managed a smile when Sam proposed a toast to the beautiful bridesmaids.

As soon as dessert had been served and orders taken for coffee, Dru made her excuses and slipped out to the terrace for some fresh air. She needed to get away from the crowd and try to calm herself. Her insides were wound as tight as a coil and she'd found it difficult to eat.

Revisiting that time had been a foolish thing to do. Despite her firm resolution in the Bungle Bungles, no matter how much she tried to calm herself, the panic was building. All she wanted to do was head to the airport and get back to the place where she felt safe.

She gripped the edge of the railing and looked out over the garden below. Fairy lights had been draped over the trees and a couple of small children were playing hide and seek at the edge of the garden. Their excited voices drifted up through the gathering darkness. She looked up, trying to ground herself, but the desert smog obscured the night sky.

No diamonds in the sky tonight, Dad, she thought. Her hands clenched as the painful memories filled her mind. Making a conscious effort to relax, she visualised each muscle relaxing.

Toes, calves, and up to her diaphragm. Slow, deep breaths. Dru shook her fingers to get rid of that awful tingling feeling in her hands. Slowly her heartbeat resumed its normal pace and she put a hand up and smoothed her hair. She walked along to the edge of the terrace and glanced at her watch. There was still about an hour before she could leave without being rude.

She looked to the north, wondering if she could see the construction on Bluewater Island. She craned forward but it was too dark to see the *Ain*. In all directions, spotlights were on the new luxury apartment blocks being constructed. From the hotel and along the main road down the centre of the island of Palm Jumeirah, each street of the residential section had been reclaimed from the sea and built up in the shape of palm fronds.

Her work had been interesting, but subsequent events had killed any attraction Dubai held for her. The sooner she was on the plane back to Australia, the better. Coming to the wedding had been a mistake.

A huge mistake.

Footsteps crunched on the bricks behind her.

'You look very lovely, tonight, Drusilla. You are wearing my favourite colour.'

Dru froze and her breath stilled in her throat as the familiar voice whispered past her ear. At the same time she recognised the cloying men's cologne. She held herself rigid, staring out into the velvet darkness of the night. For a moment, she thought it was her memory playing tricks on her but the grip on her arm was real . . . and painful.

She forced herself to look down. The tanned hand lightly sprinkled with dark hair was edged by a snowy white cuff studded with sparkling diamond and gold cuff links. Finally she drew in a shuddering gasp as he eased the pressure a fraction. As she watched, the fingers ran up her forearm to her shoulder. Zayed lifted her chin so that she was forced to look at him.

'I taught you something about lovely clothes, didn't I, Drusilla?' The voice was almost like a caress and his breath puffed on her lips. Fear held her in its icy grip, and she closed her eyes, fighting for breath. Through the doorway came the strains of a slow romantic song as the evening wound to a close.

'Do you know how much I've missed you?'

The smell of his cologne was musky and Dru fought the gag reflex that she knew was more from fear than the smell. He was wearing a dark tuxedo and a white shirt with a frill down the front.

Determined to play it cool, she stepped back. She had to get off the deserted terrace. It was her only chance. She glanced back into the restaurant. People were moving about but no one was looking out this way.

'Well.' Dru forced a smile to her face and tried to remove her arm from his grip. 'Hello, Zayed, this is a surprise. I didn't realise you were a friend of Sam's.'

'I own the company he works for, Drusilla. And he is very fortunate to still have his position there. As you well know.' His head lowered to hers and his fingers maintained their relentless grip on her arm.

Dru's mind was racing. If he tried anything, she'd scream blue murder.

Or faint.

Or vomit on the floor.

Anything to make a scene and get someone's attention. But she made the mistake of staring past Zayed to the door, and his fingers tightened painfully on her wrist.

'You look stunning tonight, my dear.' His breath caressed her cheek.

Swallowing the lump in her throat, she fought desperately for calm and steeled her voice. 'I wasn't aware you had been invited to the wedding, Zayed.' Finally she found the courage to look up. His dark eyes bored into hers.

She'd been wrong. All of that thinking she'd done under that moonlit sky in the Bungle Bungles, all of that time she'd spent convincing herself that she was imagining the danger and seeing shadows where there were none. All that time spent looking over her shoulder, even in the wilds of the Kimberley; deep down she had known Zayed would never give up.

How bloody stupid she'd been to come back here.

'Sadly, I wasn't invited.' His voice was smooth.

'So,' she said injecting a lightness into her voice that was far removed from the heaviness that was settling into her limbs. 'What are you doing here?'

'I heard about the wedding, so I took the opportunity to come and give them my sincere congratulations, personally.' he said. As usual, his speech showed his British public school upbringing. 'A friend of yours told me you were in Dubai. I've missed you so much, Drusilla.'

What friend? Dru pressed the fingers of her other hand over her throbbing wrist.

'I know you came all this way to celebrate so I gave you some time to enjoy yourself at your friends' nuptials.' The lilt in his accent made his words sound even more formal. 'Although you did look miserable in there. You were missing my company perhaps?'

Her voice came out in a croak. 'It was quite hot inside.'

'I am very pleased you decided to come back to me.' Zayed ran his fingers across her cheek and a stray lock of hair fell onto her forehead. Dru's hand was shaking as she reached up to brush the hair from her eyes. Zayed shook his head and reached for her again but she stepped back before he could touch her.

'Oh, no, no, no, my fearsome Amazon.' The hard railing at the edge of the terrace cut into Dru's bare skin as she took another step back. She clenched her teeth together, biting back on the fear that coursed through her veins. Meg had neglected to mention that the pants suit had a plunging backline that was barely decent. Luckily the Dubai hotel catered for Western guests and turned a blind eye to inappropriate dress. Zayed leaned over her and held her shoulders, gradually pushing her further against the railing. His body pressed against hers and the railing cut into her lower back until the pain was unbearable. Dru looked down; the gardens were two levels down and her head spun.

'You thought you were very clever leaving me that day.' His voice was low and caressing but the threat was there. 'And you *have* been very hard to find. But I knew you would come back to me. I just had to wait for the right time, didn't I, my little dove?'

He was crazy.

How the hell had she ever fallen for Zayed's charm? The handsome, charismatic man who had introduced her to the social scene in Dubai had been a fine actor. And stupidly she had fallen for his flattery. Thank goodness he had never succeeded in getting her into his bed.

'You are a woman. A woman from the West, and it appears you have their greedy ways. Have you spent all of the money I gave you so soon?' This time his voice was harsh, and any hint of gentleness had gone. 'Do you want more? I kept our apartment. If you want more of that money, you will come back to me.'

'I don't want any more money. What you paid me was only what I was entitled to under the terms of my contract.' She shook her head. 'I have only come back for Megan and Sam's wedding. That's all.' Dru knew her voice was getting desperate and she looked across at the door.

'Pfft. You wanted to see me. I know.' He gripped her shoulders and pulled her closer to him, his voice soft.

Fear held Dru rigid as Zayed dropped one hand from her shoulder and caressed her neck, and then trailed his fingers down to the V of her silk suit. She drew in a sharp breath as his fingers squeezed her breast and tears filled her eyes from the pain.

'I knew you would come back to me if I was patient.' He lowered his head and his lips pressed against her forehead. 'I told you, you are mine. No one else will have you.'

'No!' Dru looked around wildly and tried to pull away. They were still alone on the terrace and the music coming from the restaurant was loud; no one would hear her if she screamed for help. 'I have to go back inside. Megan will be throwing the bouquet soon and I have to be there. I'm the bridesmaid.'

'No. You will come with me now.' He held her firmly with one hand and jerked his head to the left. A tall man in Arab dress appeared out of the shadows at the end of the wall. Dru's heart almost stopped beating. There was a door recessed in the brickwork that she hadn't noticed before. They wouldn't be going back through the restaurant. She had no chance of escaping him.

'No one else will have what is mine. No one.'

Dru tried to pull away. 'You're hurting me.' He was holding her so tightly she would bruise.

'Najeeb, take her down to the car. I'll meet you there.' Zayed looked away from her to the swarthy man who was approaching them.

Her leg muscles tightened as the flight reflex took over. It was now or never. With a fierce effort Dru pulled away from his grip and rushed across the terrace towards the doorway. But before she got there, another tall figure stepped out and a firm hand snaked around her waist. Images of what would happen if she crossed Zayed flashed though her mind. He was ruthless. All she could see was her father hanging in the shed.

Her ears buzzed and her head spun as fear spiralled through her. Dark spots clouded her vision and her heart thundered in her chest. She looked back at Zayed and saw his dark eyes gleaming malevolently in the low light shed by the fairy lights.

He stepped towards her.

***

'Hello, sweetheart. I've been waiting for you in the foyer for ages. You did say to pick you up at ten o'clock?' Connor held Dru firmly and stepped back towards the door, pulling her along with him. He held his body tense and kept his attention firmly fixed on the two men on the other side of the terrace. The taller one, who he had recognised as Zayed Al Tayer, gave a brief hand signal and the short man slunk away into the shadows. It looked like they meant business.

Dru was letting out short distressed sounds. Eyes wide and with no colour in her cheeks, her breath was coming in rasps. Her body was rigid but her chin was trembling. She was trying to speak but could only manage a shaking sob. The abject terror in her eyes slammed into him. No matter what he thought she was guilty of, he'd seen the nasty side of Al Tayer.

He gathered her closer into his side; an unfamiliar protective instinct kicking in. He dropped his head and brushed his lips against her forehead as he stared at Al Tayer. 'Play along with me,' he whispered.

Finally, she managed to speak and her voice trembled. 'I'm sorry. I lost track of the time . . . darling.'

The confident Dru Porter that he knew from Matsu had disappeared and had been replaced by a woman who was scared senseless.

Connor had been watching her though the window of the bar since the wedding had begun. He had been biding his time, waiting for Dru to hand over a package to Al Tayer. But their interaction on the terrace had been nothing like what he expected. Something had obviously interrupted their deal. When Al Tayer had pushed her against the railing, he had seen her distress escalate and had moved closer to the door. He'd been about to intervene when Dru had made a run for it.

'You owe me a dance,' he said in a loud voice as he steered her inside. Her body was shaking and he could smell the fear coming from her. 'Do you want your friend to have a drink with us?' He looked over his shoulder. Al Tayer had followed them to the door and he stared at Connor, his lip curled in a sneer.

Dru shook her head. 'No. We've caught up. Goodbye, Zayed. It was . . . good to see you again.'

'Remember what I said, Drusilla. *No one* else.' His voice was vicious and he called after them as they went back inside. 'And Mr Kirk, remember what I said to you earlier.'

As they stepped into the restaurant, music and voices surrounded them as the guests moved as one towards the dance floor.

'It's time to farewell our lovely couple.' The MC's voice boomed over the microphone.

Connor pushed Dru in front of him, his hand gentle on her back. 'Straight to the door. Quickly.'

'I need to tell Megan where I'm going.'

'No.' Connor guided her along to the door as she looked back over her shoulder. 'We need to get out of here quick smart. There were more than the two of them on the terrace. You can tell *me* what went wrong when we get upstairs.'

Dru didn't answer and he stepped in front of her and pulled her along behind him, holding her hand firmly in his. The long marble corridor that led to the main entrance of the function room was deserted but Connor turned to the left and headed towards the other restaurants. He'd sussed the building out earlier, in case he needed to disappear quickly and his gut feeling had been spot on. There was a lift at the back of the Ossiano bar that led up to the hotel rooms.

The corridor was roped off at the end and the security guard put his hand out to stop them. 'Please to go around to the main entrance and use the main elevators.' His voice was heavily accented.

Connor pulled his room key from his pocket with a worried smile. 'My wife is feeling ill and we need to get back to our room quickly.' He held the key up. 'We're in this wing. May we use that elevator? He gestured over to the bank of elevators behind the guard, nodding at Dru as she put her hand over her mouth.

'Ergh, I'm going to be sick.'

'Quickly then, please. Follow me.' The guard dropped the tasselled rope and led them to the elevator. 'Fifth floor?' He looked at the key.

'Yes, please. Come on darling, you'll be fine.' Connor smiled at the guard. 'Appreciate it. Thank you.'

The elevator pinged and he led Dru into it. The security guard pushed the button for the fifth floor.

'Thank you,' Connor said as the man stepped back and the doors slid closed silently. He let go of Dru and to his surprise, she leaned against the mirrored wall before sliding down to a sitting position.

Her hand was over her mouth. 'I really am going to be sick.'

'Hold it in. We're almost there.'

'What are you doing here?' Her whisper was harsh. She shuddered as great heaving gasps wracked her body, and she lifted wide eyes to Connor. She stared at him without speaking again as her hand trembled. The doors opened with a soft ping at the fifth floor and he helped her to her feet, taking her arm and leading her to his room.

He held her firmly beside him with his left arm as he put the key on the door.

'I'm not going in there.' Her voice was low and she tried to tug away from his hold. 'My room is up the corridor.' She tried to pull away.

'Your room is on the next floor.'

She stared at him mutely.

'And from what I observed on the terrace, I wouldn't be surprised if there was someone knocking at your door very shortly. Or they might be in there already.' Connor pushed the door open. 'Come on. You'll be safer in here.'

Dru took a deep shuddering breath and stepped inside ahead of Connor. He followed her and the door closed behind him quietly. By the time he had lifted the security bar and slid it across, she'd disappeared into the bathroom and shut the door behind her.

He strode over to the window and drew the drapes closed, then he crossed to the sofa and sat checking his messages, waiting for Dru to come out.

After a while, he heard the sound of water running. A few minutes later, the double doors to the bathroom opened slowly and she stepped out. Some colour had come back into her cheeks and she seemed more composed.

'Sit down,' he said.

She shook her head and looked at the phone in his hand. 'Did you call Zayed and tell him I was up here?'

'Now why would I do that?' Connor put his phone on the table and stood. He crossed to the glossy black cupboard and opened the door to the mini-bar. 'Do you want a drink?' He lifted up a small bottle of brandy. You look like you could do with one.'

'I don't drink spirits.'

'Okay. A hot drink?'

Dru pushed away from the wall and edged around him towards the door. Her face was white and her eyes were wide. Connor stepped out and stood in front of her. 'Oh no. Not so fast, Dru. I've got some questions for you. You're not going anywhere.'

'Leave me alone.' Her voice was shrill. She shoved at him with both her hands.

Connor reached up and grabbed her wrists firmly. He was surprised by her strength as she twisted from his hold. Her right shoulder dropped as she lifted her knee but he saw it coming and stepped back.

'Oh no, you don't. We're not going to play rough.' He lifted his hands to her shoulder and steered her firmly to the chair in the corner near the window. 'That's not the way I operate, unlike your boyfriend.' He pushed her down into the chair but gently.

'My boyfriend? The way *you* operate?' She spat the words at him as she grabbed the sides of the chair. 'I'm not interested in how you operate. This whole safety officer thing? Why did Zayed set up such an elaborate cover? And why did you follow me all the way here? It would have been easier to grab me in Kununurra.' She dropped her head into her hands and her voice was muffled. 'Although I suppose it's easier if I'm already here. So, are you taking me to the apartment?'

'What apartment?' Connor looked at her curiously. 'And why would Al Tayer hire me?'

'To bring me back here, of course.' Her voice hitched on a sob and she raised a shaking hand to her face. 'I should have known better. I'll scream blue murder the instant you take me out of this room. Someone will hear. Just open the door and let me go.' Her eyes were wet with tears and her head was moving from side to side as she looked around his suite. 'Please?'

Connor shook his head. 'You're learning the hard way that crime never pays, aren't you, sweetheart? You play in the big league and you'll always get caught out . . . or worse. '

'Crime? What the hell are you talking about?' Her eyes welled and she bit her lip and Connor tried to ignore that blasted flash of sympathy that kept surfacing. He stood and crossed to the cupboard, keeping an eye on her in case she tried to make a break for it.

'And don't call me sweetheart!' she hissed.

'Where are the diamonds,' he asked casually as he plugged in the electric kettle.

'Diamonds?' Her voice was high-pitched. 'What diamonds?'

Connor ignored her and held up a coffee bag. 'Coffee or tea?'

'Nothing.'

'Whatever.' He shrugged. 'It's going to be a long night. We're going to have a chat and then we're going to go to the airport. After I call Australia. John Robinson can decide when he wants the police involved.'

'What? What the bloody hell are you on about.' The blood had come back into her face and two spots of colour sat high on her cheeks. 'You're crazy.' She leaned back in the chair and tipped her head forward with one hand over her eyes.

All remained quiet as Connor made two coffees, and stirred two sugars into hers. He flicked a curious glance at Dru as he crossed to the chair beside hers and put the mug on the small coffee table. 'So, we can do this one of two ways. You can tell me the truth straight up, or we can sit here all night. I won't give up.'

Her eyes narrowed and her lips were set in a straight line. 'I have no idea what you are talking about.'

'There's no point denying it, Dru. The evidence is stacked up against you.' He lifted his mug and stared at her over the rim of the cup. 'Where are the diamonds?'

She sat up straight in the chair. 'What diamonds? What evidence? What the fuck are you talking about?'

Chapter 27

Dru swallowed. She had to get out of Connor's room. Her muscles were screaming with tension and her pulse was racing. Why the hell had she ever come back to Dubai? She'd been kidding herself that she'd been overreacting. As soon as Zayed had appeared on the terrace she'd known she was in trouble. *Big trouble.*

What she couldn't get her head around was Connor being here and that he kept asking her about diamonds. She stared at him and he held her gaze without blinking. The light was behind him and the angles of his jaw were shadowed. Her stomach clenched as her thoughts kept circling back to Zayed. He wouldn't give up. If she got out of this room, where would she go? She couldn't get Sam and Megan to help; it was their wedding night for Christ's sake.

'Well, are you going to do it the easy way? Or are we going to be here all night?' Connor put his hand up to his face and rubbed it across his chin.

She'd humour him while she figured out what to do.

'Okay. But please tell me honestly. I need to know what's going on here. I don't understand.'

'You and me both.' Connor's voice was deep and steady.

Dru looked around the room as her mind raced. 'Why are you here? What were you doing at the wedding?'

'I've already told you. I'm looking for the diamonds.'

'What bloody diamonds? I have no idea what you are talking about.' Dru's thoughts were going round and round in her head and the confusion was making her head spin. She took another deep gulping breath.

'If you keep breathing like that you'll hyperventilate. Calm down.' Connor put his coffee cup on the table and dropped his hands between his knees. Dru watched him carefully, ready to jump up if he made a move towards her.

'The only thing I haven't figured out is how you're getting them off site,' he said in a slow drawl. 'You've got me beaten there. I've watched you go through the body scanner and I know your bags were X-rayed. And your car was searched each time. Tell me. Is Rocky Cardella taking them out the back way for you?'

'I am going to say this once more and that's it.' Dru stared at him and her words were slow and clear. 'I have no idea what you are talking about. I know nothing about any diamonds. I'm only here to see my friends get married.'

'Do you want me to go through the evidence? There's enough to have you arrested.'

Dru laughed. 'Call the police. I'd love that. It's one way I can get out of this horrendous situation.' She pointed to his phone. 'Go on, call them.' As much as she appeared confident, Dru was terrified he would call the police; although ending up in jail in Dubai might be marginally better than being kidnapped by Zayed.

Connor's smile was cruel. The bastard was enjoying this. 'Why did you leave your job in Dubai and take an almost fifty percent salary cut to go to Matsu?'

How did he know so much about her?

'Because of Zayed. I tried to tell him that I was in Dubai to work, but he wouldn't take no for an answer.'

'An answer to what?' Connor's eyes were fixed on her, and Dru raised a shaking hand to her face.

'To moving into the apartment he set up.'

'You've lost me. Why wouldn't you want to move into a luxury apartment? Why did you quit your job?'

Dru took a deep breath. 'Because I was here to work, not have a relationship with a controlling man—a married man—and I didn't quit. He terminated my contact. He told me I was the perfect addition to his collection. The apartment was where he kept his collections.'

'What collections?'

She focused on her breathing and waited till she could speak without fear making her voice tremble. 'He loves beautiful things. Art, jewellery, and he decided he wanted me.' Dru closed her eyes and dropped her head. 'God knows why.'

The first time Zayed had told her she was beautiful, she'd laughed at his words and it had taken a moment before she'd realised he was offended. She'd soon learned that Zayed didn't like anyone disagreeing with him.

Connor frowned. 'That sounds very farfetched.'

Dru opened her eyes and stared at him. 'That's the way it was. I wasn't willing to be the trophy mistress of a married man.'

Connor's eyebrows rose. 'So you left your job to get away from your overzealous boyfriend, and moved to the Kimberley?'

'I refused to do what he wanted so I no longer had a job.' The silk of her pants suit slipped against the leather as she shifted in the chair. Dru put hands on the sides of the sofa and pulled herself up straight. Her throat was tight from holding back the emotion and fear that was surging through her. She tried to swallow it down but it didn't move.

'And a few days later almost a million dollars appears in your bank account, and then disappears again very quickly.' His grin was sardonic.

'That's correct.' She raised a shaking hand to her face and wiped away the first tear that slid down her cheek. 'Hang on. How do you know what's in my bank account?'

'Oh, Dru, you'd be surprised what I know about you. Have you still got the diamonds with you?' His voice hardened. 'Or have you doublecrossed Al Tayer? Did you get a better offer? Is that why he was so aggressive towards you? I couldn't hear what he was saying but it was obvious that you were in trouble here.'

Connor was crazy. What the hell was he playing at?

'What he was saying to me?' This time her voice shook. 'He was going to take me to the apartment, and this time God knows what he would have done if I'd refused. No one disobeys Zayed Al Tayer. What he wants, he gets.'

'And he wants more diamonds.'

'No. Listen to me. *Please* Connor. Listen to what I'm saying. I'm telling the truth. As hard as it might be to believe, he wants *me*. And I rejected him. I don't know who told him I was here.' Dru gave into the tears that were aching behind her eyes and in her throat. She rolled over and buried her head in the soft fabric of the lounge as shuddering sobs racked her body.

Finally, the storm of weeping eased and she sat up and stared at him, her voice finally calm. 'He was my boss but he's a monster. He hurt me. One time he locked me in his car until I almost passed out. He told me what to wear, he manipulated me until I found myself doing things, going places, I didn't want to. When he forced the issue, I stood up for myself and he took my job away from me. I am telling you the truth. You have to believe me. I have never been so frightened in my life.'

Her arms were tingling and even though she was sitting down, she could feel her knees trembling. She put her feet firmly on the ground and folded her arms, rocking back and forwards on the chair.

Tears threatened again and Dru let them fall. 'I don't know why you took me away from him, but if Zayed had got me off that terrace, I was in big trouble.' The tears were hot on her cold cheeks and she scrubbed angrily at them. She couldn't abide weakness; it had been years since anyone had seen her cry.

Connor shook his head. 'So tell me where the money came from if you weren't stealing diamonds.'

All of a sudden she began to make sense of his words. She sniffed and swallowed as she forced herself to calm down. 'You really don't have anything to do with Zayed?'

'No.'

'Really?

'I give you my word.'

'You're investigating a diamond theft from Matsu?' She spoke slowly.

'Clever lady.'

'Oh, thank God.' Dru pressed the palms of her hands to her eyes. He had nothing to do with Zayed. Hysterical laughter threatened; she had a chance of getting away, but Connor thought she was a diamond thief!

She struggled to speak, searching for the words to convince him. 'You're wondering about the money in my account?'

'That's correct.' His face was closed as he stared at her over the rim of his coffee cup.

'I can prove to you I'm not stealing or selling any diamonds. I have a letter that explains that payment in my apartment in Darwin. In fact if I can access my Gmail, I can show you an electronic copy now.'

Connor's forehead wrinkled in a frown. 'Okay.' He held out his phone.

'No, no. I'll use mine.' Dru reached for her bag and pulled it out. She groaned as she saw all the texts from Megan; she would call her as soon as she calmed down. Her hands shook as she accessed her email and scrolled back a few months.

'My contract with the engineering firm over here was for five years,' she muttered as she flicked through page after page of emails. Having something to focus on grounded her, but her hands and legs were still trembling. 'I was here two years. Ah, got it.' She opened the email and held the phone up triumphantly. 'Not that I'm happy about sharing my financial affairs with you, but as you already know about them I don't suppose it really matters, does it?'

Connor reached out and took the phone from her. Dru watched him as he read the payment notification. No expression crossed his face, not so much the flicker of an eyelid.

He handed the phone back to her and sat back, his face closed.

'Under the terms of my contract, if I left early and it was a mutual decision, I was entitled to the salary for the remaining term of my contract. Almost three years.' She flopped back in the chair as exhaustion started to creep into her body. 'So when my position was terminated by the company owner himself—*Zayed Al Tayer*—I was paid out. Eight hundred thousand dirham converts to just under three hundred thousand Australian dollars per year. I bought a unit in Darwin almost immediately. That's where the money went. The money I was owed was mine, fair and square, and not from any diamond thieving.' Her speech was rushed, she knew she was babbling but she was desperate for Connor to believe her. She could see the lines deepen on his forehead; he was listening to her.

She shook her head slowly from side to side. 'You think anyone would be crazy enough to try to take diamonds off site from Matsu? You thought *I* was crazy enough to?'

'Somebody is.'

'Well, that somebody is not me.' She folded her arms to try and stop them shaking. 'You've added up the evidence incorrectly and picked the wrong person, Connor. If there have been diamonds stolen I can assure you it's not me.'

'I'll make a couple of calls and double check what you've said.' His voice was low and determined; almost as though he didn't want to believe what she was saying was true.

Dru rolled her eyes. 'You think I have a fake email on my phone just in case the mighty Mr Connor Kirk questioned me about the contents of my bank account? Give me a break.' The immediate threat seemed to be over, and the anger building in her was welcome. Cathartic, refreshing, and replenishing her energy. She rose from her chair and moved across to stand in front of him. 'Who the heck are you? Who can you call and check things like that? From Dubai in the middle of the night?'

His expression remained unreadable.

'You know what? I don't really care what you can do or who you are.' She poked her finger into his chest as she leaned over him. She felt a combination of huge relief at Connor rescuing her and anger that she was so vulnerable.

'Give me five minutes. Wait here.' He stepped away from her hand and ignored her words.

'You think I'm going to go back out there?'

'Sit down and finish your coffee.'

Dru remained standing while he pulled his phone from his pocket and moved across to the entry foyer to the suite. He turned his back to her. The conversation was long and she could only hear the occasional word. Eventually he turned and ran his hand through his hair before he slipped the phone into his shirt pocket.

'So?' Dru's voice was steady as she looked across at him.

He ran one hand over his face, seemingly in frustration. 'It appears you are most probably telling the truth.'

Chapter 28

Connor listened as Dru talked to him all night. The small things that Al Tayer had done; things that she had given no thought to at the time but in hindsight formed a picture of an emotional bully. Disgust filled him, as well as self-recrimination that he had added to her distress.

'He's a very rich man.' Connor recalled what he'd read when he'd been looking up Al Tayer. 'He owns quite a few companies in the Emirates.'

'Yeah. And there I was thinking he was just another international engineer when I first met him at the welcome do.'

'He was educated in England,' Connor commented.

'Yes, he always dressed as a Westerner, and I always assumed he was British. His accent was very plummy. Not that it matters, I suppose. I made a poor judgement of character, irrespective of his nationality.' She dropped her chin and he had to lean across to hear her soft words. 'I've never been good with people . . . or in social situations. Anywhere really. He introduced me to this whole new world. My confidence grew the more time I spent with him and he sucked me right in. But Zayed . . . well, he's used to getting what he wants. I knew he was determined but I never realised the lengths he would go to.' She lifted her head and looked back at Connor.

'I can remember staring at him in a restaurant one night. I was shocked by the way he spoke to the waitress and I just had to say what I thought. He reached for my hand and held it so tightly my skin was bruised the next morning. But then I'd get to thinking, that he couldn't possible have done it deliberately. He always had an answer for everything. As much as he is a bully, he is very charismatic. Sometimes he would look at me, his eyes probing into mine, and I felt as though I could stay his friend forever. And Connor I want you to believe me. I never slept with him.'

Connor nodded at that point; it seemed important to her that he believed her.

'He was only a friend to me—and my employer. He was a generous employer and I had such freedom to implement my ideas. I loved working in the Ain.'

'What happened?'

'It built up so gradually, I didn't notice what he was doing. I was so bloody gullible; nothing in my life had prepared me for a person like this. He manipulated me and towards the end he controlled me. He told me that if I complained to anyone, he would make sure that my friend Sam didn't have a job anymore.'

'Sam?'

'I worked with Sam on the Ain. That's how I met Megan. It was their wedding that I came over here for.' Dru covered her face with her hands and her words were muffled. 'He was even jealous of me being friends with Megan. How could I have ever been so stupid as to come back?'

Twice she broke down again and Connor made her more coffee. The second time, she sat there with tears rolling down her face and Connor couldn't help himself. She looked like a frightened child. He put the coffee cups down on the table. 'Move over.'

Dru was sitting on the double sofa and he sat beside her and held out his arms. With a choking sob, she leaned against his chest and he held her, stroking her hair as she soaked his shirt with tears.

'I have a confession to make. I was the one who told Zayed you were here in Dubai. I was trying to get a reaction out of him—I thought you were bringing more diamonds to him—but I was wrong. I underestimated him. I didn't know what he was like.'

She didn't lift her head but his confession resulted in a fresh storm of tears. Once she'd calmed, Dru drifted off into a light doze and Connor held her as she slept. He gave more thought to what she'd said about Al Tayer. Listening to her account of his extreme behaviour and emotional harassment, he decided it was too risky to try to take her out through Dubai International Airport. He'd already put her in extreme danger by telling the bastard she was in Dubai. The brash confidence that she'd always displayed had disappeared.

Dru stirred in his arms and woke after half an hour. She looked up at him and her cheeks flushed. Connor let her pull away and she stood and pulled the pins from her hair. It framed her face in a wild tangle of blonde locks.

'They were hurting,' she said quietly.

'I've been thinking,' he said. 'Maybe you should fly home from Abu Dhabi instead of Dubai. It'll be safer.'

'How will I get there? I'm terrified of stepping outside this hotel.'

'I'll take you.'

'Really? So, you *do* really believe me now?'

Connor regarded her silently. He'd seen Dru's email for himself, and he'd listened to what she had told him. Yes, he believed she was telling the truth. If she was lying, she was in the wrong profession. The fear she'd displayed was an Oscar-worthy performance.

'I do. And I'll help you get a flight home.'

Dru reached out and grabbed his hand. 'Thank you.' Her voice was intense. 'Oh, God. Thank you.' Her eyes welled with tears again and guilt flooded through Connor for the way he had misjudged her.

'You have your return flight today with Emirates.'

She shook her head slowly and stared at him. 'Do you know every last detail about me?'

'Only what I need to. Leave it with me. I'll make a couple of calls and cancel your booking.'

He rang Greg again, wondering how he'd got it so wrong. Everything he'd focused his investigation on was incorrect. He was on a bloody wild goose chase over here, and the identity of the diamond thief was still a mystery.

'Sorry, Kirkie. We should have gone deeper.' Greg's voice boomed over the line. 'Can I do anything else for you before you come back?'

'Probably. But I'll get back to you. I've got a bit of a situation here at the moment.'

'When are you going on to Antwerp? I've got some more information there for you. It's still not quite what you were looking for. But it's a bit of a lead.'

'I need more of that. I'm going there tomorrow.' Connor couldn't believe that he had been so wrong. 'Keep digging. I'll call you later.' He disconnected and called the airline before he turned back to Dru. 'Let's go straight away.'

'Suits me.' She shrugged. 'Before we go, I need to call Megan and tell her I'm all right and going home. She's frantic. I've ruined her wedding.' She pushed herself up from the sofa and crossed to the window, then slid open the heavy drapes. A sheer silver curtain hung over the window and a soft light filtered into the room. 'The sun's not up yet. Maybe it's too early to call. I'll text her.'

Connor crossed the room and stood beside her.

Dru's arms were folded across her stomach and her shoulders were hunched over. 'It's an ugly dawn, isn't it,' she said.

He looked to the east. A heavy pall of sand-laden smog hung in the morning light. Between the hotel and the Persian Gulf, a row of cranes lined the shore. As they watched, the sun cleared the horizon in a ball of red-orange flame, giving the smog an eerie amber glow.

Connor put his hands on the low windowsill. 'Not the prettiest view I've seen.'

'It's very quiet down there now. Maybe it's a good time to leave.

'Give me your key and I'll go to your room and get your stuff.'

Dru shook her head. 'No! I know Zayed. He'll be watching it. He's probably paid off the desk clerk. It's not safe.' Her eyes widened. 'If he knows your name, he'll know where you are too. He'll be waiting for you too. Watching this room. And me.'

'Are you sure?' Connor was willing to risk confronting Al Tayer. In fact, it would be a pleasure to come face to face with that arrogant sleaze again after what Dru had said about him.

'Yes, I know him. Don't go to my room, please.' She reached down and pulled a calico pouch from beneath her evening clothes. 'Passport, phone, money, credit cards. Deep down, I guess I always knew I'd made a mistake coming back. That's why I carried it with me. After I get home, I'll ask Megan to come and collect my stuff. Although it's only a few clothes and bathroom stuff.' She waved her hand. 'I won't even worry about them.'

'Okay, then give me your room key and I'll leave it in the room with mine.' He narrowed his gaze and looked at her. 'You'll need some new clothes.'

She looked down at her wedding outfit and grimaced. 'You're right. I can't fly in these.'

'The shops in the hotel foyer are open twenty-four seven. What size are you?'

For the first time that night, Connor smiled as Dru's laugh bubbled out. 'Tall. Big.'

After extracting a promise that she'd leave the chain on the door and not open it to anyone until he returned, Connor headed for the elevator. He kept his wits about him as he left the room, but there was no one to be seen apart from the housemaid pushing her trolley towards the end of the corridor. His mind was working fast, trying to reconfigure the information that he'd collected at the mine and take Dru out of the equation.

In the large shopping area in the foyer—he'd never seen a complex like this hotel, it was almost a mini-city—he found a pair of jeans, a couple of T-shirts and a pair of sneakers in the sizes she'd given him. After he made his purchases, he took the main lift back up to their floor. As he swiped the card security square in the door, he could hear Dru's voice, low and husky. He waited till she came across to the door and lifted the chain, the phone to her ear.

'I've got to go now, Megan. I'll call you from Darwin.' The white towel that she'd wrapped around her damp body covered her torso, but her long legs were bare. Another towel was wrapped around her hair. Her face flooded with colour and he looked away as he handed her the bag from the shop.

Connor crossed to the window to give her privacy as she went back to the bathroom.

'Megan called me,' she said through the door. Her voice was much lighter now. 'She's okay now that she knows I'm all right.'

'That's good. As soon as you're ready, we'll go.'

'Thank you.' Her voice was soft. This was a Dru he wasn't used to.

As they made their way down to the underground car park in the lift, her body was rigid with fear. Her cheeks were flushed, her eyes wide, and her knuckles were white where she clutched her phone to her chest. Another wave of protectiveness ran through him, and before he could think, Connor reached over and took her free hand and squeezed it, not letting go as they stepped from the lift to the car park. 'It'll be okay,' he murmured quietly, trying to reassure her.

The car park was poorly lit and his car was three rows along. Dru's breathing quickened as she hurried along beside him and she flashed him a tremulous smile as he hit the remote and the doors unlocked. Before he could open the door for her, she had it open and was in the car. Connor passed Dru his baseball cap. 'Put your seat right back and pull the cap down over your eyes.' She looked at him without speaking but did as he instructed.

Connor finally let himself relax as they exited the car park without incident. He hadn't said anything, but had half expected they might run into a situation before they left the hotel. He didn't think she'd exaggerated the threat from Al Tayer; he'd seen the guy's aggression, and he'd seen him call his offsider over before Connor had shown himself on the terrace last night. He glanced in the rear-vision mirror and took note of the cars behind them as they motored away from the hotel towards the main road off the island. A couple of dark SUVs; he'd keep his eye on them as they travelled.

He glanced over to the passenger seat. Dru's feet were tucked beneath her and her hands were clenched in her lap. She'd put the seat back and closed her eyes as soon as they'd driven out of the underground car park of the hotel. Long dark lashes fanned out on paler than usual cheeks. Her eyes were circled by mauve shadows and he looked away as anger—and guilt—filled him.

He was slipping. To make such a wrong call was disastrous; he had lost his touch. Connor turned his attention back to the road as the light turned green and the traffic moved forward. As the sun rose higher in the morning sky, the haze thickened and left a dreary pall over the barren landscape dotted with half-finished apartment buildings.

As they drove the busy stretch of motorway from Dubai to Abu Dhabi, Dru fell asleep. His thoughts churned through his head and he castigated himself for misjudging her. If he was honest, it was the fact that Dru was female—a strong woman—that had formed his certainty that she was involved in the theft from Matsu; the evidence had been purely circumstantial.

The sky darkened as they approached the northern city and Connor braked as a row of tail-lights appeared ahead. 'What the –?'

'It's a sandstorm.' Dru sat up and stretched her legs out. It was the first time she'd spoken since her quiet thank you a few hours ago. 'We could be held up a while.' She pulled her seat up, and rubbed her eyes before she looked ahead. 'It doesn't look too bad.'

He stopped the car and put the hazard lights on.

'We haven't been followed.' Connor wanted to reassure her. She nodded but still turned around to look out the back window.

Her eyes were wide as she craned her neck to look at the cars behind them. 'You know, I had begun to suspect he had me followed when I wasn't at work to see what I was doing. He has eyes all over the city.'

'He's very rich man.'

'How come you know so much about him?' She looked at him curiously in the strange dim light.

Putting arms on the steering wheel, he looked across at her.

'I guess a huge apology is in order.' Connor turned away and looked straight ahead at the darkening road; it wouldn't hurt to tell her what he knew. 'This is where it becomes very complicated. Zayed Al Tayer is the man who bought the diamonds stolen from Matsu.'

'And you thought I was getting them for him?' It was more of a resigned statement than a question.

'It was the connection that wrongly convinced me you were involved. And for what it's worth, I'm sorry. I made a mistake.' His voice was emotional.

'So what are you really? How do you have access to so much information? Like my bank records? Her eyes fixed on him and he turned to look at her. 'And what flights I was on, and where I was staying. Who are you, Connor? Who are you working for?'

'I'm an investigator. I work for myself. Matsu hired me.'

'And you can just access anyone's records? Anything you want? Find out what you want about innocent people.' Her voice was rising.

'I said I was sorry. Look, I have connections. I was in the Federal Police once.' He lifted his hands from the steering wheel and rubbed his jaw. His skin was bristly; he'd not showered or shaved before they'd left. 'A long time ago.'

'How legal is what you do? Accessing my accounts and stuff?' Her voice was suspicious.

'I do what I have to.' He didn't want to say too much. 'You don't have to worry about it. I'll take you straight to the airport and put you on the first flight we can get back to Australia.'

'What about you? Aren't you flying back too?' Her voice was hesitant.

The sky lightened ahead and the traffic began to move slowly. Connor turned the hazard lights off and followed the traffic ahead.

'I'm going to Antwerp. There's someone I have to talk to there.' He glanced over, taking his eyes from the road for a brief second. Her hands were pressed against her stomach. 'What's wrong now?'

'I don't want you to leave me alone.'

'I'll see you all the way to the boarding gate. You'll be fine.'

Chapter 29

Dru waited in the car as Connor crossed to the car rental agency booth across the underground car park at the airport. The sleep she had snatched in the car during the trip from Dubai had left her feeling doughy. Her hands were tingling and her stomach was a churning mess, and her mouth kept moistening with saliva as though she was about to throw up.

She closed her eyes and concentrated on her breathing, and gradually her stomach settled. Reaching down for the water bottle Connor had placed next to her before the trip, she took a tentative sip and fought for calm.

Her emotions were a mess. Fear clenched at her chest and stomach from that close call that she'd had on the terrace. Zayed's eyes had held hers and it was just like a predator stalking his prey. Her fingertips tingled as fear skittered along her nerve endings. She'd never forget the look on Zayed's face when Connor had stepped up behind her and put his arm around her waist. His lips had pulled back into a frightening snarl and in that moment, she had known he was capable of anything. God, she didn't know what she was going to do about that. She couldn't spend the rest of her life looking over her shoulder or hiding in the wilds of Australia.

Anger was bubbling up there too. Anger that she had been foolish enough to come back to Dubai and leave herself open to all this. Anger that Connor had inadvertently put her in danger at the wedding. Anger that he had suspected her of stealing from Matsu. And anger that her banking records—and goodness knew what other private information—had been accessed by someone as he'd investigated her background. But more than anything it was the uncertainty spiralling through her that was feeding her anger.

She didn't know if she would be capable of boarding a plane and travelling twelve hours back to Darwin alone.

Emotionally or physically. Her confidence had taken an almighty hit. Could she even trust Connor? He said he'd been in the police force. But was he telling the truth? He was at Matsu under false pretences and he'd carried that lie off like a consummate professional.

Could she afford to trust him? Dru put her hand to her head and closed her eyes.

She had no choice.

She jumped as her door clicked open and a whoosh of hot air came in.

'You right to go?'

She looked up at the man who had saved her from being held against her will. Connor stood beside the car, his stance relaxed and an encouraging smile tilting his lips. For the first time since last night, she took a long hard look at him. Dru tried to decide what to do. He returned her look easily and held his hand out.

'When you're ready ...' His voice was calm and soft but beneath his friendliness she sensed he was as wary as she was. But she had no choice. She'd put herself in his care and she had to trust him.

'Where are we going?'

'I thought I'd book a room at the hotel here at the airport. If you're comfortable with that? You can freshen up and have something to eat while I get my contact in Australia to chase up a flight for you.'

Since he'd decided she wasn't the thief, there'd been a change in Connor. A softening in his attitude and a glimpse of compassion that she'd not seen him display before. But a confident strength still emanated from him; a strength that had her teetering on the edge of trusting him.

'That's fine.' She reached to the floor and picked up the small bag of clothes he'd purchased for her, and the bottle of water.

Dru looked about uneasily as they crossed the exposed car park to the lift that would take them up to reception. Connor put his hand beneath her elbow as if he sensed the fear that was clawing at her throat again.

The doors of the lift closed quietly and she leaned back against the mirrored wall and caught sight of herself in the opposite mirror. Her lips were bloodless and her face was pale, and there were dark shadows circling her eyes. Dru rolled her lips together, trying to get some colour back into them.

Connor leaned on the back wall. 'My flight to Antwerp is late tomorrow afternoon, so hopefully we'll be able to get a flight for you before that and I can see you on board safely.'

She lifted her chin. 'I want to talk to you about that.'

He raised his eyebrows. 'Antwerp? Or your flight?'

'Both.' Dru's stomach rumbled. 'What time is it anyway? I've lost track today.' She put her hand against her waist and the waistband of her jeans was loose beneath her fingers. The jeans that Connor had purchased were too big and needed a belt.

'We were pulled up for a couple of hours, and we've missed lunch.' Connor glanced down at his watch. His skin was tanned and sprinkled with fine dark hair. As Dru watched him a strange jolt ran through her and her fingers tingled again.

'It's almost three-thirty.' He lifted his head to meet her eyes, and his gaze was steady. 'No wonder your stomach's rumbling. I'll get a meal sent up as soon as we get a room.'

'About that. I'd rather not be alone so see if you can get a two bedroom suite. I'll pay half.'

He raised his hand in a dismissive wave. 'No need. This is a business expense.'

'Okay. Thanks.'

Dru waited on a soft leather sofa in the foyer as he crossed to the reception counter. It was only a couple of minutes before he came across to her. 'We're in luck. A two-bedroom suite on the top floor.' He held up the key card and this time his grin was wide. Crinkles appeared next to his eyes and for the first time, Dru noticed the hazel flecks in his green irises. 'Come on, let's go order some food.'

This friendly Connor was going to take some getting used to.

***

The door closed behind the room service waiter and Connor lifted the white cloth covering the trolley. The last few hours had been exhausting. Remaining upbeat and keeping a friendly smile on his face and a constant relaxed stance had been hard work. He knew Dru was at breaking point and he didn't want her to crash before he put her on the flight. He had tried hard not to let concern cross his face.

He lifted the silver cover from each plate as she stepped from the bathroom next to her room. The rich aroma of garlic teased his nostrils and his stomach let out a gurgle.

'I'm glad to hear that. Makes me feel less embarrassed.' Dru pulled out the chair on the other side of the table.

'This is either a very early dinner, or a late lunch. But I think we both need it.' He tipped his head to the side. 'You've got a bit more colour in your face. How are you feeling now?'

'Honestly? Stupid. Embarrassed. ' Her gaze was direct and a glimmer of the Dru from the mine reappeared. 'Shaken, but better. Food will help. My stomach has stopped churning.'

'That's good.' Connor picked up his knife and focused on his steak. Dru reached for the glass of water on the table and he noted her hands weren't shaking as much now.

'So . . .' Her voice was casual as she reached for her knife and fork. 'Can I ask you something?'

'Yes?'

'Why did you leave the police force?'

That wasn't what Connor had been expecting. He lifted his head and looked at Dru for a moment while he gathered his thoughts. Her expression was intense and he hesitated for a few more seconds before he replied. He didn't normally talk to anyone except Greg about that time, but he'd done Dru a disservice by assuming she was responsible for the diamond theft. He spoke slowly. 'I left the force after a case went . . . very wrong.' He put his cutlery onto his plate; his appetite had suddenly gone. 'Dishonesty, corruption and lies that led to some arrests overseas that should never have occurred. I didn't want to stay in an organisation that valued personal ambition over human life. I learned that integrity wasn't where I expected to find it.'

Dru nodded and stared past him towards the window and her voice was full of feeling. 'Human greed is a dreadful thing. It must have taken courage to step away from a career like that because you were disillusioned.'

'It was more than that.' Connor reached for the wine bottle that was sitting in the cooler beside the table. He hadn't ordered it with the meal; apparently a complimentary bottle was part of the welcome. He poured a glass for himself and raised his eyebrows as he pointed to the other glass on the table.

'Why not?' Dru said with a shrug. 'It might help me relax.'

Connor reached for her glass and he poured the ruby red Shiraz. 'I loved every minute of my training. They put me through a degree in international security studies at night, and I worked the Canberra beat by day.' He let a mirthless chuckle escape his lips. 'I thought I had it all. I was driven by ambition and I was in a group of colleagues who felt the same way.' He picked up the wine and sipped it and Dru did the same. 'We lived and breathed the force.'

'Sounds like dedication to me,' Dru said. 'Nothing wrong with that.'

'While it lasted.' Connor shook his head. 'I had a great life over those ten years. Good friends, great work colleagues and my future all mapped out.' He sipped his wine and the strong berry flavour burst on his tongue. 'A house and a partner.'

More than he'd intended to say.

He lifted the glass and held it up to the light. 'Not a bad drop.'

'So what happened that killed your ambition?' Dru had cleared her plate while he'd been talking.

'You *were* hungry.' Connor smiled.

She nodded as she reached for the bread in the middle of the table. 'I was . . . and I still am. Was it really so bad that you ended your career over it?'

She wasn't going to let it go. Now that he had started talking about what had happened, a strange feeling ran through Connor and he didn't want to hold back any more. It was almost as though he owed it to Dru to tell her how he'd come to Matsu. He got the impression that she would understand; sadness had filled her voice when she had spoken about human greed.

'I was involved in investigating a couple of young drug couriers who were running drugs to Thailand.' His voice was cynical. 'I'm sure you've heard of the case. It's been in the papers constantly for the last few years.'

Dru's eyes widened. 'I think I know the one you mean.'

'My colleague, Greg, and I had been tipped off about what was about to go down. Greg had set up the travel alerts for when they hit customs.' The familiar flash of anger was there. Nina had shafted them both, well and truly. 'We were ready to arrest them before they boarded the flight but at the last minute a directive came through from the boss. We were told to let them board.'

'And then they were arrested at the other end?' Dru's voice was full of sympathy.

Connor took a huge swig of his wine and looked down at the glass as he twirled it in his fingers. The last few drops stuck to the glass like a stain. Just like the feelings that he carried since Nina had walked right over him that day.

'That's right.' Connor's voice was terse. 'And the worst part was that my superior had lied to us. She told us there wasn't enough evidence to arrest them. But we knew there was. We'd been watching that group for a while and we knew what they were carrying to Phuket.

He lifted his head as the bitterness tainted the taste of the last sip of wine. 'It was all about her, and her climb up the greasy pole of promotion. It was politically expedient at the time to have a big international bust. With that one investigation—that she had very little to do with, apart from letting them out of the country—she achieved the recognition that she wanted. She's Deputy Commissioner now. This time his laugh was laced with bitterness. 'It didn't matter to her who she used on the way up. And Greg and I? Look where we ended up. Makes you wonder if it's all worth it, doesn't it?'

Connor stared past her to the window. He'd not spoken to Nina since that day. He'd gone to the house, cleared out what he wanted and left town in disgust.

Dru put her elbows on the table, and her voice was quiet. 'Where did you and Greg end up?'

'Greg lives in a humpy in the wilds of the Kimberley coast.' Connor reached for the bottle and filled his glass again.

'And you? You went straight into private work?'

'I did. A one-man crusade trying to end the drug trade. I figured if the police force was so corrupt, I could bring integrity to the process and make a difference. But I was kidding myself, wasn't I?' Connor was talking to himself as he stared past Dru. A bright shard of sunlight pierced the window and hit the crystals hanging from the standard lamp beside the desk. Rainbow colours danced across the ceiling and she turned to see what he was looking at.

'You sound very cynical,' she said softly when she turned to face him again. 'Is that why you moved across to the different sort of work you're doing now?'

'You know what, Drusilla Porter?' He rolled her name around his tongue. He liked the sound of it. Her blue eyes were wide as she stared at him, and her face had lost its pallor completely. Her cheeks were now tinged with a soft pink and loose strands of hair fell across her forehead; she was a beautiful woman. Connor put the wine down and fought the attraction that had taken hold of him. He wasn't going to make any foolish wine-fuelled mistakes with her. He'd already stuffed up enough. He couldn't believe that he was actually telling her about his past.

'What's that, Connor?'

'I think I took this job on because I was tired. Tired of trying to do the impossible for almost ten years. Tired of trying to make sense of what happened back then.' Regret flitted through him. 'And because I wasn't on my game, I've stuffed up big time. I'm sorry I assumed the worst of you, and we—*I*—misinterpreted that information.'

'No.' Dru shook her head and smiled. Connor dropped his gaze as her smile jolted him into hyperawareness of her. Her whole face came alight when she let herself smile like that. 'I'm pleased you took the case on, and I'm even pleased you followed me to Dubai. God knows where I would have been by now if it weren't for you. Probably in Zayed's bloody penthouse overlooking the Persian Gulf.'

Her smile wavered and he saw her clenched hands.

'If you didn't have a successful track record, Matsu wouldn't have hired you. But nobody's perfect. Everyone makes mistakes.'

This time his laugh was harsh. 'You want to know what led me to my wrong assumption? Why you pushed my buttons?'

Her expression was wary. 'Why?'

Connor stood and put his glass on the table. 'I made more than one mistake. More than the assumption about your finances. What really drove me was that fact that you were a confident, successful woman. And you didn't let anyone get the better of you.'

He crossed to the single sofa and sat down. Leaning forward he dropped his face into his hands. ''I took one look at you and jumped to a conclusion. I assumed you were just like Nina Smythe. My boss and my one-time fiancée.'

Dru stood slowly and crossed over to where Connor was sitting with his hands over his face. There was a lot more happening here than him suspecting her of a diamond theft. She sensed there was a more to his distress than what he was letting on.

Her limbs were loose and relaxed and the tension had left her body. Maybe it was the wine, maybe it was talking to him, but she felt a flood of sympathy towards him. She sensed his strength and after what she'd seen from him over the last day, she knew she could depend on him to keep her safe. She crouched down in front of him and he jumped when she touched his hands. He stared at her, his eyes shadowed.

'You are being way too hard on yourself,' Dru said. 'I don't care how you got here, or what you thought about me. You made a mistake. But listen to me. If it wasn't for you, I would be in big trouble now. But I trust you and that's a feeling I'm not used to.' She kept hold of his hands. 'I've always had to look after myself, and having you take care of me today—despite what you suspected me of—was something I really appreciate. So forget about it and move on. I'm going to help *you*. I hope you'll let me.'

'Help *me*?' A glimmer of a smile crossed Connor's face and Dru squeezed his fingers. Warmth settled in her stomach as he held onto them. Since she'd eaten and had that glass of wine, her confidence was returning. The shakiness was going, and knowing that Zayed was a couple of hundred kilometres away added to the peaceful feeling.

'Yes. I want you to think about this carefully before you answer. I want to go to Antwerp with you.' She let go of his fingers and put her hand up. Her eyes were level with his. 'I'm assuming the reason you're going there is something to do with the diamonds. Am I right?'

'That's right. That's where the diamonds first turned up.'

'If I went with you, I could help. Would it make your investigations more believable, having a woman with you?' A cramp grabbed Dru's thigh and she dropped his hands and sat back on the floor stretching her leg out. 'I don't know what you're planning to do there, but I'm sure I can help somehow. Please? You helped me. I owe you this.'

He looked at her as if he was considering what she was asking. She tipped her head to the side and brushed her hair back impatiently as it fell across her eyes. 'Look I'll be totally honest. I can't bear the thought of going home alone. I can't do it. Even if I can't help, please let me stay with you.'

Connor nodded slowly before he stood and held his hand out to her. He pulled her up to her feet and she stood in front of him. 'First up, you don't owe me anything.' His breath brushed against her cheek and she could smell the fruity wine on his breath. 'God, I put you in this situation.'

Dru lifted her shoulders in a shrug. 'I would feel much safer if I went back with you after you go to Antwerp.' Connor opened his mouth to speak but she lifted her hand. 'I know I'm a coward but I'm going to follow my gut feelings. I won't feel safe on my own . . . away from you.'

She stared at him and waited for his answer.

Chapter 30

Antwerp, Belgium

Connor looked through the plane window wondering whether he'd made the right decision. Had he been sucked in by his emotions? He was finding Dru far too unsettling. He was consumed by the need to protect her, and he had rationalised letting her come to Antwerp by telling himself it would ensure her safety. If Al Tayer was as determined as she said he was—it might be a stretch—it was possible he'd send someone to Australia to chase Dru down.

She had fallen asleep almost as soon as they'd taken off from Abu Dhabi and her head was lolling forward at what had to be an uncomfortable angle. Even though she'd assured him she was feeling better, her eyes were dark and those mauve shadows tinged the hollows above her cheeks. He gently lifted her chin, slipped his arm behind her and moved her head onto his shoulder. Settling back into the seat, he leaned his head back and listened to Dru's breathing. The lights dimmed and he closed his eyes, wondering what the hell he was doing taking her to Antwerp.

Maybe after all this was over, he'd go back to Dubai and confront Zayed. Make him too terrified to ever contact Dru again. He deserved a shake-up after the way he'd treated her.

In the space of twenty-four hours, she had gone from being his prime suspect to someone he was now convinced was totally blameless. Speaking to Greg earlier, Connor had told him to search for a company called GCH. It was about all he had until he talked to Hughie Van Hoebeek.

Dru moved in her sleep and nestled her head further into his shoulder. Connor opened his eyes and looked down at her; the feeling that ran through him was no longer sympathy or protectiveness but a straight hit of potent desire. He dropped his gaze to her mouth, resisting the temptation to lift his fingers and run them along the soft curve of her lips.

Jesus, what is wrong with me?

He was interested in her, way too interested, and to be honest, he had been since the first minute he'd laid eyes on her in the mess at Matsu a few weeks ago. But he wasn't going to do anything about it.

Just like him, Dru carried emotional baggage and that was the last thing he needed in his life. He didn't have the energy or the inclination for a relationship.

'Connor?' Her soft voice made him jump and he moved his eyes from her mouth up to her eyes. They were intense and wide open, uncertainty clouding her expression.

'What were you thinking about?' Her voice was soft, and he kept his head turned to the side as she left her head on his shoulder.

'Why?'

'You had a strange expression on your face.'

Discomfited at being caught out staring at her, Connor lifted his arm from behind her head. 'I was trying to make you comfortable.' He didn't answer her question.

'Thank you.'

He leaned his head back and closed his eyes so he didn't have to make further conversation. He'd already told her way too much.

***

When Dru woke for the second time, the plane had begun its descent into Brussels. She stretched, feeling refreshed. One of her feet hit the back of the footrest under the seat in front of her and she bit back the grunt of pain that threatened. Her shoe had come off and she had no chance of finding it without getting out of the seat. The 'fasten seatbelt' sign was already lit up for landing and the stewards were into the usual spiel about tray tables and window blinds. Connor had the headphones on and was staring at the television screen in front of him.

If he'd noticed she was awake, he didn't let on. She reached past him and pushed his tray table up and locked it into position but he didn't move.

The way he'd been looking at her when she'd woken up before had almost made her toes curl. The feeling that coursed thought her had been unfamiliar, but had replicated that breathless anticipation that she'd felt before she'd been kissed when she was a teenager. She let out a small huff. It was a long time since she'd had that feeling. It was a wonder she could remember it. She'd sensed Connor's embarrassment when she'd caught him staring, and a little smile tilted her lips. Even though he'd seen her at her worst, he made her feel attractive, and feminine. That was something that didn't happen very often.

Dru pushed the feeling away. She snuck a sideways glance at him. He hadn't shaved since they'd left Dubai almost thirty-six hours ago, and the dark shadow on his face gave him a rakish look. As she stared he glanced over and caught her eye, and they both looked away at the same time. Dru's smile grew. No matter what he'd said before, he wasn't immune to her.

He lifted the headphones from his ears and turned the screen off. 'We're about to land.'

'I know. That's why I put your table up.'

She leaned back in her seat and neither of them spoke. The silence was awkward. They'd gone from nonstop talking to a tension-filled silence. All because of a couple of adolescent-type looks. They were two adults acting like immature teenagers.

She leaned forward as far as she could and searched around for her missing shoe.

Connor's breath brushed her cheek as he spoke. 'What are you doing?'

'I've lost my damn shoe.' Embarrassment made her voice tense and she looked up surprised when he unfastened his seat belt and stood.

'We're about to land,' she said.

'Still got a few minutes.' Connor's seat was on the aisle side of her and now Dru had room to lean over and look under the seat. She didn't notice him crouch down to help until their heads collided.

'Ow,' Dru said with a chuckle.

Connor turned his head and his face was only a couple of centimetres from hers. She was close enough to see the fine lines etched beside his eyes. Connor held her gaze for a few seconds before he whispered. 'Don't move.' He reached forward, grabbed her shoe from beneath the seat in front and passed it to her.

'Thank you.' She slipped it on and as she sat back she heard the landing gear lock into place.

***

'Do you want to freshen up while I get my bag,' Connor asked once they had disembarked. Since they had butted heads, the tension had gone and their conversation had become easier.

'Thanks.' Dru reached up to push a few loose strands of hair from her face and Connor shoved his hands in his pockets, tempted to reach up and touch her hand.

'I'll be over there at the rental car counter. You okay?' He cleared his throat.

Her smile was easy. 'I'm good.'

He watched as she walked away from him, her blonde head above the crowd, tall and proud. With a shake of his head, he walked over and waited for his bag to appear.

By the time she rejoined him, he'd finished the paperwork and the car rental service officer was handing him the keys. 'Take care, sir. There's light snow on the road,' he said.

'Snow?' Dru's voice was excited. 'I've never seen snow.'

Connor turned slowly. Dru's face was scrubbed clean and her cheeks were rosy. Her complexion was unblemished, and her dark lashes and eyebrows contrasted with her blonde hair and blue eyes.

Her eyes were glowing with excitement and her lips were tilted in a smile.

'What's wrong?' She put her hands to her face. 'Did I miss something?'

'No. You look beautiful.'

Her cheeks flushed red and Dru dropped her gaze for a moment before looking up at him. 'Thank you.'

The woman he had found so brash and sassy at their first meeting had disappeared. It was hard to reconcile this shy Dru with the aloof engineer from Matsu Diamond Mine.

Connor cleared his throat again. It was time to stop mooning about; there was work to be done.

'It looks cold out there.' He gestured to the door where the snow was falling lightly.

'I'll have to do some shopping before we go and visit your jeweller. So what's the plan?' she asked as he stooped to pick up his bag. Dru had carried the small bag that held the few clothes she had with her onto the plane.

'Wait up a minute.' Connor flicked open his bag and removed the leather coat that was lying in the top. 'This'll keep you warm till we reach the hotel.' He planned on heading straight to the diamond district in Antwerp from Brussels. He'd left it to Greg to find a hotel but there was no voicemail message on his phone when he'd turned it on after they'd landed. He held up the coat and Dru slipped her arms into it. It was a little big for her and the arms were a bit long.

'Thank you. That should do the trick.'

He picked up his bag and looked at her before holding out his hand. She slipped her fingers into his. 'Don't want to lose you,' he said gruffly.

'Don't worry. You're stuck with me.' She laughed and shook her head. 'Till we get home anyway. The level of banter held an undercurrent of tension and Connor hoped that Greg had booked them two separate rooms. He had to focus on why he was here and get this attraction to Dru out of his mind.

For the time being anyway.

Maybe when they got back to Australia, they could become friends. Maybe it was time he opened himself up to people again. They descended a level and found the rental car with little trouble. As he opened the boot to stow their bags, Dru's husky laugh reached him.

'What's wrong?'

'I feel like a tourist.' She looked at him across the top of the car. 'Since you saved my butt, all we've done is stay in hotel rooms and ride in rental cars.'

'Shame it's not a real holiday,' he said. 'Have you been to Belgium before?'

This time her laugh was loud and a couple of people walking past to another car looked over.

'Belgium? Mate, I haven't been to Europe before. Dubai was it. I was broke when I was at uni, and I've worked ever since.' Dru's voice sobered. 'I guess I could have travelled with the payout from the *Ain* but I don't know that I would have had the courage.' Her choice dropped lower. 'That experience did a fair number on my confidence.'

'I can see that now, but you put on a pretty good show at Matsu. And not just at the poker table.'

She shrugged. 'There's a job to be done there and I can focus.' Her lips tilted in a smile. 'When I'm not planning to steal diamonds, of course.'

Connor opened the door and slid into the driver's seat. He waited for Dru to get in before he answered. 'You're not going to forgive me for that for a long time, are you?'

'A long time? How long have I got? How long are you going to be at Matsu?

Connor shrugged as he looked for the ignition switch. 'Until this case is sorted.' He shook his head ruefully. 'The way I'm going I could be there for a long time.'

'You could become the real Safety Officer. You do a great job reading those policies.' This time Dru's smile was wide. Connor flicked her a glance and his lips tilted. Her sense of humour was making an appearance.

The trip from Brussels to Antwerp took less than an hour. Dru peered out the window most of the way; she almost had her nose glued to the glass. The snow had stopped falling and the road was wet with a grey sludge covering the edge.

'I've always wanted to travel through Europe. Have you been before?' she asked.

Connor nodded as he slowed down for the exit into Antwerp. 'Several times.'

He'd tried to call Greg from the airport with no luck so he pulled over just before they reached the business district. Dru was still looking from left to right and taking in the scenery. The afternoon was closing in quickly and as they approached the city, Christmas lights began to appear. A myriad of white and golden-coloured lights were draped over the peak of the stores across the road from the parking spot he'd pulled into.

'I'm just going to see if Greg has left a message while we've been driving,' he said. 'He was going to book a hotel for us but he hasn't left a message.'

'Almost like your own PA,' Dru said lightly.

'Almost.' Connor grabbed the phone. It was getting dark quickly and light snow had begun to fall. 'Ah, there's a text.'

Twin at 26 *Mercatorstraat*. Check email.

A twin? He entered the address into the navigation system and started the car.

'Everything okay?' Dru's voice interrupted his worry. Knowing Greg, he would have booked a twin room on purpose just to be a smart-arse.

'Yeah, fine. All good. We'll be there in a few minutes.' The building was highlighted on the digital map on the screen and Connor glanced at it briefly before turning his attention back to the traffic.

'Oh, look at that!' Dru pointed ahead excitedly. A square was edged by rows of outdoor stalls all festooned in Christmas lights, and crowds of people were milling about. Connor indicated to turn right and they turned away from the night market. He shook his head. 'You surprise me, Dru.'

'How?' She stared at him.

'I suppose I need to confess before I tell you why. Promise you won't get mad.'

'Hmm, I'll see.'

Connor spotted a parking spot up ahead and pulled into it. 'The hotel should be only a couple of doors up,' he said.

'Okay, so what's this confession?'

'We did a lot of background checking on you when you were a suspect.' He glanced at her as he removed the keys from the ignition. 'Make sure you put my coat back on. It'll be icy out there.' He got out and walked around and opened the door for her. Reaching in, he picked up his coat and held it while she slipped her arms in. 'Turn around.' She turned slowly and he held the bottom of the coat together and joined the zip links before pulling the zipper up firmly.

'Thank you.' She lifted her braid and flicked it out over the coat collar. 'Now finish what you were saying.'

It was hard to pick her tone so he spoke carefully. 'I was just going to say that you're very different to the woman I thought you were—you know, from your interests and things.

'Like what?' This time her voice was hard.

'All that risk-taking stuff. The things you did at uni. The abseiling, the sky diving. And then your choice of career.'

'You did do your homework thoroughly, didn't you?' Her tone was as icy as the wind swirling around the street.

Chapter 31

'Christ, Dru. Don't take what I'm saying the wrong way.' Connor ran his hand through his hair in frustration before he walked around to the back of the car and got their bags. 'Come on, this isn't the sort of conversation to have in the street.'

He wished to God he hadn't started it. Dru strode along in front of him.

'Wait up. You'll slip,' he called.

'What number are we going to?'

'Number twenty-six.' He looked up at the building ahead and to the right. 'That's it. The Leopold.'

The building was a grey brick edifice with dirty windows. The front door was locked so he rang the bell. Dru stood with her back to Connor rubbing her arms. The wind had picked up and although it had stopped snowing, the air was crisp and cold. Finally, the door opened with a creak and a small man with a wrinkled face peered around the metal frame.

'We have a booking,' Connor said. 'Kirk.'

The man stood back and opened the door and ushered them in. There was a small office set off to the side and he shuffled over to the counter where a large book sat. 'Ah yes.' He nodded. '*Tweepersoonskamer.*'

He reached up and took down a large key. Connor pulled out his credit card. '*Nee*, all good. All paid.' He shook his head.

Greg must have paid for the room when he'd booked it. Connor took the key and put his card back in his wallet. 'Thank you.'

'Fourth floor.' The man held up four fingers and pointed into the building towards an elevator with a wire-grilled gate.

'Come on, Dru.' Connor bent to pick up the bags but Dru already had hers in her hand and was walking towards the hall. She beat him to the lift and pushed the black metal button on the wall. Neither of them spoke as the elevator creaked and groaned with a screech of grinding metal as it came down from the floors above. It hit the ground floor with a jolt and they waited for a moment before Connor realised that the metal door had to be opened manually. Connor stepped past Dru and pushed it open and then stood back for her to step inside.

At the fourth floor he pulled open the gate. Dru sighed when it clanged against the metal frame. 'I can't believe this,' she said.

Relief filled Connor. Good, she was talking to him again.

'It's archaic but I kind of like it.' She stepped past him into a narrow dark hallway and peered around the corner.

'Okay.' Connor looked around the dilapidated interior of the hotel and then looked at the room number on the key. 'This way.'

He waited for Dru and muttered beneath his breath. 'This does not bode well for the room, Greg.'

***

Dru had been furious when Connor mentioned checking her background but her anger had burned out quickly. There was no point being upset with him; he was only doing his job, and that was why she'd offered to come to Antwerp and help out. The sooner they went to the jeweller and found whatever he was after, the sooner they could go back to Australia and she could slip back into her safe life at the mine. Although if she was completely honest, as long as Connor was around it was a different sort of safety she'd be looking for. He unsettled her—but not in a bad way.

He was a strong man who exuded authority and confidence. A good-looking man, with dark hazel-flecked green eyes. The last few times she'd caught him looking at her, it had been hard to look away. The strange feeling that had run through her was one she wasn't used to. Like that hand tingling, but this was a feeling that jangled every nerve ending in her body.

She followed him down the hall until they reached the room. He opened the door and stepped back and allowed her to go inside ahead of him.

'Oh . . . my.' She stopped suddenly and Connor ran into her back. He grabbed her by the elbows and her nerve endings sizzled.

'Sorry.' He looked over her shoulder and the expletive that escaped his lips spoke volumes.

Letting go of her arms, he stepped past her. 'Bloody hell. Wait till I ring Greg!'

Dru put her bag on the floor and placed her hands on her hips and surveyed the room. In both Dubai and Abu Dhabi the rooms they had shared had been the height of elegance, with luxurious bathrooms and tea-making facilities and a refrigerator in each one.

Here, two single beds with iron bedheads and obviously sagging mattresses were covered by mustard yellow throw overs. They were almost the colour of the mango chutney Mum had made when Dru was at high school. In one corner was an old pedestal sink in a dull pink, and beside it stood a table with an old-fashioned kettle.

She turned to Connor and couldn't help but laugh at the horrified look on his face.

'Where's the bathroom?' he said.

'Looks like there isn't one.'

'Bloody hell.' He took hold of her arm. 'Come on, we'll go and find somewhere else.'

'Hang on.' Dru stepped from his gentle hold and opened the door. She stepped into the hall and continued along to where it ended in a blank wall. On each side was a door. One was marked *vrouw* and the other *mannen*. She'd found the bathrooms.

It was cold in the corridor and Dru scurried back down to the room. Connor was still standing there. 'Come on, we're out of here.'

'No.' Dru shook her head. 'It's fine. We're here now. We can go and find something to eat and then wander around those gorgeous markets in the square.' She smiled. 'I'm experiencing the true Europe, not a sanitised version. I love it.'

Connor folded his arms, a stubborn look on his face. 'I can't expect you to stay in this.'

'Honestly, it's fine. It reminds me of our farm where I grew up.'

Connor unfolded his arms and walked across to her. He put his hands on her shoulders and looked at her. 'Are you for real, Dru Porter?' His voice was soft as he held her gaze intently. 'Most women would run out of here screaming for luxury.'

She lifted her chin and stared him down. 'I'm not most women.'

Suddenly the mood switched to something deeper and Connor dropped his forehead gently onto hers. He lowered his arms and put them around her waist. Dru leaned into his hold, unable to resist.

'No, you're not, are you.'

It was a long time since a man had held her close like that.

Dru rested her head against Connor's cheek. He smelled manly, with just a hint of cologne. His cheek was rough against hers and Dru closed her eyes, taking comfort from his embrace.

Without thinking, she lifted her finger and traced it along his jawline and then onto his lips. Then she wrapped her arms around his neck and lifted her mouth to his. Her eyes were closed but she heard and felt the gentle sigh he expelled. She stood still, waiting to see how he would react. He leaned closer, sliding slowly into the kiss as he ran his hands down the leather jacket to settle around her waist again.

They stood there for a few moments with their lips pressed gently together, not moving. Dru stiffened when Connor stepped back and removed his hands. She opened her eyes to a solemn regard.

'As much as I would like to, we're not going to take this any further, Dru.'

'Why not?' Her voice was soft.

'Because you're vulnerable right now, and I'm not going to take advantage of that.'

Disappointment filled her but she reached out and touched his cheek again. 'No matter what you might think, you are a decent man, Connor.'

***

Stepping out of that embrace was one of the hardest things Connor had ever done. Dru had been soft and pliant in his arms, and her lips sweet against his. If he ever made love to Dru—and he was not averse to the idea—it wouldn't be when she was in a fragile emotional state, and it certainly wouldn't be in a hotel room that looked like it hadn't been updated since the nineteenth century.

'Come on, we need to go eat. And you can go and enjoy the markets. Tomorrow we'll be busy chasing a diamond thief.'

'I'll just go and have a wash.' Dru was out of the room before he could reply.

Connor took a deep breath. God, he hoped he hadn't upset her again. He gathered his thoughts and pulled out his phone. Maybe he could find a better room around here somewhere.

Dru pushed open the door a few minutes later. 'Are you ready?' She reached for her purse. 'Do you think I'll find a clothes market down there?'

'What, my coat's not good enough for you?'

'You might need it,' she said drily.

Connor held out his arm and she put hers through it as they left the room. This time they found the steps and bypassed the elevator.

***

Connor looked at the map on his phone and steered Dru towards the *Shupstraat*. Dru was like a child at Christmas as they walked through the markets. The square was filled with people and the noise was high as various musical performers vied with each other for the attention of the crowd. Every few minutes they'd stop at a stall as she insisted on trying the Belgian waffles, fries, chocolate and beer, much to Connor's amusement.

Finally, they left the Christmas lights behind them and turned into the *Shupstraat*.

'I definitely need to buy some warmer clothes,' Dru said. She looked at him but her face was in shadow.

'I just want to check out the address Greg emailed. Number fifty-three.'

Soft light shone from the windows of the diamond merchants as they strolled along the street. Dru walked beside him, her sneaker-clad feet silent on the cobblestones. 'There it is.' She pointed to the shopfront across the road. 'Van Hoebeek. Is that it?'

'Yes. That's the one. Come on.' Connor took her arm, and didn't let go once they were across the road. The shopfront was old but elegant with thin black bars covering the glass panes. He looked up into the red light of a CCTV camera just above the window. The name of the proprietor was painted along the top of the glass in ornate, curled letters. The window itself was simply decorated with diamond jewellery nestled in red velvet. Behind the display, he could see antique furniture in a small showroom.

'Okay, we'd better get you some classy clothes to wear tomorrow,' he said.

***

The next morning, Dru woke first and slipped down the hall to the bathroom. After a very cool shower where the water stopped and started in time with the creaking of the water pipes, she dressed in the clothes they'd purchased for her at the market. Connor was awake when she returned and he went down to the bathroom while she waited. He'd slept on top of the bed in his clothes but when he returned he was wearing fresh clothes and was clean-shaven. They found a small cafe for breakfast before heading to the exclusive establishment of Van Hoebeek.

When they arrived, Connor introduced himself as a representative of John Robinson, CEO of Matsu Diamonds. Hughie Van Hoebeek pulled at his collar. He was a man with a mournful face and a brow furrowed with deep worry lines. He looked at Connor then led them through to the office behind the showroom.

They spoke for half an hour while Dru sat back and sipped her cup of steaming hot chocolate and Connor took notes in a small notebook.

He had prepared his questions very carefully. 'Please tell me about your interactions with Mr Al Tayer. When was your first contact with him?'

'The first set of stones was brought to me in May of this year.' The jeweller frowned. 'I wish to reiterate that I have reported the unetched stones to the World Diamond Council.' His Belgian accent thickened as he ran his finger around his collar again. 'I explained that when Mr Al Tayer's assistant arrived, I had allocated a junior craftsman to the creation of the earrings. They were small gems and due to the inexperience of my junior staff member he did not notice that the stones were not etched. I have accepted full responsibility for this error and will pay the appropriate fine.'

Connor nodded slowly. 'Please tell me what happened when you took delivery of the second set of stones.'

'I thought it was strange that once again the shipment was personally delivered. We do not see that happen very often. As the quality of the violets was so high, and the stones were so large, I would have expected them to be delivered in the usual way with very high security. Under the circumstances I insisted that I meet with the man who delivered them—I still do not know him by name, just that he is Mr Al Tayer's personal assistant. There was no security and he merely pulled them from his suit pocket and handed them to me. I found that quite strange. The diamonds are of exquisite quality and I have since valued them at more than a million dollars each.'

He took his handkerchief and mopped his brow. 'He also brought the earrings back so that the necklace could be matched to them exactly. That was when I noticed our mistake.'

'How long was it between the first and second visits?'

'There was only three months until his second visit with the large stones. When I saw their quality, I examined them and the lack of etching was a shock to me. I called John Robinson immediately. It is a difficult situation. Mr Al Tayer's assistant provided a registration certificate, but of course it is forged. Interpol have been notified.'

'Where are the diamonds now?'

'In our bank vault. John has requested we keep them secure until the thief is caught.'

'Is Mr Al Tayer aware of that?'

'No, he has been told that there is a delay in crafting the necklace. He is expecting it back imminently.'

Connor and Dru exchanged a glance. Dru knew Zayed well; if he'd legitimately purchased the six violet diamonds, he would want them back, and he wouldn't give up until he had them in his collection.

'Thank you. That information is very useful.' Connor closed his notebook with a snap. He held out his hand to Van Hoebeek as he stood. 'Thank you for your time. If there is anything more that you do think of, please contact me.' He handed over his business card.

'Whatever I can do to help. Please convey my apologies to John once again. I take full responsibility for the delay in identifying the first set of stones as stolen. If I had not allocated that job to my junior, the theft would have come to light months earlier.' He put his hand up. 'Wait. One more thing I had forgotten. While I was taking the earrings from Mr Al Tayer's man, he moved away to take a phone call. At first I thought he said something about a cat, and then I realised it was the name of the person he was talking to.'

Cat. That was the name Najeeb had mentioned during the interview with Zayed.

Connor's smile was broad this time. 'Thank you.'

Chapter 32

Darwin – Northern Territory

Connor followed Dru along the corridor that ran along the outside of her apartment block. When he'd talked about booking into a hotel in Darwin, she'd insisted that he stay at her apartment.

'God, Connor, we've been sharing hotel rooms and sleeping next to each other on planes for days. I insist.'

Their relationship had relaxed considerably since their escape from Dubai, and Dru's confidence had improved. By the time they'd landed, she was back to her confident, sassy self—almost. Connor had been quiet; he knew he shouldn't have accepted her invitation. But he'd enjoyed the banter that had sprung up between them, and was getting used to Dru's company. And if he was honest with himself, he didn't want to leave her on her own.

She'd opened up to him on the long flight home—they'd flown Singapore Airlines to avoid a transit stop at Dubai—and she'd told him about her father's murder and the impact she now realised it had on her life.

'It must have been a very hard time for you,' he said. 'Then that bloody Al Tayer. You've done it tough, Dru.'

'It was. I find it very hard to trust anyone.'

'I know what you're saying. My experiences turned me into a loner.'

Dru had lowered her gaze for a moment. When she looked up at him, she reached for his hand. 'Me too. But you know what? Despite all the drama in Dubai, and your investigation –' a cheeky smile lifted her lips and her eyes lit up '– and the superb accommodation in Antwerp, I've really enjoyed your company over the past few days. I feel comfortable with you.' She squeezed his fingers and Connor looked down at their joined hands. A strange feeling settled in his chest.

'You make me comfortable being me. It might sound funny, but that's how it feels,' she said. 'And I haven't felt like that for a long time.' She leaned back in the seat and looked at him. 'In fact, I don't know that I've ever felt like that. Not since Dad died anyway.'

'I know exactly what you're saying. You're very comfortable to be with too.' Connor squeezed her fingers back and held her gaze. 'Not something I'm used to either.'

Dru was the first to look away. 'Look, we're coming in to land.'

But Connor wasn't thinking about the journey, or the comfortable feeling that Dru had described. For the first time since he'd left the Federal Police—and Nina—he was attracted to a woman. And the feeling wasn't exactly what he would describe as comfortable.

Now as Dru put the key into the door of her apartment, guilt trickled through him. He knew he had to tell her that he had broken in here a few weeks back. It was the right thing to do. If they were to remain friends—or maybe more—he had to keep things completely open and truthful between them.

Dru opened the door and stepped inside before ushering him in. 'I'm not going to be much of a hostess. I don't know what's here in the way of food or cold drinks. I haven't shopped for ages.' She covered a huge yawn. 'Anyway, welcome to my place.'

'It's okay, we're only here for one night. We can eat out. Looks like there's plenty of restaurants close by.'

'I'm too tired to go out again. Let's order in.' She dropped her keys on the coffee table and put her bag on the floor. 'It'll be good to have some clean clothes.' An expanse of bare, pale skin appeared above her jeans as she lifted her arms and stretched. 'And I am looking forward to getting back to work. I miss the place.'

Connor turned away. Forget work, forget diamond investigations and forget dinner. All he wanted to do was slide his fingers over that bare skin and hold her close. 'Dru. I need to tell you something.' He cleared his throat.

'Yes?' She tipped her head to the side and Connor took a step towards her. He held his arms rigid by his side so he couldn't touch her.

'I want to be totally honest with you.' Connor drew his breath in as Dru stepped closer. 'I'd like to stay friends after this is all over.'

'That sounds good. I'd like that too.'

If she touched him, he was going to be a goner. He stared over her head at the view of Darwin Harbour and took another deep breath. 'You need to know I was in your apartment a few weeks back.'

'What?'

He clenched his hands as confusion filled her voice.

'I was here. When I thought you were involved in taking the diamonds.'

'How did you get in?' Cold laced her words. When he looked at her, her blue eyes were glacial and her mouth was set in a straight line.

'I broke in.'

'You bloody broke in to my apartment?' Now her hands were on her hips. 'What did you look at when you were here?'

'Not a lot.' He shrugged. 'You don't have much here.'

'Did you go through my personal things? My underwear? My toiletries.'

Her voice was shaking; he hated seeing her distressed again.

'I was looking to see if there was any evidence that you were involved.'

'So did you find it in my knickers drawer?' She shoved at his chest with both hands and Connor grabbed them. 'Jesus, Connor, I don't know if I can forgive you for that.'

Connor held her hands firmly as she squirmed against him. 'It was part of my job. I needed to tell you. I wanted to be upfront with you.'

She pulled one hand free and hit at his shoulder. 'I am just so bloody cranky. I don't know what to think.'

Connor grabbed her hand again and held it tight. 'Settle down.'

'Settle bloody down? What else do you have to *confess*?' She narrowed her gaze. 'Was it you creeping around in my apartment at the mine last week?'

'No. What do you mean?'

'I told you I was going to leave the door open, so you waited till I went to sleep and then you came in.' She tried to jerk away from his hold. 'So, did you have a good look? Didn't find any fucking diamonds there either, did you, Connor.'

'I didn't come into your room. When did that happen?'

'The night of Rocky's accident. I thought I'd dreamed it but it was you, wasn't it?'

'No. It wasn't. I promise. I've been honest with you. There's nothing more to tell.' Anger simmered in his chest. 'I won't apologise for doing my job. And just for the record I didn't get my jollies going through your underwear.'

Dru put her head back and glared at him. The sexual tension in the air was so thick Connor found it hard to catch his breath. He put his arms around her and pulled her hard against him. When she reached up and grabbed his head, her lips were a breath away from his. He lowered his mouth and her lips opened to welcome him.

He walked her backwards until she was up against the wall, and then he slid his hands up under her shirt. The skin of her back was warm and soft beneath his fingers. 'I'm sorry, but I have to touch you.'

'Don't be sorry,' she murmured against his mouth. Her voice was low and husky and the spark of desire fired in Connor again.

He lifted his head and rested his forehead against hers. 'You've gotten into my blood, Dru, you know. What are we going to do about it?'

***

'Yes, what *are* we going to do about it?' Anticipation and desire had dispelled Dru's tiredness. '*I* think we need to go and lie down. You already know where my bedroom is.' She couldn't help the smart-arse comment. Connor was hard against her stomach. Pushing herself against him, Dru lowered her hands to the clasp on his jeans, but before she could undo them, he put his hands beneath her bottom and lifted her.

She wrapped her legs around his thighs. 'Do you know how much I weigh?' she said with a laugh.

'Don't worry, I work out.' He carried her into the bedroom before gently lowering her to the bed. He grabbed the bottom of his T-shirt and pulled it over his head.

Dru let her eyes feast on his muscled bare chest. 'Obviously.'

A shiver of exquisite pleasure ran through her as he stepped out of his jeans and stood before her.

'Commando?' she murmured.

****

The light reflecting on the window woke Dru the next morning. She opened her eyes slowly and rubbed her cheek against the soft pillowcase before she rolled over. Connor was on his side, facing her and breathing evenly, still sound asleep. Dru sat up slowly and leaned back against the bedhead. They'd ordered in a pizza delivery just after midnight, and not gone to sleep until the early hours. Her body ached deliciously in all sorts of unfamiliar places and her skin was tingling where Connor's stubble had scraped over it.

'Good morning, Drusilla.' His voice was lazy and she looked down at him with a smile.

'Good morning, Connor.' She knew her lips were swollen and her hair a tumbled mess around her head.

He looked bright and his eyes were clear. A sexy smile crinkled the skin around his eyes. 'You look like you had a busy night.'

'Let's say it beat watching termites.'

Connor rolled over onto his back with a mock groan. 'Oh, you're a cruel woman. What a comparison.'

Dru slid down in the bed and put her head on his chest, listening. 'Maybe it was the best thing that's happened to me for the last few years. But I don't want you getting a big head.' She lay there quietly listening to the steady, slow thump of his heart. 'Want to go out for breakfast?' she murmured sleepily.

'I thought we'd have breakfast here.' His voice was full of amusement and Dru smiled against his bare skin.

'What did you have in mind?' She lifted her head and arched her back as his lips trailed up her shoulder and along her neck.

'More of the same. What time's our flight to Kununurra? Noon?'

With a slow nod, Dru lowered her mouth to his. 'Then I guess, breakfast in bed, it is.'

Chapter 33

Matsu Diamond Mine

On the flight back to Kununurra, Dru and Connor had both agreed it was necessary and appropriate to resume a professional relationship while on site. Sounded sensible but in the time they'd been back, Connor was doing it tough. He was finding it hard to stay away from Dru.

After two intense days of investigation and several conversations with Greg and with John Robinson about the mysterious Australian woman, they were no closer to the thief. As well as following up the woman in Antwerp as best he could with such scant information, Greg was digging up what he could seeing what he could find out about the GCH company.

'Jesus, mate. You're giving me the hard stuff. GCH!' Greg had been vocal in his protest. 'There's probably hundreds of companies with those initials.

'Add it to your bill,' Connor said drily. He had no doubt Greg could crack it eventually. Although a connection had been set up with Interpol, Connor was frustrated. It was difficult to share some of the information they had, as Greg's methods of gaining it were highly illegal. Similarly the flow of information from Interpol back to John Robinson was almost non-existent. On the bright side, Zayed Al Tayer was being grilled by Interpol, but that still didn't aid in the identification of the thief at Matsu.

He turned the ute into the car park beside Dru's demountable office. He was heading for the tailings dam on the pretext of dropping off an updated safety document. He also wanted to talk to her about Rocky and suss out the area around the dam where the older man seemed to be spending a lot of time. But if he was honest, the main reason he'd come across here this afternoon was to see her.

Dru's ute was parked at the northern side of the dam and she was walking along the edge of the water with one of the workmen. Every few metres they would stop and Dru would crouch down and examine something on the ground before resuming her walk and stopping again a little bit further along. As he watched, her hat blew off and when she bent to retrieve it the sun caught the silver glints in her hair. Connor could still feel the soft silkiness of her long hair against his fingers.

He leaned back in his seat and waited till they walked around the dam; it was too hot to leave the air-conditioned vehicle.

The heat was messing with his head. With his concentration. It was the looming wet. What did Greg call it the other day?

Mango Madness.

That was a good explanation for why he was working so slowly, and visiting the tailings dam when he didn't really need to. The whole trip was a bloody pretext just to spend a few minutes in Dru's company. It bothered him that he couldn't control this feeling; he'd never felt this way about a woman before.

His relationship with Nina had been different. It was clinical, logical—a natural progression after a year spent working together and seeing each other socially. But he realised now that his emotions hadn't come into play back then.

This intensity that heated his blood, the constant craving to be with Dru was unfamiliar to him. When he was with her, he felt invincible, and there was another unfamiliar emotion that he guessed some people would call happiness. She made him laugh; she made him *feel*. He'd tried to rationalise it, and when his emotions let him think rationally—usually when he was away from her—he was putting this feeling down to a guilty conscience for judging her, and the need to protect her.

Whatever it was, it had forced him over here today; he could have seen Dru after work in the mess tonight. He reached over to start the car. There'd be an opportunity to talk in private sometime after dinner.

Last night, he'd slipped into her room after dark. He hadn't intended to stay long but it was after midnight before he'd gone back to his room to work. Sex in a single bed brought back teenage memories.

Damn it, he was here now, he might as well stay. He pulled the key from the ignition as someone tapped on the window.

'Connor!' Dru had walked over to the car while he'd been bloody daydreaming. He pressed the button to open the window and the burst of heat that slammed in was almost solid.

'I don't know how you work out in that heat all day.' He waited till she stepped back and he opened the door and climbed out to a welcoming smile.

'What can I do for you?' She flicked a glance at the workman who was gathering the tools and putting them in the back of her ute.

'A couple of things.' He reached into the passenger side and pulled out a folder. 'This is the report I was telling you about.'

'Ah,' she said with a smile. '*That* report.'

Connor pointed to the dam. 'What were you doing over there?'

'Come and I'll show you.' Dru called out to the guy who was standing beside the ute. 'Mick, can you take that vehicle back to the demountable please? I'll get a lift back with Connor.'

'Okay, boss.'

As they walked across to the dam, the sound of crunching gears drifted down the hill.

'Uh, maybe not such a good idea letting him drive,' Dru said with a grimace. 'I might need a new ute.'

Connor ignored the feeling that ran through him when she touched his arm and pointed across the dam with her other hand. She left her fingers on his arm.

'See over there. That's the fence line where the traditional owners want the new boundary to run.'

'It won't take much land from the site at all, will it?' He stared out over the flat land surrounding the dam.

'No, just the dam and a small area where we've finished the rehabilitation work. Rocky's behind the whole push to get the site back.' Dru was pensive. 'Something worries me about his attitude, the way he's gone about it. I'm not really convinced about his motivation.'

'So why are they so interested in that land?'

'The tailings are a major pollutant on a mine site. That's why we've focused the rehabilitation work over here to begin with. When Rocky and those two lawyers presented their proposal, I did a bit of hunting around in the literature. If the new processes that are used in South African diamond mines were put into place here with the advances in separating, sorting, and crushing equipment, very small diamonds could be recovered from the residue of the original diamond-bearing ore. Almost a million carats of diamonds were recovered that way in one year at just one mine.'

He glanced over his shoulder. The other two workmen were far enough away not to hear them. 'Do you think Rocky wants the tailings dam for the diamonds that could be in there? Is there any chance he could have got the Antwerp diamonds from there?'

'No, none at all.' Dru shook her head. 'It's only residue. Only tiny diamonds.'

'John Robinson said there was a possibility that some big diamonds might still be in the dam.'

'I doubt it,' Dru replied.

Connor looked over at the dam where the shimmering heat was lifting from the ground. 'So, what's your gut feeling about Rocky?' There'd been no sign of him since they'd come back from overseas, and when Dru had asked one of the workmen, he'd shrugged and said he was on leave. He reworked his question. 'What I meant to say was, do you think there's a possibility that we will find evidence that Rocky took the diamonds.'

'Not a chance. I'd put money on it. And besides, he doesn't have the contacts to be selling diamonds in Dubai or Antwerp. Whatever he's up to, it's got nothing to do with the missing diamonds. He wants that sacred site returned to his people.'

'Back to square one. I hope to God Greg comes good with something soon. He's working through the security staff again, and looking for GCH.'

Dru smiled up at him. 'Come on, let's go grab some lunch. I've got the makings of a sandwich in the fridge in the demountable. Bring your paperwork with you and we can make it look like a meeting.' All thoughts of missing diamonds fled as Dru smiled up at him and whispered, 'I missed you today.'

***

Dru yawned as she walked up the hill to her apartment later that same afternoon. They'd been back on site for almost a full roster and Connor's frustration with the progress of the investigation was obvious. She'd racked her brains trying to think of ways that the diamonds could have been stolen but they were no closer to a solution even with her knowledge of the plant and the staff. Tiredness dogged her footsteps. She'd slept in her own room last night. Connor had spent all night on the laptop in his donga, trawling through the information that his friend had gathered. Looking for something he may have missed.

Her sleep had been fitful, and around 3.00 am she had jerked awake. Connor had gone back to his room but it had sounded as though someone was trying to open the door to her donga. Heart pounding and mouth dry, she'd climbed out of bed, switched the light on and tiptoed across to the door before switching the outside light on as well.

'Connor,' she'd whispered, but there'd been no reply. Finally, she'd taken a few deep breaths and worked up the courage to open the door but there had been nothing to see apart from the moonlight spilling across the road to the car park. There was a slight breeze coming from the Matsu Range and a loose sign at the edge of the pool building creaked as she watched and listened. Finally her heart rate returned to normal, but when she went back to bed, she couldn't sleep. Zayed's face and voice filled her thoughts and she made a conscious effort to block him out. She was at Matsu, and she was safe. She was home in Australia, and she was safe. He wouldn't risk coming here.

A smile had lifted her lips as she tucked her hand beneath her cheek and drifted back to sleep.

Connor had vowed to keep her safe too.

After lunch with Connor, Dru had spent the afternoon going over the summer schedule in her demountable office. It was too hot to work outside. By the time she got back to the donga, the sun had set and she was tired. She threw her hat on the table and lifted her heavy braid up from her neck; perspiration had soaked the collar of her work shirt.

There was a knock at the door, and she wiped the perspiration from her face with the back of her hand as she crossed to open it. Connor stood on the top step. All thoughts of being hot and tired fled. He came inside and she closed the door behind him with a smile.

'Hey, you,' she said.

'It's stuffy in here. Why don't you have your air conditioner on?' he asked.

'I thought I did.' Dru frowned and lifted the remote from the cradle next to the door. She hit the power button and it came on with a roar. 'It must be playing up again. The maintenance guy said he'd fixed it.' She let her eyes linger on Connor's broad shoulders as he reached for her. He grabbed her by the waist and pulled her closer. She lifted her face and his lips settled gently on hers.

'Hello,' he murmured softly.

Dru pressed closer to him as his hand trailed down her back. A pleasant sensation ran through her as his fingers caressed the bare skin between her shorts and her T-shirt. 'I'm all hot and sweaty.'

'You feel all right to me.' He stepped back but kept his hands on her waist. 'I only called in for a minute. I'm going to keep working. Greg thinks he's making some progress with the GHC link.'

'Are you sure you don't want to stay for a while?'

'No, I've got work to do, and besides –' he nibbled his way down her neck '– there's barely enough room for one in your bed, let alone two. My back is still aching from the other night.'

'I'll move over.' Dru smiled and cupped her hand around the back of his neck but he shook his head with a smile.

'You are a temptress, but I can't. I'm waiting for Greg to call back.' His voice turned serious. 'And *you* are too much of a distraction. I need to focus.'

'Do you think you'll be able to come back to Darwin with me tomorrow night? If you've solved the case by then . . .'

'And pigs might fly.' He touched his hand to her face gently. 'If Greg's info isn't what I'm hoping for tonight, I'll head out to Wyndham to see him. I called John Robinson this afternoon and he's as frustrated as I am. Whoever is doing this is a top operator. But I reassured him; slow and steady and we'll get him.'

Dru knew Connor's frustration was building as every lead he'd followed had come to a dead end. 'If you do go to Wyndham, maybe I could come with you?' The thought of going back to her apartment in Darwin alone held little appeal. 'It's not far from Kununurra, is it?'

'It's only a short drive. And I'm happy for you to come if I go. Depends on what Greg's found out today.' Connor wrapped his arms around her and pulled her close.

Dru leaned on his chest; she loved being in his arms. 'So how long till he gets back to you, do you think?'

Connor sighed and leaned back against the door. 'He had a lightning strike and his router got fried. He said he was picking one up at Wyndham Post Office today. So, soon I hope.'

'Well, you'd better go back now. I've got an early start in the morning.' Dru bent down to unlace her boots but she stiffened.

She felt the cold tiptoe across her shoulders and deliberately fought the reflexive shiver as she looked around the small room. 'Someone's been in here.' She walked across to the table under the window where she kept her bag and her keys.

Connor pushed away from the door and followed her. 'What do you mean?'

'Last night I thought I heard someone at the door but I put it down to my overactive imagination giving me a bad dream. But I have been making doubly sure the door has been locked since we came back.'

'Are you sure?'

'Look. My bag's unzipped. I always keep it zipped up.' Dru leaned over the bag and pulled the zippered opening apart and rummaged through the contents. A couple of T-shirts and pairs of shorts and her sandals were in there, where she'd left them when they'd come back from Darwin. She frowned as her fingers encountered something hard. She lifted the bag up and brought it over to the large table.

'What the –' She reached in and lifted up the edge of the stiff layer of vinyl covered padding that formed the base.

'What's wrong? Is something missing?'

'No, there's something under the base.' Dru worked her fingers beneath the hard edge. A small box was wedged beneath the base in the back corner of the bag. She pulled it out and held it up.

'It's the face cream I bought in Kununurra. But it was gift-wrapped.' She frowned and shook her head as she looked at the white box covered with gilded writing. 'How the heck did that get in my bag?'

'What do you mean?'

'I didn't buy this for me. It's not mine.'

'But you did buy it? You've lost me, Dru.

'I bought this as a favour for Adam. I gave it to him and now it's back in my room. How bizarre. I'm sure I gave it to him.' She put her hand to her forehead. 'Maybe I was jet-lagged. Maybe I just thought I had?'

She opened the box and peered inside.' It's wrapped in different paper. How strange.'

Connor reached out and took the dark blue package from her hand. 'It's carbon paper,' he said slowly. Unwrapping the paper from around the jar, he set it on the table with the carbon paper beside it. The lid was gold and the label was embellished with gold ink.

'This is definitely the cream I brought back from Kununurra for Adam. But it *was* gift-wrapped. And I *did* give it to him,' Dru said.

'Adam Hennessey?'

'Yes, I was confused because this is the second time I've bought it for him.' Dru said. 'The first one was for his wife's birthday and this one was for her sister.'

'Are you absolutely sure you gave it to him?'

'Yes, I am now. I picked it up in Kununurra on the way to Dubai. I offered to post it for him, but he said he'd post it from here.'

'Tell me more,' Connor said thoughtfully.

'I remember now. I gave it to him on the way to the mess the other night when you were in the processing plant.' Dru screwed her nose up. 'So how did it get back in my bag? And why is it wrapped in carbon paper? It doesn't make sense.'

Interest flared in Connor's eyes. 'That's the bag you always take off site when you go off duty?'

'Yes. I don't take much because everything I need is in my apartment in Darwin.'

Connor's whole body was tense and Dru could see his mind ticking over. 'What are you thinking?'

'Maybe you're onto something here,' Connor said.

'What do you mean?'

Connor took the jar from her and twisted open the lid. A sweet smell pervaded the small room.'

'Hey, that's a gift.'

'If it's really a gift, why is it back in your bag? And more to the point, how did it get there?' Connor crossed to the table and picked up a magazine from the pile on the floor. 'Can I tear this?'

'Sure.'

Dru watched as he carefully pulled two centre double pages out and spread them over the table. Kim Kardashian stared back up at them.

'What are you doing?'

'Bear with me. I have a theory.' Excitement filled Connor's voice and Dru stared at him. His eyes were bright and a faint flush stained his cheeks. As she watched he placed the jar on the paper, and then carefully dipped his forefinger in and moved it around.

'Smells nice,' she said.

Connor shook his head with a grimace. 'It's sickly sweet and it's slippery.'

'It's supposed to be brilliant for the complexion.' Dru watched as Connor moved his finger slowly around the edge of the jar. Finally, he lifted his hand; his finger was covered in soft pink cream. He reached for the box of tissues on the table and went to wipe his finger.

'Hey, no. Don't waste it.' Dru held out her hand and opened her palm. 'You're holding four hundred dollars' worth of cream there.'

He slowly ran his finger across her palm, leaving a trail of the diamond cream. Dru ignored the warm feeling that shimmied up her arm. 'Might as well get some of his money's worth, since you opened it.' She sniffed her hand and then rubbed the cream into her skin. 'A bit of a con I think. It smells and feels just like Olay. Except it's got sparkles in it.'

Connor grunted and inserted his finger into the jar again. Excitement flitted through Dru when a satisfied smile crossed his face.

'Pass me another tissue, please.'

She pulled a tissue from the box and held it out.

'Hold out your hand and spread the tissue over it.' Connor's voice was soft but she could hear the excitement in it. He stood still as she spread the white tissue on her hand.

This time he put two fingers into the jar and frowned as he worked his way to the bottom. 'Yes! Got it!' Connor withdrew his fingers from the jar with painstaking slowness and Dru held her breath as he lifted his hand triumphantly.

He opened his fingers and dropped a glob of something solid onto the tissue.

Dru gasped at the two large violet diamonds nestled in the white bed of tissue. As she lifted her hand, the light caught them and reflected a pattern of violet light onto the wall.

'Diamond fire,' she said slowly, lifting her eyes to meet Connor's intent gaze.

'I think we've found our thief.' Connor's voice was tight with satisfaction. 'You bloody beauty.'

'Adam?' Dru shook her head. 'No, it can't be. He's a lovely guy.

'Many criminals are,' he said drily.

'But why would he take the diamonds and then put them in the jar in my bag?'

'To get them off site. You're driving out tomorrow. I'd put money on there being camera interference at the front gate, and I'd say Adam—or his offsider, I'm sure he has one—will be down there when you leave.'

'But what about the X-ray machine that our bags go through?'

'That's where the carbon paper comes in.' Connor's expression was one of satisfaction.

'What?'

'Carbon paper blurs X-ray images. With the cream already having diamond flakes in it, the larger diamonds will appear distorted as the jar goes through the machine. Very, very clever. But he has to be working with someone else on site.' Connor frowned. 'How long have you known him?'

'Since I started here. Nine months now.'

'Is he extra friendly with anyone that you've noticed?'

'Not really. He does play cards with us very occasionally.'

'Anyone in the card game you've noticed he's palled up with? Rocky? Liam? Dave?

Dru shook her head. 'No I don't think they like him very much. He's not really a guy's guy if you get my drift. He's a hard worker.' Dru narrowed her eyes. 'But hang on, I do remember Adam and Dave talking once about how they both lived on the Gold Coast. I vaguely remember them organising a squash game here once.' She shook her head again. 'I think it was Dave. Or maybe it was Liam. Sorry, I'm not really sure. I didn't take much notice at the time.'

'Okay. We can check Dave out. We haven't looked at him yet.'

Thinking back about conversations, Dru suddenly widened her eyes as her mouth dropped open. 'Oh my God!'

'What? What's wrong?'

'When Adam first asked me to buy this stuff, he said it was for Cathy. His wife's name is Cathy. *Cat*. Is that a coincidence?'

They looked at each other at the same time, eyes wide.

'Cat?' Connor's voice was full of suppressed excitement. 'You said Cat?'

'I did. Cat! Isn't that the name Van Hoebeek heard?' Dru shook her head. 'My God! Not Adam. I can't believe it.'

Connor grabbed her and kissed her hard. 'Cat is the name I was given by Zayed's personal assistant. That, sweetheart, is another awesome link.'

'I'm sorry I didn't think of it before.' Dru couldn't believe how far they'd come in just a few minutes. So, what are we going to do now?'

'First up, I need to talk to John Robinson and Don Finlayson.' Connor glanced at the diamonds still sitting on Dru's palm. 'But before that, we need to secure these diamonds.' He took the tissue from Dru's palm, holding the diamonds carefully. 'I'll let John know what's going on and then we'll set up a plan for tomorrow when you leave the site.' Connor frowned and then walked across to the window. 'You know what this means don't you? Somewhere out there, someone is going to try to access your bag.'

Dru could see his mind ticking over. Here was the ex-cop, the consummate professional, planning and preparing for any eventuality.

'As soon as you're through the front gate security and off site, I'll follow you closely. That way, if he tries anything before you get to Kununurra, I'll be right behind you.'

'Adam wouldn't hurt me.'

Connor's stare was serious, his mouth set in a straight line. 'Dru, don't be naïve. After what you've just been through, you of all people should know that what you see is not always what you get. More often than not.'

Dru dropped her head as a small tingle of fear shimmied through her. 'So what do you think he'll do? Just try and get to my bag?'

'Does he know where you stay in Kununurra?'

Dru thought, trying to remember past conversations with Adam. 'I don't think so.'

'I'll get John to alert the Kununurra police. Have them on standby. The minute Hennessey makes his move they can arrest him. I'll be with you and the bag every minute once we get to town.' Connor ran his hand through his hair. 'But we can't afford anyone else on site knowing about the diamonds. Just in case there's someone else working with him. The most important thing is that you're safe. I wish I could travel with you in your vehicle but I don't want to alert Adam to anything different as you leave.'

'Do you think he'll be the one to take the cream from my bag?'

'I'll bet anything you like that Adam will be down there waiting for you to leave tomorrow. He'll be watching like a hawk when you go through X-ray to make sure you have your bag and that the jar of cream shows up nothing. With any luck, I'll be able to spot his accomplice there too.' Connor reached over the table and took Dru's hand. 'I want you to promise that until I catch you up on the road to Kununurra tomorrow, you'll do exactly as I say.'

'I can look after myself, Connor.'

A smile hovered around his lips. 'Okay. Grab your stuff. My swag's still in the ute. You can have my bed and I'll sleep on the floor in my room. I'm not going to risk anything happening tonight.'

Dru looked at him from beneath her eyelashes. 'I won't take up much room in your bed. There's room for both of us.'

Connor stood and came around beside her. He rested his hands lightly on her shoulders and her nerve endings tingled as he chuckled. 'You're incorrigible, woman.'

His eyes were alight with satisfaction. It looked like they were about to solve the case.

But where would he go then?

Chapter 34

The following afternoon Connor sauntered over to the security booth outside the airport terminal. The guard looked at him and pointed to the building.

'Boss is inside, mate. If that's who you're looking for.'

'The boss?' Connor raised his eyebrows.

'Adam Hennessey. He's in charge here.' The guy raised his hands. 'You're the safety guy, aren't you?'

'I am.'

'Well, no point talking to me, mate. Adam's your man.' The guy looked past Connor as another ute drove into the car park. 'He's inside.'

Connor nodded his thanks and crossed to the building. So far his suspicion was right; Adam was on duty. Dru wasn't going to head out until just before the outgoing plane was due to leave so he had plenty of time to engage him in conversation and watch closely as she went through security.

He knocked on the door and opened it. The room was empty apart from a man sitting at the X-ray machine. Connor kept his expression blank. Things were going down exactly as he'd expected.

'Hey, Steve, isn't it?' Connor injected a friendly tone into his greeting. Steve nodded at Connor as he walked over and then turned his attention back to the screen. 'Adam around?'

Steve jerked his head to the closed door. 'There's someone in there with him. You'll have to wait.'

'Thanks.'

As Connor spoke, there was a bang from inside the office and the sound of raised voices. Steve shrugged and ignored Connor's raised eyebrows. The door opened and Liam Carruthers hurried out with a scowl on his face. He pulled his car keys from his pocket and headed for the exit.

'Hey, you leaving the site, mate?' Steve called out after him.

'Yeah, what's it to you?' Liam's mouth was turned down in a sneer.

'Grab your bag out of your car and join the X-ray queue. You know the rules.'

Liam shifted his gaze to Connor and laughed. 'Ah, following procedure in front of our safety guy. I'm in a hurry. Gotta plane to catch.'

'Don't care, mate. Join the queue.' For the first time, a grin crossed Steve's face as the door opened and a crowd of workers began to fill the building. 'Boom gate won't open until I clear you.'

'Shit.' Liam glared at them both, and then shoved the door open and headed out to the car park.

Connor turned his attention back to the office, wondering what the yelling had been about. The door was slightly ajar but Adam hadn't emerged. He watched for a moment as Steve flicked on the conveyor belt and stared at the screen of the X-ray machine as the first worker reached the body scanner adjacent to the metal bench.

As he crossed the scuffed lino tiles towards Adam's office, Connor watched Liam through the window. He pulled a bag from the back of his ute just as Dru's small dark blue sedan turned off the main road from the mine. Liam waited behind his vehicle until Dru had parked her car. As she got out and crossed the road, he didn't take his eyes from her.

Sleaze, Connor thought.

When Dru was inside the security building, Connor tapped on Adam's half-open door and stepped inside. He was staring intently at the screen in front of him.

'Adam. Got a minute?'

'Hey Connor, what can I do for you?' Adam took his eyes from the screen for a second before turning back to concentrate on it.

'Just wanted a chat with you about a couple of things. You're a hard man to find. I've been looking for you for a while.' Connor leaned forward slightly until he could see the screen.

***

Dru's sweaty palms slipped on the steering wheel as she turned onto the approach to the front security gate of Matsu. She needed to keep calm; if Adam was watching she didn't want to alert him to anything being different. Her bag was sitting on the back seat of her car where she always kept it when she travelled to Kununurra. A small measure of relief eased her tension when she saw Connor's ute parked next to three others in the small car park adjacent to the security building. She recognised Connor's and Liam's but the other two were generic Matsu utes.

Maybe Adam's, maybe not.

She had no idea when or where they would try to retrieve the diamonds from the bottom of her bag. Dru was on edge and trying not to act nervously. She relaxed and smiled, trying to look like someone who was about to enjoy their rostered days off.

The bus with the departing staff on board was parked at the airport terminal and as the workers disembarked, the crowd outside the terminal grew. Connor had deliberately timed her arrival to coincide with their departure to lessen any attention on her. She pulled up at the gate and the security officer gave her a nod.

'Grab your bag and come across to the scanning room, love. Jump on the end of the queue.' He flicked her an apologetic glance. 'Hope you're not in a hurry. The bus just unloaded about fifty workers for the flight out to Perth.'

'No, it's okay. I've got plenty of time.' Dru smiled as she climbed out of her car and grabbed her bag off the back seat. From what she could see, the security process was in full swing and everything appeared to be working today. Her hands slipped on the vinyl handle of the bag as nerves took hold of her again. The jar of cream—wrapped in the carbon paper but without the diamonds—was safely wedged back underneath the lining in the bottom of the bag.

She pushed open the door and joined the end of the queue, forcing herself to stand casually.

The guy in front of her looked at his watch. 'Plane's late.'

She nodded and shot him a smile, taking the opportunity to look around without appearing obvious.

No sign of Connor or Adam. The doors to the two offices in the terminal were both closed.

***

'Yeah, what's up?' Adam's attention was firmly on the screen again. Connor waited until he could see Dru's blonde hair at the end of the queue. He intended keeping a close watch as her bag went through X-ray. He wouldn't have to watch Hennessey for much longer.

'Equipment playing up again, is it?' Connor moved his chair closer as he nodded towards the screen. Adam's face was flushed and his short hair was standing up in spikes as though he'd been running his fingers through it. He pulled a handkerchief from his pocket and wiped the back of his neck.

'No. All good. We've fixed that, I think.'

'What was the problem?' Connor settled back into his chair as the queue on the screen moved forward.

'Electricity supply.' Adam watched as Dru neared the front of the queue. His voice was distracted. 'It was spiking and interfering with the cameras.'

'An easy fix, then.' Dru's bag moved through the X-ray machine as Connor answered.

***

The queue began to move through quickly, and the X-ray conveyor belt came into her sight. The guy manning the camera looked familiar.

Dru reached the metal-topped bench near the camera and lifted her bag up. Her hands were tingling, but she ignored the discomfort.

As her bag slid closer to the X-ray machine, the queue shuffled forward to the body scanner arch.

'Hey, Dru.'

Her head flew up. Liam Carruthers had joined the queue behind her. She put her hand to her chest and forced her voice to normality. 'Hi. You off shift too?'

'I'm outta here. Flying to Japan for a ski. Getting away from this heat.' He was still wearing his hi-vis jacket and Dru wondered why his ute was in the car park if he was flying out.

She nodded with a brief smile; her nerves were on edge because there was no sign of Connor.

'I'm meeting Jules in Darwin. What about you?'

Dru shrugged and kept her voice nonchalant. 'Just going home for a few days.'

The second security guard called her across to the body scanner and she gave Liam a wave. 'Enjoy the snow.' She stepped up to the scanner and stood there until he waved her through. 'Next,' he called to Liam.

Dru's knees were shaking as she picked up her bag and crossed the room to the exit door. Nobody called her back. There was still no sign of Connor; the door to the office was still closed. He must be in there with Adam. She stepped outside into the blistering heat and crossed to her car.

She flinched and pulled her hand back from the door. 'Shit.' The handle was burning hot even though it was late afternoon and the sun was low.

'Car's been checked over,' the guard in the small building called out. 'You're right to go.'

'Thanks.' Dru climbed into her car and turned the fan onto high. She fiddled with the dials for a moment, marking time, and then pulled out her phone to check whether Connor had messaged to say how long he'd be. A horn tooted and she looked up; there were two more work utes waiting to park in the small bay for a security check. Reluctantly she nudged the automatic lever into drive and pulled out onto the road.

***

The screen flicked to another view and Steve Jarvis's face appeared. It was as though he was looking directly at them. If Connor hadn't been watching so closely, he would have missed the almost imperceptible nod. Adam reached over and switched the screen off. 'Looks like everything down here is working okay. So what can I help you with?'

'Just a couple of the procedures in the safety manual for the recovery room. I just wanted to let you know I've suggested a couple of amendments.'

'I'll make a coffee and you can tell me about them now.' Adam pushed his chair back.

'No thanks. I'm fine.' Connor was anxious to get to his ute and follow Dru now that she was through security without a problem. 'Short of time, sorry. I'm heading out today for a break, and I'm about to hit the road. I'll email you.'

Adam crossed to the coffee machine. 'A coffee will keep you awake,' he insisted.

Connor glanced at the closed door. He didn't want to alert Adam to there being anything amiss so he nodded. 'Okay, just a quick one.'

Adam opened the cupboard and took out two cups and the jar of coffee before he slowly filled the kettle.

Connor tried to hide his impatience. 'What was Carruthers' problem before? I noticed him in the mess a couple of weeks back. He's got a short fuse.'

Adam shrugged as he flicked the switch on the kettle. 'He's a dickhead. Always has been, always will be.'

'What was he so upset about?'

'Just a family matter. Nothing to do with work.' Adam pulled out the chair and sat down again.

'Family?' Connor stilled.

'Yeah. Didn't you know he's my brother-in-law? Our wives are sisters.' Adam laughed. 'You know what they say; you can pick your friends but not your family. I lucked right out there.'

Holy fucking hell. Adam Hennessey and Liam Carruthers were related. The implications hit Connor like a sledgehammer. Liam would be through security by now and on the road behind Dru. And he'd watched her so closely when she'd left her car.

No wonder Hennessey was so keen for him to stay now.

'Just remembered something. I have to go.' Connor didn't look back as he hurried from the office and out to his ute. As soon as he was on the road, he'd call John and get the police involved.

'You haven't been cleared from inside, mate. Sorry. You'll have to go back and take your bag.' The security guard leaned out of his booth and the boom gate stayed down.

Bloody hell. The very security system he'd been so focused on was going to hold him up now. Connor grabbed his bag and ran back into the terminal. The office door was closed again.

Chapter 35

Before Dru reached the turn-off to Smokey Creek Road, a Matsu ute sailed passed her with a toot of the horn. But it was Liam, not Connor; he must be flying out from Kununurra. The red dust kicked up by his tyres obscured her vision and it gave her a reason to slow down. Connor had said to drive slowly so he could catch her up. Her palms were slick with sweat and she wiped them one at a time on her cargo shorts before reaching for the bottle of water.

'Come on, Connor,' she whispered under her breath. 'Hurry up.'

In the next few minutes two more Matsu utes passed her car but neither of them were Connor's vehicle. Dru forced herself to stay calm and reached down to switch the radio on, taking her eyes from the road for a brief second. If Connor hadn't caught up to her by the time she reached the Great Northern Highway, she'd park and wait there for him.

The radio blared on and she turned her attention back to the road. A vehicle was stopped ahead of her. She hit the brakes and her car slewed to the shoulder, its front wheels grabbing on the edge of the slight incline.

When she got closer, she saw that it was Liam's vehicle; the M was missing from the tailgate. He had stopped almost in the middle of the road.

She pulled up beside him and put her window down. 'Jeez, Liam, I almost ran into you. What's wrong?' He was crouched beside the back wheel of the ute.

He stood and wiped his hand on the back of his trousers. 'Bloody nail in the tyre! I haven't got time to change it. My flight to Darwin leaves at eight o'clock. If I miss it, I'll miss my international connection. Shit.'

Dru's blood ran cold as apprehension took hold. She'd been flying to Darwin every fortnight for over six months and she knew the schedule. There was no night flight out of Kununurra. She kept her voice bright and casual, although she knew full well he was lying. 'You've got plenty of time to change it. It's only an hour and a half from here. It's just gone five o'clock now. You won't miss your flight.'

He strolled over to her car and leaned in the window. As she stared up at him, she saw his glance flick to her bag on the back seat. She swallowed as he looked back at her.

'You're going to Kununurra, aren't you?' He laughed. 'Of course, you are. Where else is there to go in this godforsaken place? Hop out and give me hand, will you?'

She shook her head. 'Sorry, haven't got time. I'm going down to Wipporing and calling into Rocky's place on the way out.'

'Rocky's at work.'

'Oh?' Dru swallowed. 'I thought he was on leave.'

'He was heading up to the processing plant as I drove out.'

'Are you sure?' Dru tried to stall for time. 'Anyway, I have to go. I know there's a couple more utes coming along behind me. One of the guys can help you.'

'I thought you *were* one of the guys, Dru.' Sarcasm laced his voice as Liam opened her car door. His expression was set and his eyes were cold.

Dru's mouth dried as she looked up. She reached for the handle to pull the door shut again but he held onto it firmly.

'Get out of the car, Dru.' His voice was hard.

'No. I have to go.' Dru put all of her strength into an attempt to pull the door closed. Liam flung the door open again and then reached in and grabbed her shoulder with one hand and her braid with the other.

'Get out of the fucking car.'

Her head jerked back and tears sprang to her eyes as Liam pulled her out of the car by her hair.

'No!' Dru struggled against his hold, but he was too strong for her. 'What the hell do you think you're doing?' She jerked her head to the side and tried to escape his punishing grip.

'Don't make me hurt you, Dru.' Liam pulled a knife from his pocket with his other hand and Dru's eyes widened as he flicked it open.

'Bloody hell, Liam. What do you think you're doing?'

'Who's coming behind you?'

'I don't know.'

'Answer me, bitch.' He let go of her braid and stared at her.

Dru reached a shaking hand up to her stinging scalp and glanced back. In the distance towards the mine, a cloud of red dust swirled into the sky. 'Connor Kirk and a couple of others were in the car park.'

He looked along the road as she looked back at him.

'Put the knife away,' she said softly.

'You're coming with me,' he growled.

'No.'

Liam took a step towards her and Dru put her arm up instinctively. He slashed at her and pain lanced through the inside of Dru's forearm. She froze as he lifted the knife again.

'Get in the fucking ute.' His voice was a snarl.

Dru pulled away from him and shook her head. 'Why?'

'Do as I say or you'll be fucking sorry.' Liam grabbed her arm and dragged her across to his ute. He shoved her up and into the passenger side and slammed the door behind her. The locks clicked shut as Dru sprawled across the passenger seat.

Dru pulled herself back up to a sitting position and looked out the window. Liam was running back to her car about twenty meters away. Her arm felt wet and she gagged as she looked down. Blood was streaming from a long gaping wound. Her head spun but she forced the nausea down as she scrambled across to the driver's side.

I have to get away.

Liam's ute was the same as hers back at the mine and she knew that the unlock override for the door was on the driver's door next to the window buttons. She pressed it and then opened the driver's side door and half climbed, half fell into the fine red dust in the middle of the road.

'Hey! Stop!'

Dru stumbled to her feet and took off. She sprinted up the middle of the road, cradling her injured arm against her stomach, fighting the dizziness that was threatening to overcome her. She couldn't believe that Liam had slashed her arm. She had to get away from him. If he'd cut her once he would do it again, now that she knew he was the thief.

'Stop there, you bitch.'

Dru slowed for an instant and looked back over her shoulder. Liam had her bag and was throwing it into the back of his ute.

Her breath came in harsh gasps as she tried to put more distance between herself and the two vehicles. The dust cloud up the road had disappeared and there was no sign of any cars between them and the mine.

Where the hell are you, Connor? This was exactly the scenario that he'd expected. Dru had thought that they wouldn't try anything until Kununurra. And Connor and Greg had discounted Liam.

But now that he had showed his hand, Liam wasn't going to let her get away from him. A door slammed, followed by the rattling roar of his diesel engine. Dru turned away from the road and jumped down the slight incline. Perspiration dripped from her forehead into her eyes, and she reached up with her good arm and brushed it away as she ran down the rocky hill as fast as she could.

Desperately looking around, she noticed a narrow ridge off to her left and she ran towards it. Her feet slipped on the small rocks on the side of the hill, and she stumbled as she began to climb again, managing to regain her balance before she pitched headfirst onto the uneven ground. Between the Matsu Range and the Purnululu National Park, the semi-arid savannah grasslands rolled in waves of volcanic ridges and hills riddled with caves and gorges. If she could get over the lip on the edge of the ridge there would have to be somewhere to hide and it would give Connor time to get here. Her phone was in the car so she couldn't even call for help. Her breath hitched and her head spun as she stumbled up the hill. In the distance, Liam's motor stopped and a car door slammed. Rough branches scratched at her face and legs as she pushed her way through the scrubby bush.

God, she'd hoped that Liam would take off once he had the bag. But now she knew he wouldn't let her get away.

Dru's chest burned with the effort of climbing the steep hill. Each gasping breath of hot air she took in burned her throat and dried her mouth. If she could just get to the edge before he caught up with her.

Come on, Connor!

Taking the final step to the top of the ridge, Dru gasped as a deep, sloping drop on the other side yawned below her.

Not a blasted cave to be seen.

For a moment she stood looking down the steep hill to a gully dotted with boab trees. A shout from behind spurred her on and she jumped down, putting her good arm over her bleeding forearm to protect it.

Over and over, she half rolled, half slid down the slope. Sharp rocks and sticks bruised her body until her right leg jarred against the rough edge of a fallen log and she came to a sudden stop near the bottom of the hill. Lying there, trying to catch her breath, Dru looked up. Liam was up on the edge of the ridge, with his hands on his hips. She watched as he carefully climbed over the edge and began to make his way down towards her.

Dru blinked and swallowed as the view in front of her shimmered and faded. Her arm was throbbing. Blood and clear fluid were seeping out of the cut. The edges of the long wound gaped open, sticky with red dirt; her cargo pants and shirt were damp with blood. She had to fight this faintness that was pricking at the edges of her vision; she'd got this far and there was no way she was stopping now.

Pushing herself up to her feet, she took off at a slow run, bent over, desperately looking around for somewhere to hide. A pile of dead branches from a large boab tree blocked her way and Dru skirted around them. She took a moment to look up; Liam was picking his way down the hill, and not looking directly at her. Ahead was a stand of boab trees and she ran quickly and pressed herself behind one with a huge trunk. Shuffling around it, she noticed a smaller tree with a narrow opening at its base. She stared at it for a moment before glancing back at Liam. He'd stopped about a third of the way down and was looking back up the hill. As Dru watched him, working out if she could dive across to the tree before he looked back down to her, the sound of another vehicle coming along the road reached her.

Thank God.

She scurried across to the tree and used her good hand to push away the cobwebs that covered the tiny space. Trying not to think of spiders and snakes or other creatures living in the tree, she crawled into the hollow. As Dru lay back, the dead leaves crackled and a roaring buzz filled her ears as her vision faded to black.

Chapter 36

Connor grunted with frustration as he planted the accelerator to the floor. The back of the ute fishtailed and by the time the boom gate came down behind the vehicle, he was a hundred metres down the road. The bitumen turned to gravel but he didn't slow as he turned off the entry road and headed east across the desert.

Bloody hell.

Dru was on the road ahead . . . and so was Liam Carruthers. He would never forgive himself if Carruthers hurt her, He would never forget the feeling that had coursed through him when Adam revealed their connection. The moment he realised that Liam was out there in the desert, chasing after the diamonds he believed were in Dru's bag.

He gripped the steering wheel and stared ahead. In the far distance a pall of dust indicated that a car was on the road ahead. Perspiration ran down his face and Connor brushed it away angrily, resisting the temptation to drive faster. He'd be no use to Dru if he rolled the car. The road was getting worse the further he went.

'Shit!' The exclamation left his lips as he crested a slight incline. Dru's car was parked at a crazy angle and its front wheels were hanging over the incline at the edge of the road. A few hundred metres ahead, a Matsu ute was roaring away, heading north. It was Carruthers' ute; Connor recognised the tailgate with the missing letter. He slammed his foot on the brakes and swerved to a stop. Opening the door, he jumped out and ran to Dru's car. The driver's side door was open but she wasn't there. Her phone was on the passenger seat with her small pack. He looked into the back; the large bag was no longer there. So the bastard had taken her and the bag with him. Connor slammed his fists on the roof of the car as anger coursed through him. He turned to run back to his ute but stopped as he noticed what looked like blood on the road beside Dru's car. He crouched down and touched the damp soil. It was still warm and sticky. He looked around but couldn't see any more.

Rage consumed him. He'd kill the bastard if he'd hurt Dru. He ran for his ute and this time he pushed it to its limit as he tried to catch up to the vehicle in front of him.

***

When Dru woke, it was pitch black and her arm was stiff and throbbing. She blinked and opened her eyes wide but she couldn't see anything. Tendrils of panic wound their way around her chest. She'd hated the dark ever since Dad had died.

Her mouth was parched and her head was sore where Liam had pulled at her hair. Her arm was burning and when she tried to move it, it was stuck to the front of her T-shirt. She ran her tongue around her mouth but it was as dry as her lips. All was quiet around her but she wasn't game to move in case he was still out there.

Dots of light danced across her eyes and she wondered if Zayed had a torch and was looking in all of the trees. A bubble of laughter threatened as she imagined him walking from tree to tree in the desert. How did he get here? Had he finally found her? Then she realised if she closed her eyes, the lights were still there. And it wasn't Zayed looking for her, it was Liam. Hot tears splashed her cheeks and Dru put her finger up and tried to catch one but she was too tired and it hurt her bad arm. Closing her eyes, she let sleep take her into its soothing depth.

Something ran across her bare leg and she jerked awake again. She didn't have enough energy to crawl away from whatever creature was in here with her. She closed her eyes again and whispered, 'Connor, come and find me . . . please.'

But the night was still and there was no one to hear her.

***

Connor held back his temper and focused on the best strategy to approach Carruthers. He wouldn't put Dru in any more danger than she was already in. When Carruthers' ute appeared ahead, he eased back on the accelerator. As hard as it was, he made sure he stayed at least a kilometre behind. After they had both turned onto the sealed Great Northern Highway, Connor kept half an eye on the road and pulled out his phone. He hit speed dial for Greg and flicked the phone onto Bluetooth.

'Come on, mate, pick up, pick up.' It was late and Greg was probably on the turps by now. A surge of relief ran though him when Greg picked up and his voice was clear and not slurred. 'Hey, Kirkie, how's it hangin'? Sorry, I've got nothing more for you, mate.'

'Forget that. I need your help, Greg. It's Liam Carruthers and he's got Dru. I'm going after them now.'

'Jesus! Where are you? What do you need me to do?'

'We're on the road from Matsu to Kununurra. I'm behind the bastard, and he's just turned onto the highway north. I know the mobile service drops out on this part of the road. Can you call the Kununurra police and tell them what's happening? If they won't listen to you, insist they call John Robinson in Perth. He was going to put them on standby anyway. We're about an hour to the south of town.' Connor took a breath. 'After that, call John Robinson and tell him it's Liam Carruthers who's running the diamond racket. Tell him I've got evidence and at least one accomplice—maybe two: Hennessey is involved, and possibly Steve Jarvis as well.

'Rightio, I'm on it. Be careful, mate.'

Connor tagged Carruthers's ute all the way to Kununurra; it frustrated the hell out of him that he was too far back to see if Dru was in the vehicle with him.

Monotonous red desert and scrubby bush flashed past his window in the fading light. It seemed as though everything was in slow motion. The time dragged and Connor pushed away the worst scenarios that kept filling his thoughts. All he could hope was that

Carruthers hadn't yet looked for the diamonds in Dru's bag. He gripped the wheel until his knuckles were white.

It was almost dark when they caught up to a line of caravans on the highway close to Kununurra. Connor eased back his speed. As he pulled further back, flashing lights appeared from the north. As Connor watched, a police car turned across the road and blocked Carruthers' path. Connor's grip on the steering wheel relaxed and he pulled over to the side of the highway behind the police car. By the time he was out of his ute, they had Carruthers face down against the bonnet of his vehicle. Connor ran to the front and looked inside. It was dark but Dru's bag was the only thing inside.

'Where is she?' He turned to Liam and reached to grab him, but one of the policemen stepped between them.

'We'll deal with this, sir.'

'What have you done with her?' Connor put his face close to Carruthers but the man stared at him, a scowl on his face.

'The woman whose bag he has in his vehicle –' Connor choked on the words as he approached the senior policeman '– her car is abandoned about eighty kilometres back on the Matsu road and there's blood on the ground. She's not there. He's done something to her.'

This time Connor couldn't help himself. He grabbed Carruthers' chin and pushed his head back against the ute. Two of the policeman turned away and the senior guy moved closer.

'Where is she, you lowlife?' Connor growled. 'What have you done with Dru?'

'This is assault. Get him off me.' Carruthers jerked his head away from Connor's grip.

'What the fuck have you done with her?' He yanked Carruthers' shirt with his other hand.

'You can't pin it on me. She took off into the desert.'

Connor's mouth dried. 'Where?'

Carruthers shrugged. 'Back there somewhere.'

'I'm going back to find her,' he called to the senior officer as he shoved Carruthers back against the ute. 'Can you get a search team together?' Connor ran back to his vehicle and slammed it into gear. He threw it into a U-turn when the road was clear and dialled Greg again. 'Greg, Dru's not with him. I'm going back to where her car was.' Frustration gripped him. It was at least an hour back there.

'Shit, that's not good.'

Connor cursed as he came to a line of slow traffic. 'Jesus, there's a bank of traffic heading south.

'I'll get there as soon as I can,' Greg said. 'I'm on my way into town. I'll be behind you.

'Do you know anyone who knows this area well?' Connor glanced in the rear-vision mirror and pulled out, overtaking three long caravans. 'The desert, I mean.'

'Not really. But Wipporing's not far from the mine. There's an aboriginal settlement there. Do you know any of the local blokes at the mine?'

'Jesus, yes. Rocky Cardella, but I don't know where to find him.'

'Leave it with me, mate. I'll track him down. See you in an hour or so.'

The trip back on the Great Northern Highway was frustrating; a couple of times Connor had to slow as kangaroos crossed the road ahead of his car. Once he turned onto the dirt, there was no traffic and he put his foot down. He glanced back; one of the police vehicles was behind him. He let out a relieved breath. At least there'd be someone to help him until Greg turned up.

Eventually his headlights revealed Dru's sedan in the distance. He pulled up, raced across and flung open the driver's side door. He scrabbled around in the dark, looking for the lever that popped the boot. Finally his fingers found it underneath the left side of the steering column. By this time, the two policemen had crossed the road and stood beside him with a torch. He flicked the lever with a click.

'What are you looking for, mate?'

All sorts of scenes had run though Connor's head as he'd raced down the highway.

'He might have locked her in the boot.' Connor's mouth dried as he walked around to the back of the car and lifted the boot open.

He put his hand to his face as he stared at the space faintly lit by the interior light.

It was empty.

Chapter 37

'Thank you.' Connor nodded at the policewoman who handed him a bottle of cold water. He leaned back on the ute and stared past her. The sky was gradually lightening on the eastern horizon. Shards of gold lit the clouds hovering over the desert and the inky darkness of the sky began to fade.

Frustration held him rigid; they had searched all night to no avail. His clothes were stiff with perspiration and his legs were aching from climbing up and down ridges. The group of searchers had grown as the night had progressed; more police had arrived and John Robinson had ordered the mine rescue team to join the search. They had mapped a search grid; five kilometres up and down the road and three kilometres into the desert on each side. A couple more blood splatters had been found, but nothing more.

'How you going, mate?' Greg appeared beside him as Connor wiped his mouth with the back of his hand.

'It's like looking for the proverbial needle, isn't it?' Connor put the empty water bottle on the roof of the car. He stretched his leg out as a cramp seized his thigh.

'You need to have a rest. You've been going nonstop all night.'

'We don't even bloody know if we're looking in the right place, do we?' He slammed a fist into his palm. 'Christ, she could be anywhere.'

'Calm down, Kirkie. You'll be no use to anyone if you lose the plot. Didn't you follow Carruthers all the way from here?'

Connor nodded.

'And you didn't see him pull up, so she has to around here somewhere. She might have headed back towards the mine.' He looked at Connor quizzically. 'Hold on. There's more to this than just a missing person, isn't there?'

'Yeah, I owe Dru for thinking she was in this.'

'It wasn't that bad a call. That money in her account was a flag. It would have fooled the best.' Greg regarded him intently. 'Is that all?'

Connor looked at Greg as the sun cleared the horizon in a burst of golden light. His old partner had shaved and had a haircut since he'd last seen him, and was looking a lot closer to normal than he had for a long time.

'Dru's a pretty special person. She's been through a lot over the past few years.' He shook his head and pushed away from the ute. 'Come on, we're wasting time. It's going to get bloody hot in the next couple of hours and she's been out there all night without water.'

'Wait.' Greg grabbed his arm.

A vehicle was coming in quickly from the west. They both stood and stared as the dust cloud got closer. Connor started forward as it slewed to a stop.

'It's Rocky!'

The aboriginal man climbed out of the ute and crossed the road to Connor. 'Sorry, I was visiting some family over on the other side of the Bungle Bungles. I only just got the message.' He looked around at the group of people, waiting for instructions. 'I guess she hasn't turned up yet?'

'No.' Connor took a deep breath. 'I'm heading out again now.'

'No. Wait here with me. Tell me exactly what happened and where she went into the desert.'

'That's the fucking problem, mate. We don't even know for sure if she's out there. Carruthers won't say a word.'

'Liam Carruthers?' Rocky's brow furrowed in a frown. 'What's he got to do with Dru?'

'Long story. All we know is that Dru is missing and her car is here.' Connor's voice shook. 'And there's blood on the road.'

Rocky knelt beside Dru's car. He squatted there for a long time and Connor's impatience grew. He took a step forward but Greg stayed him with a hand on his arm.

'Be patient, mate. This is our best chance. We've done no good by ourselves and we've had hours to search. This bloke will know the desert better than any of us.'

'What's got into you, Greg? You're usually too cynical to believe in anything like that.'

Greg's reply was short. 'You can be an arrogant prick at times. You always did think you knew it all, Kirk. Now settle down and wait.'

Rocky moved to the side of the road and stood at the edge of the incline with his hand to his eyes. He stared ahead across the terrain and eventually he turned to Connor and the police sergeant who had walked across to stand with them.

'I believe she's still out there, and she's injured.'

'Clever deduction, mate.' Connor's voice was full of frustration.

'I know you're hurting for her.' Rocky's dark eyes stayed on Connor. 'Dru knows this landscape. She's been working here for a while now, and she grew up in the bush. She would have known where to hide when he chased her.'

'Chased her?' Connor said.

'That's the easy part.' Rocky gestured to the road. 'You can see that easily.' He put his car keys in his pocket and pulled out a torn baseball cap and pushed it onto his head. 'Bring some water. We have to find her quickly.' He met Connor's gaze and Connor frowned at the worry on the aboriginal man's face.

Rocky turned to the policeman. 'Make sure there's an ambulance here when we bring Dru back. I'm worried about how much blood she's lost.'

Greg and Connor stared at each other and Connor shook his head as a feeling of doom settled over him.

***

Dru was dreaming of her father. His arms were around her and he was keeping her safe. The familiar smell of his aftershave soothed her. He pulled her back against his hard chest, just as he had when she was a little girl. She tried to turn around to see him but her eyes wouldn't open. The softness of his flannel shirt tickled her face as she turned into his chest. Licking her lips, she tried to speak but her voice wouldn't come. Her arm was throbbing and the heat had gone up into her shoulder. She woke with a start and opened her eyes; a soft filtered light was coming in through the hole in the trunk. She lowered her head and a sharp pain ran down her neck as she looked at her arm. Slowly, she pulled her forearm away from her chest and as it came away from her T-shirt, the cut started to bleed again. Dru gagged as her stomach roiled and a cold feeling ran through her blood. This time she welcomed the blackness as the pain took over.

***

Connor and Greg followed Rocky down the hill and then across to the ridge slightly to the east.

'This is the right way.' Rocky's tone was full of confidence.

'We've already searched down here. We've searched every bloody ridge, and every cave for three kilometres.' Connor's frustration was growing. He closed his eyes and made a deal with himself. If Dru was all right, he would change. He'd give up his investigation work and think about his future. Rocky's quiet triumphant cry interrupted his thoughts.

'She's down here.'

Connor ran over to him.

'How do you know that?' Greg asked quietly.

'I just know. The land tells me,' Rocky said with a shrug. 'I can see where she has walked up here but it was before dark last night.'

'We've been here already. We've called her till we were hoarse and we had searchlights on the hills all night.' Connor slipped and caught himself as the small stones skittered under his boots. He was so bloody tired but he wasn't going to stop until they found Dru. 'I'm going back up the top. We've got to look on the other side.'

'No. Stay here. We're going to need a few men to carry her up.' The aboriginal man walked around in a circle at the edge of the ridge, looking at the ground. He let out a grunt of satisfaction. 'This is where she went down.'

Rocky climbed carefully over the ridge and Connor followed him with Greg close behind. Rocky paused halfway down the hill and stared ahead. He stood for a few minutes without moving and Connor chafed with impatience.

'That way.'

Connor followed the direction of Rocky's arm but there was nothing to see apart from rolling hills, each one with a ridge that dropped off before the next hill rose. He wiped sweat from his brow. The sun had climbed higher and the heat was becoming intense.

'We have to find her quickly. It's getting too hot.' Rocky's words held an urgency that hadn't been there before and he took off like a mountain goat, running down the rocky slope. Connor and Greg followed him as quickly as they could. At the bottom of the hill there was a small clearing with a few trees scattered along the gully. Connor looked at the next ridge; it was at least a hundred metre climb up a steep slope. He crouched down as he caught his breath.

'Dru? Can you hear me?' Rocky's voice was soft as he almost crooned the words. 'She's here. I can feel her. She's in a bad way.' He moved slowly through the clearing, his gaze firmly on the ground. Connor looked at Greg and then took off after Rocky. He kept his attention on the ground as he followed the smaller man; the grass was long and there were a couple of dry creek beds running along beside of the copse of trees. They reached the base of the next hill and Rocky shook his head.

'I was wrong. She's not here.' He took off up the hill and Greg followed him but something held Connor back. Behind him was a large boab tree surrounded by dead branches. He walked towards it, listening intently; he could have sworn he'd heard a soft sound. He held his head still and listened, but the only sound was the gentle sigh of the wind in the trees. As he approached the fat boab, a pile of dead branches blocked his way. Behind it was a smaller tree with a gaping hole in its trunk. He crouched down and looked inside. Elation filled him as he saw Dru's blonde hair moving in the slight breeze.

Getting her out of the small space in the trunk of the tree was tricky but Rocky climbed in and managed to move her to the opening. Connor and Greg worked together to lift her out. To Connor's concern, Dru didn't stir as they moved her onto the flat ground between the trees. Her eyes stayed closed and her cheeks were flushed and dry, her breathing shallow. The front of her T-shirt was stained with blood and her injured forearm was red and swollen.

Connor fought to stop his hands shaking. 'Come on. We have to get her out of here.'

'Patience, Connor.' Rocky dug into his small backpack and handed a bottle of water to Connor. 'Put some water in your hand and get as much around her mouth as you can while I make a sling.' He took his T-shirt off and formed a sling to protect her injured arm. Meanwhile Connor dipped his finger into the water bottle and wet Dru's lips. Fear gripped him when she didn't move.

God, let her be okay.

'Okay, let's go,' Rocky said. Connor lifted her into his arms.

As they made their way up the hill, Greg helped him support Dru and Rocky ran ahead to alert the search team and the paramedics. Each time Connor stopped to catch his breath, Greg took some of the weight. By the time they reached the road, his legs were burning and his chest was tight. Perspiration was running down into his eyes and blurring his vision.

At last, the paramedics lifted her from his arms. Connor turned to follow them across to the mine rescue ambulance but Greg grabbed his arm and shoved a bottle of water into his hand. 'Drink that. You look like you're about to flake out.'

'I'll kill the bastard,' Connor growled in a hoarse voice.

'You can queue up behind me.' Rocky's eyes were dark and glittering. 'What happened? Why was she with Liam in the first place?'

Connor shook his head. 'Later.' When the paramedics had finished assessing Dru, he hurried over. 'Is she going to be okay?' His voice broke but he didn't care.

'We're taking her into Kununurra. She's badly dehydrated and the wound on her arm needs stitching. It looks to be infected too.' The paramedics exchanged a concerned glance.

Connor watched helplessly as they closed the back of the ambulance and walked around to the front. No matter how worried he was, he had no claim on Dru; he couldn't ask to go in the ambulance with her.

'I'll drive you to town, mate. You're too knackered to drive yourself.' Greg gestured to his beat-up vehicle and Connor nodded.

'Thanks.' He ran over to his ute, picked up his bag from the back and locked the vehicle.

'I'll be right behind you,' Rocky said.

Chapter 38

Kununurra Hospital

It was late afternoon before Connor was allowed into the private room where Dru was sleeping. She had regained consciousness and her wound had been flushed out and stitched. Before he and Rocky went to the waiting room outside the ward, Connor spoke to the police sergeant.

Greg had headed back home to Wyndham to finalise the evidence for Connor's report, now that they knew Adam Hennessey and Liam Carruthers had masterminded the theft. Once Connor had explained everything to Rocky, they sat quietly together waiting for the doctor. Finally, the doctor walked up the corridor and Connor stood to meet him.

'Is Dru going to be all right?'

'We're rehydrating her and she's on an IV drip for the infected wound. It'll take twenty-four hours or so till she starts to feel a bit better but she'll be fine.'

'How long till I can see her?'

The doctor stared back at him. 'Are you a relative?'

Connor lifted his chin. 'I'm her partner.'

Rocky looked at Connor. It was hard to read the expression on his face but after a moment he nodded and mumbled something that Connor didn't catch.

'You can go in now then. She's asleep but you can sit with her.' The doctor looked at his watch. 'I'll be back to check on her later tonight.'

Connor paused outside the room to scrub his hands and arms with anti-bacterial gel. As he rubbed his hands together, Rocky sidled over to him. 'You tell Dru I said to get better quick. She's a good woman.'

Connor nodded. 'She is.'

'And you take good care of her.' Rocky pointed at him as he turned to leave, but he was grinning. 'Or you'll have me to deal with. Tell her I said you're all right.'

As Connor was about to open the door to Dru's room, his phone vibrated in his pocket. He paused and picked up.

It was Greg. 'Kirkie, I've got good and bad news.'

As Connor listened to what Greg had discovered, he stared at the closed door in front of him. 'Thanks, I'll call you later tonight. Keep at it.'

'How's Dru,' Greg asked.

'She's going to be okay.' Connor slipped the phone into his pocket and pushed open the door. He walked across to the bed, conscious of being quiet. Dru was propped up on three pillows and her head was to one side, her eyes closed. The red flush had left her cheeks and her colour was good. Her lips were shiny where they had been smeared with a lubricating gel. One arm was in a sling, and the other had a cannula inserted in the back of her hand.

Connor pulled the chair close to the bed and sat down, not taking his eyes from her. Her chest rose and fell softly and he reached out and touched her hand lightly. She murmured softly in her sleep but he couldn't make out her words.

He put his head in his hands. This case had almost lost him the first person he had cared about in a long time. He sat there for a long time with his eyes closed, thankful that Dru was going to be okay.

Eventually Connor lifted his head and looked at Dru as he thought about his future. He took her hand. Life was about to change for him; it was time to move on to something else. The only problem was that he didn't have anywhere to go. It had been a long time since he'd had a place he called home. Weariness pulled at every muscle in his body. He yawned and leaned his head back against the wall.

If the truth be known, he didn't want to be anywhere else.

***

Dru opened her eyes slowly. Her left hand was warm and she couldn't move it. She turned her head slowly and looked down. A tanned hand held hers firmly on a white pillow on the side of the bed. She looked around; when she'd woken up earlier the doctor told her she had been brought in by the mine rescue ambulance. It had taken a few moments to remember what had happened. The last thing she recalled with any certainty was climbing into the cavity of the boab tree.

Slowly she lifted her gaze from their joined hands to the man sitting in the chair. Connor's head was back against the wall and his eyes were closed. 'Connor,' she whispered softly.

He didn't move; he was fast asleep. Dru let her eyes linger on his face. Dark stubble dotted his strong jawline and his eyes were shadowed. His mouth was relaxed in sleep. A rush of feeling filled her chest. Her eyes ached with unshed tears and she swallowed them back.

The safety that she had sought in the remote Kimberley had proved elusive, but now that she was safe from Liam, and Zayed couldn't reach her, her life would settle back to normal; the same daily routine with a fortnightly visit to her sterile apartment in Darwin.

But that wasn't what she wanted anymore.

The isolation that she had once craved now frightened her. The ice that had encased her heart had cracked while she had been with Connor. She wasn't used to the long-forgotten emotions that now flooded through her; she'd managed to keep herself immune from feeling anything at all since Dad had been murdered.

But they hurt.

Hot tears ran down her cheeks, but with one arm strapped to her chest and the other hand firmly in Connor's grip, Dru couldn't do anything about them. She put her head back and sniffed.

'Dru.' Connor let go of her hand and rubbed his eyes with his fists like a small child. 'Thank God. You're awake. How are you feeling?' He pulled his chair closer to the bed.

Dru scrubbed at her cheeks, still embarrassed. She never cried in public; but this was the second time she'd broken down in front of Connor. The tubing attached to her wrist brushed her face and she put her hand down carefully onto the pillow. 'Tired. But I'm okay.'

'Is your arm hurting?' Connor's mouth was set in a straight line.

'A little bit of a throb now and then but it's not too bad.'

Connor's eyes were bleak as he held her gaze. 'I thought I'd go crazy when we couldn't find you.'

'I'm fine.' If she said it often enough, she would believe it too. The raw emotion coursing through her was scaring her. 'You found me, didn't you? I opened my eyes and you were there. I knew I was going to be okay then.'

'I wouldn't have found you without Rocky's help. He said to tell you to get better quick.' Connor's lips tilted in a small smile. 'Don't cry, Dru. It's all okay. You're going to be fine. You'll be back at work before you know it.'

Her voice wavered with the embarrassment of not being able to stop the tears. 'And what about you? Where will you be?'

Connor stared at her intently. 'I'll be trying to clean up this mess of a case.'

Dru sniffed and reached for a tissue. 'I thought it was all sorted. We were wrong, weren't we? It was Liam after all, not Adam?'

'No, it was both of them. They were working together.' Connor shook his head. 'That's why I was late following you. Adam must have suspected something. He did his best to hold me up. As soon as he told me Liam was his brother-in-law, I took off after you. But I wasn't fast enough. I'm sorry I put your life in danger. I should have been with you on the road.'

'It's not your fault.' Dru focused on Connor's words and pushed away the thought of him leaving. 'If it weren't for you, the diamonds would still have been in my bag. Who knows what would have happened to me if you hadn't been here investigating? This is the second time you've saved my life. If you hadn't intervened, I'd probably be in Zayed's penthouse in Dubai, trying to figure out a way to get home.' Her voice was muffled as wiped away the tears. As she squeezed the now-sodden tissue in her fingers, Connor reached over and took her hand. She looked down at his fingers wrapped around her hand, while he waited for her to regain her composure.

'Can I get you a drink?' His quiet and steady voice calmed her.

'Yes please.'

Connor stood and poured some water into the plastic cup on the table beside the bed. He passed it to her and Dru drank deeply.

'Now tell me,' she asked. 'You know who the thieves are.'

Connor sat back in the plastic chair, his body tense. Dru's fingers itched to reach out and touch him but she resisted the temptation.

'Liam Carruthers and Adam Hennessey are brothers-in-law, married to two sisters. Cathy Hennessey—the "Cat" from Antwerp—and Julie, Liam's wife, set up GCH, Gold Coast Holdings, a couple of years back. Hennessey started at Matsu before that, and that must have been when they hatched the plan. Carruthers was the one getting the diamonds from the recovery room while Hennessey was interfering with the cameras. The Kununurra police have interviewed Steve Jarvis this afternoon, and he has admitted letting Liam Carruthers through a few times without following proper procedure. Hennessey caught him drinking on the job and threatened him with dismissal, so on Hennessey's orders he turned a blind eye to Carruthers being in the recovery area when he shouldn't have been. He claims he wasn't directly involved, but Greg said there's been a few deposits in his account he can't explain.'

'So where's Adam now?'

'I left him at the office in the airport when I took off after you and Liam.' Connor rubbed his chin with his hand. 'Hennessey caught the flight to Perth as soon as I left him. He was arrested when they landed.'

'What about the sisters?'

'They've done a runner apparently. Greg took a call from John Robinson a little while ago.' Connor's laugh was dry. 'They've alerted the Federal Police and informed Interpol.'

'And Liam?'

'In the lockup at Kununurra.'

'There's a lot of things I still don't understand.' Dru put her hand to her head.

'What don't you understand?'

'Why did they bother with the cream? Who put it in my bag and why did they use me as the courier?'

'John Robinson called me earlier. He's already been to police headquarters in Perth and was allowed to talk to Adam. Apparently he's singing like a bird and trying to blame the whole thing on Carruthers. He claims that Liam smuggled the first few diamonds out while Steve Jarvis turned a blind eye. But when Don Finlay told Adam that they were overhauling the whole security procedure, they had to come up with another way of getting the diamonds out. Hence, they planted it in the cream. That way if something had gone wrong on the way out, you would have got the blame. As for who broke into your room; my money's on Adam—he would have had keys.'

'What about Zayed? How is he involved?'

'You know what? I really believe he was an innocent player the whole time—or at least, he had no direct knowledge that the diamonds he'd bought were stolen.' He smiled. 'But even if they can't pin anything on him, he's still six million dollars out of pocket and I doubt if he'll see the money for a long time.'

'If at all. Couldn't happen to a more deserving person.' Dru pulled a face. She looked down as Connor picked up her hand and smoothed his thumb over her skin. 'So . . .' Dru spoke slowly. 'Your job here is done? Or at Matsu, I mean.'

'I suppose it is.' Connor stared past her as though he found the blank wall behind her suddenly interesting.

'So where to now?' She kept her voice bright, even though her heart was splitting into icy shards. 'More diamond thefts or back to chasing drug runners?'

'I don't know, Dru.'

The look on Connor's face and the slump of his shoulders tore at her.

'We made a good team, didn't we?'

'We did.'

A tendril of hope flared when Connor lifted her hand to his lips. He held her eyes with his. 'I'll be honest with you. I don't want to leave.'

The hope burned a little brighter in her chest. 'So, stay.'

Dru pushed away the uncertainty that was telling her to just be quiet and let it go.

Let *him* go.

But she couldn't. She swallowed and squeezed his hand. 'I've got a perfectly good apartment that sits empty half the time. It would be good to have someone there when I'm at the mine.'

Connor stood and moved closer to her. His breath brushed against her cheek as he lowered his head to rest against hers. 'What about when you're home?

'That's when it would be *really* good to have you there.'

Dru closed her eyes as Connor's lips brushed against hers.

Chapter 39

24   *December*
Darwin

Dru stood back and surveyed her once bare apartment. She had surprised herself. In the corner of the living room was a huge pine tree that Connor had helped her decorate. She grinned as she reached up and adjusted the angel on the top. A small grimace ended her smile as the healing cut on her arm pulled tight. The stitches had come out but the wound was still tender. The smell of pine wafted around her. Who would ever have thought you could buy a real Christmas tree in Darwin in the heat of the tropical summer? But something she was discovering about Connor was that once he set his mind to something, it happened.

The red table napkins on the white tablecloth were in stark contrast to the all-white minimalist decor in her apartment. The low coffee table was covered with wrapping paper and sticky tape and ribbon where she was almost done with wrapping the gifts.

Last Christmas she had been in Dubai. She had spent the day alone in her apartment and had a 'Christmas call' with Mum and Emma and Jeremy. This year was going to be very different. The doctor had given her a month off work, and she'd added a month's annual leave to that as well—it was too hot to work on site in summer.

The buzzer announcing someone at the door downstairs brought her out of her daydream and she crossed to the intercom on the wall.

'Only me, Dru.' Connor's voice was clear.

He'd decided to take some time off and settle in Darwin for a while before he looked for a job. She was getting used to having him around, and their relationship was unfurling slowly. The night in Antwerp had been the catalyst of change for them both and she acknowledged that they were still learning to trust again. A smile crossed her face as she buzzed him up.

It was time he had a key.

Connor had refused to move in with her. He'd insisted on renting a small unit on a short lease across in Cullen Bay, but he spent more time at her place than he did over there.

She crossed the room, opened the door and waited for the lift to come up. The door to the lift pinged open and Connor stepped out, his arms full of parcels and shopping bags.

'Where the heck are we going to put all that stuff?' she asked with a smile. 'We have to leave for the airport soon.' He juggled a couple of parcels and she went to grab the one that was falling but he shook his head.

'Uh-uh, not that one.'

Connor's face was tanned and the shadows that had etched his face when she'd first met him had gone. Talking through his undignified exit from the Federal Police had been cathartic for him.

She held the door open and he dropped the bags on the coffee table next to her mess.

'How long have we got to get these wrapped?' He still held onto the small parcel that had slipped.

'What's in that one?' She tilted her head to the side.

'Never you mind.' Connor slipped the package into his shirt pocket, and she reached for it playfully. 'You're worse than a kid at Christmas.'

'It'll be the first Christmas we've all spent together since Dad died.'

Connor grabbed for her fingers and she looked up with a smile as he pulled her closer to him.

'I hope it's a happy one for you.'

'And for you, too.' She spoke softly as he held her gaze. 'I owe you so much, Connor.

He shook his head. 'No you don't. This path to getting our lives on track is a joint effort. No debts anywhere. Okay?'

'Okay.' Dru closed her eyes as his lips brushed against her mouth.

***

Connor stood behind Dru in the arrivals lounge at Darwin airport. She was hopping from foot to foot, barely able to contain her excitement as they waited for the flight from Cairns to arrive. She kept looking over at the door and then at her watch. Her sister, Ellie and her partner, Kane were supposed to be meeting them here at the airport. They were driving in from the family mango farm out near Kakadu.

'It's not like Ellie to be late.' Dru's voice was worried and she started to shake her fingers.

'It's Christmas Eve. The traffic will be bad.' He rubbed his hands down her arms and held her hands. 'And what did you forget?'

'Okay. I'm not worried. I'm calm.' She took a deep breath. 'I won't worry about things I can't control.'

'Good girl.'

'Dru!'

They both turned at the same time. A small woman with dark hair was hurrying across the concourse, followed closely by a tall guy.

'Ellie.' Dru's voice was a little reserved. She waited for the couple to reach them.

Dru's sister stopped and put her hands on her hips. 'Well, little sister, you're looking very well.'

'And so are you, little mama.' Dru's reached out and touched Ellie's heavily pregnant abdomen. Connor was surprised at the reticence between them for two sisters who hadn't seen each other in more than a year.

'Hello, Dru.' The tall guy reached down and kissed her cheek. Connor was surprised to see a blush stain her fair skin. She turned around to indicate Connor.

'Ellie, Kane, this is Connor.'

Ellie held her hand out and grasped Connor's in a firm shake, and Kane did the same.

'Sorry, we're a bit late. Traffic was heavy,' Kane said.

'Told you.' Connor nudged Dru and smiled.

Dru looked up at the arrivals board. 'It's landed,' she said, her voice wavering.

Ellie looked at her sharply. 'You okay?'

'I will be when all my family is here.' Dru's voice was firm again. She held out her hand to Ellie.

Ellie looked at Dru for a moment and then her face broke into a huge smile as she took Dru's hand. Kane and Connor stood back while the two women crossed to where the disembarking passengers were gradually appearing at the top of the escalator that came up from the tarmac.

As he and Kane stood and watched, a small older woman with blonde hair came through the door, followed by a man and a woman.

Connor smiled. The younger woman was a shorter, darker version of Dru; she had the same nose, same brow, and the same look of determination on her face. It had to be Emma, the oldest of the three sisters, and Jeremy, her fiancé.

The older woman let out a loud yell. 'Drusilla!'

'Mummy.' Tears were streaming down Dru's cheeks as she held her arms out to her mother and sister. The women ran towards each other, oblivious to the passengers smiling at them. Connor clenched his jaw as emotion clogged his throat.

The four Porter women stood in a circle, arms around each other.

Dru was going to be okay. He'd make sure she was.

He patted his shirt pocket as he crossed the room to meet the rest of Dru's family.

He hoped she would see the diamond pendant not only as a reminder of what had brought them together but as a promise of the future.

Their future. He had no doubt there would be one.

Acknowledgements

The East Kimberley in Western Australia is one of the most remote and beautiful locations in Australia. In 2015, we flew over the Purnululu National Park (more often known as the Bungle Bungles) and into the Argyle Diamond Mine on a day trip. As I listened to our guide talking about security, the idea for *Diamond Sky* was born.

The writing of *Diamond Sky* has been another leg of my fabulous writing journey, fulfilling my lifelong dream. Seeing my third book come to print, and on shelves in Australian and New Zealand book stores has been just as exciting as the first two times. My goal is to fill a whole library shelf!

I have been supported by so many people in the writing of this book. I would like to acknowledge them here.

To the many friends I have made in the writing world who constantly support me on my journey; I often say I have found my 'tribe' and I value the daily contact with like-minded people all over the world. Again, a special mention and thank you goes to my critique partner, Susanne Bellamy, and to my proof reader, Roby Aiken.

It would be impossible to write without support in your personal life:

To Ian, the love of my life and my partner in research as we travel this magnificent country seeking stories each winter. I could not do this without you.

To our children and their partners, and our grandchildren: thank you for your love and support.

Again, my love and appreciation goes to my wonderful aunt, Maureen Smith, who not only supports me, but supports so many Australian writers by reading, loving and sharing their stories.

I would also like to acknowledge and thank the *Gija* and *Miriuwung* people, the traditional owners of the East Kimberley.

And to you, the reader: Thank you for choosing this book. I hope when you read, that you love it and talk about it, and that maybe you will want to visit this wonderful part of Australia. I hope you enjoy Ellie, Dru, Dee and Sandra's stories. Drop me a line at annie@annieseation.net I would love to hear from you.

Reviews on Goodreads are always welcome and much appreciated!

All Annie's books are available in print at Annie's store

eBook links:

https://www.annieseaton.net/books.html

Print Store:

All books are available in print at Annie's store and on Amazon in paperback

https://annieseatonstore.ecwid.com/

Look for Annie's next series: **THE AUGATHELLA GIRLS**

Drop me a line at annie@annieseaton.net. I would love to hear from you.

Book 4 of the Porter Sisters series: Hidden Valley

Prologue
Darwin - Casuarina Shopping Centre

'Mum? What are you looking at?' Ellie McLaren tried to keep the impatience from her voice as she stared at her mother. At the same time, she attempted to prevent James, her eighteen-month-old son from smearing ice-cream on her cargo pants.

Honestly, it was easier to control a helicopter in a dive than get a determined toddler to do what he was supposed to do.

'James, stop it. This instant!' Ellie snapped as her mother ignored her question, and her son squirmed on her lap, his sticky hands smearing ice-cream over her navy-blue cargos.

'Give him to me, Ellie, and go and get some paper towel from the restroom.' Mum's voice was patient as always, and Ellie wished for the thousandth time she had that same patience.

Rolling her eyes, she passed James across. 'What were you looking at then, Mum?'

A head shake. 'Um. Nothing.' Her mother's voice held a slight tremble. 'No one. Go and get the towel for Mr Sticky Fingers here.' Mum dropped a light kiss on James's upturned face.

'More ice-cream, Nanny?'

Ellie smiled at her son as she stood and headed towards the restroom at the shopping centre. She had to queue to get inside; it was a week before Christmas and the crowds at the Casuarina shopping plaza were large, noisy and impatient. By the time she got back to her mother and James, her little boy had a clean face and was resting his head on her mother's shoulder, his thumb in his mouth.

Ellie's heart melted as he looked up at her with an angelic smile. 'Mumma.' He held his arms out to her.

'Clean hands first, little man.' She gently wiped his sticky hands with the damp towel. 'Now, come here.' Ellie nuzzled her face into her son's sweet-smelling neck and breathed in that wonderful smell. As she always did, she found it hard to believe that she and Kane had created this perfect child.

'More ice-cream, Mumma?' James insisted.

'No, it's time to go home. I don't know about you, Mum, but I've had enough of crowds for the day.'

'Oh my God! Not again, dear God, not again.' Her mother's cry was almost a scream.

Ellie's head flew around and she caught her breath as she looked at her mother. Jagged fear sliced through her and as she gripped James tightly, he let out a cry. Mum's cheeks had lost all colour, her eyes were wide, and her bottom lip was trembling. It had been over three years since Ellie had seen that terrified expression on her mother's face.

'Mum, what's wrong?' She kept her voice even and soft as she stood, hitched James onto her hip and reached out to touch her mother's clenched hand. 'Talk to me. Please.'

'It's happened again.' Mum's eyes were bleak, and her fingers relaxed and trembled beneath Ellie's touch. 'I saw him again.'

'What has? Who?'

'Peter. Your father.' Mum's voice hitched on a sob. 'I keep seeing him. Everywhere I go.' She lifted her shaking hand and pointed to the games shop across the concourse. 'He just went into that shop. It was him. I think I'm going crazy. Again.'

'What do you mean? You can't see Dad. You know you can't.' Ellie tried to swallow her fear. Since Dad's death and the discovery of the truth of his murder, her mother's mental health had improved and for the last year, it had seemed as though her recovery was finally complete. Knowing that her husband hadn't committed suicide had been the catalyst for Mum's recovery. The grieving had started, and Ellie and her sisters, Emma and Dru had made sure that one of them was always with Mum as she worked through her grief. Dru lived in Darwin with Connor, and Emma and Jeremy were still in the Daintree, but they had all been there to support Sandra.

When James had arrived, Mum had eased back into her old self; she was so good with him, Ellie had gone back to casual relief work on the helicopters out of Makowa Lodge where she and Kane had met, while Kane looked after their mango farm.

Thank God, Emma and Jeremy are coming over to the Territory for Christmas. Ellie was no good at this psychological crap. With Emma and her husband both being doctors, Ellie had ready access to good advice on how to deal with Mum on her bad days.

Now Mum's hand gripped Ellie's fingers. 'I'm sorry, love.' Her eyes were awash with tears as she lifted her head. 'Of course, I know that. But I've seen him a few times. And it scares me. I know Peter is dead. I miss him so much I must be hallucinating.'

'The man went into EB Games, you said?'

Mum nodded. 'Just ignore me. I'll go back to the doctor and get some more medication. Or I'll wait and see Emma. She'll be here in a few days.'

'Here, take James.' Ellie pushed her son into her mother's arms. 'I'll go to the shop and take a look around. That should ease your mind. What was he wearing?'

'Jeans and a black T-shirt.'

Without a backward glance Ellie strode over to the EB Games shop and walked through the door. There was a crowd inside, and she stood and scanned the group at the counter waiting to be served. They were mainly young guys, but a taller man in a dark T-shirt at the other side of the display shelves caught her attention as he walked past them towards the door.

Ellie blinked and then stared. He was the same height as Dad had been, and his hair was longer and a lighter blond, but it was the guy's walk that held her attention. The same loose-shouldered swagger like Dad's. As she stared, he lifted his hand and smoothed his hair back with his right hand; the same gesture that Dad had used when he was nervous.

Before Ellie could step forward, he walked out of the shop and disappeared into the milling Christmas shopping crowd.

HIDDEN VALLEY and all Annie's books are all for sale on the store on her website… in print and e-book… free postage
You can find them here: https://annieseatonstore.ecwid.com/